Absence
of Rules

By Joe McCoubrey

ABSENCE OF RULES

Text copyright © 2013 Joe McCoubrey

The right of Joe McCoubrey to be identified as the author of this work has been asserted by him in accordance with the Copyright, Designs and Patents Act 1988.

A CIP catalogue record for this book is available from the British Library.

ISBN: 978-0-9576965-1-8
Cover Art copyright © 2013 Book Graphics

Dedication & Thanks

I am lucky to have four important women, and two very special young men, in my life. This book is dedicated to Teresa, Brenda, Lynda, Lisa, and the next generation, Alfie and Rory. A special mention to my God-daughter, Norma Ennis – I promised not to forget her.

Finally I owe a lot to friends and colleagues, too numerous to mention. You know who you are, and you have my heartfelt thanks.

About the Author

Joe McCoubrey is a former journalist who reported first hand the height of the Northern Ireland "Troubles" throughout the 1970's and 1980's, firstly as a local newspaper editor, and then as a partner in an agency supplying copy to national newspapers and broadcasters. He switched careers to help start a Local Enterprise Agency, providing advice and support to budding entrepreneurs in his native town, and became its full-time CEO. He retired to concentrate on his long-time ambition to be a full-time writer. He lives in Downpatrick, County Down, and is proud of its historic connections to St. Patrick, Ireland's Patron Saint.

Chapter 1
New York

THE LAST THING Mike Devon needed right now was to get involved in an argument likely to attract unwarranted attention from local police. He had far more pressing things to worry about than the behaviour of two drunken yobbos, wedged into an adjoining small cubicle in an all-night cafeteria on Manhattan's waterfront.

Ordinarily he would pay his bill, bang two heads together on his way out the door, and march straight back to his hotel for an early night.

The effects of jetlag were beginning to settle in after a seven-hour flight from London, and he wanted to be fresh for his early-morning meeting with one of the city's high-flying investment brokers. Yep, no reason to get involved. Besides, throwing in your two-cents' worth always had a way of coming back to bite you in the ass. Despite the fact that the other diners dotted around the small room looked decidedly uncomfortable at the raucous commotion, you just never knew if one or two might take exception at some do-gooder visiting violence upon their fellow man.

Better to stay out of it, he told himself, than risk someone speed-dialling the boys in blues and tying him up with awkward questions for the next few hours.

As the decibel levels grew, he avoided eye contact with the two men, aware that they were spoiling for a fight with anyone stupid enough to look in their direction. An elderly couple had already been subjected to a torrent of snide remarks, and two teenage girls had slipped out the door, disappearing quickly into the gloomy night.

Devon decided to follow suit.

He had just drained the last dregs of his coffee, and was preparing to slide out of his seat when one of the men shouted at a nervous-looking waitress standing station at the end of a semi-circular counter.

"Haul your ass over here bitch, and bring us some more coffee."

The woman looked to be in her early forties, with her hair tied in a tight bun at the back of her head. She wore the look of someone for whom life was one daily grind, her shoulders hunched and shadows darted across sad, tired eyes. She remained rooted to the spot, fear etched across her face as she turned towards the kitchen area looking for help from some unknown source.

One of the two men banged his fist heavily onto the table. "Are you deaf?"

Both men broke out in loud guffaws of laughter as the waitress jumped in a nervous reaction to the noise. After glancing again at the kitchen, she picked up the coffee dispenser and slowly came around the counter to approach the table.

Devon watched the shake in her hand as she tried to fill the cups. Then he noticed one of the men slip his hand up her skirt. "What have we here?" He smirked at the woman's attempt to wriggle free.

Game changer. Devon inwardly sighed.

It was one thing to ignore bad behaviour and the

decibel-busting antics of two petty thugs, but when it came to an assault on a defenceless woman, that was entirely something else.

Devon thumped a ten-dollar note on the table, shuffled out from behind his table, and walked forward to the waitress. When he spoke, his voice was laced with sweetness and affability. "Thank you for the service, Ma'am. Would you mind telling these two gentlemen that I'll be waiting outside for them? I think it's time someone taught them some manners."

Without waiting to see the reaction, he strode confidently out through the door and walked to the end of the block. Behind he could hear the cafeteria door crashing open. "There he is," a voice shouted over his shoulder.

Traffic was heavy, but the pavements were deserted as Devon kept walking fast, grateful to see the dark shadows of an alley entrance less than twenty yards away. Behind he could hear the pounding of feet on the concrete walkway.

Devon turned into the alley just as the two men came running round the corner. By this time he was ready, standing sideways ready to face his assailants, feet spread apart and fists balled.

The first guy didn't stand a chance.

Devon waited until the last second.... waited until the man's momentum would do most of the job for him. He unleashed a vicious straight-arm, palm-open jab directly into the bridge of the man's nose and was rewarded with the sound of bone splintering. The thug's rush was halted by the strike, his feet lifting frontways into the air before he collapsed heavily onto his back. He moaned once and fell unconscious.

The second assailant was not so foolhardy. He had held back a few yards and had already withdrawn a flick-knife, which glistened in the light thrown by nearby street lamps. He advanced cautiously on Devon, the blade swishing in a jerky sideways motion ahead of him.

Devon quickly removed his jacket and wrapped it around his left arm, thrusting it forward to ward off any possible strike from the wicked-looking blade.

The two men danced in a semi-circle, each looking for an opening to deliver a telling blow. Twice Devon had to jump back as the knife flashed downwards, tearing strips from the protective coat. Confident he could judge the man's movement, Devon moved to the left to offer an opening to his unguarded right side.

The assailant seized his chance and rushed forward, this time with the blade held in a stabbing downward thrust position. Devon shifted again and shot out his right foot to connect with the attacker's kneecap before raking its way down the leg bone.

The man roared in pain and bent over, offering Devon full access to the side of his head. It was not an invitation Devon was about to pass up. His fist crashed into the man's temple, sending him face down onto the concrete. Devon dug his fingers into the man's hair, lifted his head, and unleashed another piledriver which ended the contest.

Devon looked down at the unconscious figure and bent forward to prise the flick-knife from a chubby grip. Then he spread the man's hand on the tarmac, stood up, and stamped heavily twice across the knuckles. He moved across to the other assailant and repeated the stamping.

Satisfied he had broken at least several bones, Devon marched out of the alley, confident it would be several weeks before either of the men could even think about attacking anyone else.

***

Twelve hours later, at precisely 9am, Devon walked into a plush downtown office and strode across the room. From the moment he took in the surroundings, with a floor-to-ceiling glass view over the Manhattan skyline, he decided he didn't like the figure perched behind the oversized mahogany desk.

Maybe it was the way the man waved a dismissive arm towards an empty chair in the centre of the room, or maybe it was the way he continued to bellow down the cordless phone at some unfortunate underling. The amount of expensive jewellery adorning his fingers and wrists didn't help either.

Hell, give the guy a break! Could be I just got out of the wrong side of the bed this morning?

The phone was slammed back on its cradle. The man swivelled on a high-backed leather chair that must have cost more than Devon made in a month, and then he spoke.

It was right about then that Devon decided there was nothing wrong with the way he had gotten out of bed this morning.

The man in the chair fixed Devon with one of those looks usually reserved for when you discover you've got dog-shit on your shoes. "I don't know how you wormed your way into my appointment book this morning Mr *Devlin*, but I can tell you we've got nothing to discuss. Why do you Government-type agents think all you have to do is show up and the rest of us will go weak at the knees? Well sir, you'll find I'm cut from an altogether different cloth."

Devon looked down at the oversize nameplate on the desk. It had to be large to accommodate inch-high gold-embossed lettering that read *Denvir Montgomery III – CEO*. He wondered if Denvir the First and Denvir the Second were just as self-important as this little pipsqueak.

But he had long ago learned to control his emotions. He spoke with a slight London accent, and threw in a beaming smile. "First off the name's Devon, not Devlin. I'm sure you already know that, since you don't strike me as a man who would tolerate his staff getting things wrong. I can therefore only assume that you deliberately mispronounced my name in the hope of provoking a reaction."

"Second," Devon continued without waiting for a response, "I'm not some Government-type agent. I'm working with Homeland Security on a matter of the utmost gravity. We need your co-operation and I figured, wrongly as it turned out, that the best way to go about this was to make an appointment, and give you the opportunity to do the right thing."

Montgomery held up a hand. He wore the look of someone who recognised a lecture when he heard one. "I can guess what you're after, Mr *Devon*, and I can assure you it's out of the question. I run one of the largest investment houses in America. We pride ourselves on offering customers complete confidentiality. The idea of you taking a look at our books is preposterous. You've made a wasted trip."

Devon drew his seat up to the desk, pushed aside the prized nameplate, and fixed the man opposite with a glacial stare. The knuckles on his right hand felt sore from last night's altercation in the alleyway, but he fought down a temptation to throw just one more right cross into the face of the smug bastard sitting opposite.

Instead, he slipped into a mild-mannered tone of voice. "The reason we need to see your books is because we believe one of your investors is channelling funds for al-Qaeda, and those funds are helping to put together a rather nasty terrorist operation in Europe."

It was a statement intended to evoke a more animated response than the one Devon got. Montgomery smiled benignly, as if addressing a child. "Our investors are among the world's most wealthy and influential people. They are fully screened, and we know at all times where the money comes from and where it goes. What you suggest is simply not possible. If I may say so, Mr Devon, you people are watching too many movies."

Devon decided on a cool response. "Let me paint you a picture. Suitcases full of money, together with hundreds of apparently innocuous wire transfers, have been making their way into various clearing houses in Paris and Switzerland for the past few years. This money is bounced around a few times, before ending up in a small, outwardly respectable London bank, which in turn sends it off on yet more electronic travels. We have traced one of its destinations to Manhattan or, to be more precise, to this very same building."

Devon watched the confident façade of the CEO

of Montgomery Holdings drop a notch, but to be fair to the guy he tried not to let it show. "Even if what you say is true, there would be no way of tracking these kinds of transfers, no way of knowing their origins. I've told you, we deal only with reputable investors. I should have thought it was obvious that you should be in London grilling the bank you say you've identified. You'll get nothing here."

Devon smiled. "Let me explain something to you. We have the London end fully covered. We know what's going out from London but we need to learn what happens to the transfers after they reach you. In short, we need to follow the trail from here."

"Financial investment portfolios are rather more complicated than that, Mr Devon. I simply can't have you people tramping through our business in the hope of finding something that probably isn't there."

"Ever heard of The Patriot Act, Mr Montgomery?"

"Of course I have and this has nothing to do with what we're discussing."

Devon rose and walked across to the large windows. Perched on the twentieth floor of one of the borough's newest buildings, it was easy to see why Denvir Montgomery III saw himself as king of all he surveyed.

He spoke over his shoulder. "Under The Patriot Act it is now legal for Homeland Security to intercept and investigate anything which threatens the national wellbeing of America. That includes looking at financial records."

Despite allowing the man to think otherwise, Devon was not with Homeland Security. A former operative of Britain's Secret Intelligence Service, better known as MI6, he was now attached to an elite anti-terrorist group answerable only to the British Prime Minister. He worked regularly with a similar group set up in America under the Office of the President. Both groups had a certain carte blanche when it came to dealing with the enemies of democracy. And both freely walked on the toes of other agencies, including Homeland Security.

Montgomery sprang from his chair. "This is nonsense. I think you'd better leave. You can deal directly through the company's lawyers."

Devon smiled again. "I'm afraid you're missing the point. One phonecall by me will bring a hundred agents into this building. We'll cart out records by the truckload, and make sure CNN get a nice view of us doing it. You and I both can both figure out what will happen then."

There was no response, so Devon continued. "Alright, let me take a guess. Your investors won't like the public exposure. They'll probably move elsewhere. And then there are your stockholders to consider. I'm betting you'll get a run on selling, and when the dust settles there'll be nothing left of Montgomery Holdings."

Denvir Montgomery III slumped back into his seat. He twiddled with a few desk ornaments before glancing up at Devon. "Okay, tell me what you need."

Four hours later, Devon had what he wanted. Cloistered in a side office, he was given unique access to the company's computer database of financial transactions stretching back to its formation. He concentrated only on the last two years, and watched mesmerised as a printer spewed out more than three hundred A4 pages.

He took the opportunity to scan through the lists, knowing he was unlikely to spot anything. He comforted himself by the fact that a team of forensic auditors would spend the next few weeks combing through every detail, which he copied onto a pen-drive before also sending an encrypted email attachment back to his London base. When it came to computers, Devon believed in the belt-and-braces approach to saving and storing vital information.

Financial skulduggery was not his cup of tea, and he would be happy to hand everything over to the spreadsheet wizards.

What he did know, thanks to a tip-off from a well-placed investment-guru friend of his boss, was that large sums of money were funnelling across Europe into one particular London bank that had previously been credited only with low-level deals. The fact that it had suddenly become awash with mountains of cash was enough to suggest that something stank to the high heavens.

And that kind of money could mean only one thing - someone was trying to manipulate world trading markets.

Initially, Devon had been sceptical about involving his agency in matters outside their normal remit. But he had been persuaded that any attempts to destabilise Britain's fragile economy were every bit as important as chasing down some gun-toting terrorist.

Satisfied that he had done all he could, he turned his attention back to the other operations currently stacked on his in-tray, and wondered how his second-in-command was getting on.

Chapter 2
London

ALAN DOYLE HELD the butt of the Glock firmly in his left hand and loosed off every round in the magazine. Then he reached out a prosthetic right arm to a switch, and started the target moving towards him on a slide rail. He noted with satisfaction that half his shots had found the target photo's head, whilst the rest were neatly grouped around the heart.

Not bad for a cripple, he mumbled to himself.

He moved the Glock into his prosthetic hand and neatly ejected the magazine. Then he reloaded, racked the slide to chamber a round, and stuffed the weapon into a shoulder holster.

It was his usual routine at 8:30 every morning.

Doyle crossed the basement floor to a lift and punched the button for the fifth floor. He stepped out into a world of opulence, a richly carpeted area covered with expensive office furniture and the kinds of striking wall murals more suited to a museum of modern art.

As he looked around, Doyle knew the surroundings were not what people would expect in the offices of a private security agency, but with annual turnovers running into the multi-billion-dollar stratosphere, it could almost be forgiven for the rather visible signs of its success.

To be fair, Doyle thought, the frills had nothing

to do with the pretensions of the owners; they were simply one more way of disguising the true structure of *LonWash Securities*, a name chosen to underline the base of the company's activities in London and Washington.

He was well aware he had joined a company different from any other.

Its income came not from a wide base of private customers, but directly from the British taxpayer, although the mechanism for payments could never be traced.

Set up under the offices of the British Prime Minister, the agency was the brainchild of General Sir John Sandford (Retired), a member of the government's elite COBRA committee, who had persuaded the PM that more direct action was needed against the enemies of state. Sir John envisioned action away from political oversight, and the constraints faced by established agencies such as MI6, MI5 and various other strands of anti-terrorist groupings in the UK.

LonWash Securities came into being ostensibly to handle a number of private government contracts in places like Iraq and Afghanistan. The cover allowed the Civil Servants at Whitehall to channel funds into the agency, though no one ever checked what was actually delivered for the large sums involved.

Financial support was also provided by Washington, where a similar organisation set up by President Barack Obama, worked closely with its British counterpart in rooting out world terrorism threats.

Doyle had to concede that Sir John had chosen

well for the agency's London location. It was a large five-storey block on Charterhouse Street, not far from the Victoria Embankment, and within easy access to all major city routes. The clincher was the availability of a large underground car parking area where the agency could store and operate a fleet of specially-converted vehicles, including highly sophisticated, armour-plated surveillance cars and vans.

Beneath the car park was another level for the building's maintenance machinery, with large rooms for generators, electrical switchboxes, and a water filtration plant. One room on this level was converted into a large, fully soundproofed firing range.

It was here that Doyle spent the first hour of every working day.

The past few years had been a rocky ride for him. He had lost the use of his right arm in an IRA shootout in Dublin a number of years back, as part of an undercover team led by Mike Devon. The team had tracked the IRA's top men to a farmhouse, and in a bloody gun battle Doyle took a round into his right elbow. It shattered the socket and forced surgeons to amputate most of his arm.

His life in Special Forces ended then and there. Pensioned off to live in his parents' cottage near the Brighton shoreline, Doyle retreated into a world of pity and a continuous diet of whiskey.

It was here that Devon had found him almost a year later. Living alone after the death of his parents, Doyle knew he cut a sorry sight for his old comrade. The once-proud little cottage was strewn with litter and empty bottles. A prosthetic arm was discarded on the floor.

He remembered with embarrassment his first words to Devon. "I don't want your fucking charity, leave me alone."

He was thankful now that Devon persisted, calling by every morning for almost a week. It was during one of these visits that Devon had explained the setting up of his new unit and begged Doyle to join him.

"Come off it, Mike. What use am I to anybody?"

"For a start, you're the best tactical planner I've ever come across. I need you. I'm not offering charity, this is too important for that. I'm offering a way for you to help and if I didn't think you could do it, I wouldn't be here. You can either sit here wallowing in your own shit or be the man you always were. Let me know if you want to join the human race again."

He could still see Devon's back as he slammed the door. Something snapped inside him. Looking back, he knew it was the realisation that his last chance had just walked out of his life.

He had rushed outside just as Devon was about to climb into his car. "Don't go Mike, I need your help."

That began one of the most gruelling periods of his life.

Over the next three weeks, Devon supervised Doyle's physical rehabilitation, starting with gentle jogging sessions along Brighton beach. Gradually the strength grew back into his legs, and by the end of the third week he was undertaking punishing country runs with weighted rucksacks strapped to his back.

When Devon wasn't around, Doyle remorselessly built up the strength in his left arm with punishing daily one-armed press ups. He went back to his local hospital to be fitted with a new prosthetic arm and started to master the mysteries of its robotic movements, eventually gaining full control over all its functionalities.

When he walked into the London offices of *LonWash Securities* seven months later he was transformed.

The agency's basement gun range was heaven-sent for Doyle. He began familiarising himself again with all manner of weaponry, re-learning gun stripping and reloading with the aid of his prosthetic. When he was satisfied he could handle most of the armaments he decided to be the master of one.

He settled on a Glock compact G19, fastened into a holster mounted on his right shoulder for easy release with his left hand. After pummelling the targets with thousands of rounds, he reached a level of marksmanship that he had never achieved with his good right hand. He was ready for some real action again.

He didn't have long to wait.

As part of a routine surveillance operation on a radical cleric operating out of a London mosque, Doyle intercepted a package that was to set *LonWash Securities* on its latest venture.

Doyle knew he was being eased back into the action by being handed what was little more than a babysitting assignment, but he was grateful to be back in what he considered to be the real world.

More out of a whim than for any real purpose, Doyle broke from his routine to pay a visit to a Royal

Mail sorting office in Romford. His credentials got him immediately in front of the manager and from there to unrestricted access to the items being sorted for delivery in the area in which the mosque was located.

Over three late evenings, Doyle rummaged through the mountain of flyers and junk mail that were set aside for next-day delivery to the offices of the cleric known as Almahdi Hashemi. Doyle wasn't sure what he was looking for, and several times had to resist the temptation to rip open a number of envelopes.

On the third evening, just as he was about to call off his vigil, he glanced at a brown parcel with a Paris stamp.

After filling in various forms he removed the parcel from the office with a promise to return it before delivery time in three hours. The technicians at *LonWash Securities* swiftly got to work, and within one hour provided a full report to Doyle.

The contents of the package were hardly significant, but something piqued Doyle's interest. There was probably nothing unusual about a cleric ordering a run-of the-mill Zane Grey Western novel, but why go to the trouble of ordering it from a book store in Paris? It was not a limited edition, nor did it appear to be a rare or out-of-date publication. A simple online search of Amazon showed the book among all the author's listings, so why not order it more directly and cheaper from this source?

Doyle smelled a rat, but had to wait until the following morning when Devon returned from his trip to Manhattan to brief him about his discovery.

He watched now as Devon read the short report

before animatedly slamming it down on the desk.

"Great work, Alan. You might just have something here. Let's see what my old friend, Claude Bartran, makes of a Paris book shop delivery turning up among the belongings of a suspected al-Qaeda cell leader."

Chapter 3
Paris

HALFWAY DOWN A Paris side-street, just off the Rue de l'Quest, is a small cellar book shop accessed by eight steps leading from the pavement. Located close to Montparnasse on the left bank of the River Seine, the area attracts more than its fair share of tourists, and is considered by many to be the heart of the city's intellectual and artistic life. None of that, however, rubbed off on the little book shop whose volumes of rare books and first editions hardly produced a liveable income for the owner.

He was a thoroughly harmless-looking man, small and rotund with striking bushy eyes in marked contrast to a bald pate, tanned and weathered by seventy years of life. He wore a frumpy woollen cardigan, thick with grease and zipped over a gut that hung out well beyond his faded old jeans. Heavy black-rimmed glasses, perched at the end of a bulbous nose, gave him a quirky professorial look.

He could be seen most days shambling between the rickety rows of shelves, duster in hand, and a pencil sticking out from behind his right ear. Cleaning and cataloguing was all he ever seemed to do.

Odd therefore that he should be under the constant surveillance of GIGN, *the Groupe d'intervention de la Gendarmerie Nationale*, the country's premier counter-terrorism unit. To them, Monsieur Jacques Basquey, owner of *Le Dépositaire Livre*, was more than a person of interest; he was considered an important middle-man for some strange operations in France and farther afield.

Acting on Mike Devon's tip-off, the French agents had been watching Basquey for two weeks. A permanent stake-out had been established in a first-floor rental apartment opposite, with six men assigned on a 24/7 basis to chart the comings and goings at The Book Depository. Behind the louvered six-section window frames of the stakehouse, false two-way glass sheets allowed the watchers to set up sophisticated video and sound equipment, without the danger of anyone seeing what they were up to.

Very few customers graced the little shop, though it seemed to do a thriving business. Regular deliveries by vans bearing the logo of a blue bird inside a yellow ellipse, the recognisable mark of the French national postal service *La Poste*, pulled up to the shop at least twice a week.

On other occasions Monsieur Basquey could be seen shuffling down the little narrow street heading for a postbox, where he usually deposited a small brown cardboard package containing a single book.

The odd thing about this aspect of the business was that *Le Dépositaire Livre* did not have an internet site, and did not advertise its goods in any newspapers or magazines, or in the French equivalent of Yellow Pages, *Pages Jaunes Groupe*. To the world outside the Rue de l'Quest the little shop didn't exist. So how could it be receiving so many regular orders for its goods?

The agents of GIGN decided to find out. Using its considerable powers, the agency intercepted the packages and brought them for analysis to their headquarters in Versailles. There a specialist team opened the packages and subjected the contents to a rigorous series of tests, before resealing them and allowing them to continue on their journey.

The methods used at the lab were perfected by the FBI in Quantico, Virginia, and shared with friendly agencies across the world. The skill of opening letters and packages had gone well beyond the use of steam irons. When the FBI "tampered" with goods they could boast with certainty that it couldn't be spotted, even under the most microscopic of inspections.

Quantico housed the world's most sophisticated cataloguing systems for just about anything that might help in the detection of crime. Fingerprints, DNA and photographs were just the tip of the FBI iceberg. They had a database for every known car-tread pattern, and every make of shoe or boot print. They used the latest in mass spectrometry and electromagnetometer analysis to break down the structure and particles of all known compounds. They had databases for adhesive substances, various inks and papers in use around the world, and a complete breakdown of materials, fabrics, soils, and grasses.

Using painstaking techniques and instruments calibrated beyond human understanding, they could disassemble the most elaborately packaged item and reconstruct it to the last detail.

However, the standard brown cardboard wrappings used by the *Le Dépositaire Livre* needed no such skills. The fold-over flap was easily unglued and resealed. Even if by chance a mistake was made, the package could be simply replicated by buying a similar off-the-shelf brown cover. They also had handwriting experts who could re-address the item in Monsieur Basquey's shaky penmanship.

What the French technicians found inside the packages was also rather less challenging than they had hoped for. There was always a different book, each an obscure English-language publication, together with a single A4 sheet that appeared at first glance to be an invoice statement.

They started with special X-ray equipment and laser imaging to scan for any hidden watermark messages or micro-dot implants. There were none.

It was at this point they brought in two of the group's top cryptologists who examined titles, author names, publishing house details, anything that might throw up a coded sequence or subliminal message. Nothing.

They turned their attention to the invoice itself. At the top of the page was the handwritten name and address of the customer, followed by a lengthy reference number, always a clue to the existence of a potential coded message. The remainder of the sheet was taken up by a simple two-line scrawl: *Your order has been processed and is enclosed. Please send payment at the first opportunity after the 4th of next month.*

Each of the messages was almost identical except for distinctive changes in the reference number. They followed no logical sequence, nothing to suggest an orderly process of product identification. They seemed to be totally random, and therefore an obvious code.

The cryptologists subjected the reference number to a series of computer decoding logarithms, starting with basic assumptions and working up to more complex formulae. They eventually concluded that the series of numbers referred to pages and lines within the books, but without a basic key from which to start they got nowhere in a hurry.

It was only after opening the third intercepted package that the cryptologists noted a subtle change in the date for payment. Instead of the 4th of the next month, the other invoices referred to the 5th and 2nd. They quickly deduced that the coded pages and lines started after either Chapter 4, 5 or 2. The first number in the invoice gave them the position of a word on each line.

Applying the key to the first book's lengthy reference, they found the coded words they were looking for. The first message in full read simply – *Manchester Piccadilly locker twenty take to London by train contact waiting Friday end month*.

After that the decoding was simple. To date they had amassed fourteen separate messages. They also had the names and addresses of four recipients of the packages.

All were based in various locations in England.

In the modern world of highly encrypted passwords and secure satellite transmissions, it seemed strangely odd to the men of GIGN to come across a simple antiquated system. But too often, would-be experts found that governments around the world, not to mention individual hackers using programs that could run up to twenty million passwords per second, usually ended up breaking the most sophisticated coding.

Satellite listening stations such as Echelon, a signals intelligence network (SIGNET) employed initially by America, the United Kingdom, Australia,

Canada and New Zealand, were now capable of picking up the most obscure "trigger" words that crossed the airwaves.

Since the 9/11 attacks in New York, America alone had contributed billions to updating existing software, and introducing new orbiting satellites to provide live Intel across the globe. Many countries friendly to the USA had gladly come on board and were constantly feeding into the new global war on terrorism.

Little wonder then, that email traffic of the nefarious kind, as well as the use of mobile phones for directing clandestine operations, had all but dried up. Perhaps the clumsy, outdated methods of Monsieur Basquey were understandable after all.

The GIGN agents relayed their findings to bureau chief, Claude Bartran. He picked up the phone and dialled Mike Devon's special number. It was usually answered. On the occasions there was no reply, he left a voicemail message simply giving his first name.

He never had to wait long for a reply.

Chapter 4
Manchester

THE OWNER OF THE Iridium satellite phone number, which was on the speed-dial list of Claude Bartran, was climbing through a garden fence at the rear of a rundown bedsit not far from Manchester city centre. Acting on Bartran's information, Mike Devon had spent the last two days keeping watch on the rented locker area inside the Manchester Piccadilly train station.

Late on a Friday evening, a woman dressed stylishly in a brown suede half-coat, designer jeans and high-heeled boots, approached locker number twenty and removed a holdall.

Discarding his Network Rail cleaner's uniform and handcart, Devon followed the woman to a taxi rank, and watched as she climbed into the first cab. He took the next one available and avoided ordering the driver "to follow that cab." Instead he told the man he was a private detective on the trail of an unfaithful wife, and asked if he could keep a discreet distance behind the taxi in front.

The ride took him through half the city and into a run-down area noted for boarded-up shops and walls covered in graffiti. *Hardly the legitimate haunt of a fashion-conscious lady.*

He watched from more than three hundred yards away as she alighted and walked purposefully down a narrow laneway.

Devon paid the driver and sprinted across the road, attracting a few blaring horns from passing drivers as he skipped out of their way. He arrived at the entrance to the lane in time to see the woman open the door of a building and disappear inside.

He waited a few minutes then walked past the doorway, noting its dirty bronze plaque mounted on the wall and containing the illegible names of the bedsit occupants. He already knew the address of the location, but this was his first time on site.

He wandered to the rear of the street premises and counted off the buildings. He was just climbing through the fence into an overgrown rear garden when he caught a movement to his right. Someone was crawling about the tall weeds.

"You'd better be who I think you are." There was menace in the voice.

"That you, boss?"

Devon let out an exaggerated sigh. "Jeez, if it was anybody else, they would have shot you by now. Don't you know how to keep quiet?"

The weeds parted and a figure rose in view about twenty yards from Devon's position. He recognised the features of Mason Hunter, one of a two-man surveillance team ordered to the location when the address was revealed by the French interception of the bookstore packages.

Despite the apparent friction of their opening greetings, both men shook hands warmly and hunkered into the grass. Devon had deliberately made enough noise for Hunter to hear as he climbed through the fence, not wanting to take a hit-first-ask-questions-later blow across his skull.

"Give me a sit-rep," Devon ordered in a friendly

manner.

"There are four possible hostiles, all men, and all currently in situ. A blonde woman has just joined them. Is that who you followed from the train station?"

"Yes, keep going." A hint of impatience.

"They are all in their twenties, all with swarthy complexions, could be Middle Eastern. Don't go out much, mainly to the supermarket around the corner for fags, newspapers and a few groceries. Different one each time, like they're taking turns for fresh air. Always looking around them."

"What about visitors?"

"None, until this blonde showed up. And another thing boss, they never seem to use the phone and never talk about anything but football. We've had a listening device in for two days and you'd think their whole life was about Manchester bleedin' United. I'm sick hearing about Giggsy, or Nani, or Chicharito as if they're the only footballers ever played the game. As a Spurs man meeself it's hard to take."

"Careful Hunter, you're letting your London upbringing take over your cover," Devon told him playfully. Then he added more seriously: "Who's watching the front?"

"Alfie Cheadle, he's one of our best new recruits. Brought him up from Norwich last night and I'm impressed. Guy knows what he's doing. He's rented a bedsit at the head of the intersection and has eyeballs on the front door at all times."

Devon considered his options for a few moments, and then came to a decision. "Here's what we're going to do. I'm sending over another man to bunk in with Cheadle. My guess is that the blonde will leave sometime soon and I want her followed. From what you say, Cheadle is just the man for the job."

"Then what?"

"Then we find out what was in that holdall and what our footie-loving friends have to say for themselves".

***

The Royal Mail Parcelforce van drew up outside the entrance to the bedsit shortly after eight the following morning. Mike Devon jumped from the cab, walked to the rear of the vehicle, and extracted a medium-sized cardboard box. He slammed the door shut, strode onto the pavement, and hit a feeble-looking doorbell halfway up the cracked wood structure.

"Whatya want?" a tinny voice barked through a small vent underneath the bell.

"Parcel delivery for Terence Stone."

"Leave it on the step. Some people arc trying to get some sleep here."

"Can't do that sir, it needs to be signed for."

There was a pause for a few seconds and then the tin voice started up again. "Press the bell four times. The man you want is on the fourth floor." The voice cut off.

Five minutes later, after the four-ring code was angrily pushed twice, the front door opened haltingly to reveal a sleepy-eyed youth wearing only a pair of boxer shorts. "Is that a parcel for me?"

Devon read out the full name and address and the youth stepped forward to retrieve the parcel. He signed an offered clipboard and was about to disappear inside when Devon explained he had another parcel for him in the van but he needed help to carry it.

The youth looked at him quizzically and then shrugged his shoulders.

Devon couldn't help but wonder at the way people react to receiving parcels. It's like rushing to open a present at Christmas. Even people who should be tuned into danger are often thrown by the urge to investigate. It was no surprise to him therefore that the youth meekly followed him to the rear of the vehicle.

Devon opened the doors and stepped aside for the youth. There was just about enough time for the hapless young man to register the presence of Mason Hunter in the back of the van before a vicious downward chop to the back of his neck rendered him unconscious.

Hunter caught the body as it fell forward and Devon pushed it all the way into the van. Hunter then joined Devon on the roadside and both men walked back to the open door of the house. No one was on the deserted street, and no curtains moved in any of the nearby properties. They went inside and closed the door behind them.

Devon removed a Sig Sauer P226 from his rear trouser waistband. It was an impressive piece of kit, with a custom-design silver frame and walnut grip. It had a threaded barrel, which neatly accepted the Impulse II compact sound suppressor that he screwed into place as he made his way towards the stairwell.

He had relieved the weapon from an IRA

assassin after a shoot-out at a Dublin farmhouse a number of years previously, and carried it everywhere he went. It held a 15-round magazine of 9mm Parabellums and favoured a handy release mechanism for easy reloading.

Behind him, Hunter was carrying an Austrian Glock black polymer pistol with a longer barrel Gemtech suppressor. The pistol also held 9mm Parabellums, but with a shorter 12-round magazine.

As far as semi-automatic ordinance was concerned, the lethal firepower of these two weapons, particularly in confined spaces, was almost unmatchable. Devon and Hunter would rather not have to use them, but if they did, there was only going to be one winning side.

Devon's rubber-soled combat boots provided him with a noiseless ascent up the threadbare stairs. At the fourth floor he paused at the top and peered around a wall down a short corridor. The stale smells of old cooking, cigarette smoke and alcohol fumes were almost overpowering in the unventilated space.

A single door hung slightly open and the soft sounds of an early morning radio show could be heard from within. He moved quickly down the corridor, taking up position on the right side of the door, with Mason going left.

Devon silently counted off 3-2-1 with his fingers and then rammed his foot against the door.

The sight that greeted him inside the bedsit was almost farcical. One man was lying on makeshift bedding in the centre of the room, blowing smoke rings towards a heavily-stained ceiling. A second man was propped with his back against a wall, his legs covered by a sleeping blanket, and his fist wrapped around a beer bottle.

A third man was just emerging from a nearby room, probably a walk-in kitchen Devon guessed, carrying a mug of coffee. He too was dressed only in shorts.

All three froze in shock and couldn't take their eyes from the menacing barrels pointed towards their heads. Devon had seen it all before – the initial numbness, followed by a realisation of what was happening, then the overwhelming urge to do something, no matter how futile.

He tried his best to let them know that any movement would be folly. He fired two rounds into the radio, sending shattered pieces across the room. Then he barked an order with as much threat as he could muster. "Move and you die. Don't be heroes."

But there was always one.

The man lying on the makeshift bed turned towards Devon with his right hand coming out from under the blankets. Devon waited until the last possible moment, waited until he could see the barrel of a revolver clear the soiled linen sheet.

And then Devon fired.

The man's head disappeared in a spray of blood and grey matter. His body simply tumbled over and crashed on the wooden floor.

Everything in the room went quiet.

Then the man with the mug of tea hurled it in Devon's direction and turned to run back into the kitchen.

Devon casually sidestepped the flying crockery and watched as Hunter fired into the back of the fleeing man's right knee, bringing him crashing to the floor, his head thumping heavily against an inner wall.

The third man's hands shot into the air. His voice carried all the fear and conviction of someone who knew he was staring death in the face. "Don't shoot, please don't shoot!"

***

Two hours later the bedsit was fully sanitised. A special team arrived in a large furniture removals van to clear the area. As far as any nosey residents were concerned, their neighbours had decided to move South to find work, and no one paid too much attention to the large cardboard boxes carried down the stairwell.

The dead man was wrapped in polythene sheeting and stuffed into one of the boxes, whilst his injured companion was treated for his leg wound, knocked out with a non-lethal injection, and put into another box.

The third man was allowed to get dressed and accompany the team under his own steam to the waiting van. The threat of certain death was enough to ensure full compliance.

Devon led the search of the premises and found the holdall stuffed in a small cupboard under the kitchen sink. It was crammed full of British Sterling notes, American dollars and Euros. Devon estimated the total value at around a quarter of a million pounds.

There was also a wallet crammed with papers, including passports, entry visas to the USA, and various maps of locations in London and

Washington. He stuffed everything back into the holdall for detailed inspection at headquarters.

The remainder of the bedsit yielded an assortment of handguns and knives, but no explosives or more sinister materials.

On top of a small fridge, an opened brown package revealed an obscure book, together with a handwritten invoice from *Le Dépositaire Livre* in Paris.

Chapter 5
London

MIKE DEVON HAD just finished the latest round of interrogations on the prisoners picked up in the raid on the Manchester bedsit. He was beginning to make progress, but nothing made sense.

He now knew he was dealing with an al-Qaeda cell, but in typical fashion the surviving three members didn't seem to know what was expected of them. They had been holed up in Manchester for more than six months before receiving the package and the holdall of money. All they knew was that they were to travel to London to make contact the following Sunday with a man on the Embankment overlooking the Houses of Parliament.

Devon knew from experience that there was always one person likely to break under extreme interrogation. The trick was in finding which one.

To help matters along, he brought all three to a secluded wood outside the city of Nottingham, and made them watch as their dead friend was unceremoniously buried in a crude lime-pit that would serve as his eternal grave.

It was designed to show the captives they were not dealing with the normal forces of law and order. They needed to know that the men who held them appeared to act independently and were capable of killing them without the prospect of a trial.

Devon would have no qualms about ending the lives of these men, but not like this. He was not an executioner. If any of them came at him, or were threatening the lives of innocents, he could squeeze the trigger without batting an eyelash.

For now he just wanted to instil in them the fear of God, or Allah, or whoever the hell they worshipped when they weren't forcing their crazy beliefs down everyone else's throat.

Instead of shooting them and disposing of them in the same grave as their comrade, he ordered them to be bundled into a waiting van.

Back in the basement of *LonWash Securities* they were each given one last chance to talk. One of them did.

"This is just not the normal modus operandi of al-Qaeda," Devon told Alan Doyle at a late evening briefing. "We know they operate in cells so that one hand doesn't know what the other is doing, but why ask this group to travel to London to meet with what appears to be someone from another cell? It goes against the grain for al-Qaeda."

Doyle looked at his boss. "Maybe they were sent to pick up weapons or bombing materials?"

"That's just the point Alan. Why not have these delivered to Manchester? They were able to receive a holdall full of cash, so why not arrange a similar drop for whatever munitions they need? Why risk one cell exposing itself to another cell? It's got to be more than that."

"It would make sense," Doyle responded, "if something big is being planned, something that requires a lot of manpower. We could be looking at the next major al-Qaeda operation in London."

Devon knew that ever since the infamous 7/7 attacks on three London underground trains and a double-decker bus on July Seventh 2005, authorities in the capital had been on edge. Those atrocities were carried out by a single-cell group of four men who acted without the support of other known cells dotted around the country, so why was this latest activity veering away from the proven modus operandi of al-Qaeda?

It was a question nagging away at the back of Devon's mind.

He turned again towards Doyle. "Consider this. In the post 7/7 era a lot of the existing al-Qaeda cells were rounded up and to this day both MI6 and the GCHQ believed they had broken the back of the threat from groups already based here. Now we are finding the existence of new groups, ones that appear to be changing the rules by apparently operating collectively."

"I take it you're talking about the groups we have so far identified through the efforts of our friends in Paris?"

"Yes, thanks to you Alan, we were able to put GIGN onto the mysterious coded messages emanating from the book store. We've now identified three groups in the UK. What we have still to discover whether there are any more we don't yet know about and...."

"And," Doyle finished the sentence for him, "we don't know what it is they're planning."

Devon knew he would have to make a detailed report to the agency boss, General Sandford, but he needed more time to unearth additional information. He came to a series of quick-fire decisions.

"Here's what we're going to do. First up, we intercept the Manchester cell's mysterious appointment at the London Embankment on Sunday.

We'll see where this leads us, but in the meantime we need to take affirmative action on the remaining groups we know about."

Doyle leaned forward on his seat. "Just what do you mean by 'affirmative action'?"

Without hesitation, Devon told him. "We're going to round them up and put them beyond any threat."

Doyle looked at him quizzically. "Shouldn't we continue to monitor them and see if they lead us to any other cells that we don't yet know about?"

"No, we've been watching them long enough. It looks like they're getting ready for action and we can't risk them slipping the net. The safest thing is to get these people off our streets. The shit would really hit the fan if they did something whilst we were supposed to be keeping an eye on them."

A knock on the door interrupted his flow, and Mason Hunter stepped into the room without waiting for an invitation. "Sorry about the interruption boss, but I thought you'd want to hear this."

"What is it?"

Hunter crossed the room and placed a large colour photograph on the small coffee table situated between Devon and Doyle. "Remember her?"

Devon twisted the photograph to look down at an image of a blonde woman entering through the glass revolving doors of a city centre bank. "That's the woman I followed to the bedsit in Manchester."

"Yeah, and if you remember you delegated Alfie Cheadle to follow her? He's just sent in this surveillance snap. It was taken an hour ago here in London. The premises she's going into are the offices of TriStar Global Securities…."

Alan Doyle immediately cut in. He turned towards Devon. "Isn't that the investment bank you were investigating in Manhattan?"

Devon stared at the photograph and then theatrically slapped his forehead with the palm of his right hand. "Dammit! This opens up a whole new can of worms."

Both Doyle and Hunter waited for more, but Devon stared off into space, trying to get his thoughts into some kind of order. After a few moments he spoke again. "This bank has been moving large sums of money around the world over the past year and I was investigating whether there were any possible links to potential terrorist funding."

"Now you know that there are," Doyle said.

"No, that's what puzzling. What I discovered on the trip to the Manhattan clearing house was that the funds were tied up with Russian-owned companies suspected of involving themselves in attempts to undermine some of the world's most fragile economies. There was no inkling of any terrorist undertones."

"This can't be coincidental Mike," Doyle told him confidently.

"I agree, but I honestly can't see how the two are related. Five minutes ago I was running two entirely separate investigations, one into the murky world of big business, and the other into al-Qaeda. Somehow the two have come together, but I'm damned if I know why."

London's Victoria Embankment is always a lot

quieter on Sunday afternoons than it is at busy weekday periods, but only just. Its lure as a prime vantage point for a great tourist viewing angle to the River Thames and the Houses of Parliament meant that sizeable crowds of people are always milling about.

Technically-speaking, Victoria is part of the Thames Embankment, a road and river link that that was built on reclaimed marshland way back in 1870. Its four-mile route attracts a heady mix of joggers, pram-pushers, business people and daytrippers, all catching a taste of the countryside in the middle of one of the busiest city precincts in Europe.

The Embankment, as it is more commonly known, always has its fair share of intrigue. Beloved by television and film directors, it appears regularly as the location for a diverse range of productions, from live news broadcasts to cookery programmes, and just about everything in between. It is seen by scriptwriters as a perfect cloak-and-dagger location, be it clandestine meetings between spies or the perfect getaway spot for afternoon love trysts.

There was nothing vaguely romantic about what had brought Mike Devon to one of the many walkway benches on this particular Sunday afternoon.

He had a full team in place with back-up bodies in various disguises along the stretch identified as the location for the delivery of the holdall taken from the bedsit in Manchester.

One of the men captured along with the holdall was persuaded to carry it down the long pathway beyond Waterloo Bridge.

Devon's main concern was that the youth

handing over the holdall did not know how to make contact with the pick-up man. All he had been told was to be at the Embankment by two o'clock, and continue to walk up and down the main pathway until he was approached.

Devon's team therefore had no idea of what the pick-up man looked like or where precisely he would chose to intercept the courier. It was a situation fraught with danger. All they could do was keep on their toes, and be ready to react to whatever happened.

The youth made his first full journey along the designated section of pathway. Thirty minutes later he was repeating his walk, this time from the opposite direction. Still no sign of any contact.

Devon scanned every face in the area for possible targets. A case could almost be made for any one of more than twenty single men who loitered about taking pictures, reading Sunday newspapers, or just lounging against the long walkway wall.

On more than one occasion Devon had to fight the urge to bet on at least two potential targets.

One was a swarthy-complexioned man in his thirties. He wore sunglasses and seemed to be transfixed on the imposing parliamentary structure hugging the riverside. The man hadn't moved from a bench seat for more than thirty minutes and displayed all the classic traits of a patient operative.

Devon was about to use his throat mic to bring some of his team tighter into the area where the man was sitting, when a petite brunette rushed forward and threw her arms around the man's neck. The two could be heard arguing about her lateness before they moved off in the direction of the Strand, heading towards Trafalgar Square.

The second possible suspect had spent most of the time hanging over the wall watching various river craft cut through the calm waters, breaking his concentration only twice to glance backwards at the walkway pedestrian traffic. But he too was eliminated when he suddenly moved away from the wall, crossed the grass island separating the pathway from the main road, and hailed a taxi.

The contact, when it came, was from an unlikely source.

A Metropolitan Police beat-bobby entered the walkway shortly before three o'clock. He was fully rigged in the familiar yellow-fluorescent jacket and wrapped in a duty belt that held a familiar array of equipment, which included handcuffs, a baton, a CS spray unit, and a short leather holster with a button-down strap over the butt of a small automatic.

He had the relaxed and assured manner that is a hallmark of his profession, a highly visible presence to reassure the public that the forces of law and order are watching over them.

Devon was about to shift his eyes away from the policeman when two things caught his attention.

It struck him as odd that the officer, standing at over six foot and with the youthful features of a new recruit, should be walking the beat on his own. It was standard police practice - particularly in high-profile city tourist areas - that foot patrols were two-person assignments.

And, the last time Devon looked, British Bobbies were not allowed to be armed!

The policeman was about a hundred yards from Devon's location and walking with his back to him towards the youth with the holdall. Devon leaned forward in his seat and whispered into his throat mic. "It's the policeman. Our subject is the policeman!"

Everyone had been warned to keep a watching brief only. The job here today was to identify the pick-up man and follow him back to perhaps the location of another cell.

The bogus policeman held up his hand and stopped the holdall youth, under a casual pretence of wanting a chat. The youth placed the holdall on the ground between himself and the policeman, and as the two carried out what appeared to be a friendly conversation, the policeman's hands surreptitiously wrapped around the handles of the holdall.

Two things happened at once.

The policeman unbuttoned his pistol and brought it into the gap between him and the youth. Before Devon or any of his team could react there were two short cracks and the youth's eyes widened in shock and pain. His hands involuntarily jumped against the policeman for support, but couldn't stop his slow slide to the pavement.

He was dead by the time he reached it.

At the same time the "policeman" pivoted on his left foot and turned to scan the area for danger.

Devon's line of sight was blocked by a noisy group of youths who appeared to be screaming along with some banal lyrics feeding out through their iPods. He had no option but to jump to the side of the group for a better view. His sudden movement must have alerted the policeman. The gun was now swivelled towards him.

Devon knew the whole situation had just turned

into what he loved to call a *clusterfuck*, a crude US Marine expression to describe that the worst thing that could happen had just happened.

His first thought was for the innocent bystanders. He cleared the Sig from his rear waistband, fired two shots into the air, and shouted at everyone in the area to get down.

There was instant pandemonium. People started rushing around in circles, bumping into each other, and screaming at the top of their voices. One youth crashed into Devon, pushing against his gun arm as he fought to bring the weapon to bear on the threat ahead of him.

The policeman stooped to place one knee on the ground, aiming his weapon directly at Devon and the flailing bodies around him. Devon could see the finger contracting on the trigger.

Shots rang out.

But they came from a direction different to where the policeman was standing.

Devon looked to his right and saw Alan Doyle hold a steady aim as the policeman crumpled to the footpath, his yellow jacket already heavily stained with blood from the gaping chest wounds inflicted by Doyle's well-placed, three-round burst.

The policeman rolled onto his back as Devon fired twice into the exposed yellow uniform, intent on making sure the gunman couldn't fire into the panic-stricken pedestrians around him.

By the time Devon reached his target, the man's eyes had glassed over and were staring unseeing at a bright-blue London sky.

Chapter 6
Pakistan

OSAMA BID LADEN was a fading star long before a pair of Chinook CH-47D helicopters dropped two dozen members of the Naval Special Warfare Development Group into a compound in Abbottabad, close to the capital of Pakistan. Guided in by an Air Force RQ-170 pilotless drone, the members of the group, better known as Seal Team Six, cornered and killed bin Laden in less than four minutes.

The man who was responsible for the 9/11 Twin Tower attacks in New York, and who had attained among his people a mystical status that was every bit as awe-inspiring as the Allah they worshipped, was sent to an ignominious end after years of unremitting pursuit by the Pentagon and CIA.

For the previous decade, bin Laden could find refuge only in the deep bowels of a crude cave network in the remote mountainous border region between Afghanistan and Pakistan. He moved among his people mainly at night, revelling in the near-idolatry status that the attacks on America had bought for him. He became the de facto leader of the Muslim militant world, and began to build dreams and plans for a second 9/11.

But slowly he began to lose touch. His cave exile dulled his ability to move between the disparate groups of mullahs who wanted to press home more and more attacks on America and its Western lackeys, particularly the United Kingdom. Constricted and hounded, bin Laden gradually saw the rise of other leaders who refused to turn to him for sanction of their operations.

Bin Laden knew he had to move again to the forefront, be seen by his people, and take his rightful place as the one true voice of Allah. Even as he prepared to take more and more chances, he was encouraged by the pathetic attempts of America to discover his location.

On one occasion the Americans carried out a major night-long bunker-busting bomb raid in the Hindu Kush mountain range. At the time, bin Laden was three hundred miles away in a mud hut on the Hari River heading for North West Pakistan.

The same American ineptitude was repeated over and over again. When they claimed they had cornered bin Laden in one place, he was usually in an altogether different place. The chances of them actually finding him were looking more and more remote.

Emboldened by the mistakes of the Americans, bin Laden sought to retrieve his power by moving closer to the source of the challenges against him. These were to be found in the streets, marketplaces and mosques of Pakistan, where the battle for the hearts and minds of young Muslims was being fought out on an almost daily basis.

But he had misread the carefully-crafted disinformation that was allowed to circulate concerning the apparently inept attempts to locate him.

Far from being confused by his likely

whereabouts, the CIA had him pinned to within twenty miles for almost the past two years. By carefully disseminating false trails and reports of near-misses, the Americans sought to lull bin Laden into a false sense of security.

When bin Laden thought they were looking one way he moved another way, usually under the watchful eye of a constantly retasked satellite. Eventually he was funnelled towards Islamabad, the country's capital, where he felt safe enough to establish a base in a large self-contained compound that brought him untold comforts denied for the past ten years by his "most wanted" status.

And that's where they found him.

A man, who prided himself on self-discipline and a God-like instinct to see into the hearts and minds of his enemies, was looking the wrong way when death came calling.

There was never a chance that he would be taken alive.

Quite apart from the massive security-cost implications, and the increased profiling that a long-drawn-out trial process would engender, the American authorities knew they would face almost daily protests and upheavals from the large Muslim communities dotted around America. Civil unrest would be at a scale never seen before in the country.

And so the bin Laden operation was stamped "terminate with extreme prejudice" long before the Chinooks left the ground. The Americans were confident they could deal with whoever stepped into take bin Laden's place.

They would not have been as sure of themselves had they known that bin Laden had been forced out of the picture more than two years previously, and that not one, but two new leaders had emerged in that time under their radar.

***

Asif Changwani and Yousaf Hasni were brought up in poverty in a remote tribal village west of Lahore in the Punjab province. They were cousins, both the eldest in their families, and both with strikingly athletic features handed down by their fathers, two of three brothers who achieved legendary status as military leaders in the country's fight for independence from the British Empire in 1947.

Asif and Yousaf loved to hear the campfire tales of the adventures enjoyed by their fathers and uncles, adventures that instilled in them a sense that they too were destined for things greater than minding sheep.

The first time they travelled into the big city of Lahore on the crowded Karachi Circular Railway, they were hooked.

When they both reached the age of twelve they were apprenticed to a small engineering company owned by a friend of the family. They quickly took to life in a big city. Not only did they continue with their religious study and prayers, they spent more and more time attending the local mosques to hear about the history of their country and its intended place in the world.

After a day's work they spent two hours each evening learning the arts of self-defence and how to make the most sophisticated bombs.

As the years rolled by, they were often parted

on missions around the world, but always found time to meet up again when they returned to Islamabad, which they had made their base.

They were now respected commanders, but as their influence grew they feared a confrontation, a struggle for ultimate control, would erupt between them.

It was Asif who found a solution. "Yousaf my brother, if we are to truly claim our destiny we must walk a separate path. We must not fight each other, but only the common enemy. We are each too determined, too set in our ways to yield to the other, so we must find a solution."

"Tell me what you have in mind."

Asif had rehearsed his speech for more than a year, and knew that he could convince Yousaf to go along with him. "We all know that the real enemy is the Great Satan, America. But we have other enemies and we must also take the fight to them. We cannot leave them unpunished for their crimes against Allah, praise and blessings be upon Him."

"Are you talking about Britain and the dogs of war that foam at the mouth in their Whitehall?" asked Yousaf.

"Yes, my brother. One of us must concentrate on Britain whilst the other is free to deal with the Great Satan."

"And how shall we decide this?"

Asif looked at his cousin and allowed a smile to wash over his features. "It's really quite simple Yousaf. You decide, and always remember that we must be ready to help each other when the circumstances call on us to do so."

Asif broke from the meeting more than two

hours later, satisfied he had secured the best deal possible.

He knew Yousaf harboured a similar competitive streak to his own, and would want to make a bigger impact by his actions. For that reason he did not tell his cousin he had an ace up his sleeve, a benefactor who provided him with access to untold cash and contacts that would make his task much easier.

Chapter 7
Dzerzhinsky

A LARGE SPRAWLING mansion sits incongruously among the forlorn hills overlooking the town of Dzerzhinsky on the banks of the Moskva River. The twenty-bedroom palace, with garage space for a dozen limousines, and surrounded by acres of manicured lawns, is out of keeping with the bedraggled landscape over which it stands sentry.

The 400-acre estate has its own runway for a Gulfstream G450 private jet capable of flying anywhere in the world. It shares luxury hangar space with a Sikorsky S76B helicopter, used for in-country flights, usually no more than frequent short hops to Moscow.

The man sitting in a large study overlooking his domain could afford all the frills that oil revenues had brought him over twenty years of a business career that had seen him plunder his country's most valuable commodity. As a self-made oligarch, he was ahead of the queue during Russia's mad scramble into privatisation – and he cared little about the backs he climbed on or the lives he terminated to get where he was.

But Gennady Anasenko was always mindful of one survival strategy on his rise to the top, and his determination to stay there. Quite simply he knew how to cultivate political power, ploughing untold millions into diverse regimes, and greasing the engines of change that constantly swept his homeland.

A major player on the world's financial stage, Anasenko also helped whoever sat in the power seats of the Kremlin to maximise the country's investments, sometimes by supplying shrewd market intelligence, other times by downright manipulations that left many leading-edge Western companies on the brink of collapse.

These days he enjoyed diplomatic status as a roving envoy, a neat title he engineered for himself to help with the movement of certain goods and cash transfers that could be transported with impunity anywhere in the world. Wherever it was parked, the Gulfstream was considered sovereign Russian Federation territory, and the diplomatic bags that were removed from it could not be challenged or searched.

As he sucked on a Cuban Behike cigar, he considered his latest project while studying his two most able lieutenants, luxuriating in two deep leather armchairs, and engrossed in American *Soldier of Fortune* magazines.

Igor and Yevgeni Borimov cut hugely menacing figures. Both weighed in at over eighteen stone, stood six foot five tall, and had shoulder spans that tended to make most people feel physically inadequate. Their heads were polished domes of pink granite, reminiscent of grotesque Telly Savalas lookalikes on a bad day. Their bodies were honed to physical perfection with the kind of spare-fat absence of heavyweight boxers preparing for a title fight.

The Borimovs were twins, born into an

impoverished family on the edge of Siberia. At the age of six they knew what it was like to work fourteen-hour shifts in a hellish coal mine before returning home to the meagre plates of food their mother could rustle up. What little money they earned was grabbed by their wasteful father, who spent his days throwing cheap rot-gut Vodka down his throat, and his nights beating up on his wife or his two sons.

When the boys reached their twelfth birthday the beatings stopped.

They arrived home from the pit to find their father slapping their mother brutally about the face because, once again, she couldn't find any meat to go with the stewed vegetables that were the family's staple diet.

Igor reacted first, sprinting across the small room to grab his father and fling him violently against the bare brick wall of the kitchen. There was a sickening crunch of bone and a trail of blood as the father slid down the rough wall surface to collapse onto the stone floor.

Had he stayed down, the matter might have ended there.

But fuelled by drink and a carthorse strength, which he had passed on to his sons, the father rose and fixed Igor with a murderous stare. The young man held his position.

By that time the twins had grown to almost six feet, and were beginning to understand that they were vastly different than anyone of their age. They had begun to notice they had even overtaken most of the adults with whom they worked down the treacherous mine shafts.

As the father advanced on Igor he failed to see Yevgeni coming in from his right side. The second twin had gone to the aid of his mother, but recognised immediately the danger Igor had put himself in. He sprang across the room and delivered a roundhouse blow to the side of his father's head.

It was delivered with such force and venom that it broke two of Yevgeni's knuckles. It also lifted his father off his feet and flung him across a rickety table and onto the floor.

This time he would not be getting up.

As if with the telepathic understanding that is inherent in twins, both boys immediately sprang towards the fallen figure. For almost five minutes they kicked and stomped on their father until, exhausted by the effort, they moved silently away.

Beneath them the corpse was not recognisable as a human being. The face was flattened into a mushy pulp of blood and brains, the neck was twisted at an obscene angle, and one of the arms was almost torn from the torso.

The following day the twins were behind bars in a brutal Moscow detention centre that was to make their lives down the pits seem a picnic by comparison. But as the years rolled past they adapted, and by the time they reached their seventeenth birthday they had pretty much the run of the place.

Fellow inmates and guards alike were fearful of the psychopathic brothers who bent most people to their will.

Early one morning their period of incarceration came to an end. A guard opened the cell door and ordered them to gather together what meagre belongings they had. They were escorted into a snow-covered courtyard and put on a truck with twenty other prisoners bound for conscript to a Russian infantry division suffering appalling losses against the Mujahideen of the mountains and plains of Afghanistan.

Whilst those around them cursed their luck, the Borimovs revelled in the limitless opportunities to kill their fellow man. They became particularly efficient and ruthless at it.

It was little surprise to anyone around them that they were recruited into Spetsnaz, the country's elite Special Forces unit, and it was there they met Gennady Anasenko, who was then a battalion commander.

Anasenko cared little for the war against Afghanistan. His time was devoted to pilfering army stores and trading guns with the rebels in return for high-grade cocaine that was secretly shipped back to various gangs for sale on the streets of Moscow. It was of no consequence to him that the armaments he used in his dealings were later used to kill his own soldiers, or that the expensive white powder was doing the same to the growing addict population back home.

He was making money, and lots of it. He saw the Borimovs as ideal enforcers and bodyguards. Over time he grew peculiarly found of the twins, recognising that their blind devotion and loyalty to him was not the kind of personal relationship he was used to.

For their part, the twins saw in Anasenko a man they could look up to, a father figure they never had.

When he judged the time right, Anasenko quit

the military and engineered freedom for the twins. He arrived back in Moscow to begin building a financial empire on a scale none of them could have envisioned in even their wildest imagination.

Anasenko was fortunate to have capital at a time when the Russian state was crying out for funds. The implementation of privatisation allowed him to snap up huge oil and gas assets at a fraction of their true value. Virtually overnight he became a billionaire many, many times over.

Using his new-found wealth, he turned to the outside world. He always had a head for business, and saw immense opportunities in ploughing his capital into some of the biggest names in Western commerce. Through time he constructed a tangled web of companies across Europe, then into China and Japan, and finally into the United States.

He hid his ownership behind countless subsidiaries, and started to wield immense worldwide business influence. His success brought the Kremlin to his door, and once again he saw an opportunity to expand still further.

He embraced the overtures, ploughed vast sums into shoring up political leaders, and helped the Politburo to maximise its overseas investments. In return they left him alone to operate freely from his new base at Dzerzhinsky, and granted him full diplomatic status to further his various illegal activities.

All along the way the Borimov twins stood at his shoulder, eliminating rivals and clearing the way for yet more business takeovers. They had benefitted greatly from his mentorship, becoming vastly wealthy individuals themselves, and enjoying the jet set life their association with Anasenko had carved out for them.

The trio spent only three months of the year at Dzerzhinsky, the rest of the time being taken up at a private palace in Gstaad, Switzerland, or on the biggest of the big yachts moored at Monaco. From these locations they reached out into every aspect of meaningful business and political life on the planet.

Anasenko drew longingly on his cigar again. "Tell me my sons, how are things going with our al-Qaeda friends?"

Igor was the first to respond. "We have now persuaded them to implement the first stage of your plan. Asif Changwani is on his way to America as we speak. The cells have been activated for him, and the money and weaponry has been delivered."

Yevgeni cut in. "I spoke with his cousin, Yousaf Hasni, two hours ago. He has arrived in Paris to carry out the first part of his mission before crossing over to London. We are awaiting your signal to commence operations."

"Excellent. We are getting very close to our dream of putting mother Russia back on top as the world's major superpower. All we need now is to be patient and let all the little pieces fall into place."

Anasenko thought back to two years ago when the plan first took root in his mind. Since the 9/11 attacks on New York he had waited patiently for Osama bin Laden to follow through with yet more atrocities that could well have tipped America over the edge. But nothing happened. The so-called great leader had shrunk into his caves, taken his foot off the pedal, and allowed America to recover its footing.

When it became obvious that nothing was being planned, he decided to take a hand. He reached out through a cabal of middlemen to the large Muslim population of Chechnya, and used his wealth to make them put him in touch with the power-brokers among the Afghan terror groups. He wanted men capable of taking over bin Laden's mantle, young men unafraid of action, and willing to die for their cause.

In all the reports he received, the names of Asif Changwani and Yousaf Hasni came up as two determined warriors who were commanding the respect of the next generation of martyrs. Although they were cousins, and had built seemingly very strong bonds of friendship, Anasenko decided to cultivate each of them separately. It was the way he had done business all his life, the rule of divide and conquer had been learned from an early age.

He had started to ply the cousins with money and equipment for their various enterprises, and made it easy for them to move around the Middle East and Europe. At the same time he had ensured a constant stream of praise was heaped on them by his sources within Afghanistan. Gradually he built up their profiles as the next natural leaders of al-Qaeda.

The cousins had believed their new-found status was due to the influence of powerful Russian Muslim connections. They were separately warned, however, that they must never reveal the true source of their support.

Only one problem had remained for Anasenko. The continued existence and influence of bin Laden hampered the chances of independent actions by the two cousins. He decided to put matters straight.

Using his many in-country contacts he began to carefully plot bin Laden's movements, even going so far as to pass on suggestions that he should relax his self-imposed exile and be seen among his people again.

When the American RQ-170 pilotless drone guided Seal Team Six to bin Laden's lair, few people in the world realised that it was Anasenko who passed on the information that led the drone to Abbottabad.

With bin Laden out of the picture, Anasenko was free to manipulate his own plans against America and its European allies. He would have his private al-Qaeda army launch a series of devastating attacks against Washington, Paris and London, and watch as the already dangerously unstable economies of these countries teetered over the brink.

He cared not a jot about Muslim fundamentalism or what the al-Qaeda terrorists were prepared to fight and die for. What he cared about was using the resultant mayhem to further his own megalomaniac dreams. Whilst the so-called superpowers battled to deal with the latest attacks on their freedom, he intended to slip under their defences to deliver an altogether different kind of knock-out blow.

Chapter 8
Monaco

MOST PEOPLE LOOK AT the familiar harbour scene in Monaco and draw the immediate conclusion that here is the playboy backyard of all playboy backyards, a haven for the world's idle rich. Most of that is true.

But away from the casino life and the endless yachting parties, Monaco has a serious side. It is estimated that more than a third of the world's big business and sports deals are transacted within this tiny municipality. It attracts the highest of the high rollers who use the pleasure backdrop for far more serious matters than the outward and visible signs would suggest.

As Gennady Anasenko sat back in the stern of the small power boat that ferried him out to his luxury yacht, he reflected that it was good to be back among the action. The deals he intended to put together on this trip would dwarf all his other accomplishments.

The small boat manoeuvred expertly between a mind-boggling collection of the world's most expensive boating structures, and came to rest alongside a solid-silver ladder reaching down to the water from the most impressive craft of them all.

Anasenko looked lovingly over his creation. Built at the Blohm and Voss shipyard in Germany, and measuring over 160 metres, the five-deck superstructure had its own 16-metre swimming pool, together with covered accommodation for an on-board Sikorsky S76B helicopter, the twin of the craft sitting in the hangar back in Dzerzhinsky. Despite his great wealth, Anasenko believed in getting discounts for job-lot purchases whenever possible.

There was nothing job-lot however about his yacht. The interior design went way beyond anything to be found in a five-star hotel, nothing having been overlooked for the $700 million dollar cheque that Anasenko wrote off as casually as if paying for a second-hand car.

In a rare moment of self-indulgence for a man who normally preferred to move in the shadows, Anasenko entered its name as *Gennady1* in the Lloyds Register of shipping.

He was welcomed aboard by the yacht's resident captain, a Danish-born sailing master whose career had taken him in all types of vessels to all parts of the maritime world. At sixty-five years of age, Benny Christensen couldn't believe his luck when he landed this latest job at a time when he was being passed over in favour of younger men for just about every posting he had applied for.

He had tried marriage once when he was in his twenties, but knew even then that a relationship was not possible for a man who spent at least ten months of every year with a deck under his feet and the open skies above his head. He agreed to a divorce after less than six months, and had never sought to repeat the mistake.

He was a large jocular man who ran a tight ship, encouraging his crew as much with kindness as with a steely determination to strive for perfection. His head was still covered in a mass of copper hair, and he had never been seen without his matching trademark goatee beard.

Even during the long absences of the owner, Christensen put his crew through a daily ritual of cleaning and maintenance chores, and for two hours every day he ran the two vast Rolls Royce Bergen V16 engines, each capable of delivering 4,000 horsepower and sending the craft hurtling at top speeds of up to seventy knots.

The annual running bill for *Gennady1* was more than five million dollars - and Benny Christensen was intent on ensuring that the owner got full value for his money.

He was grateful for the trust that had been placed in him and was more than happy to accommodate his owner's wishes, even though at times he knew some of the activities that took place on board could not be considered lawful within any usual definitions.

"Good to have you aboard again sir," Christensen flashed his usual greeting.

"Good to be here Benny. I'm afraid you'll have us around for longer than usual, perhaps as much as the next four weeks."

If Christensen was surprised he didn't show it. Anasenko's usual visits never lasted more than two weeks before he was off again on his many travels. A month-long stay was not something Christensen could have imagined.

"That's good news, sir. I'll await your schedule."

Christensen watched the remainder of the party climb on board. As usual the Borimov twins stood off to each side, watching for any threats, and preparing to rush in to protect their mentor. Behind them was a short stern-looking woman whose face seemed to be covered in large horn-rimmed spectacles, and whose curly black hair was tied up into an old-fashioned bun that did little to accentuate her porcelain features.

Anna Bobkov was thirty-five years old and considered by many to be the power behind the Anasenko throne. She was the old man's personal secretary, business manager, and, it was rumoured, his constant bedtime companion, though both took great pains to hide the intimate side of their relationship. She was a financial wizard who had helped add many billions to the Anasenko crock of gold.

Next up the ladder was a resident chef who followed the world with his boss, and delivered cuisine unparalleled even among the famed Michelin-starred fraternity he spurned. Life for Dieter Hochstetler was one long creative journey, a daily challenge to present food in a way others could not imagine. Few things gave him more pleasure than to hear Anasenko's guests wax lyrical about the delicacies he placed before them.

He was followed aboard by a large woman who acted as housemaid and cleaner in all of Anasenko's residences, and a young valet who was left to struggle alone with a pile of suitcases that covered the deck of the motor launch.

Bringing up the rear was a middle-aged man with a lean build, a buzz-cut hairstyle that had shorn his former mop of black curls to number-one shortness, and a pair of reflective sunglasses that added to his general air of cockiness and indifference. He was Anasenko's resident chopper pilot, and was looking forward to showing off his Holywood looks to the female population of Monte Carlo.

The two pilots who had flown the Gulfstream G450 from Dzerzhinsky to Nice Cote d'Azur, barely fifteen miles away, would remain with the jet at all times and be prepared to take off at a moment's notice. The jet's on-board luxuries, including generously-appointed staff bedrooms, meant they wouldn't be slumming it.

In addition to the group which boarded the yacht there were eight full-time crew members. Those working above-deck were required to wear crimson tailcoats and white trousers at all times. The jackets were emblazoned with a white eagle, the logo of Anasenko Worldwide Enterprises.

Anasenko swept ahead of his party into the yacht's master lounge, an enormous open-plan space adorned with luxurious soft white-leather seating, and dominated by a large bar area that ran down one side.

An intercom buzzed on a table close to where Anna Bobkov was seated. She lifted the handset to her ear, listened intently for a few moments, and then returned it to its cradle without uttering a word. She looked across at Anasenko. "There is a priority-one request from Paris."

He rose from his seat, crossed to the closed doorway, and pushed his face against a retinal imager. It blinked green and the single mahogany door swivelled open noiselessly. He stepped into the passageway and headed for his office.

Inside the large room he moved to a massive bookcase panel and pushed a finger against one of the delicately-woven wooden carvings that ran down the length of the bureau.

There was an audible click, followed by the whirring of an inner mechanism. The whole bookcase seemed to fold into itself, bringing forward hidden shelving that contained what appeared to be a large radio. It was in fact a state-of-the-art satellite transmission and receiving system, fully encrypted, and safe from any interference from the most sophisticated listening devices.

Anasenko twiddled a few knobs, hit a series of numbered buttons, and waited as the machine ran through its database. Within a few seconds there was a pulsing sound followed by a distinctive voice. "Eagle Four, please acknowledge."

Anasenko's reply was just as brief. "This is Eagle One. You have information for me."

He knew the man at the other end of the line was seated at his desk in the Ministere de l'intérieur offices in central Paris. He had been on Anasenko's payroll for more than ten years. "We have a problem. Members of GIGN are keeping watch on the little store. I fear it has been compromised."

Anasenko cursed at the news. The last thing he needed now was any slip-ups. His ordered mind immediately dismissed a batch of questions about how this part of his operation had been uncovered. There would be time later to find out the whys and wherefores. Now was a time to remove emotion from the equation.

He spoke quickly and without pause. "Our friend

is due to arrive in your city in twelve hours. Change his accommodation plans and arrange for his friends to meet him in a different location. Make sure that this time there are no foul-ups."

"What about our friend with the book shop?"

"That is no longer your concern. You should already have ended this conversation. You have work to do."

For several minutes after he stowed away the equipment, Anasenko sat staring out through the cabin window towards the magnificent hills of Monaco. He finally came to a decision, and retraced his path back to the main cabin.

All eyes turned towards him, recognising that something was wrong. However, when he turned towards the Borimov twins he had a smile on his face, and he spoke in a quiet, measured tone.

"I have a little job for you both. You leave for Paris immediately."

Twenty minutes later Anasenko watched as Captain Christensen pressed a knob in the mammoth console in his state-of-the-art wheelhouse. The deck roofing at the ship's aft opened in two sections and slid across into special recessed paneling on either side of the superstructure.

From below could be heard the muted sounds of hydraulics and a large circular platform rose slowly into view, pushing the Sikorsky S76B skywards, its four rotor blades drooping downwards in their usual position of unrest. The platform continued rising to a height more than thirty feet above the deck, a large ladder opening up on concertina legs as it settled into its final position.

As soon as the hydraulics stopped, the pilot

scaled the ladder, entered the cockpit, and began his pre-flight routine. The sound of the engine awoke the rotors, which stretched their arms and began a slow clockwise turn. Gradually the rev counter rose and with it the turning motion of the rotors, now a continual blur against the bright blue Monaco skyline.

Anasenko nodded at the Borimov twins as they walked across the deck, climbed the ladder, and disappeared into the passenger compartment of the helicopter. There was barely time for them to strap into the suede seating before the craft lifted clear off the platform and rose fifty feet into the air. It seemed to hover motionless for a few seconds, but then its nose dipped and it accelerated across the harbour, creating irritating small waves for the other yacht owners.

Within minutes the sound dissipated, and the chopper was lost to view over the mountain that was a natural shelter for Monte Carlo Bay.

Chapter 9
Paris

THE GIGN AGENT showed remarkable fortitude for a man nearing the end of a mind-numbing eight-hour shift, spent looking out through a window at a scene that barely changed. Down on the street there was little night-time traffic and no, absolutely no, comings and goings at the book depository shop across the way.

Shortly after six in the morning that all changed.

The agent's attention was drawn to movement at the top of the street leading to his location. Ordinarily he would pay little attention to early morning pedestrians, knowing most had emerged from the many small apartments in the area in search of first-baked croissants at a delightful patisserie around the corner on the Rue de l'Quest.

What was unusual was the size of this particular individual. He was quite simply the biggest sonofabitch the agent had ever seen. Tall, wide and menacing, the figure stomped his way down the cobbled pavement, brushing aside advertising hoardings, and ignoring the stares of a couple who had to jump out of his way to avoid being run over.

A shiny bald head sat between enormous shoulders, and he wore a tailored blue suit with the ease of a walkway model. The cut of the expensive cloth perfectly hugged the contours of a well-honed body, and, despite his bulk, he carried the easy grace of an athlete. He stopped at the steps leading down to the door of *Le Dépositaire Livre*.

The agent in the room opposite quickly turned backwards and hammered his fist against the stockinged feet of his colleague, who was lying snoring on a makeshift camp bed in the centre of the room. It took three good blows to bring the man awake.

The two agents watched as the bald giant descended the steps and hammered on the shop door. It took almost five minutes for a bedraggled-looking Jacques Basquey to tentatively open the flimsy glass-covered structure and peer out at the unexpected intruder.

The giant crossed the threshold, roughly brushing past the little man.

The agents immediately turned their attention to a voice-activated sound recorder mounted on a small table near the window where they sat. The listening device was put in place some weeks earlier, but had failed to pick up anything of interest.

Until now.

The familiar voice of Monsieur Basquey was the first they heard. "Who are you, why are you here at this ungodly hour of the day?"

There was a momentary silence and then a second voice entered the recorder. "I have been sent by your master to take care of a little situation. It seems you've been careless, your position has been compromised."

"Ce n'est possible"

"Oh I'm afraid it is possible, and now you must be silenced."

The two agents looked at each other as if willing the other to make a decision. They finally seemed to agree that they needed to stop whatever was about to happen across the street.

Suddenly, there was a booming crack behind them. They turned to look incredulously as the door to their room crashed off its hinges and tumbled onto the floor. Standing in the gap was the man who they had just watched enter the book shop and whose voice they could still hear booming through the recording machine. How was it possible?

Igor Borimov smiled as he lifted a T-33 Tokarev and fired twice at the nearest man. The agent grew two new holes in his forehead and fell against the camp bed, his stockinged feet twitching for a few seconds before going still.

The second agent was reaching for a pistol still strapped in its shoulder holster over the back of the chair when Borimov shifted his aim fractionally and fired a single round into the man's stomach. He crossed to his victim who was writhing on the floor trying to staunch the flow of blood with both hands clenched against the wound.

The smile never left Borimov's face. There was no rush with this one. It was a long time since he had the up-close pleasure of watching a man die. Might as well make the most of it, he mused.

Through the recording machine he could hear his twin brother Yevgeni goad the little shopkeeper. "It is time for you to depart this world. I have been asked to thank you for your help, but we can go on from here without you."

Monsieur Basquey's plaintive cries were cut short by a gurgling sound as the giant's hands encircled his throat and pressed against the airways. Even through the recording device, Igor could make out the snap of bone as his brother crudely twisted his victim's neck.

He turned his attention back to the GIGN agent and pushed the short barrel roughly into the man's mouth, breaking two front upper teeth in the process. A look of pure malevolence crossed his face as he squeezed the trigger.

***

Asif Changwani had to move quickly after landing at the Charles de Gaulle airport shortly after midnight. He didn't expect to find a telegram paged in the name of his alias at the arrivals counter, much less be prepared for what it contained.

His Russian benefactors had somehow learned that the two Paris cells might have suffered a breach of security, and he was ordered to a new location to await further instructions.

It was not news to unduly faze Asif. Throughout his life he had always prepared for the unexpected, knowing that seldom, if ever, any operation worked out exactly according to plan. He trusted his Russian sources fully, and knew he could rely on them to put matters right. Hadn't they come through for him so many times in the past?

He walked casually through the concourse building and out to the taxi rank. He gave the driver the address of one of the biggest hotels in central Paris, and settled back to enjoy the twenty-minute hop across town.

Outside the hotel he paid the driver and climbed six steps to a large revolving door. Ignoring the attempts of several brightly uniformed hotel staff to help with his single suitcase, he pushed through into the foyer, and stood looking around at the unbelievable opulence of the place.

After waiting two minutes, he pushed back through the revolving doors, descended the steps, and hailed a separate taxi. Again he gave the destination of a landmark hotel and repeated the same in-out manoeuvre as he had at the first hotel.

On his third taxi ride, he ordered the driver to stop in the suburb of Saint-Denis close to the Stade de France, the country's national football stadium. Satisfied he hadn't been followed, he spent fifteen minutes walking down narrow streets and lanes before emerging onto a large pedestrian square, full of late-night revellers spilling from various bars dotted around the perimeter.

He weaved his way through the throng and entered a small corner hotel. The directions provided by his Russian friends were, as usual, impeccable.

Inside his room, he settled easily on top of the bed and waited. Within minutes he was asleep from the exhaustion of a long journey, and the knowledge that ahead of him lay one of the most challenging periods of his life.

It was one that would demand all his resources and energy.

Chapter 10
London

MIKE DEVON AWOKE to the afternoon sounds of traffic outside his Bayswater home. His head thumped from too little sleep, not to mention the half-bottle of Bells whiskey he demolished in the small hours of the morning. He had stumbled into the house shortly after 3:00 am, having spent most of the previous evening trying to cover the squad's tracks following the debacle of the Embankment shooting.

General Sandford earned his money with a series of phone calls, which persuaded the Met police to accept credit for an outrageous story about the interception of a major drug deal. A substantial stash of heroin had even been produced for the benefit of the media cameras, together with a carefully constructed press release boasting the success of a major undercover operation.

As far as the great British public was concerned, two contemptible drug dealers were killed and a haul, with a street value in excess of two million pounds, would not now be polluting their sons and daughters.

It had taken the intervention of the Prime Minister to get the Met to play ball. Their commissioner was hell-bent on rattling cages about not being informed of an undercover operation on his doorstep, until it was pointed out to him that a joint terrorist task force was involved, and unless he shut his mouth, his resignation would be accepted before the close of day at Downing Street.

To help ease any loss of face with his men, a Downing Street statement made clear that the commissioner was involved from the outset in the planning of the operation.

Everyone ended up happy. Everyone, that is, but General Sandford who gave Devon the mother of all tongue-lashings for his failure to control the handover of cash from the Manchester courier to the bogus policeman.

Devon didn't argue. He knew the death of the al-Qaeda cell's London contact had deprived them of the next piece of the puzzle, a chance to discover where the man was holed up, and who he was working for.

In a debriefing that lasted through the evening and into the small hours, it was agreed to suspend action against the three London addresses they still had from the Paris book deliveries.

Devon reasoned that the bogus policeman was unlikely to be from any of the known locations. It was certain he was a middle-man, responsible for activating individual cells to suit whatever purpose he had in mind. They now needed more time to discover if a replacement go-between emerged on the scene.

On the chance the cells might be contacted and ordered to break up as a result of the Embankment shooting, Devon put extra men on the surveillance of the properties. All they could do now was sit and wait.

It had been almost a week since Devon was last home. It was a large three-storey Georgian house handed down to him by his parents. His father died two years ago after a cruelly long battle with cancer, and his mother followed two months later from loneliness and a broken heart.

Devon had rarely been around during the last years of their lives. Always stuck in the middle of assignments, and usually far from London, he made do with a handful of telephone messages and twice-a-year visits, when he could spare the time.

The guilt over his absences set in after their deaths. He knew if he could turn the clock back, little would change. As an only child he couldn't remember a time when they didn't pamper and cosset him. He loved them deeply for it, but he had chosen an occupation that demanded his full attention and commitment. There was little left to share, even with the two most important people in his life.

They had left him a moderately wealthy man. The house was mortgage-free, and with it came a substantial cash nest egg in their bank and savings accounts, as well as a 1963 Austin Healey 300 MkII in mint condition. When he had the time, he loved to tour it around London and turn heads, as his father had on many Sunday afternoons. He had received numerous offers from collectors, but turned down temptations that were well north of £30,000 in favour of keeping the memories.

The same was true of the house. It was much too big for a bachelor, but he loved the smells, the familiarity, and the security of coming home to it.

He pushed back the sheets on the bed, swivelled his legs onto the carpet, and gingerly tested his equilibrium by standing up. Surprisingly he experienced only a slight dizziness from which he quickly recovered, and marched towards the bathroom. Later, as he stood in a tracksuit drinking a cup of coffee, he suddenly remembered Emma.

Jeez! He had a date last night and didn't ring her to explain! There had been many short-time flirtations over the years, but Emma came closest to rekindling the love he once had for Pauline Brown, an MI6 operative he met on assignment in Chicago many years ago, and who was taken from him by an IRA assassin. He had avenged her death in the shoot-out at a Dublin farmhouse where Alan Doyle lost his right arm, but he had never truly gotten over her.

Until the evening he literally bumped into Emma Saunders walking through the foyer of the Dorchester Hotel. His mind absorbed by other matters, he knocked the poor girl's shopping bags from her grasp, spilling the contents for all to see.

On a reflex he had mumbled an apology, and stooped to gather up her belongings. It was only when she knelt beside him that he had taken his first look at her. Long brunette hair framed a face full of smiles, and missing any form of make-up. She didn't need any. She was stunning.

Devon had paused in the motion of handing her a perfume box and stared into bright blue eyes that penetrated into his soul. Without realising it, his eyes had roamed all over her, drinking in the white sports t-shirt, faded blue denims, and the three-inch wide brown belt that cinched her midriff to elfin proportions. It was only when he had noticed the blushing of her freckled cheeks that he realised he was the cause of it.

"I'm so sorry, I didn't mean...." For the first time in a long time, Mike Devon was slightly tongue-tied.

She broke the awkward silence hanging between them with a smile and an impish admonishment. "If you've seen quite enough perhaps you can help me gather the rest of my belongings. I'm not used to people gawping at my little personal knick-knacks."

Devon's uneasiness evaporated. For some reason he had felt comfortable in the presence of this stranger, lifting her bag to return her smile, and inviting her to a cup of coffee as a way of saying sorry. It was not something he had done for a long time. To his surprise and delight she had readily accepted.

That first meeting lasted almost two hours, each lost in the moment, each anxious to learn as much about the other as they could. They had agreed on a dinner date the following evening and so began a romance that was still strong after almost eighteen months.

There were no commitments on either side. She had slept many nights at his home, but always returned the following day to her own apartment. He told her just enough about his job for her to understand that he would be out of London for long periods, often at short notice. It seemed to suit her own desire for independence, her need for freedom to pursue a career that also demanded lost evenings and weekends.

Thinking about it over coffee, he remembered that he had texted her the previous evening to break their theatre date while he mopped up the Embankment operation. He had also promised to call her later but, in the buzz of meetings and deliberations, it had gone completely out of the window.

He lifted his cell phone and tentatively hit the speed dial for her number. She answered immediately, almost as if she was patiently awaiting his excuse. "Emma, I'm sorry, I got totally wrapped up last night and couldn't get away." He stumbled over the words.

"Not even to make a call?" In anyone else it would have sounded like a reprimand, but Devon knew her moods and could guess the tone was light-hearted.

"Let me make it up to you," he pleaded with equal good humour. "How about I order a takeaway and we curl up together tonight?"

"Mike Devon, if you think a few barbeque spare ribs are going to get you off the hook, then think again. At the very least a girl needs pampering when she's stood up. I've been stuck in the office all morning waiting for a delivery of flowers and chocolates, not to mention a note expressing undying love. What do I get? A quick Chinese and the promise of a roll in the hay."

"We could skip the Chinese."

Her laughter came down the phone. "You don't get off that easy, buster. Make sure the wine is chilled and the flowers are on the table. I'll be round at seven o'clock."

He smiled, said his goodbyes, and climbed the stairs to the top floor. The entire floor space was converted into a home gymnasium. Partition walls had been removed, new wooden flooring installed, and an array of keep-fit equipment dotted the area. The pavements of London were not user-friendly for joggers so he had hit on the conversion as the best way of maintaining his keep-fit regime whenever he was in residence.

Forty-five minutes of running the treadmill at various speeds brought out beads of sweat that loosened him for an attack on the weights. Thirty minutes of pushing himself to the limit was followed by his usual stint in front of the punchbag, a professional piece of equipment that wouldn't have been out of place in the best boxing gyms.

He was working towards a final series of combination punches when his mobile chirped on a bench. He frowned when he saw the name on the display, and his mood darkened still further when he heard what the caller had to say.

Tonight's date with Emma had just gone south.

Chapter 11
Paris

CLAUDE BARTRAN MUNCHED on an unlit cigar and stared at the corpses of his agents. Standing at a little over five-seven and showing all the signs of his sixty years, the little GIGN chief was as agitated as at any time in his life. Thinning grey hair was plastered on his wrinkled pate, and a once-full matching beard was now more akin to a three-day stubble full of gaps.

He was less than eight months from completing forty years of service, a milestone that meant he could take a full pension, get away from the capital, and enjoy the delights of Provence where he owned a small holiday cottage.

Bartran was one of those people who wore a permanent scowl, a face covered with age and worry lines that gave him a hangdog look. First impressions of him were always of a man whose company was to be avoided at all costs. Nothing could be farther from the truth. Claude had a laconic wit which emerged when he was in a storytelling mood. He had an encyclopaedic knowledge of all sports, particularly horseracing, and reckoned the *Pari Mutuel*, France's betting Totaliser, owed him payback for a lifetime of coming out second best. Before he hung up his boots he promised himself he would beat the odds to supplement his pension with a windfall.

He had been on his way to the betting shop to place his daily *Trifecta* when the call came through about the deaths of his agents.

He had called first at the book depository to inspect the body of Jacques Basquey, still dressed in pyjamas, his neck twisted at an unnatural angle. Both the shop and the small upstairs apartment had been thoroughly ransacked, the floors littered with upturned drawers, discarded clothes, and piles of books. If there was anything that may have interested GIGN, Claude knew it was probably long gone. He couldn't figure out, however, why the place hadn't been torched. Why take the risk that something might have been overlooked? Although it seemed likely that whoever was behind this gratuitous killing had gotten what they came for, he ordered a leave-no-stone-unturned search of the premises.

When one of the crime scene technies offered the view that it was unlikely they would turn up anything of significance, Claude fixed him with a withering stare, and launched into a tirade that left the poor man with no illusion that anything less than way beyond thorough, would cost him his job.

Claude marched angrily out of the shop, crossed the street, and steeled himself for the sight that awaited him. He knew both dead agents; knew of their families and of their hopes for the future, knew about their dedication and the hard work they had put in for him over the past six years. He took the loss hard.

As he sat on the edge of the bed, trying to picture what happened, he came to a sickening conclusion. There was no doubt in his mind this was a betrayal. Someone had learned that the bookseller had been compromised, and was under permanent surveillance by GIGN. Someone had passed that information to a third party who had set about cleaning house.

What rankled Bartran the most was the certainty that the information could only have come from within. Someone inside his organisation had turned renegade, and was responsible for these deaths. Someone had sold out their colleagues, not for some highbrow ideal, but for a filthy pay-off. Find the money and you find the man, he told himself.

A tear was forming in the corner of his left eye as he remembered his men in a jumble of lifelike images. Their laughter, the way they walked, the way they talked, the odd stupid things that spring to mind when you suddenly realise they won't be repeated. He turned away from the bodies to look out the window in a movement to mask his emotions. Staring across the rooftops of Paris, he was hit by a sudden thought.

What about the houses his other men were watching? What about the suspected al-Qaeda terrorists who were holed up there?

He turned quickly into the room and barked orders at a number of agents milling around. They broke off and began scrambling for satellite phones strapped to their belts. Bartran interrupted the urgent chatter. "Forget surveillance. Tell all squads to move in and arrest everyone they find in those houses. Tell them to do it now!"

***

Asif Changwani woke to a bright Paris morning, the sun filtering through a flimsy lace curtain choked with dirt and cobwebs. He didn't need time to assimilate to the unfamiliar surroundings of a nondescript hotel room – too often he had gone to bed and arisen in strange rooms in strange hotels in strange lands. He was well used to a life lived in the shadows, and was able to adapt quickly to wherever he found himself.

He knew that by now his benefactor had arranged to move the two cells from their safe houses, and he would meet each of these four-man groups separately in two prearranged locations later this morning. He was fastidious about his hygiene and appearance, and allowed himself almost an hour to bathe, shave and change into a new suit, which was among a small wardrobe conveniently left for him the previous afternoon. He missed wearing the beard of his religion, but it was a small price to pay for having to blend in with these Godless heathens who would feel his wrath for their decadent ways.

He consumed a small oatmeal breakfast and left the hotel shortly after eight o'clock. A taxi took him within twenty minutes walking distance of the address he had been given for a lock-up garage in a back street off Avenue Charles de Gaulle, due east from the Eiffel Tower. He carried with him a set of keys that would provide access to the third garage in a row of ten.

As expected the garage contained a large Citroen van, in the back of which he found four ready-packed rucksacks. There was no need to check the contents; he knew everything would be as it should.

Ten minutes later he heard the tap-tap-tap of the coded knock on the garage door. He quickly opened a small wicker gate and admitted four men. He had never before met any of them, but was confident they knew what was expected, and would obey without question whatever assignment he set before them. All they knew was that today was to be their last day on earth; today was to mark their ascension to join Allah in his heavenly kingdom where he would bestow the many bountiful delights awaiting all martyrs in the afterworld.

"Salaam Alaikum", he reverently said to each man as he entered the garage. It was the traditional *Peace be Upon You* greeting of their faith.

"Alaikum Salaam," was the response from each.

The five men climbed into the back of the van, and for more than forty minutes Changwani outlined their mission. He went carefully over every step, explained what was expected of them, and set out a series of likely events that might arise as a result of their actions. Satisfied they were ready for what lay ahead, he took his leave with a final ominous message.

"In the unlikely event that any of you find a means to escape from the situation, you have a duty to Allah to seek the chance to live to fight another day in his name. Otherwise you are to embrace your death, and go towards your meeting with Allah in the certain knowledge that your eternal rewards await you. You must not, under any circumstances, allow yourselves to be captured."

Just over an hour later he was setting out another mission to his second group. This was also in a lock-up garage, and also in the back of a fully-stocked van.

By two o'clock in the afternoon he was in the air

en route to London, knowing that he would be safely in another hotel in another city before the actions he had planned would kick off in Paris.

***

A fully-armed assault team of six GIGN agents broke down the doors at the front and back of the first house under surveillance. They expected resistance and were fully prepared to kill anyone who showed the slightest hint of making a fight of it. They knew the men they would find in the house were connected in some way to the deaths of their colleagues in the stake-out opposite the Book Depository shop. It was a connection that meant there would be no mercy.

What they didn't expect to find was an empty house.

The agents on duty throughout the previous night had reported that all four men were still inside. They had monitored the usual late-night music-playing and television-watching, followed by the usual ritual of lights being turned off, and the occupants retiring to the bedrooms shortly after two o'clock. A constant vigil was kept on the front and back doors and no-one had left until the agents burst into the deserted rooms. But how could this be?

The group leader had the unenviable job of contacting Claude Bartran to break the news. Bad as the news was, he couldn't believe that Bartran had just received equally bad news from the second house to be gate-crashed that morning.

The birds had flown from that address as well.

Immediate all-points bulletins were issued to

every Paris law-enforcement agency. Detailed dossiers, including high-density enhanced photographs taken during the stake-outs, were issued to all counter-terrorist agents, city detectives, patrolmen, train station security details, and airline checking staff. Public notices were posted around the city, and the main television companies broke into their regular broadcasts to issue appeals for help in finding what one announcer called "dangerous terrorists" who were plotting imminent attacks.

Back at the site of the first house, the agents discovered how the terrorists slipped the net. A hole hidden behind a large picture was cut into the wall adjoining a vacant property. It must have been carefully excavated over many weeks and provided a simple means for the occupants to move into the second house and exit under the cover of darkness. Mounds of rubbish strewn around the exterior would have made it easier to avoid detection from the watching agents – even in the unlikely event they had shifted their gaze away from their primary target.

There was nothing subtle about the way the second group had vanished from the other house. In each of the two adjoining homes the agents found families trussed up in their beds. One man had died from a horrific throat-cut, but his wife and ten year-old daughter were still alive, bound, gagged and stuffed in a wardrobe.

In the second house an elderly couple were hog-tied to chairs, suffering from little more than the effects of shock on their frail bodies.

The terrorists had simply climbed into the roof-spaces, cut their way through to the adjoining houses, and descended through attic hatches to confront their unfortunate victims. Unlike the first group, they had decided to put two houses between them before calmly exiting through the rear of the third building.

Claude Bartran was called to a meeting at the Ministere de l'intérieur where he briefed ministers on the events of the past few hours and outlined his fears for what could be happening. Everything he told them was pure conjecture, but his reputation was such that no-one was about to question the need for such a high-profile response to the sudden disappearance of eight suspected members of al-Qaeda. Within an hour a decision was taken to supplement the search for the men with a squad from the *Commandment des Operations Speciales*, a Special Operations Command based at Taverny. They were placed under the immediate command of Claude Bartran.

The operation was the largest ever mounted within the inner-city limits of Paris. Roadblocks brought traffic to a standstill and train departures were delayed as agents combed through carriages and waiting-area platforms. Scores of officers descended on hotels and guesthouses. Pedestrians were stopped in the streets, and large department stores were ordered to close their doors. Everything that could be done to restrict the movement of these eight men was being done.

All things being equal, the forces of law and order were about five steps behind and two hours too late.

Just before the first of the roadblocks were

maneuvered into position, a blue Citroen van pulled over to the pavement on the Avenue Gustav Eiffel close to the main visitor entrance of Europe's most iconic structure. The vehicle occupants cared little about parking restrictions or about the curious looks caused by the squealing of their tyres on the dry road surface. Four men alighted casually onto the pavement, each pointing Israeli-made Uzi sub-machine guns in the air, and each fired a sustained burst into the clear Paris sky.

A crowd of more than one hundred people was milling around the tarmacked forecourt, heavily shadowed by a light sun that failed to break through the Tower's latticed framework. Men, women and children taking their turn to queue for the turnstiles or to visit the wooden gift shop sitting to the right of the entrance doors, were oblivious to everything, save for the expectation of sampling a once-in-a-lifetime viewing experience from more than a thousand feet in the air.

At first no-one seemed to react to the noise of the gunfire, but seconds later there was pandemonium. Played in real time it looked like everyone broke away at the same split second, screaming and stumbling into each other in a mad panic to escape what they could only initially register as something that shouldn't be happening. Played in slow motion, a middle-aged woman was the first to recognise the danger confronting the crowd, and it was her hysterical screams that galvanised the rest into action, many still trying to understand why they were suddenly very, very frightened.

The four gunmen advanced in a line across the

forecourt, their weapons slowly brought back to the horizontal and pointing directly at the mass of bodies scurrying for safety in all directions. The gunman to the left of the group opened fire again, his weapon pointed at a security guard rushing forward to see what was happening, and armed with no more than a flimsy directional baton to control the normal queues of visitors. The burst of 9mm rounds almost cut his body in two.

Another of the gunmen also fired towards a man dressed in a dark blue security uniform. The burst not only felled the unfortunate guard, but cut down two women and a fourteen year-old boy standing beside him.

The remaining two gunmen began firing indiscriminately at the entrance doors before raking the exterior of the gift shop where small groups of people huddled for safety.

The body toll was horrendous.

By now more than sixty people had taken flight up and down Avenue Gustav Eiffel, or crossed the road towards what they hoped was the safety of a public park opposite the main Tower entrance. Most ran as fast as their legs could carry them, but incongruously many travelled at a much slower pace, some dodging and weaving, and holding their hands over the backs of their heads in a pathetic gesture intended to stop the penetration of bullets into their skulls.

They needn't have worried. By that stage, the gunmen had turned their attention away from the fleeing mob. Two of the group unshouldered haversacks at the west base of one of the Tower's giant legs, and removed more than twenty blocks of brick-orange Semtex plastic explosive. They began placing the blocks around the quadrangular iron structure and joined the blocks with a web of det cord feeding back to a sinister black box, left on the ground close to where they worked.

Meanwhile, their two colleagues herded what remained of the cowering group of visitors into the entrance foyer, and slammed the doors against their screams. One of the men placed his haversack on the ground, removed two hand grenades, and pulled the safety pins. He casually stepped out onto the road, and tossed one grenade twenty yards towards a parked minibus; the other was sent sailing over a wrought-iron fence marking the boundary of the park.

Without waiting to see the results of his actions, he walked back to join his comrades, barely flinching as one explosion followed another. There were no casualties, if only because by this time anyone who could have left the scene was long gone. Had anyone chanced to look back, all they would have seen were thick palls of smoke, adding to the macabre shadows dancing around the Eiffel Tower. The detonation of the grenades had only one purpose – to further alert the security forces and bring them rushing to investigate.

Time appeared to be of the essence to the terrorists.

The leader of the group positioned his men in a wide circle around the base of the Tower structure. Each man carried six thirty-two-round spare magazines for their Uzis, together with a dozen pineapple-shaped Mk II American-made hand grenades. They placed the piles in front of them and waited behind the ironclad protection of the Tower's massive feet. The leader kept the control box for the Semtex charges close to his right hand.

It was three o'clock on a balmy Paris afternoon.

***

Thirty minutes later Claude Bartran was racing towards the scene in the back of an armoured Land Rover. The gridlock he had earlier ordered throughout the city conspired against his best attempts to make better progress after being rousted from his meeting with the country's top brass. For most of the journey he shouted furiously into a command phone, ordering local Gendarmerie to clear the route ahead of him. When that didn't work, he barked at his driver to ram into parked cars, mount pavements, and shoulder their way past any obstructions.

He arrived at the Avenue Gustav Eiffel to a scene he didn't believe possible in his nation's capital. Hasty police cordons were thrown across the road and pavements two hundred yards from the Tower entrance, and more than fifty officers in a variety of uniforms cowered behind their vehicles. He could see the burnt-out remains of a minibus, palls of smoke rising slowly in the windless air, and people waving frantically from all the Tower's vantage points. Then his eyes fell on corpses littering the road ahead and on the Tower's forecourt.

He leapt angrily from the vehicle, demanding to know who was in charge. He was greeted by a measured burst of machine-gun fire that pitted the road surface ahead of him, stopping well short of the makeshift vehicle barricade.

A tall man, dressed in full Gendarmerie uniform topped with gold epaulettes, emerged from a group standing behind an armoured Renault police station wagon. He held a bullhorn in his left hand while extending his right in a greeting to the well-known GIGN chief.

Bartran ignored the offered hand. "What's going on here? Why haven't we moved in?" he shouted at the unfortunate police commander.

"Sir, there are at least four heavily-armed individuals encamped at the base of the Tower. We estimate more than eighty hostages trapped in the building, and we have been warned that if we move any closer they will be killed."

Bartran fixed him with a stare of pure contempt. "Good God man, take a look around you – they've already started killing. How many bodies will it need to convince you that these terrorists aren't here to talk? They've already stepped over the boundaries of negotiation."

To his credit the policeman didn't flinch. He held Bartran's gaze and calmly told him: "They have rigged the tower with explosives, and I think they've already proved that they will detonate if we take pre-emptive action."

Bartran snatched binoculars from another policeman, and trained them on the building. The officer directed his search to the base of the west stanchion, and Bartran could see through the sharpening image the tangle of explosives wrapped around the ironwork. He swivelled the binoculars slowly across the compound, following the trail of wires, which ended close to a figure half-hidden behind a crossbeam. Bartran could see part of the man's face, and the unmistakeable mocking grin which covered it.

He continued to watch the terrorist for several minutes, taking in the calm composure, the sneering look, and the sense of serenity that he felt was emanating from his enemy. There was little doubt in Bartran's mind that these were the features of a martyr. Little doubt that no matter what was about to happen, here was a man already embracing his own death.

Bartran knew then what he had to do. Every instinct in his body told him this was no stand-off situation. There would be no demands, no bargaining, no bullhorn diplomacy. The men facing him had already proved themselves capable of killing, and they looked in the mood to add to their gruesome tally.

He would have to end this, and he would have to end it quickly.

A half-hour later, the group leaders of four squads assembled by Bartran began to radio in that they were in position. Despite feeling a knot of dread and apprehension tighten in his stomach, Bartran calmly flicked a switch to open all channels and mouthed *"It's a go"* into the voicebox of the command radio.

Almost immediately, the growing staccato sounds of four army helicopters assaulted the still air to the east of the Tower. Heads everywhere turned skywards to pick out the noisy intruders. From the north and south approaches to the tower, separate groups of armed assault troops raced towards the hidden terrorists, one of whom swivelled from his position to shout across at his leader.

"Haseem it has started. We must detonate the bomb before it is too late."

The man he addressed calmly rolled up the sleeve on his left arm and stared at his wristwatch. "No it is still too early. We must hold them off. We must fight like tigers my brothers, and we must use the time that has been allocated to us."

They were the last words he ever spoke.

A marksman, lying prone and camouflaged behind a bush fifty yards from Bartran, squeezed the trigger on an FR-F2 sniper rifle and sent a 7.62mm full metal jacket round into Haseem's throat shattering the spinal cord on its path out of the base of the neck. During the previous ten minutes the sniper never once had sight of more than half Haseem's neck, but he judged the width of his target to be at least an inch more than he was used to dealing with. At a distance of less than two hundred yards it was almost an insult to his prowess.

The hapless terrorist didn't have time to register that anything had happened. His body simply folded and dropped to the ground, all life instantaneously extinguished. The control switch to the bomb was less than a foot away from where he fell. It would have mattered little if at the moment of his death he was holding a finger over the top of the switch – the killing shot sent an immediate paralysis through his body, making any movement impossible to activate.

The three remaining terrorists were as yet oblivious to their leader's death. They were laying down a barrage of return fire towards the advancing Special Forces soldiers, and trying to avoid a deadly corridor of death that kept them pinned down behind their barricades.

One of them glanced across at the leader, instantly blanching as he spotted the corpse lying twisted behind the fretwork of iron. Without pause, he rose to his feet and dashed across the open ground towards Haseem's body, his mind seared with a single thought – detonate the bomb!

Halfway to his target he was poleaxed by incoming fire, taking two rounds to his exposed back and one through his left arm. He cartwheeled across the tarmac, coming to rest barely two feet from the black control box. With his last remaining dregs of energy he inched forward, reaching out his right hand towards a flashing-green switch on top of the console.

The extended hand, with the index finger pointed directly over the button, suddenly disappeared in a vapour of red and white mist.

The sniper, who had concentrated his attention on the control box while the storm raged around him, coolly slid forward the bolt action lever on the rifle, and waited for any other attempts at detonation by the remaining terrorists.

The action lasted barely another three minutes. The north and south Special Forces assault teams were joined by a third team of GIGN agents who burst in from the west side, and added to the torrent of murderous fire peppering the base of the Tower structure. The eastern approach was kept clear on Bartran's orders to provide the sniper with a clear line of sight to the bomb control box. The two remaining terrorists were ripped apart by the fusillades that rained in on their positions.

It took more than twenty minutes to secure the area. A bomb disposal squad cleared the Semtex devices and groups of agents poured into the Tower to evacuate hostages, and look for any remaining terrorists. A corridor of heavily-armed security personnel escorted the sightseers from the building to a containment area in the park opposite. There they would be individually screened and interviewed before being released. Bartran was taking no chances that any terrorist was hiding among the rescued civilians.

One by one his squad leaders came to him to report the successful mop-up of the operation. "Are you quite sure there are only four terrorists accounted for?" he asked one of them.

"Quite sure, sir."

"And none of the civilians reported seeing anyone else with the terrorists before or during the incident?"

The officer fixed him with a gaze that showed a mixture of curiosity and exasperation at having to repeat himself. "We got them all, sir."

Bartran thumped his fist on the bonnet of a car he was leaning across. "Damn, damn," he cursed in tempo with his banging.

"What is it, sir?"

"I'm afraid we didn't get all of them. There are at least another four terrorists unaccounted for, and right now my guess is that we're about to hear from them."

Bartran turned away from the assembled men and ran fingers through his thinning hair. He stood in that pose for several minutes, his mind trying to compartmentalise a jumble of thoughts. Finally he turned back to his men. "I want this area cleared as soon as possible. Leave only the necessary numbers to control the scene, and order everyone else back on duty. All road blocks are to stay in place and step up the search for the missing members of that second terrorist cell group. I want this city locked down, I want those men found."

As his men dispersed in all directions Bartran pulled a satellite phone from his combat jacket. His friend in London would need to be brought up to speed on what had just happened.

Chapter 12
London

MIKE DEVON WASTED little time after his conversation with Bartran. The news from Paris was grim, with twenty-three bodies so far accounted for, and the activation of the terrorist cells giving a clear warning that something similar could soon happen in London.

Not on his watch, he told himself.

General Sandford was watching the first pictures streaming in from Sky TV when Devon burst into the headquarters building. He had phoned ahead to mobilise all available manpower and knew the General would waste little time in bringing together the other security agencies, and approving immediate action. "The Met's been put in the picture and they've already begun an evacuation of the areas under surveillance. I don't want any slip-ups on this. If none of these targets remain alive, I can live with that."

Devon was strapping on an all-purpose combat webbing belt whilst eyeing the General's calm demeanour. "Are we taking the lead on this?" he asked.

"Yes," the General told him, "it's your show. Just make sure we don't have another Paris on our hands."

Devon racked the slide on his Sig and pushed it into a special holster at the back of his belt. On either side of the holster, four spare magazines were slotted into purpose-built pouches, alongside two cylindrical flash-bank grenades, two standard fragmentation grenades, and a Ka-Bar Army-issue knife. He wedged the belt to a tight fit over his hips and turned to Alan Doyle, already suited-and-booted. Their eyes locked in a knowing glance.

"Alan, I'll take target Alpha, you've got target Bravo. Don't take any chances out there. Bring everyone back safely, but make sure all tangos are put down."

"Don't worry boss, "Doyle responded with a grin, "I'll count 'em all out and I'll count 'em all back. Make sure you do likewise."

Devon was in the first group which took up position at either end of Tudor Street in the south-west district of Blackfriars. With him was Mason Hunter and four other agents, one of them a burly Scotsman, Bill Carlisle, whom Devon recruited from MI6 when he first put together the squad under the direction of General Sandford. Including the resident three watchers of the terrorist house, Devon knew he had enough manpower to deal with the situation.

***

Across the city at a terraced street in Hatfield, Alan Doyle was in charge of a group that included Alfie Cheadle, John Dyson and Bob Mortimer, all experienced men with Special Forces CVs. Doyle's orders were explicit – move in when ready. There would be no attempt at co-ordinating the two raids.

Members of the Metropolitan Police Special Terrorist Unit provided substantial back-up at both locations, and streets leading into the areas were cordoned off away from the views of any onlookers from the watched houses.

Doyle's squad was the first to move. The action was prompted by the opening of the front door of the house and a man emerging onto the street. He was a medium-build individual with slicked-down black hair atop a bronzed face. He wore a dirty brown anorak and carried a white plastic bag. One of the watchers reported that it was a usual shopping routine at this time of the day.

Doyle ordered Alfie Cheadle and Bob Mortimer to follow the man and take him down when he was out of sight from the house.

Fifty yards before he reached the corner that would take him into the High Street shopping area, and into full view of the police cordons, Cheadle noticed the man suddenly stop and look around him, his face full of quizzically worry lines.

Cheadle guessed his target had become alerted by the unusual silence in the bustling street, no doubt trying to figure out why no neighbours were standing around, why no window cleaners were about, or why the traffic had stopped running up and down what was normally a well-used thoroughfare.

He watched as the man's eyes turned in his direction, the eyebrows lifting up in fear as he recognised something else wasn't quite right.

Cheadle pulled Mortimer behind a car and withdrew his Glock 19 before crawling to the back of the vehicle. He edged onto the road and raised himself level with the boot of the car just as the gunman swivelled towards his direction.

The man had dropped the plastic bag on the pavement, reached inside his coat for a weapon and spun to face the two men following him.

"Stop! Armed police!"

The shout was lost in a burst of semi-automatic fire which raked the car, shattering glass from the side windows onto the street. Cheadle held his two-handed grip across the boot, ignored the incoming rounds, and fired a three-round return at the gunman. The tightly-controlled grouping all found centre mass and the gunman stumbled backwards to crash against the wall of a corner building.

Cheadle immediately broke cover and ran towards the victim, closely followed by Mortimer, who angled in from the opposite site. There was little doubt the man was dead, but Mortimer roughly kicked the gun from his grasp and turned the body over to face downwards on the pavement.

A hundred yards away, Alan Doyle jumped into action. "Fuck it, we've been made. Everybody move in. Go. Go!" he shouted, and sprang from his hiding place in a walled garden next to the target house. Six men rushed up the small pathway, the leading two attacking the door with the soles of their boots. The door crashed inwards and splintered against a wall. A similar sound could be heard from the rear of the building as agents kicked against a flimsy kitchen door.

John Dyson was first through the front door and into a narrow unlit hallway. He would have died there had Doyle not roughly pushed him aside with his prosthetic arm while aiming his Glock up the stairwell at a figure crouched behind wooden slatted railings. Because of Doyle's action, one of the gunman's rounds caught Dyson on the shoulder instead of the top of the head, leaving the former SAS soldier to fall away from the line of fire. Even as the gunman tried to shift his downward aim towards the second man through the door, he knew he had lost the race.

Doyle's left-handed grip, honed to rock-steadiness by hours spent on the range, was sighted perfectly at the threat from above. He calmly squeezed the trigger and the terrorist's head disintegrated.

Another member of Doyle's team tossed a flash-bang grenade into a small living room where two gunmen were sheltering behind large armchairs, and firing blindly towards the kitchen doorway. The thunderous noise and blinding light sent the men scampering to the floor, already suffering from burst ear-drums and eyes that had lost focus. Their end came quick.

Two agents, with MP5s on full auto, raked the room until the breach bars of their weapons locked on empty. The terrorists' bodies were found curled in foetal positions, unseeing eyes staring at each other in a look of utter desolation.

***

Mike Devon was unaware of Doyle's success. Standing behind a large builder's skip alongside a house renovation, he was cursing the news he had just been given by one of the resident stake-out teams. "How long ago was this?" he shouted at the figure squatted beside him.

John Templeton, who had racked up a sixteen-hour shift, rubbed his eyes and turned towards the main street. "He left the house shortly after three o'clock. There's a betting shop about ten minutes away and he usually spends a few hours there before returning. We had no way of knowing what was going down and no reason to stop him. It's a daily ritual and one…."

Devon cut him off. "If he comes out of that bookies and spots the roadblocks, he'll make a run for it. You know what he looks like so take two men and get over there. Let me know if he's still inside."

Templeton motioned towards two other agents and all three set off at a crouching run.

Devon swivelled back towards the target house and radioed his squad to move forward. The house was a two-storey affair, situated midway along a small residential street crowded with parked cars. There were no front gardens to the houses, just three steps leading directly from the pavement to the front doors. Using hand signals Devon manoeuvred his men to within twenty yards of each side of the front door.

And that was as far they got before all hell broke loose.

Glass shattered outwards from an upstairs window where a wicked-looking barrel was now pushing through the gap. Talk about advertising your intentions, Devon thought as he hurled himself to the ground before the first burst of automatic fire raked the pavement around him.

"They've spotted us!" Mason Hunter shouted above the din.

"No fuckin' kidding, Einstein," Devon responded testily.

As he crouched on the pavement, Devon became aware of a window opening in a house opposite. He watched bemused as a green-coloured tube protruded through the gap and sighted itself towards the target house. He recognised the familiar outline of an RPG and the *whoosh* of the missile as it arced across the roadway, disintegrating the upper part of the building where the terrorists had fired from.

Devon was as surprised as anyone by the use of the heavy armament. "Who the fuck brought an RPG to a knife fight?"

Hunter's face was widened by a silly grin. "It's Bill Carlisle. That big Jock doesn't believe in subtlety and, after all, you did tell the squad to draw whatever they wanted from the arsenal."

Devon returned the grin, but his mind was focused on a shower of debris that was still cascading onto the pavement around them. He waited a few moments longer before rising to his feet and barking orders at the men around him. Instead of rushing the door, the men flattened themselves against the wall of the building. One man fired a burst that shattered the downstairs window, whilst two others hurled flash-bang grenades past torn, flowing curtains into the room beyond. The same thing was repeated at the rear of the building.

Devon waited a full minute before ordering the door to be broken down. Despite the cramped interior, six men burst into the hallway aiming MP5s ahead of them in sweeping motions designed to lock onto any movement ahead. Their progress was unchallenged.

In a small front living room littered with upturned furnishings and broken ornaments, Devon found a figure lying behind a settee, his left leg at an odd angle as a result of being cartwheeled across the floor by the concussive blast caused by the two grenades. The man was either unconscious or dead, so Devon moved his gaze around the remainder of the room, wary of any other bodies suddenly jumping up from behind a discarded chair.

As he turned back towards the prone figure he heard a sharp intake of breath. The man's eyes shot open and his right hand fumbled on the floor for a pistol that was wrenched from his grasp during the explosions. Whether by luck or some inner sixth sense of its position, the flailing hand settled on the butt of a weapon partly hidden by a torn piece of cushion material.

Devon took one step forward, raised his Sig, and shot the man in the centre of the forehead. Today was not a time for the rights of suspects or for the taking of prisoners, who probably didn't know very much of what was going on outside their compact cell structure, and who would only cause logistical problems in terms of wasted interrogation and being granted access to willing lawyers.

No, today was a day for closure.

Mason Hunter stepped into the room looking totally disinterested in what had just taken place. "Two bodies upstairs, not much left of them after dancing a set with an RPG. The rest of the building is clear."

Devon thanked him and ordered him to take charge. "Search this place from top to bottom. Bag and tag anything of interest and then let the Met take over. Take the squad back to HQ and wait for my instructions."

"Where are you headed?"

Devon was already halfway out the door,

pushing the Sig back into its holster as he stepped onto the pavement. "We still have one man on the loose."

Just then his phone vibrated in his trouser pocket. He flipped it open and continued walking up the narrow street while he listed to John Templeton report that the fourth terrorist was still inside the betting shop, oblivious to what was going on less than five hundred yards away.

"Where are you now?" Devon asked.

"Outside on the opposite footpath looking directly across at the shop entrance. Bill Hastings is still inside the shop and Frank Butler is outside stationed at my nine. If he makes a move we have him covered."

"I'm on my way. Do nothing until I get there"

"If he comes out of that shop he'll spot the roadblocks down the street and know that something's amiss. There's a large crowd gathering at the junction and it's only a matter of time before someone goes into the shop and announces what's going on."

"I know John, but we're going to let this one run. We need to find out where he'll go." Devon cut the connection and called back to the ruined house. He spoke urgently to Hunter and gave instructions for the full team to break off the search and take up positions at various parts of the High Street.

Two minutes later he walked up to Templeton's shoulder. "Is he still inside?"

"Yes."

The door of the betting shop opened and Omar Massoud walked out, counting a wad of money grasped in his left hand. After a moment he looked up, saw the crowd at the junction, and made his way down the street to investigate. He burrowed his way into the throng of people until he could see down the avenue where his house was located.

He visibly blanched.

Staying within the protection of the crowd, Massoud glanced around him in all directions, trying to see if anyone was looking for him. He couldn't understand what had happened since his absence, but he was smart enough to realise that his friends had been either killed or captured and, but for the intervention of Allah, he would have been with them. He must get away from this place.

He stayed inside the crowd for another five minutes until he was sure no-one was looking for him. People were constantly running towards the scene, but others were going about their business, disinterested in anything that might interrupt the flow of their lives. He couldn't spot anything out of place and decided to break his cover. He strode slowly from the crowd and made his way back up the High Street, intending to get as far away as possible.

His first thought was the underground tube train, but as he walked he began to ration that that was one place where his photo could be plastered, and where he could be trapped if he was recognised. On a whim, he turned and marched through the revolving doors of a large Marks and Spencer department store.

"He's on the move, he's headed towards the underground station," a helpful radio voice informed the eight agents dotted around the area. "No, cancel that. He's gone into the Marks & Spencer store."

Devon decided to add to the chatter. "You all know what to do. Keep him under tabs, but don't let him spot you. If you think you're compromised break off immediately. Nobody is to follow. Does anyone know if there are any other exits?"

"Yes boss. There's another main entrance leading in from Carlisle Street to the rear."

Devon issued instructions to disperse his team to various locations overlooking the store and then took off at a sprint towards a junction that would lead him to Carlisle Street. All around him shoppers were still thronging the pavements oblivious to what was going on.

Inside the store Massoud took the escalator to the first floor, got off and completed a full circumference around the various aisles of men's clothing racks. He mounted the escalator for the second floor, this time manoeuvring behind a large display of kitchen utensils to make sure he had an unobstructed view of anyone being disgorged from the staircase.

He waited ten minutes, satisfied no-one was taking any interest in his presence. Then he casually made his way to the down escalator, all the time watching everyone around him. Back on the ground floor, he strode slowly towards the rear exit and emerged into a typically busy London shopping street. He walked barely a hundred yards before approaching a taxi that had just deposited two passengers outside a toy store. He climbed into the back of the cab and allowed himself a long sigh of relief.

It was only after a few moments that he thought about his comrades, pre-occupied as he was in making his escape. Nervously he removed a mobile phone from his pocket, and called up each of the numbers stored in the names of his friends. One by one the phones rang, but each time he heard the familiar *"The caller is not available"* message. By now he feared the worst.

Panic began to set in with the realisation that he knew no-one in this infidel city, he had nowhere to go. His only contacts were the men with whom he had shared the house as they awaited further instructions from an unknown man. He had no way of getting in touch with this mysterious figure. All that he knew was that the group had been ordered to a new address the following afternoon. He would have to get off the streets and lie low until then.

He had asked the taxi driver to drop him off in the middle of Piccadilly, if only because he had heard his friends say it was London's busiest district. He wanted to lose himself in the crowds, and began wandering up and down side streets until he came to a building advertising itself as a low-rate hostel. He walked through the door and up to a reception counter that was completely encased in wire mesh.

An elderly man, barricaded behind the counter, was engrossed in the sports section of a daily newspaper and seemingly uninterested in a cigarette that was burning dangerously close to his lips. "Whatya want?" he rasped through a fog of swirling smoke.

"I need room for the night," Omar told him.

"If you've got the money we've got the room. But

mind we don't allow parties, pets or ponces."

Massoud looked blankly at him, unable to translate what was said.

"Do you want the room or not? I haven't got all day."

Massoud took a handful of notes from his pocket and pushed them through a small grill that mysteriously opened in the mesh. The old man counted them several times and then pushed a key back through the opening. "Number 23 top of the stairs on the left."

Five minutes later Massoud was stretched out on a flimsy single bed, staring at the ceiling, and fighting back tears that welled up behind frightened eyes. Slowly he recovered his composure by telling himself to be strong and that he still had a mission to complete. Whatever that mission was, he would know about it tomorrow and he would honour the memory of his friends by carrying it out to the best of his ability.

Suddenly remembering that switched-on mobile phones could be traced to exact locations, Massoud began disassembling the unit. He now knew his friends had been caught, and the security services would check their mobiles for incoming and outgoing calls in an attempt to track down any associates, but he was too smart for them. He ripped the small battery from its bed and removed the Simcard. He lay back contented that he was now safe.

At that precise moment, Mike Devon was downstairs deep in conversation with the old man behind the reception. His team had tracked Massoud across the city, surprised at the ease of the operation which led them to the hostel. Their quarry seemed alert enough to look constantly around him, but it became obvious that he lacked even the most basic counter-surveillance techniques.

Devon requisitioned one room adjoining Massoud's and another directly across the corridor. Special listening equipment was ordered up and brought to the hostel, and agents silently gained access to both rooms. Satisfied they were probably in for a long wait, Devon headed back to headquarters to review the events of the past twelve hours.

Chapter 13
Paris

IGOR AND YEVGENI Borimov sat in a car parked in an underground garage, beneath an eight-storey office building equally divided between two large, unrelated companies involved in various world financing ventures. The top four floors were the most expensive to lease, but when your business is bankrolled by Saudi Arabian oil revenues, there's not much point in worrying about minor expenses. *Kalnay Petro* was responsible not only for maximising those revenues through the manipulation of oil pricing, but also for investing in a staggering portfolio of some of the world's bluest of blue-chip companies.

Headed up by Sheik Kalid Abu-Nayyan, a sixty percent shareholder, the company was noted for the ruthlessness of its business practices and its success in annually quadrupling the bottom line of its balance sheet. Any investments that failed to hit the yearly target were jettisoned in favour of fresher pastures, with little care given to the effects on stability, or the subsequent job losses caused by suddenly dumping shares on jittery world stock markets.

But lately, Sheik Abu-Nayyan had been hoist on his own petard. More than thirty percent of his business was sunk into banks and investments houses where toxic debt took root more than a year ago. So far he had lost more than $100bn despite his best efforts to shift the exposure into other areas.

The banking sector, once a gilt-edged fallback, was now a polluted chalice spurned by all but the reckless investor.

To make matters worse, he had become aware of a stalking horse company that seemed to exist to undermine his many interests. Months of expensive investigations helped him zero in on a Russian by the name of Gennady Anasenko, who seemed to be cleverly setting himself up to grab *Kalnay Petro* for his biggest acquisition to date. This Russian peasant would soon realise he was out of his depth. He would come to regret meddling in affairs that soared way above his limited understanding.

Abu-Nayyan was running through these thoughts in his palatial eighth storey office when the first sounds of gunfire reached him from the street below. His initial thought was to rush to the window to investigate, but his secretary quickly drew him into the centre of the room and pressed an intercom sitting on a large marble-topped desk. Three heavy-set bodyguards immediately burst into the room.

"We must exit the building immediately," the secretary told Abu-Nayyan.

"Nonsense, we are perfectly safe here."

The secretary had served his master too long to worry about anything less than plain speaking. "We don't know what's going on outside, but we could be trapped here if terrorists are targeting this building. We've just been looking at what happened at the Eiffel Tower this morning and I'm not prepared to let you take any chances. If they set bombs around this building it could fold like a deck of cards."

Abu-Nayyan thought for a few moments. He knew he had private-elevator access to the underground garage situated to the rear of the building, away from the gunfire raging at the front of the complex. Once in the garage, he could be whisked quickly away in his armoured limousine to a secure complex on the outskirts of the city, free to continue his business dealings without worrying about terrorists. He couldn't imagine for a moment that the attack near the offices had anything to do with him, but why take any risks?"

Coming to a decision, he turned back to his secretary. "Okay. We will leave. Bring the folders from the safe and switch off all our computer servers. We will work from the back-ups at the house."

Five minutes later one of the bodyguards emerged from the elevator gripping a machine pistol. He scanned the deserted car park and, satisfied that it was secure, he signalled for the rest of the party to make their way to the limousine. With one bodyguard to the front and the others walking on either flank, Abu-Nayyan strode unhurriedly towards the parked vehicle, sitting underneath a wall light less than fifty yards from the elevator entrance.

None of the party heard the muted *phut* of the silenced weapon that poleaxed the guard walking on the right side of the small group. As they turned towards the falling figure, the guard on the left also suddenly threw up his arms and collapsed to the ground.

The guard leading the group instantly knew something was going down. He spun to his left and loosed off a full burst of automatic fire in the general direction he believed the first shot was fired from. As he swept his weapon across the dimly-lit area he could not pick out any sinister figures lurking behind the parked cars, many of which suffered wicked punch-holes in their bodywork as a result of his panicked reactions.

"Nice try asshole," came a voice to his rear as his gun locked on empty.

He spun round to look into the cold eyes of Igor Borimov, and knew that death was not far away.

"It's not him you should be worrying about," Yevgeni shouted from his right. The man spun again, this time looking at.....it was the same person! The look of bewilderment froze permanently on his face, his body destroyed by simultaneous volleys fired by the twins.

Sheik Abu-Nayyan could not believe what was happening. He was crouched behind his secretary in an attempt to avoid the bullet-fest, all the while cursing his highly-paid bodyguard contingent for allowing themselves to be neutralised so comprehensively. He watched in fear as the two assassins walked across the park, sporting the widest grins he had ever seen. Slowly, but surely, recognition set in.

"The Borimov twins," he whispered a lot louder than intended. He had seen these faces among photographs in a dossier compiled on Gennady Anasenko and knew, with a growing tightening of his stomach, that his nemesis had struck before Abu-Nayyan could put the wheels in motion for his destruction.

"It's nice to know that we're known, brother," Yevgeni said to Igor. "I hadn't realised we were so famous."

Abu-Nayyan rose from his crouch in a show of defiance. "I know who sent you and you can tell him that I'm not easily frightened. I am not going to sit back and let a backstreet gangster take away everything I've worked for. You can tell him from me it will be over my dead body before he gets a dime from the businesses I've built up over twenty years."

As soon as the words left his lips he knew he had misjudged the situation. These men weren't here to scare him off.

"Funny you should say that," Yevgeni smirked. He racked the slide on a Heckler & Koch MP5-N and stitched a row of bullets from Abu-Nayyan's groin to the top of his head. As the body was sent hurtling over the still-crouched secretary, Igor stepped forward and callously raked the trembling little man with a six-round burst.

The MP5-N is a distinctive variant of the original German-made submachine pistol. Developed especially for the American Navy, it has a collapsible stock and a threaded barrel to take a stainless steel sound suppressor favoured by the Seals. It's rarely seen outside America, which was why it was chosen for the attack on the *Kalnay Petro* premises.

The four al-Qaeda terrorists who stepped out of a van in front of the building were each carrying MP5-Ns from the same batch as the ones used by the Borimov twins. Their leader had an added noise suppressor, which would provide roughly the same shell scoring marks as the rounds discharged by the Borimovs. The plan was to fool the authorities into believing that Abu-Nayyan and his party were unfortunate to stumble into the terrorists, and were little more than innocent casualties.

Any hint of criminal wrongdoing would freeze the assets of *Kalnay Petro,* and effectively protect the company from the kind of hostile takeover that Gennady Anasenko now planned to launch against it.

The al-Qaeda cells were little more than pawns pushed around Anasenko's financial chessboard. The attack on the Eiffel Tower was merely an initial diversion to pull the security forces away from a rapid response to the attack on the Paris financial sector in which the *Kalnay* building was located.

Anasenko knew from detailed intelligence-gathering that Sheik Abu-Nayyan's likely reaction to violence being perpetrated anywhere near his postcode, would be to scarper back to his well-protected fortress residence on the outskirts of the city. A lot of assumptions were built into the conclusion that the Sheik would exit his eighth-storey office via the underground car park. As it turned out, it was a prediction that would have carried very short odds.

The orders given to the terrorists were explicit; they were to cause mayhem around the building, killing anyone in their path, and after twenty minutes, they were to move to the rear of the building to take refuge in the underground park. There they would wait and engage any security forces sent to apprehend them.

The twenty-minute deadline was calculated to provide the twins with enough time to carry out their mission. If the Sheik had not descended to the car park before then, it was likely that he would not be coming at all.

After mowing down ten hapless people doing little more than going about normally-humdrum lives, the terrorists made their way around the building and piled in through the opened doorways to the car park. The sight of five bodies strewn around the asphalt surface immediately sent them scurrying for cover, trying to understand what had taken place.

After five minutes of rushing from the cover of one parked car to another they worked out that they were alone. Whatever had taken place here would have to be put out of their minds. They had a job to do and, as if to emphasise the point, the screams of police sirens drew their attention back to the exterior of the building.

They were told their mission would send shockwaves through the world's financial institutions and perhaps lead to the final crippling of a number of economies which were little more than lapdogs to America. Should that happen, Allah would be well pleased by their sacrifices.

Chapter 14
Monaco

WISPY CIGAR ENTRAILS curled lazily upwards from the open deck and hung suspended in the still Mediterranean air beneath a necklace of pole-mounted lights that accentuated the man-made clouds. Beneath the smoky canopy, the chatter from a dozen people was occasionally interspersed with the sounds of laughter and the tinkle of glasses. The party mood had well and truly taken hold aboard *Gennady 1*, the host showing more signs than anyone that all was well in his world.

The news from Paris couldn't have been better. Everything had gone off without a hitch, leaving Gennady Anasenko to stretch out on a leather recliner and savour the success of his latest venture. He relished thoughts of the days ahead, the inevitable coming together of his plan to dominate the world's oil markets - and with it the prospect of bankrupting some of Europe's major economies.

He missed the company of the Borimov twins, not least because his security was guaranteed when they were around. He felt vulnerable without them, but it was a small price to pay for having them in charge of the next phase of his operation. His private jet had been sent from Monaco to Orly to ferry the twins to London where they would already be in position to carry out their next assignment. All being well they would return to the yacht the day after tomorrow.

He turned his attention to the men gathered

around the open-air deck. He had wined and dined them beyond extravagance, knowing that the fare served up was immeasurably better than could be found even among Monaco's many famed harbour restaurants.

Now it was time for them to pay the piper.

They were an eclectic mixture of bankers, investors and politicians, all with hands in Anasenko's pockets, and all owing their status to the benefactor role he had played over many years. During that time, he had made sure he received ample returns for the vast sums of money he had diverted into their private coffers, so much so that he owned them down to the very shirts on their backs.

It was the first time he had brought them together as a group. Before now they had each insisted on the anonymity of their relationship with him, aware of the dangers that would be caused to their professional reputations should such an association be made public. Before now they had acted in vacuums separate from each other, not knowing, or wanting to know, who else had sold their souls to this devil.

Anasenko cared not a jot about their sensitivities – he was entering a crucial stage of planning and needed these men to understand fully how they fitted into the big picture and the part they each had to play in the events that would follow.

Afterwards, when he no longer needed their services, he would decide what to do with them.

Anasenko rose from his seat, signalled the yacht's waiting staff to disappear, and invited his guests below decks to a soundproofed boardroom. When they were seated he outlined his plans to gasps of amazement.

Sitting farthest away from Anasenko was a man who, more than most, had looked decidedly uneasy all evening. He fidgeted nervously for several minutes with his cut-glass tumbler of cognac and, as if reaching a decision, he thumped the glass down on a nearby table and rose from his seat. He spoke directly to Anasenko. "You are talking of financial matters of which I have no understanding. I should not be here, so with your permission, I will leave."

Anasenko's reaction was that of a schoolmaster scolding an unruly child. "Sit down Minister, and shut up. I'll get to you later, but for now you will listen and say no more until I tell you to speak."

"You cannot talk to me that way. Do you know who I am?"

Anasenko burst out laughing. "The last time I looked you were the French Minister of Interior who sat twiddling his thumbs while Paris erupted yesterday. No, that's not fair. You played an active part in those events and would be hanged for treason if your Government knew about it."

Andre Fabron's face developed a sickly pallor in stark contrast to the bulging red veins on his neck. His was the voice on the other end of the encrypted phone link to Anasenko several days ago. He knew that his tip-off about the book store had led to the violent deaths of the owner and two policemen but, until now, his mind had refused to make the connection to the terrorist attacks at the Eiffel Tower and the financial district of Paris. The enormity of his involvement, and the subsequent hold that it give this man on him, slowly sank in. He collapsed into the chair, covered his face with his hands, and wept uncontrollably.

"Pull yourself together you pathetic excuse for a man," Anasenko shouted across the room. And then, as if the interruption was no consequence, he turned smilingly to the rest of the group and began issuing instructions for the purchase of shares in every known subsidiary of *Kaynay Petro*.

It was to be the first assault in a line of hostile dealing that would lead all the way to the main company itself.

***

For the first time in his life Asif Changwani began to question the reasoning behind an operation. Lying atop a bed in a hotel in Bayswater, London, he watched the Sky News images flowing into his room from Paris. The Eiffel Tower cell had killed many people, but failed to detonate the bomb. Although he cursed their stupidity he knew the primary objective of the attack was to act as a decoy for the attack on the financial district and, in that respect, it had been successful.

He would have liked to have seen the Tower fall to the ground in the same way the Twin Towers collapsed in New York ten years ago. That would have been a lasting remembrance of the power of Islam, a reminder to the world that they could strike anywhere they chose. If it had been up to him, he would have made sure of the success of the mission against the Eiffel Tower – this surely would have sent shockwaves once again around the world.

Instead what were they left with? A meaningless attack on financial institutions that Changwani was convinced served no useful purpose. How could the deaths of a few bankers be more important than demolishing one of the world's best known landmarks? Something wasn't right, and Changwani felt uneasiness towards the unknown Russian benefactors who were guiding his hand.

He lay for a long time trying to make sense of his thoughts. His targets in London followed much the same pattern as those in Paris, but what if the same outcome was achieved? What if a planned decoy attack on Trafalgar Square left that symbol of decadence still intact while his brothers martyred themselves for the sake of a few bankers? If these bankers were so important they could be killed at any time – why waste resources just to throw a smokescreen around the real target?

The only answers that came to Changwani were ones he didn't like. He was being used, not for some great crusade against the enemies of his faith, but for reasons that had more to do with money than with ideals.

He sat bolt upright on the bed. He had reached a decision and now he would follow it through. He would meet with the London cells tomorrow morning as planned, but this time there would be only one target – and this time he would join with his brothers.

**

"We have our orders Yevgeni. We must wait for the appointed time." Igor Borimov was trying to reason with his brother as they sat in a quiet corner of a restaurant ignoring the looks they received from other diners.

"No, don't you see that things have changed? The men who were planted here have either been killed or captured. We have no other choice."

Igor looked around him again to make sure there were no eavesdroppers. "We don't know that. We just know there has been a big security operation. The news stations say that a number of men have been killed, but they may not be the men we are relying on to mount the operations tomorrow."

Yevgeni smiled at his twin and slapped him playfully on the knee. "I keep telling you that you are too much of an optimist, my brother. What else could this be other than the fact that stupid al-Qaeda cells have allowed themselves to be compromised? We must take steps to ensure we can make alternative arrangements to complete our mission."

As if in resignation, Igor slumped back in his chair. "Alright brother you win. What do you propose we do?"

"We know the addresses where the al-Qaeda groups were staying, so we need to check out if these are the places where the security operations were mounted. Then we must make contact with our friend who is holed up in the hotel we booked for him. He must be made aware of what is happening."

Igor was quick to reply. "I say we let him rot. If the groups are out of action we don't need him. Let him make his own way back home."

Yevgeni smiled benevolently. "But what if our master has other plans for him?"

Twenty minutes later the brothers stepped out of a taxi in Blackfriars and made their way on foot towards the address they had for the safe house several streets away. There was a heavy police presence in the area, and by the time they neared Tudor Street the roads were completely sealed off. They walked quickly away from the area and hailed another taxi to take them across town.

A similar scene greeted them at the High Street. They watched as workmen shored up the front of a terraced house that looked like it had been bombed, and noticed forensic police officers carrying large sacks of materials out through a front door. Conscious not to draw attention to themselves, they stood for only a few minutes among a crowd of onlookers, and then walked back towards where the taxi had left them off.

"I've been thinking Yevgeni, how do we contact our friend? He has no phone and we can't just waltz into the hotel and ask for his room number."

Yevgeni smiled. "There are more ways than one to skin a cat."

Chapter 15
London

THE FIRST THING to grab Devon's attention as he pushed open the front door of his house, was the tantalising smells of cooking wafting out from the kitchen at the rear of the building. The next was the sound of Emma's familiar attempts to hum her way through an entire Elton John number. He wasn't sure which was the more welcome – his desire for food or the thoughts he was now harbouring of the dessert which was sure to follow.

He had swung past the house intending only to pick up a few files and a change of clothes, before spending a late night back at the office trying to grapple with an operation that was dangerously close to spiralling out of control. Far from being annoyed with the interruption, he was thankful for a piece of Emma's company. He had missed her over the past few days, something that was lately happening more and more. It also helped his mood that he hadn't eaten anything since early yesterday morning.

He crept down the hall, pushed open the kitchen door, and watched as she stood over a cooker covered with just about every pot in his possession. He silently crossed the room, pushing his way through the fog of steam, and wrapped his arms around her waist. He held tightly as she jumped in fright against the shock of the interruption, the tangle of her hair falling back against his face as she smiled upwards in recognition.

He kissed her tenderly on the forehead. "How did you know I would come home this evening?"

She turned back towards the cooker, absently stirring a pot filled with a curious mixture of beansprouts and peas. "Even the great Mike Devon has to eat sometimes," she told him. "Besides, as I remember, we were supposed to have this meal last night."

"I'm sorry, Emma, I just couldn't get away. I'm afraid I'll have to go out again."

She turned towards him, noticing for the first time the streaks of grime on his face and the spots of dust in his hair and jacket. "Looks like someone's just come from a building site? Go take a shower and change out of those filthy rags. Dinner will be in thirty minutes."

He kissed her again, this time full on the lips, and turned away to head for the bathroom. He turned the shower to the hottest he could bear, standing under the sharp needles for ten minutes before twisting the knob to ice cold. Feeling reinvigorated he dressed quickly and made his way to the dining room, just as Emma began ferrying in a series of dishes.

"Anything I can do to help?"

"Everything's good to go. Sit down and tuck in."

An hour later they were stretched out on the settee, holding glasses of wine and snuggled together in a rare moment of contentedness. She reached up and kissed him. Then she sat down her glass, swivelled onto her knees, and took his head in her hands. This time the kiss was long and lingering, her hands running through his hair and her tongue darting in and out of his mouth as her breathing rose to a crescendo.

Somewhere along the way she remembered being picked up and carried into the bedroom. What followed was a frenzied wrestling match that both seemed to need, but when the passion was spent, they locked again, this time in a long series of thrusts, each wanting to draw out every piece of pleasure they could.

Finally, close to midnight, they rolled into a comfortable stretch and began falling asleep. She leaned over to nuzzle his ear and whispered, "I love you Mike."

Emma awoke next morning to the sounds of coffee cups rattling outside the room. She was glad he was still here, but then remembered her stupid words to him the night before. She shouldn't have told him she loved him. She should not have risked pushing him away by offering a commitment that she knew he couldn't undertake. She knew he had heard her, but had chosen not to reply, and now she wondered if there was any future for their relationship.

Everything was fine for the first year or so, but gradually Mike Devon's influence on her life had taken hold. She had never been in love before and knew she would never have the same feelings for any other man. But now she wanted more, and he was not prepared to give it. Much as the prospect frightened her, she knew she would have to start thinking of a future without him. It would be better to get out now than to linger in the forlorn hope that things between them would change.

The bedroom door opened and he walked in

carrying a cup of coffee to her bedside table. "Morning sleepyhead. Some of us have been up for hours," he told her while running his hand tenderly through her hair.

Perhaps he hadn't heard her last night? Was she being too selfish in her demands? He had never tried to kid her about what he wanted out of the relationship and she knew she couldn't hope to compete against his other mistress - his job.

He straightened up and angled away from the bed. "I have to go. I'll be out of commission for a few days, but I'll call you at the weekend." With that he was out the door.

She fell back on the pillows, fighting tears that summed up her feeling of despair. Then the door opened again and his head appeared through the gap.

"By the way," he said, "I love you too, Emma."

There was none of the usual frustrated banging of fists on the steering wheel, no mouthing of obscenities against fellow motorists who usually drove much too slowly for his liking. There was not even a hint of his normally dangerous habit of jumping lanes to steal an extra precious second of time against the other idiot drivers who should know better than delay a man with important business to attend to. On this morning, Mike Devon was showing a carefree, smiling side he had hidden from as far back as he could remember.

He even managed a poor attempt at whistling along to Sinatra's *My Way* belting out from a radio more used to being firmly turned to the off-position.

He knew of course that his all's-well-with-the-world mood was down to only one thing, or more precisely one person.

He had made a huge leap into the unknown back at the house when he told Emma he loved her. He wasn't quite sure at the time how it would affect him, only that it seemed the right thing to do. He had known for some time that he had fallen hopelessly in love with her, but he didn't want to admit it, least of all to himself. Things between them had always been great and, he had to admit, he liked the space in their lives and the lack of total commitment between them. But the changes had been coming for some time.

He knew that Emma, despite her brave front, wanted more. He had disclosed to her that his job involved national security and would take him off around the world at a moment's notice. She never probed too deeply, but he was savvy enough to know that she had long since joined the dots. Yet somehow she didn't allow the danger of his profession to become a barrier between them.

For his part, he had realised she was more and more in his thoughts. The idea of not having her around, of not being able to reach out and touch her whenever he could, was unthinkable. In the end when she confirmed last night that she loved him, there could be only one response.

Yeah, he'd pretended not to have heard her, but he was only delaying the inevitable. He had risen shortly after six o'clock, spent an hour in the home-gym, and reached a decision after a long, cold shower. Now, all was well with the world!

Not quite, he chastised himself, remembering

the small matter of terrorists running round the streets of London. It was his job to catch them, and for two hours before he woke Emma, he buried himself in files trying to find some missing answers.

He had checked in with the stake-out teams at the hostel where Omar Massoud was holed up, and learned that he was still locked in his room. He had time to go to the office before returning to head up a long day of surveillance. During his earlier search of files, Devon thumbed his way back through the operation he mounted against the small London bank, which was bouncing unusually large sums of money around the globe. Because of the leggy blonde girl who worked at the bank, and who was spotted making a drop at the terrorist safe house in Manchester, that operation had now melded with the current surveillance of other terrorist hideouts unearthed by the packages sent from the Paris book store.

Devon's first order of business back at the office was to assemble a full team to keep track of the blonde. Alfie Cheadle, who had proven himself an extremely capable and resourceful addition to the squad, was put in charge. Devon left little room for guessing what he expected.

"By close of play today, I want to know everything about her. Find out where she lives, who her friends are, all known business and social acquaintances. Get our people delving into her records – bank accounts, social security, passport, and birth certificate. I want to know everything she's done from the moment she slipped out of her mother's womb until exactly five minutes ago."

Cheadle glowed at the prospect of being handed

what he knew was a top assignment. "Don't worry boss. If it's out there we'll find it."

As Cheadle turned to leave the room, Devon called him back. "Starting now she is not to be allowed out of sight. I want her tracked everywhere and I want to know who she talks to, who she meets, who she's sending emails to. You have a go for full wire taps, computer hacking, home and office video feeds, whatever it takes to learn what we need to know."

The young agent stared blankly at Devon, the first signs of the enormity of his mission beginning to paint frown lines across his face. He opened his mouth to speak, but seemed to think better of it.

Devon threw him a disarming smile. "If I didn't think you were up to it son, you wouldn't be asked. This bitch could hold the key to a lot of things, so I know that your best effort will be more than good enough. You have full authority to ask for anything you need, and don't be afraid to start ordering people around."

The frown disappeared, to be replaced by a beaming smile. "I won't let you down."

As soon as Cheadle left the office, Devon started scanning through a file that contained his notes from the visit made several weeks ago to the offices of Montgomery Holdings in Manhattan. Something was gnawing at the surface of his brain, but he couldn't yet nail it down.

Most of the names on the list of financial transactions that Devon copied from the Montgomery records were those of companies, many of which were little more than shells constructed to cover the tracks of the real companies, hidden behind a tangled web of subsidiaries and offshoots. A team of forensic accountants, armed with the best data-mining software money could buy, were still chasing around in circles trying to get to the end of a continuous loop. They reported almost on a daily basis, ending their summaries always with a note to say that given time, they would reach the end of the tunnel. But time was not something Devon believed they had much more of.

He turned his attention to the list of individual names, which to date had been disregarded, but only because it was unlikely a master planner would leave such an obvious audit trail of his activities. In any event, the sums of money sitting alongside these individuals were relatively modest amounts when set against the billions recorded against a number of companies.

Devon's attention was drawn to one name, which had four separate transactions of half a million dollars each over the past six months. It was not the amounts or the regularity which piqued his interest, it was the name. Francois Balliol.

There was nothing unusual about it, and the fact that it hadn't raised any red flags during an initial trawl of all the main criminal databases, meant there was little reason why Devon should now be staring at it. But yesterday's terrorist attacks in Paris had brought renewed focus on anything French. Could the payments relate in any way to those attacks? Could Francois Balliol be an alias for the man who activated the Paris cells? At the very least it merited a detailed follow-up.

Five minutes later he was deep in conversation with Claude Bartran. He filled him in on the background information he had on Balliol and reminded him that they had drawn a blank with criminal databases or any known associates. "Maybe from your end Claude, you can check banks for any accounts or safety deposits in that name. The money may bounce around a bit, but it has to come back and he has to be able to access it. You might get lucky."

Bartran assured him that he would put a small team onto the investigation. Devon could tell from the GIGN chief's voice that the old boy was taking to heart the deaths that had occurred in Paris.

"If only we had closed in sooner on the safe houses. Your tip-off about the book store led us directly to them *mon ami,* but we just sat and watched while they crawled out from beneath our noses to commit these terrible crimes. I will have to carry those deaths with me to the grave."

"Claude, you're being much too hard on yourself. Don't forget, if it wasn't for your prompt actions a lot more people would have died at the Eiffel Tower. I shudder to think what would have happened if you hadn't prevented those bombs from going off."

There was silence at the other end of the phoneline and for a moment Devon thought Bartran was cut off. Then the familiar guttural voice cut through the static. "I appreciate your attempts to wash away my guilt, but it won't work, it simply won't work."

"Bullshit!" Devon roared down the line. "If you hadn't had the presence of mind to contact me when you did, we might have been faced with the same scenes you had to endure in Paris. Don't forget we sat with our thumbs up our asses and would still have been watching the stake-out houses if you hadn't alerted us to what was going on."

"Did you get all the terrorists from the houses?" Bartran asked with a slight degree of trepidation in his voice.

"Yes, we got them all. Actually we're still sitting on one of them in the hope that he'll lead us to others, but the rest won't be giving us any trouble."

"Did you arrest the others?"

"No Claude, we killed the fuckers."

"Bon, tres bon."

The two men spent twenty minutes going over the details of their respective operations. The book store link to both the Paris and London terrorist cells meant these cells shared a common goal and probably a common command structure. They both agreed that among the terrorists who died they would not find the men responsible for setting them up and giving them their orders.

Devon was struck by a sudden thought. "How do you think the Paris cells were activated?"

"It was not done by phone. We monitored everything that came out of those houses and we checked the cell phones taken from the dead terrorists. There were no calls or messages."

"So what are you saying, Claude?"

After only a short pause the reply was full of authority. "They must have met their handler at a prearranged location sometime during the morning. From there they travelled immediately to their targets, since there was no time for anything other than to pick up their weapons and instructions."

It was pretty much as Devon expected. "I agree, but what I can't understand is why the London operation didn't follow the same pattern?"

"Probably because you killed the courier at the London Embankment," Bartran replied.

"No, Claude. What went down at the Embankment does not follow the pattern of Paris. The man we intercepted was little more than a courier, perhaps someone sent to pick up the address of a meeting place where the terrorists were to go for a briefing on their mission."

"What makes you think the meeting at the Embankment was not for a briefing?"

Devon knew he hadn't fully thought through his ideas but the more he talked with Bartran, the more he began to get them into order. "For one thing, there were no weapons or vehicles. If, as you say, the terrorists in Paris had immediate access to both, then why wasn't the same modus operandi used in London?"

There was no response so Devon continued. "And another thing. Why hadn't the London cells already left the stake-houses to make their way to the rendezvous? Why were they still in position when we jumped them?"

"I'm afraid you've lost me, mon ami."

Devon stretched back in his seat, aware that his thoughts were beginning to go in a direction he least expected. "What if whatever was planned for London was not due to take place just yet? What if the terrorists needed time between both planned attacks?"

Bartran cut in. "But what could possibly be gained from that? It would be much better to carry them out simultaneously. They would know that security in every major city, let alone London, would be heightened as a result of what happened in Paris.

It would not make sense to delay."

Devon smiled to himself. "What if the man who activated the Paris cells was also supposed to activate the London cells?"

"Obviously he could not be in two places at once. He would need to activate Paris and then jump on a plane to London......." Bartran tailed off as the significance hit him. "Mon Dieu, we should have been watching the airports."

Devon jumped in. "Stop beating yourself up, Claude. My guess is that this man would have already left Paris before the attacks began, and that means he's already in London. I'm guessing that whatever is planned here is not expected for at least another 24 hours to give him time to settle in and make contact with the cells."

"*Non, non,*" Bartran shouted down the phone. "Don't you see, *mon ami*, there was no contact in Paris, the terrorists already knew where to go to meet this man. It will be the same in London. He will expect the members of the cell to turn up soon at an address they already know."

The silence on the line dragged out as Devon considered the new twist. Finally he spoke again. "Claude, if you were here I would kiss that balding head of yours. Maybe he doesn't know we have eliminated all but one of his merry little bands, maybe he's still expecting them to turn up."

"And this helps you how?"

Devon smiled. "Because we're babysitting the last man standing, and he might just lead us to the fucker who's behind all this!"

Chapter 16
London

"HE'S ON THE MOVE." Mason Hunter spoke quietly into his throat mic as the door closed on the apartment opposite. He watched through the spy hole as Omar Massoud turned the corner of the corridor and disappeared down the stairwell.

"All units be advised, the suspect is heading for the street. You all know what to do." Mike Devon spoke from the front seat of a van parked at the end of the road overlooking the hostel. Beside him Alan Doyle sat cradling his prosthetic arm across his knee; in back were two agents ready to disembark and follow the target on foot. A similar van was parked at the opposite end of the street.

Devon watched as Massoud walked out slowly from the hostel entrance, blinking his eyes against the strong morning sun. He looked both ways up and down the street and then set off in the opposite direction from where Devon was located. Devon thumped the partition behind his head and the back doors of the van were thrown open.

Massoud continued walking for almost an hour, at times doubling back on his route. Watching from a safe distance, Devon surmised his movements were not counter-surveillance; it just seemed that he was lost. Finally, as they neared Trafalgar Square, the terrorist hailed a taxi, which set off towards the Whitehall district.

More than a half hour later, the taxi pulled into a kerb, neither the driver nor his passenger aware of the van which roared past and parked up a hundred yards farther on. When Massoud stepped onto the pavement, he also seemed to take no notice of a second van which had pulled in short of the taxi stop.

It was not a set-up Devon liked. Following Massoud was child's play, but sooner or later Devon knew they would be funnelled into a rendezvous area where things could go to hell in a handcart in a hurry. If Massoud was meeting the mysterious facilitator, it was likely this second man would have a lot more smarts than Massoud. It would be easy for this man to watch from an unknown vantage point, suss out whether Massoud had a tail, and abort a meeting if he felt in the least way compromised.

Devon decided he had to gamble. He ordered everyone to remain in their current position and told them he would follow the suspect alone. He had dressed down in workman's overalls and a large, slightly bruised anorak that looked like it belonged in one of the many skips scattered along the frontage of a collection of small shops.

"Do you think that's wise, Mike?" Alan Doyle asked him.

Devon quickly filled him in on this thinking and then added, "The throat mic will stay in the on position and I'll keep you posted as I go. No-one is to move forward unless I'm happy the area ahead is clear." He grabbed a hand-carry canvas toolbag from the back of the van to lend more credence to his cover, and set off on pursuit of Massoud.

At the end of the row of shops Massoud turned into a small laneway, which ran at right angles from the street and stretched a few hundred yards into the distance. Although it was a passageway that seemed to be regularly used, Devon knew he risked discovery by following immediately. Instead he ducked into the last shop in the row, asked for the owner, and explained he was an undercover policeman following a suspected pickpocket who he hoped would lead him to other members of his gang.

If there's one thing the British public doesn't like it's a pickpocket, someone who steals from them without caring whether or not they are left penniless by the callous act, someone who takes their hard-earned cash and walks away with a smile on his face. The shopkeeper brushed aside Devon's request to use a back door exit. "I can do better than that mate. Follow me."

The shopowner led Devon up a stairwell and along a short corridor to a window at the rear of the building. "This looks out on everything at the back. You can see both ways to the end of block and across the wasteland to the housing estates at the other side."

Devon scanned the area below his vantage point. For a few seconds he could see no sign of Massoud, and was just about to hit the panic button when the familiar figure emerged from behind a small wall that must have been at the boundary of the alleyway. He turned to the shopowner to thank him for his help.

"Don't thank me. Just make sure you catch those bastards," the owner told him with a passion that made Devon believe that the man, or someone from his family, had suffered personal theft of one kind or another.

As the owner retreated down the hallway, Devon turned back to watch Massoud pacing up and down on a small roadway, his eyes shifting constantly towards a row of lock-up garages to his left. Devon spoke into his throat mic: "The target has stopped behind the row of shops about three hundred yards from your location. I have full view of the area and no chance of being spotted. Everyone continue to hold."

Massoud was still pacing back and forth across a distance of no more than ten yards. He looked at his wristwatch several times before setting off towards the lock-up garages, all the time glancing behind to make sure he wasn't being followed. At the third garage he paused for a moment, and then rapped his knuckles against the aluminium up-and-over door.

Devon watched as Massoud pushed down on the handle of an inset door and stepped inside the garage.

Less than a minute passed before Devon heard the gunshots.

***

Asif Changwani stopped watching the Sky News coverage of the events in Paris and turned his attention towards a red 'Breaking News' banner that flashed across the bottom of the television screen.

Suspected terrorists killed in London shoot-out.

Changwani waited for ten minutes before the station interrupted its Paris broadcasting to switch to a live broadcast showing police roadblocks cordoning off what looked like a major shopping precinct. The camera panned the area before settling on a reporter, clipboard in hand, waiting for his cue.

It was the usual kind of report expected at a breaking news scene. *"Unconfirmed sources have told us that at least four men have died in what appears to be a gun battle with undercover police. We are also getting reports that at least another three men have died at a second shoot-out in the Bayswater area."*

Changwani didn't wait for any more information. He grabbed his coat and rushed out of the hotel room, checking his watch as he made his way to a stairwell at the end of the corridor. He passed by a group of lifts, ignoring the respite they would give him from having to walk down five flights of stairs. He never trusted elevators; there would be no time to react if someone was waiting at the other end. He preferred to have alternative means of escape.

He didn't know whether the terrorists who were killed were members of the cells he was due to meet, but he didn't believe in coincidences. He also didn't believe for a moment that they could be linked back to him, but why take chances? There were still four hours to go until the rendezvous and he decided he could make better use of the time doing something more constructive than being cooped up in a hotel room.

He strode through the hotel lobby and out the front door. Without pause he turned to his right, and disappeared into the morning rush of pedestrians. Less than a hundred yards behind him, a taxi pulled over to the front of the hotel and two men stepped onto the pavement.

"Look brother, we know the hotel he's staying in, and we know the name he is registered under. All we have to do is tell the receptionist that we have a meeting with him and get them to put a call through to his room."

Igor Borimov shook his head. "No, that won't work. He won't answer the phone and then we'll be standing there like sore fingers."

"Thumbs."

"What?"

"The expression they use here is standing out like sore thumbs."

"Whatever," Igor replied testily. "We can't risk being tied to this man. We can't give the hotel staff any reason to remember us."

Yevgeni paused in thought for a moment. "Okay, we'll do it your way. What if we get a large gift box and tell reception it's a business delivery that must be signed for in person? They're bound to give us the room number."

Igor smiled. "That's more like it, but only one of us can enter the hotel. It's your idea, so I'll wait outside for you."

A half hour later, the brothers emerged from a department store carrying a box containing a briefcase. They told the staff it was a present and asked for it to be wrapped. Then they hailed a taxi and give instructions for the Baymar Hotel.

Yevgeni walked into the foyer and strode across to the receptionist desk, cradling the box in one hand and a clipboard in the other. The clipboard was bought in the same store, but not wrapped.

The receptionist beamed a false smile and directed him to room 501. Fifteen minutes later

Yevgeni was back at reception. "There is no answer from room 501. Can you check if his key has been handed in?"

The receptionist turned towards a bank of wooden trays. "The key is not here. Perhaps he's still asleep or taking a shower."

Yevgeni knew neither alternative was right. When he failed to get a response from buzzing the bell mounted outside the door, Yevgeni had expertly gained entry with an all-purpose cardreader and quickly searched all areas of the room and adjoining bathroom. He noted the television was still on and that Changwani had obviously been watching coverage of the terrorist deaths. Had he put two and two together?"

***

Changwani spent an uncomfortable three hours squatting inside the lock-up garage. He needed to make sure his cell members would not be arriving, thus confirming they had been the victims of the police operation referred to in the television news. He had spent considerable time making his way to the location, and thoroughly checking the area for any possibility of surveillance. Satisfied the garage was not being watched, he entered the building and began preparations.

A white Transit van was parked up, and in the back he found four rucksacks crammed with explosives, weapons and spare magazines. He could almost have been back in Paris.

Looking around he noted the row of garages were cheaply constructed of basic cement blocks with no rendering. The roofs were little more than crude sheets of aluminium studded together to form an ineffectual barrier from the elements. The floor was covered in damp patches and pools of water that had formed from drips through a series of holes in the roof.

What pleased him most was that the brickwork separating each garage was built two feet shy of the roof, making it possible to climb from one garage to the next. He removed his coat, shoved a Walther PPK into his trouser waistband, and clambered to the top of the wall using the Transit as a ladder. He dropped into the adjoining garage, and found he could easily scale the next wall by bending his knees, and springing upwards with outstretched arms. He repeated the action down the row of garages, until he came to the last one.

At the end garage he checked the inset door, which was locked. It was a flimsy mechanism and yielded easily under three good blows delivered with the butt of his weapon. Satisfied he now had an escape route, he returned to the first garage and settled into the front seat of the Transit.

Something nagged at the back of his mind. According to the television news there were seven dead terrorists, which meant that one man could have escaped and could yet be on his way alone to this meeting place. The chances that this man wouldn't be followed were slim in the extreme, Changwani reasoned, knowing that if this was the case he could be cornered. Despite the dangers it never crossed his mind to leave the scene.

Shortly before the appointed time, Changwani climbed out of the Transit and hoisted himself onto the dividing wall, where he stretched across the rough brick, weapon in hand, eyes fixed firmly on the garage door.

He heard footsteps approach from outside. They stopped at the door. Two knocks, a pause and then a third knock - the agreed code. He spoke towards the door: "It is open, come on in."

Omar Massoud stepped inside and scanned around the dimly-lit interior. The large van took up most of the confined space and he could make out no other shapes. Then a voice from above startled him. "Where are the others?"

Massoud looked up at the prostrate figure of Changwani lying across the top of the wall, and aiming a pistol directly at his head. "Don't shoot! It is I. The others have all been killed."

"Why have you come here?"

Massoud shot him a puzzled look. "I am here to serve Allah. I want to follow through with our mission."

Changwani burst out laughing. "You fool, what do you think you can do alone? All you've succeeded in doing is bringing the security forces to my doorstep."

"No, no I was not followed. I was very careful."

Changwani smiled again and squeezed the trigger. He fired two rounds almost directly through the top of Massoud's head. Without waiting for the lifeless body to crumple to the floor, Changwani rolled off the top of the wall and dropped into the adjacent garage. Less than three minutes later he was standing beside the small door in the end garage.

He rubbed the dust from his clothes, shoved the

Walther into his waistband, and pushed down on the door handle. He stepped outside, resisting the temptation to look to his right towards the garage where he had left Massoud's body, and walked smartly away in the opposite direction. He was aware of the sound of running feet, but kept up an even pace as he made his way towards a gate that led to waste ground beyond. He walked across the ground at an angle that took him away from sight of the garages, and within five minutes emerged into a housing estate.

Just then a thunderous noise filled the air and Changwani smiled at the detonation of the timed booby trap he had fixed against the hidden cache of explosives in the back of the Transit. Windows shook in the houses around him and he turned to watch a fireball mushroom into the air high above the garage complex.

A narrow laneway took Changwani between two blocks of terraced houses and into a wide avenue cramped by cars parked on either side. He continued walking for twenty minutes until he reached a main road. Shortly afterwards he hailed a taxi and rode into the city centre.

Mike Devon's first reaction on hearing the gunshots was to rush down the stairs and out into the back alley. Then he realised he had a grandstand seat and looked again out the window, his eyes darting back and forward searching for movement. He shouted into the throat mic. "Shots fired, shots fired.... move in from all sides to the rear of the building. Target went into the first garage in a row of lock-ups."

His attention was drawn to a figure emerging from the end garage. Two things struck him immediately. Anyone who had been innocently pottering about in those garages would have heard the shots and would have looked towards where the sound came from. It's human nature, pure and simple. But this man didn't look - not so much as even a sideways glance.

The second thing that struck Devon was the man's appearance. Easily over six foot and dressed in what looked like an expensive suit, he was out of place as a potential owner of a lock-up in a rundown part of the city. But odd though that was, it was the calm, assured and confident manner in which the man walked away from the scene that did it for Devon.

From his vantage point he was treated only to the man's right profile, but it was enough to pick out the swarthy features, a distinctive bushy black eyebrow, and a hawk-like nose that drooped over tightly-closed lips. It was the kind of profile he would remember.

Devon spoke again into the mic. "I need someone at the north end of the site. I have a suspect heading towards waste ground. Someone get over to that section now!"

He watched as the first of his team arrived into the back street and began edging their way towards the first garage from either side of the block. Mason Hunter was first to reach the door from the left approach. To his right, Alan Doyle joined him and hand-signalled a countdown towards opening the garage door.

Above them Mike Devon watched as his men

prepared to enter the garage. He didn't know what it was that put the thought in his head; he just knew that suddenly he didn't like what he saw. He screamed into the mic. "Everyone freeze! Get the hell away from that building, there's a booby-trap. Move, move, move!"

It was pure guesswork on Devon's part, and so what if he was wrong? The alternative was to risk the lives of his crew, and that was not something he was prepared to do. He watched Hunter take off at a sprint, and smiled as Doyle easily passed him within thirty feet. He was still smiling at Doyle's ungainly running style when the garage block disintegrated, sending flying debris and dust in all directions.

Devon had already turned away instinctively, but the concussive wave tore off the window where he was standing and flung him like a rag doll down the corridor and into an interior wall at the top of the stairs. It was only then that the noise of the explosion reached him, but he passed out before it could assault his eardrums.

He wasn't sure how long he had been unconscious. He came round to the sight of the shopowner kneeling over him and pressing a cold, damp towel against his forehead.

"You alright mate? I thought you were a goner when I saw you."

Devon gently pushed the man's hand away and rose unsteadily to his feet. After a few moments he regained most of his equilibrium, the memory of the explosion now flooding back into his mind. Jesus, he thought, what about my men?

He made his way carefully down the stairs, out through the shop, and into the back alley. A cloud of dust hovered over the area. He could see men lying on the ground whilst others attended to them. An ambulance was racing away from the scene, its siren wailing as it cleared a path through a gathering crowd of onlookers. He started to fear the worst, but his spirits were lifted by the sound of a familiar voice. "Is that you, boss?"

He turned to see Alan Doyle emerge from the melee. The big man was covered in dust, his face streaked with blood. At that moment Devon had never seen a better sight. "Alan, thank God you're safe. Who was the ambulance for?"

"Big Bill Carlisle is pretty smashed up. He's on the way to hospital, but the medics say his chances are no better than fifty-fifty."

"How's everybody else?"

The sad look in Doyle's eyes told the story.

"Who?" was all Devon could manage.

"Mason Hunter didn't make it."

Chapter 17
London

SYLVIA FLYNN WAS a looker and she knew it. Despite the understandable reservations of a woman reaching her fiftieth birthday, she smiled into the mirror as she combed out the long blonde tresses flowing below her shoulders, knowing that many women half her age would sell their souls to the devil for the unblemished skin that was still pulled tightly across her face.

And yet her life to date had been one lived under many shadows. The pressures heaped on her by the various roles she had to play and which exposed her at any time to the threat of discovery and the prospect of a long incarceration, should have etched deep lines into her complexion and stolen away the vitality of watery blue eyes that drew men like moths around a flame.

In her teenage days she belonged body and soul to the Provisional IRA, first as an "active volunteer" who did her fair share of planting bombs and killing members of Northern Ireland's security forces – in local parlance that usually meant anyone working for the British Occupying Forces, or what she called their colluding friends in the then Royal Ulster Constabulary. Later she became an astute financial broker for the terrorist organisation, touring the world to raise funds to buy arms for the cause.

She was based in America in the years leading

up to the permanent IRA ceasefire in 1997. Disgusted by what she considered a sell-out by her erstwhile comrades she decided to remain in New York and carve out a new life for herself. With her looks, and an assortment of influential contacts, she had little difficulty in finding a career that made best use of her many talents.

One of her contacts was a wealthy Russian whose pockets were always open to anything that would help undermine the British Government. He made no secret of his hatred for the West or of his hopes to see good old-fashioned Communism rise again to dominate the world stage. The fact that he was one of the shrewdest and most successful capitalists she had ever met never seemed to be a contradiction to him.

For a time they were lovers and it suited both of them to play out their carnal lusts over a frenzied three-month period. But just as suddenly as it had started it was over. They had had their fun; now it was time to turn their attention to serious business. Sylvia was to travel to London to work for a small investment bank, ostensibly as an overseas finance manager, but in reality to carry out a number of other duties that wouldn't appear in any job description.

Gennady Anasenko recognised from an early stage that Sylvia Flynn was a heady mix. Thoroughly corruptible, she had a single-minded determination that he knew could be put to good use for the various nefarious activities he planned in England. Not least among her assets, she would provide the perfect honey-trap for the many unsuspecting financiers and politicians he intended to gather around him. The fact that she had proved herself to be a cold-hearted assassin was also bound to come in handy at some point.

Sylvia loved life in London. She had at her disposal an expensive self-contained apartment near Covent Garden and access to unlimited funds that appealed to an all-consuming desire to get in the fast lane, and stay there. For the first few years she loved the socialising and the thrill of bending powerful men to her will. What she enjoyed most was seeing the look on their faces when they realised they had been taken for a ride. For some it was the awful knowledge that she had fleeced their secrets and left their businesses vulnerable to Anasenko's manipulations. For others it was the look of horror when they scanned the blackmail videos and saw themselves writhing naked in her bed.

Her assignments started to change when she was asked to become little more than a courier, collecting packages and holdalls stuffed with cash and weapons and delivering them into the hands of terrorists. At first she was ordered merely to ferry the goods from pick-up point A to drop-off point B. She never saw the recipients, and guessed they were little more than urban terrorists, maybe even some of her colleagues from former days. If Anasenko wanted to help bank robbers, or blow up parts of London, that was fine with her.

She only discovered her mentor's true motives when she was asked to courier directly to residential addresses in London and Manchester. She knew that various shipments came in aboard Anasenko's private jet under diplomatic cover and that they were covertly taken off the plane and dumped in either nearby rail station lockers or vacant properties. All she had to do was pick them up and deposit them at another rail station locker, presumably closer and more accessible for the end-users.

But now she was dealing directly with the recipients. When she went to the first address, it wasn't rocket science for her to know that the Middle-Eastern inhabitants were most likely al-Qaeda, or some other fanatical faction. For a while she struggled with her emotions, trying to square her conscience with helping a bunch of crazy fuckers who thought nothing of suicide-bombing a busy train station or department store. Back in the day, she had done her fair share of killing, but the IRA tried to avoid civilian casualties, tried to give a warning when they planted a bomb. Their targets were usually buildings, not people. At least that's what she had convinced herself.

In the end, she brushed it off as just another job. Let them do whatever they wanted, as long as it didn't interfere with the cosy little world she had built for herself.

She finished her grooming, gathered her belongings into an expensive Gucci shoulder bag, and exited the apartment. She had to step around two painters busily erecting a scaffold and spreading dustsheets over the expensive hallway carpet. Good to see the management company responsible for the upkeep of the complex had finally gotten round to a bit of sprucing up.

"Morning Miss," one of the workmen jovially hailed her. She ignored him, continuing to walk towards a central foyer where a uniformed man eagerly stood holding the outer door open for her. That's another thing that could do with a change, she thought, as the elderly caretaker beamed a smile in her direction.

It had been relatively easy for Alfie Cheadle to get a dummy order typed up under a manufactured Photoshop copy of the logo and title design of the management company, which picked up the expensive rents and did little in return for overseeing the apartment complex where Sylvia Flynn was resident. It also took little to convince the doorman-cum-general-factotum that someone at head office had asked for a rush job and had forgotten to call him in advance. The pensioner had just seemed to want to get his day in with no fuss and saw no need to challenge the official-looking order.

Cheadle watched from atop a ladder as the blonde exited the apartment and sashayed past one of his men who were spreading paint-splattered sheets over the floor of the hall. He watched as she ignored the man's greeting, in the way that only the truly arrogant can achieve. What a bitch, he thought. It was alright to bounce her tits and waggle her bum at the hired help, but don't lower one's self by actually speaking to the creatures beneath her!

When he was sure she had left the building, Cheadle descended the ladder and moved quickly to the door of the apartment she had just exited. From his overalls he withdrew what looked like a gun, but was in fact an electronic key opener, which he inserted into the key slot. He waited for several seconds while the aluminium-tipped head whirred its way through a selection of calibrations before contorting itself to fit precisely into the serrated vents of the inner lock mechanism. A green light pulsed in the handle and he turned the gun clockwise. The door clicked open.

Cheadle and the man with him, a video surveillance technician who liked to be called just Mortimer, stepped into a generous-sized reception room. They expected to find a frothy pink interior, complete with multi-coloured scatter cushions, dainty ornaments, and girly knick-knacks, all the things the male mind conjured up for a woman living on her own the way she wanted. What they got was a room devoid of character, half-filled with bland furniture and a noticeable absence of pictures or personal memorability of any kind. There were no discarded sweaters or pairs of tights draped over a chair, no sense at all of a lived-in feel to the place. Apart from a faint scent of perfume there was nothing to distinguish the apartment from a functional office.

Cheadle and Mortimer exchanged a puzzled glance and then set about their appointed tasks. While Mortimer hooked up a miniature camera behind the grill of an air vent, Cheadle walked towards the bedroom. Using a pair of tweezers, he removed strands of blonde hair from a brush on a bedside vanity table and deposited them into a small plastic evidence bag. Next he unrolled a special reel of tape and began wrapping it around the handle of the brush and sticking it against a number of surfaces until he was happy with several sets of latent fingerprints.

He walked back to the main reception room just as Mortimer was reassembling a telephone, which now had an added piece of software attached to its inner motherboard. "Just a few bugs to plant, and a little attachment for the back of the laptop, then we're done," he told Cheadle.

They exited the apartment and closed the door silently behind them. Barely six minutes had elapsed, about the standard time to rig a good-sized house with state-of-the-art surveillance that would remain undetected, even after a thorough sweep with so-called anti-bugging equipment.

They gathered up their props and headed for the exit, stopping to put the doorman at ease. "We've just got a call on the mobile from head office. Somebody down there cocked up and we've been redirected to another building. Seems like the work here isn't scheduled for another month."

It seemed to satisfy the old boy. At the very least it would provide him with a reasonable explanation for his blonde resident, who had watched them set up as she left for work.

Cheadle and Mortimer had been on the go for twenty straight hours, having spent most of the night breaking into the high-security premises of the investment bank where Flynn worked. They installed a full suite of surveillance gear before heading to the car park beneath the apartment block. There they fixed a GPS locator under the wheel arch of Flynn's car, and a neat little receiver listening device into the radio console.

As they settled back into their van, Cheadle dialled up the number for *LonWash* headquarters. He had intended to report that he would head home for a few hours of shuteye and return to the offices by early afternoon. The news that greeted him drove all thoughts of sleep from his head.

"The back of his head was crushed by a piece of flying brick. The terminal velocity at impact was so great that he wouldn't have known what hit him. Death was instantaneous." The summary from the forensic scientist was cold and to the point. As if sensing he had been too aloof he added: "I'm sorry for the loss of your agent."

Mike Devon didn't reply. He watched as the last section of a black bag was zippered over the corpse of Mason Hunter, shutting him off for all time from a world that had been a better place for his passing through. Devon was one part sad, one part angry, but for the most part he was lost in a wave of emotions that were a mixture of guilt and hopelessness. He stood away from the rest of his men trying to fight down a growing need for revenge, a need he knew he would have to harness if he was to get the job done properly.

He was aware that his men were looking his way, waiting for him to take command, to give them a lead, and to help snap them out of the black hole into which they had plummeted. Hunter had been a popular figure and his death hit them all harder than they would ever admit to. It was Devon's job to get things back on track.

He turned towards Alan Doyle. "Round everybody up and head back to the office. We've got work to do. I'm going over to the hospital to check on Bill Carlisle, but I'll join you within the hour."

"Do you want company?"

"No, this is something I've got to do on my own. I'll swing past the office where Mason's girlfriend works and break the news personally. Christ, I've just remembered that they were talking about getting married next year."

Doyle shook his head. "I don't envy you that one, Mike."

Less than thirty minutes later he was walking out of the offices of a small estate agent, leaving behind the heart-breaking wail of a young girl whose world had just collapsed around her. Mason had introduced Janet Brown to him at a Christmas drinks party, and she had struck him as the kind of level-headed girl who would be a perfect foil for Hunter's live-today-hang-tomorrow approach to all things.

There had been no easy way to tell her, yet even as he had started to form the words, she sensed something in his tone and demeanour, and put her hands across her ears, as if to drown out the news that was coming.

She had collapsed into Devon's arms and he held her tightly for several minutes before the sobbing subsided and she pulled away. As she slumped into a chair, several female colleagues rushed to her side, offering the kind of support that Devon knew he couldn't. She would need these people in the days and weeks ahead, and he left her in their capable hands as he walked out of the building, feeling about as low as at any time in his life.

Back behind the wheel of the van, he threaded his way through heavy traffic heading for the hospital. His mobile phone pulsed on the passenger seat and he glanced across to see Emma's name fill the display screen. He hit the green answer button and simply said "Hi."

"Oh thank God it's not you, I mean thank God it is you. I mean...I heard on the news that an undercover policeman was killed this morning... I didn't know what to think...I thought it might be you...I thought..."

"Emma calm down, I'm alright. For the record I'm not an undercover policeman, but yes, the man who died was a colleague..."

"Were you with him? Did you see what happened?"

Devon thought for a moment before replying. There was no point in lying to her. "Yes Emma, I was involved in the operation, but I was safely away from the action. One of our other men was injured and I'm on the way to the hospital to see how he's doing."

There was silence for a moment, and when Emma spoke again, the edge had left her voice. "I'm sorry for the hysterics darling. I just had to know. I couldn't just sit in the office all day without being sure."

Although her lightened mood helped to dull some of Devon's misgivings, he began to wonder if it was fair to be putting her through this. He couldn't ask her to spend her life wondering if she was going to get a visit like the one he had just paid to Janet Brown. Despite his feelings this morning that she was a tough cookie who could handle the dangers of his job, he was beginning to have second thoughts. He couldn't turn her into a blubbering wreck every time she heard bad news on the television or radio.

Her next words dispelled his fears. "Darling, I know you're busy and you have things to do. Make sure you catch the bastards who did this and come back safe to me when it's all over."

Devon smiled to himself. "It might be a few days before I see you again. Will you promise me not to worry?"

"My only worry will be that you'll be too tired for me."

Chapter 18
Scotland

A MAN IN A THREE-PIECE pinstriped suit strode confidently towards the security checkpoint, an expensive woollen overcoat draped over one arm, leaving the other arm free to swing in tempo with his long stride. He wore a plain white shirt nipped in at the collar with a silk Paisley tie to match the perfectly angled pocket handkerchief peeping out from the breast pocket. He held out a well-used British passport to the plainclothed guard, who glanced briefly at the name, and waved him through with little more than a cursory glance.

It's a peculiarity of human nature that people do judge books by their covers. Presented with a distinguished-looking figure most people will automatically pigeon-hole the subject into a category that translates as a dependable solid-citizen. Even trained security observers are no different in rushing to rash first impressions. When the subject hands over papers which identify him as a doctor, they serve as gilt-edged confirmation of the initial instincts.

When the guard turned towards the queue of people waiting to board, Asif Changwani smiled as he walked up the ramp and merged into the safety of the throng of people hurrying to find a seat. For the remainder of the journey he would be lost in the crowd of fellow passengers, just one more person trying to pass the time during the tedium of a three-hour journey.

It was time he would use to catch up on some sleep, not that he expected to rest easy with the struggle of thoughts that had attacked him since his escape from London almost twelve hours previously.

Normally by now, he would be sitting in a private jet and contemplating the success of his mission. He would simply have dialled a special number, been picked up at a location of his choice, and whisked through the tedium of airport controls courtesy of the diplomatic status that was afforded to him by his Russian benefactors.

Two things prevented that from happening.

First off, the mission was not successful; in fact it hadn't even been launched. The exposure of his two cells not only robbed him of manpower, but also made it imperative for him to destroy the cache of arms and explosives that were to be used for the mission. He had set the charges as a precaution against the chance that the last remaining cell member would show up trailing police surveillance in his wake – in which case an explosion would not only get rid of vital evidence, but also provide him with a window of opportunity to escape.

The second reason he had not made his usual call for transportation was that he had continued to question the reasons behind his missions in Paris and London. The choice of targets just didn't make sense, and the more he struggled with finding answers, the more convinced he became that he had been used as little more than a puppet for reasons that had nothing to do with the cause he cherished.

No, he decided, he would be used no more. He

would cut all ties with these people and go to America to join his cousin Yousaf. But that was easier said than done. He was alone and cut off from support, knowing that because of his skin and his origins, he would start to attract attention in the hysteria that was bound to follow the incidents of the last few days.

He had one last card to play. He had made his way to Euston station, trying for more than an hour to blend in with the constant stream of passengers rushing to and from the various platforms, and all the while he watched for signs that anyone was paying him any attention.

Careful to avoid security cameras mounted on walls around the station, he had kept his head lowered and moved slowly towards a bank of red-coloured lockers. As he walked, he withdrew a key from his pocket, holding it ready to insert into box 57 in the middle of a three-tiered bank of lockers that stretched for more than fifty yards. Inside, he would find a holdall stuffed with cash, a weapon, and a false passport in the name of Dr Adam Seaton.

As he had turned the key he realised he was sweating profusely, waiting at any moment for a challenge or the rush of security guards to grapple him to the ground. But nothing happened. Outside the station he had hailed a taxi and directed it to take him to Oxford Street.

Clutching the bag under one arm, he had alighted from the taxi and entered a large department store, heading immediately for the toilets which were signposted on the second floor. Inside a cubicle he emptied the contents of the holdall, separating four bundles of cash and cramming them into various pockets, conscious of keeping a small wad of sterling notes to push into his wallet. He would need these for immediate purchases.

Next, he had hoisted the lid of the urinal flush and eased it gently to the floor. From the holdall he withdrew a Colt revolver, carefully wiped it down and placed it into the cistern. Much as he wanted to have the comfort of a firearm, he knew it was too risky to carry around. After extracting the passport he balled the holdall, stuffed it behind the cistern, and set the lid carefully back on top.

Over the course of the next hour he had visited various stores, careful to keep his purchases to a minimum in each. It wouldn't do to attempt to pay in cash for all transactions in one go. In the last shop he visited, he again used a toilet cubicle to change into a new three-piece suit, and emerged to begin what he knew would be a long journey.

***

Mike Devon sat across from a sketch artist, trying to recall every detail of the man he had watched emerge from the lock-up garages shortly before the explosion. The artist rested a large pad across a crooked knee and gently led Devon through his memories of hair colouring, distinguishing features, the shape of the head and countless other questions to help him form a likeness of the subject who would be at the centre of a massive police and security services dragnet.

As the artist caressed a pencil over the page Devon became increasingly frustrated. "I don't see how this is going to help. I only glimpsed one profile and I doubt you can capture even that from what I've been able to tell you."

The artist was nonplussed. He had heard enough sceptical criticisms of his profession to last a lifetime, and knew that he could eventually produce a result that might just surprise even a seasoned operative like Devon. "We're nearly done with this part," he replied, in the kind of tone a teacher would use to soothe an unruly child.

What he didn't know was that Devon was a fan of sketch artists. It was a photofit image produced in Chicago that had led Devon ten years later to cornering an IRA assassin who had killed his then girlfriend and an MI6 colleague. But back then Devon had gotten a good look at the subject and was able to guide the artist better than he was doing here.

What he didn't appreciate was that technology had moved on considerably from the days of photofits and identikits. The job of the sketch artist was made easier by the introduction of computing imagery, which produced E-Fit facial composites of such clarity, that they had to be circulated to the public with a cautionary note explaining: *This is not a photograph.*

The artist rose from his seat and crossed to a computer terminal. He played with the keyboard for a few minutes, and then dragged the mouse in and out of various boxes towards a drawing that was slowly taking shape on the main screen. Devon watched fascinated before quizzing the artist about what he was doing. "Why not use the computer before now? Why go through an initial sketch with your pencil?"

Without lifting his head, the artist explained what he was doing. "Too often people pay more attention to the multitude of alternatives the computer can offer, and this can distort the image in their minds. I like to get your first impressions down on paper and then start playing with how we can sharpen your recollections."

He finished moving the mouse and sat back in his seat, directing Devon's attention to the screen. "How's this looking?"

Devon had to admit it wasn't bad. The computer graphics offered a bit more detail and pigmentation than the pencil sketch, and he could begin to see a likeness to the image that was filed away in his brain's photo album. He sat for another ten minutes challenging various details, and all the while the artist made subtle changes to the image.

"That's it," Devon confirmed. "That's pretty close to what I remember. The only problem is that all we have is half a face."

The artist smiled and dragged the cursor into a new menu running down the left side of the computer screen. The square-on, one-dimensional image on the screen began to slowly rotate, taking on a three-dimensional shape as it mutated its other missing half. "The software is bolting on the rest of the image, making allowances for the fact that most humans do not have perfect facial symmetry, and assuming there is no unknown damage to the half that it is recreating."

"Unknown damage?"

"Yeah, the other half of the face could have a massive scar that we don't know about, or a wart growing out of a cheek, or it could be covered in a

Phantom of the Opera mask for all we know."

Devon smiled back at the artist. "I take the point." Satisfied they now had a viable photofit, he ordered the artist to rush the sketch to the printers. "I want this out nationwide within the hour, I want this face plastered everywhere, I want this bastard to realise there's no hiding place."

He got up and crossed to a small huddle of agents gathered around Alan Doyle, who was scribbling furiously on a large wipeboard and issuing assignments in a business-as-usual determination, which was designed to snap everyone out of the stupor brought on by the loss of Mason Hunter. He paused as Devon pulled up a seat and joined the circle.

"Did you get it done, boss?" one of the agents queried Devon.

"Yes, the photofit will be on the wire within the hour. Copies will be rushed here as soon as they're ready. I don't need to tell you that finding this scumbag will be our main priority."

Doyle banged his marker pen against the wipeboard. "Just what we've been discussing. Security has been alerted at all airports, train stations and channel crossings. Our only concern is that our fugitive will lie low in some safe house until all the furore dies down."

"It won't matter," said one of the agents, "we'll keep at this until we get him, or hell freezes over."

"Yeah" said another agent, "don't forget they're running out of safe houses." The remark brought a chorus of agreement and head-shaking.

Devon cut in. "Let's go with the assumption that he's trying to run. This is one smart cookie and I don't see him standing in a queue at Heathrow waiting to have his collar felt. So what are his alternatives?"

For several minutes the conversation flowed back and forth. Every possible getaway was scrutinised, from the Channel Tunnel to private airfields, from fishing boats to luxury cruise liners. The more they talked, the more furiously Doyle covered the wipeboard with scrawled notes that would have made a doctor's handwriting look legible.

"What if," Devon asked, "we're looking the wrong way? Why assume that if he's not hopping a plane, he's trying to get to the continent?"

Several of the men shrugged at each other, not understanding what Devon was getting at. At the head of the group Doyle smiled, and stared directly at Devon. "Are you thinking what I think you're thinking?"

"Only if you're thinking of a certain IRA man we chased down the length of England a few years back."

Doyle broke out into a large grin. "If I remember correctly we were watching the airports and the Channel Tunnel while the bugger made his way to Wales and jumped on a ferry to Dublin."

"The way I see it," said Devon, "getting across to Ireland is one of the safest ways of getting out of England. Once in Dublin, he can board a flight to almost anywhere without the kind of security blanket he would face here."

There was a general stirring among the men as one by one they realised the significance of what was being said. "Do we concentrate on the Welsh ferries?"

"Yes, we do, but there are also other possibilities. There are two ferry routes operating out of Scotland into Northern Ireland. From there it's easy to drive to Dublin, where he can have a choice of flights or take a ferry direct to France. I doubt though that he'll make for France."

Despite Devon's presence, Doyle continued to run the discussion. "Okay, it's decided. We keep up the high level of surveillance on our airports and train stations, but we pay most attention to the ferry crossing routes to Ireland. I think it would be a good idea to have our own two-man teams to supplement the other security agencies at these locations. You good with that, Mike?"

Devon rose from his seat. "Couldn't have put it better myself. I need to make an urgent call. Let's work on the assumption that we miss him at this end and that we're going to need some extra help from our friends in the Irish police, the Garda Siochana."

Chapter 19
Ireland

AT THAT PRECISE moment, Asif Changwani was seated against a window looking out at the Irish Sea. The Cairnryan to Belfast ferry had maintained its speed restrictions as it idled out of Lough Ryan, but was now powering up to its 40-knot capacity under the propulsion provided by four GE Aviation gas turbines. The HSS Stena Voyager was on its last trip of the evening and was travelling with almost its total capacity of 1,500 passengers.

Changwani barely noticed the throng around him as he settled into thoughts of what stretched ahead of him. It would be shortly after midnight by the time the ferry docked at Belfast Harbour, where he knew he would find a willing taxi driver to take him to Dublin. At that time of the evening he would face a rip-off fare of around £200, but it would be worth it to extricate himself from British jurisdiction. The fact that there were no longer any border checks between Northern Ireland and the Republic of Ireland meant that in less than an hour he would be in another country without worrying about being stopped en route.

Once in Dublin he would hole up in a small hotel and arrange a flight to America sometime the next day. He knew his cousin Yousaf had travelled to Chicago, although he had no clues as to his final destination. He would use local Muslim resources to help track down Yousaf, and together they would turn their attention towards inflicting pain on the Great Satan. Yousaf's previous successes had led Changwani to believe that his cousin was somehow being supported by the same people who had been helping him, and he knew Yousaf would be just as angry to learn that he too was nothing more than a pawn being moved across a board by selfish, unprincipled men.

It was almost 2am when he registered at the Dolphin Hotel located just off O'Connell Street, Dublin's main arterial route. Before heading to his room, he requested the receptionist to make a booking for him on a next-day flight to Chicago and was happy to pay the hotel's added reservation fee – better that than turn up at a security-conscious airport waving a handful of cash.

When he awoke the next morning, the computer-printed ticket was waiting for him at the reception desk. The flight time was at twelve noon which left him little time to purchase a few essential items. He rushed into Grafton Street, bought a suitcase at the first store on his left, and then filled it with various essentials, including items of underwear, two new dress shirts, a pair of jeans, three sports shirts, a pullover, a pair of trainers, a zip-up jacket, and a shaving kit. Back at the hotel he ripped the labels off his purchases and neatly packed them into the case, knowing that to travel long-haul without luggage would raise too many suspicions.

The queues at the Aer Lingus check-in desks were lengthy and he had no way of knowing whether the large numbers of policemen milling about the departure lounge were usual for this period of the day, or whether extra personnel had been drafted in for a specific reason. He had to fight to bring his rapid breathing under control and to resist the temptation of wiping clammy hands on his trouser legs.

As the queue inched forward, he could see one policeman staring in his direction. The man's eyes seemed to bore through him, and he wondered if it was possible that a photograph of him had somehow been circulated by the authorities in London. He didn't see how that was possible, but something had definitely caught the attention of the uniformed Garda officer who was now making his way down the line towards him.

Changwani tried to look casually around him, taking in exit doors and the position of other policemen. He knew it would be hopeless to attempt to escape, but all his training and all his reflexes were wired towards not being arrested. He would die here before letting himself be captured.

As the burly policeman made his way along the line of passengers, Changwani noticed the weapon still buttoned down into its holster. He could easily grab the man around the throat, snap his neck, and free the gun before any of his colleagues had time to react. With a weapon in his hand, he relished the chance to shoot it out with these infidels and go to Allah like a true warrior.

The policeman was now almost level, his hand raised towards Changwani's shoulder. Changwani tensed waiting his moment.

But then a strange thing happened. The policeman moved past Changwani and spoke to a woman standing directly behind him in the queue.

"You don't look well Madam. Let me take you to the front of the queue."

Changwani turned to notice a woman sag down on top of her suitcase. From the bulge in her coat it was obvious she was heavily pregnant, and feeling the effects of standing so long. She turned her eyes upward towards the policeman. "I don't want to make a fuss officer. I just need to sit for a moment."

"Nonsense," the policeman told her as he gently hooked his arm under hers and supported her as they began to walk away. The policeman's eyes met Changwani's and he spoke directly at him. "If you wouldn't mind sir," he said nodding at the woman's suitcase.

Changwani lifted the case and followed the policeman and the woman towards the check-in desk. The girl on duty immediately noticed the commotion and waved the policeman towards a chair near her cubicle. "I'll get you sorted immediately after I deal with this party," she told the woman in a sympathetic tone.

"I really don't want to be any trouble," the woman replied.

"It's no trouble. In your condition you should have come directly to the desk. None of the other passengers will mind you going ahead of them."

Changwani placed the suitcase beside the woman, smiled briefly at her and the policeman, and returned to his place in the queue, his cheeks deflating to expel the pent-up tension in his body.

***

A jpeg file containing Changwani's E-Fit image was

attached to an email that pinged into the Garda Siochana permanent office at Dublin International Airport. It was immediately opened by the Sergeant on duty and sent to a colour printer which sluiced out a hundred copies in less than three minutes. Two constables were ordered to circulate the copies throughout the airport, starting with staff at the checking desks, and then putting one into the hands of each policeman and airport security guard stationed around the vast concourse.

Ten minutes after that, a dozen extra policemen entered the departure lounges and began studying the faces of men standing in boarding queues or sitting in designated areas waiting for their flights to be called.

An immediate hold was placed on all flights, raising a collective sigh from passengers as they gazed at the *Delayed* messages sweeping across the screens in all areas of the airport. Annoyance gave way to alarm as people noticed the large numbers of uniforms hurrying every which way, a sure signal that there was some kind of security flap underway. Some passengers, fearful of the threat of an explosion, started to make their way to the exits, but were held back by reassuring staff.

Out on the runway, a Boeing 747 had reached the peak of its revs in preparation for starting its take-off run when the pilot received his orders to return to the holding area. There the plane was met by four armed plainclothed Garda detectives who filtered the passengers through a makeshift narrow turnstile whilst they studied the faces passing between them.

The message attached to the email had left the

Garda sergeant in no doubt that the massive show of security on the part of his men was warranted. The message read simply:

SENIOR AL QAEDA TERRORIST BELIEVED TO BE IN DUBLIN
This man is known to be behind the recent terrorist incidents in Paris and yesterday's explosion in London. It is believed he has escaped to Dublin and may be attempting to board a flight for Europe or America. Apprehend at all costs.

Whilst searches were going on throughout the airport a team of officers were directed to sit in front of large screens re-running the facial scans of all passengers who had already gone through the check-out desks. Digital photographs of passengers are taken as they stand at the check-out desk and these images are then numbered according to the flight data on boarding passes. This allows boarding staff to see instantly whether the passenger attempting to board is the person who initially checked in.

Because Dublin International had dealt with more than eighty flights and twelve thousand passengers so far that day, the officers scanning the images were in for a long shift. Their job was made easier by being able to discount female photographs, but that still left them with the thick end of five thousand print-outs to compare against the photofit pinned alongside their screens.

Two hours out of Dublin, high in the skies above the Atlantic Ocean, Asif Changwani was fast asleep aboard an Aer Lingus Airbus A330, which took off as scheduled at noon, exactly sixty-five minutes before

Mike Devon's email hit the inbox at the Garda office.

"We've got him, we've got him!" Alan Doyle couldn't keep the excitement from his voice as he burst into Devon's office. Devon was on the phone and he held a hand over the mouthpiece as he waved Doyle to a nearby chair.

Doyle remained standing, waving a piece of paper and gesticulating to Devon to cut the phone connection. Devon was about to ignore him when Doyle twisted the paper in his hands and showed Devon a print-out of a face he recognised. The phone slammed in the cradle.

"Jesus Alan, tell me that's who I think it is!"

A grin spread across Doyle's face. "This has just come in from the Garda Siochana office at Dublin airport. It's a copy of a digital photo taken of a passenger booking in for a flight to Chicago at noon today. I must say Mike your photofit was damned near the mark."

Devon leapt from his seat and grabbed the picture. "What are the details, when is the flight due to land at Chicago?"

Doyle glanced at his watch. "It won't touch down at O'Hare International for another hour. We have time to alert our American friends and have him picked up. He's travelling under the name of Dr Adam Seaton. We have him. He has nowhere to go."

Devon raised his right hand in a high-five gesture which Doyle immediately picked up on. He made a show of caressing the injury caused by Doyle's hard slap and then picked up the phone. He spoke quickly into the line and asked for Don Hill, the head of the *LonWash* operation in Washington. "Tell him to conference-call me on the laptop in five minutes. This is a code-red. I repeat code-red."

He turned back to Doyle to tell him that Hill had apparently just stepped out of the office. when his door burst open again and Alfie Cheadle stumbled into the room. He waited until the young agent caught his breath. "Boss, the woman we've been following, Sylvia Flynn, has just boarded a private jet at Heathrow. It's scheduled for take-off about now."

"Where's it heading?"

"I checked with the tower, and it has booked a flight path to Monaco airport."

Devon turned towards the office window and stared out at a greying London sky. As he looked upwards, he couldn't help but think that all his birds seemed to be in the air at the one time. Finally, he turned back towards Doyle. "Do we have any assets in Monaco?"

"No, but we can't let her disappear. I could arrange a reason for the flight to be rerouted back here. That would give us time to think of something."

It was a possibility Devon had considered, but he was wary of raising any suspicions, even if they could think of a plausible reason for turning back the plane. He looked at Cheadle. "What's the flight time to Monaco?"

Without hesitation the young agent replied: "Already checked, it's around ninety minutes."

Devon grabbed for the phone and dialled a number. While he waited for it to ring he told Doyle to keep an eye on the laptop for the incoming conference call from Washington, and then turned towards Cheadle. "Did you find out who owns the private jet?"

"It's a Gulfstream G450 registered in the name of a Russian company. I've been able to find out very little about them, but I'll keep checking."

Devon nodded his approval and was about to reply when the phone picked up at the other end of his line. The familiar voice of Claude Bartran filled the earpiece. Devon quickly filled him in on events and told him it was imperative that the woman on the plane was followed when she touched down at Monaco. "Can you get someone there in time Claude?"

"I will need to get a chopper in the air. It will be tight, but we will make it. Now I must go. Au Revoir." As he replaced the receiver, Devon smiled at the no-nonsense approach of the little Frenchman.

Just then a familiar musical beep sounded on the laptop. Doyle hit a logo on the menu bar and after a brief flash the image of Don Hill filled the screen. Whilst Doyle went through the usual introductory pleasantries, Devon spoke to Cheadle. "Go find me everything you can get on that Russian company."

By the time he bent over the laptop, Doyle had already filled Hill in on everything. As he came into view on the laptop's digital camera, the voice at the other end said, "Hi Mike, looks like you caught yourself a biggie."

"Here's the thing Don," Devon launched straight in without any hellos, "I think we need to let this man run. It looks like your cities are next on the list and if this thing follows a pattern this man will be activating a few sleeper cells that you'll want to know about."

"I agree, Mike. These things are always risky but

we have enough manpower to get the job done. I'll let you know how we'll get on..."

"No need Don, I intend to join you."

"Think we need a bit of babysitting?" It was said without any trace of annoyance.

"This bastard killed one of my men and put another one on the critical list. When the time comes to take him, I want to be the one who puts a bullet in his brain."

Don Hill smiled knowingly out from the screen. "Didn't figure it any other way Mike."

Chapter 20
Monaco

CLAUDE BARTRAN WAS sipping a coffee and looking out over the runways at Monaco when the Gulfstream taxied up to the small VIP terminal reserved for non-commercial flights. He had made the journey from Paris with fifteen minutes to spare, having radioed ahead to the airport's chief of security, a former policeman who also happened to be an old acquaintance of Claude. He brought the GIGN chief into a small office with a clear view of the disembarkation area for the numerous private jets that used the busy airport, and listened intently as Bartran filled him in on the subject of his surveillance.

The Gulfstream was finished in two shades of nondescript metallic blue, the darker royal blue colour running across the top half of the sleek craft. There were no fancy flashes or name logos, just a small cluster of letters and numbers stencilled across the tail to denote its mandatory registration identification. The jet came to a stop barely thirty yards from the entrance to the building, where the two men were positioned, and from where they had an uninterrupted view of the exit door.

Nothing happened for five minutes. Then the door, fixed to the left side of the aircraft not far from the cockpit, swung slowly open and folded down to gently kiss the tarmac below. Bartran watched as a blonde woman, carrying only a small pink valise, gracefully stepped her way down the built-in stairs. Her eyes were hidden by sunglasses, but there was no disguising the beauty of a face that could have graced the cover of any glossy magazine. From the description provided by Devon there could be no doubt that this was his target.

He watched enthralled as she glided across the gap between the plane and the administration building, thinking to himself that this was one assignment he was glad he undertook personally. He was just about to move away from the window when he caught his breath at the sight of two figures which had emerged from the jet's doorway. The size of the two men was enough to warrant a second look; they were the biggest specimens Bartran had ever seen, but more than that, they carried on their shoulders the kind of inherent menace his eye was trained to pick up.

It was obvious they were identical twins, a double dose of trouble, dressed up in expensive suits and wearing sneers that showed distain for everyone and everything around them. The sight made Bartran's blood run cold, not because he feared the men, but because he was remembering something from the aftermath of the killing of his two agents in the room across from the Paris bookstore.

One eyewitness, an elderly lady who said she was on her way to the local bakery, reported seeing a giant of a man walking on the pavement towards the book store. She described him as being over eight feet tall, and at the time her witness account had all but been discarded. Looking now at these two giants, who must be over six-six, Bartran could understand the old lady's exaggeration. Was it possible these two men were involved in the murder of his agents? Had Mike Devon once again put him onto a hot trail?

"Claude, are you coming?"

He was snapped out of his reverie by the urging of the airport security chief. He turned and followed the man towards a stairwell that took them down to the ground floor where they watched from behind a mirrored partition as the woman presented her passport to two Customs officers. She was waved through. Behind her, the Borimov twins showed their diplomatic passports and were similarly waved through without comment. A large Renault Espace people carrier was waiting at the front of the building, a uniformed chauffeur holding open the side-panel slide doors as the party emerged into the bright sunshine.

The airport security chief had agreed to loan Claude his car, which was parked at the side of the building. Claude was behind the wheel, watching as the Espace pulled away from the kerbside, and took the exit road signposted for Monaco. He eased his car forward and followed at a discreet distance, struggling with his emotions as he tried to decide what to do about the discovery of the giant twins. No matter how the girl fitted into the equation, his thoughts were now solely on making sure he didn't lose track of the two men he was convinced were responsible for the death of his agents.

He decided it was time to call up reinforcements.

Gennady Anasenko was in a rage; a foot-kicking, fist-thumping rage that was now in its second day. It started with the news that the security services in London had somehow cornered and killed the two al-Qaeda cells that were painstakingly put in place to carry out the next phase of his operation. His anger continued with the news that Asif Changwani had dropped out of sight, had not followed through with the most important target, and had not made contact through several safe channels that were established for him. Worse still, the train station locker had been cleaned out, meaning that Changwani was going it alone, cutting himself off from his mentor, thumbing his nose at all the help and support Anasenko had lavished on him these past few years.

Well, the bastard would pay! There was no hiding place on earth for him, no way for him to avoid the consequences of his treachery. His death, when it came, would be a slow and agonising one, a lesson to all who dared to double-cross the great manipulator. But for now Anasenko had more important things on his mind.

He watched from his cabin window as the small launch weaved its way through the packed harbour on a criss-cross course to *Gennady1*. It would be good to have the Borimovs back on board, but equally he was also looking forward to seeing Sylvia Flynn, and rekindling a bit of the passion they once enjoyed. It was the least he could do before sending her out on her last mission.

He left the cabin, strode through the lounge, and climbed to the upper deck as the launch pulled up to the boarding ladder. He gazed down as first Igor and then Yevgeni hauled themselves across and began ascending the steps, ignoring the ladies-first convention and leaving Flynn to fend for herself. For the first time in more than twenty-four hours Anasenko allowed a smile to drift across his face.

There was a genuinely warm greeting between the three men although Anasenko reserved his most radiant smile for Flynn. He clasped her in a rare public show of emotion, and kissed her lightly on both cheeks before standing back and casting appreciative eyes down the full length of her body. "Sylvia, my dear, it has been much too long. You look radiant even after spending so much time in the filthy smog of London."

Flynn returned his smiles, her face betraying none of the inner turmoil she felt at this sudden summons away from her job. "Gennady it's so good to see you. I've missed you so much," she lied.

Standing away from the group, Anasenko's secretary Anna Bobkov looked less than happy with the reunion. She was aware of the history between her boss/lover and did not welcome this unexpected intrusion into her cosy arrangement. This was the first time she had met Flynn, and anyone who may have caught the darkness creeping over her features would have little doubt that it was not a meeting she welcomed.

Flynn removed her sunglasses and the two women locked eyes in a moment of raw contempt. For different reasons, but with the same inbuilt instinct for survival, they let go of their moods and smiled demurely at each other for the benefit of the watching Anasenko.

Flynn turned back to face Anasenko. "You must tell me, Gennady, why it was so important to drop everything back in London and rush here? Do we have a problem?" She tried to make the question seem light-hearted, but the apprehension continued to twist knots in her stomach.

"All in good time, my dear. First you'll want to freshen up after your trip and then we'll have something to eat. I've asked Dieter to prepare something special in your honour." As he spoke he gently nudged her in the back as a signal that the conversation was over and that she should go to her cabin.

While he watched her descend the stairs his smile switched off. Turning to the Borimovs he said simply: "Come to my room in thirty minutes; we have work to do."

***

Claude Bartran was bent over a HDC observational telescope, mounted for public use on the harbour walkway. He watched as the party aboard the yacht disappeared from view below deck, aware that he had just witnessed what appeared to be a very touching reunion between old friends. His mind switched from the giant twins and the woman to the man who had greeted them aboard - a man who was clearly in charge, and someone about whom Claude knew he would have to find out everything there was to know.

He turned away from the telescope and walked towards one of the many cafés that dotted the main harbour walkway. Sitting at a table, he gestured for a waitress, certain that the first pieces of the information jigsaw would come from someone whose job it was to know the key players, not to mention the biggest tippers, who came ashore from the expensively assembled crafts bobbing on the blue waters.

He ordered a coffee and waited until she returned before starting into what must have been a conversation she had gone through many times with starry-eyed visitors. "Do you know who owns the large yacht that sits bigger than all the rest?" he asked, his head turned towards the direction of the blue-white superstructure.

She was a young girl, probably no more than twenty thought Claude, and when she spoke there was a slight trace of a German accent. "Ah the *Gennady1*, it is magnificent. It is berthed here for most of the year and everyone knows it throws the most glamorous and expensive parties."

"Do you know who owns it?"

"Everyone knows Mr Anasenko. He's a very generous man, but alas we see so little of him these days." The last sentence was said with a tinge of regret as if she were counting up the lost tips when the yacht's owner was away or chose to stay on board.

Bartran made a show of sorting through a bunch of Euros, dangling the prospect of a good tip if she could tell him more. Without prompting she continued: "People say he is a Russian billionaire, but others think he works for his Government. Sometimes there are many people from other Governments who visit the yacht, but I think his money could only come from oil, you know like the sheiks from Saudi Arabia."

Her reference to Government visitors made Bartran sit up and take notice. He decided to fly a kite. "I am a Civil Servant from France and I have heard that some of my Government officials have often come down here. You may have seen them or heard about them."

The girl looked strangely at him and for a moment he thought he had gone too far. The last thing he needed was to draw suspicion, to have word get back to the yacht that someone was snooping around. He peeled off a twenty-euro note and handed it to her with a smile. "Maybe I'm just hoping that because I work for a Government I will get an invitation to one of the parties."

The girl relaxed, discreetly pocketed the money and smiled back at him. "I'm afraid you would only qualify if you were very high up in your Government. Only the most important people are invited on board."

"I expect you're right," he replied ruefully. "A poor clerk like me would have no chance, but I suppose we can all dream."

The girl moved away from the table and then, as an afterthought, turned back to him. "You could have asked your French minister to get you an invitation, but I'm afraid you are too late. He left two days ago."

***

Anasenko was at that moment pacing up and down the carpet, listening intently as the twins reported back on their various assignments in Paris and London. Yevgeni spoke first. "We must have just missed Changwani at the hotel. When I entered his room the television was still on and was showing reports of the deaths of the al-Qaeda cell members. He must have guessed these were his men and decided to make a run for it."

"But what about the bomb in the garage, surely that was his work?" Anasenko's voice was laced with impatience.

Igor picked the conversation up from his brother. "As far as we can tell he went to the garage, perhaps to pick up the bombs and the weapons. Maybe he was going to follow through with his mission, but somehow got cornered. My guess is that he detonated the bombs as a diversion to escape."

"No, no," Anasenko bawled, "the television has reported that one terrorist was killed at the scene along with an undercover policeman. How do we account for that?"

Igor shifted uneasily in his chair. "Perhaps one of the cell members did survive and had gone to meet Changwani as planned. The fool must have been followed and that left Changwani with no alternative but to liquidate him and dispose of the weaponry."

Anasenko eyed him with renewed interest. "You may be right my son, but it still doesn't explain why Changwani cleared out the train station locker and has since gone to ground."

As the conversation bounced back and forth between his brother and Anasenko, Yevgeni Borimov continued to stretch out on the leather armchair, listening intently and trying to draw a conclusion from what was being said. Finally he spoke: "I agree that he appears to have cut all ties with us since all he had to do was contact us to arrange his extraction. If he had intended to go through with the operation alone and was compromised by an idiot who led the police to the garage, he could have no worries that you would think badly of him for his efforts. So why is he running the risk of being caught by the authorities?"

"Why indeed?" Anasenko answered before holding up his hand to stop Igor from speaking. He allowed himself a few moments before again addressing the brothers. "There is no doubt in my mind that this dog has decided to become a free agent, perhaps because he has turned yellow, which I don't believe, or maybe it's because he has finally figured out that we don't give a fuck about Allah and his divine teachings. Perhaps it has finally gotten through his thick Muslim skull that he has been little more than a patsy for the past few years."

"What do you want us to do about him?" Yevgeni asked.

"We have to forget about him for now; there are more important things to do. Don't worry my sons, he will surface again and you will have your chance to teach him the error of his ways."

Yevgeni rose from his seat and walked towards the drinks counter to refresh his glass of brandy. The move gave him time to rehearse his next words, knowing that if he approached the subject the wrong way he would incur the wrath of his mentor. "I must ask why you did not let us finish the London mission. This man you wanted killed would already be dead if you had given us the word."

Instead of throwing a temper tantrum, for which he was famous, Anasenko smiled benignly at the brothers. "The reason for using these people was to throw suspicion away from our real motives. Just like Paris, I wanted this man killed in a way that would appear he was innocently caught up in random terrorist attacks. If you had simply gone into his office and assassinated him, the world would have known it was an attack carried out for financial reasons, and that would have led to a suspension of the Stock Exchange at a time when I need to stay under the radar and manipulate various trading activities."

The brothers nodded as if appreciating the bigger picture. Anasenko knew they could not possibly understand everything that was going on around them, if only because he chose not to tell them everything. Perhaps now was the time. "In Paris you disposed of Sheik Abu-Nayyan in a way that has everyone believing he was murdered by al-Qaeda thugs. Because of that belief, we have been able to prepare the groundwork to take control of one of the most powerful oil companies in the world."

He paused to take a seat and sip appreciatively from his brandy glass. "The intention in London was to create a diversion with a terrorist attack in Trafalgar Square. This would have been followed up by another attack, apparently aimed at the Bank of England premises in Threadneedle Street, but in reality was targeted at premises in the nearby Lombard Street area. As in Paris, the terrorists had been instructed to take refuge in a particular building after lobbing hand grenades in the general direction of Threadneedle Street. Bombs were to be detonated at this secondary location with the express intention of killing the man whose offices were on the first floor."

Igor cut in. "You never told us the identity of this second man."

Anasenko smiled again. "It is really simple to figure out. This man helps control one of Britain's biggest oil companies. With him out of the picture I can make a move on the company and add it to my growing portfolio. In time I will be able to dictate the price of oil worldwide and I can tell you that the West will pay dearly for it."

"But if this man is so important to your plans he must be eliminated."

Anasenko rose from his seat and crossed the room to look out at the busy harbour scene. A cloudless sky allowed the sun to bear down mercilessly on the trapped inlet, and everywhere people could be seen sheltering under parasols, or hiding beneath a sea of wide-brimmed sunhats. With his back to the room he told the twins: "He will be eliminated and it can still be done in a way that will avoid undue suspicion."

Igor looked at his brother and then towards Anasenko's back. "But who will do this?"

"A rather remarkable young woman who will use her considerable charms to do what it would take a bunch of heavily-armed terrorists to achieve."

Igor looked at Yevgeni and then both men looked towards the cabin door as if staring through it and down the corridor to the room where their travel companion was freshening up.

**

The waitress stood at the back of the café looking out towards Claude Bartran. He seemed a harmless enough old man, but there was something about the way he quizzed her that made her think there was more to his questions than just idle gossip. Magda Schroeder celebrated her twentieth birthday two weeks ago and was due to return to her final year Art studies at the University of Nice at the end of the month. Her summer job at the little Café de Monaco paid very little, forcing her to rely on tips, which at busy times could triple her wage packet. She saw now an opportunity to add to her savings.

She had heard stories about how the owner of the *Gennady1* was extremely security-conscious and had offered generous rewards to local workers for tip-offs about any unusual activity around his yacht. She knew of one waiter at another café along the harbour stretch who had received one thousand euros for alerting the yacht to a group of exuberant youths who boasted they were going to gatecrash a party in the early hours of the morning. The small rowing boat ferrying the four drunken youths across the harbour mysteriously capsized, leaving them to spend the night drying out in local police cells, trying to convince an uninterested Sergeant that they had seen frogmen swimming under their boat shortly before it tipped over.

Magda walked across to a small noticeboard hanging above the café counter and pulled down a post-it note. She carried it with her to the rear of the building and stepped outside to a small patio area where workers often congregated during their break. She pulled a mobile phone from her apron pocket and dialled the number scribbled across the yellow scrap of paper. Most of the cafés kept phone numbers for the large yachts in the hope of getting snack orders or hiring out their staff for onboard parties.

A woman's voice answered almost immediately and listened intently as Magda described her brief encounter with the old man whom she had noticed earlier looking through the telescope in the direction of the *Gennady1*. The woman thanked Magda and told her she would be rewarded for her diligence.

As Magda walked back into the café her thoughts were only of the "reward" she might receive and how it would help with her university expenses.

She could not know there would be a far heavier price to be paid for the call she had just made.

Chapter 21
Chicago

MIKE DEVON'S PATH through customs was eased by the presence of Don Hill who brought him up to speed on Asif Changwani's movement through O'Hare International six hours previously. "We tagged his false passport, monitored him all the way through the airport to the taxi rank, and have been on his tail ever since. He registered at a fleapit hotel in the downtown area and is still holed up there."

Devon climbed into the passenger seat of a black Dodge Charger LX and looked across at Hill. "I don't have to tell you that this man is probably a master of disguise and very adept at escaping surveillance. How confident are you that he's still where he's supposed to be?"

There was no trace of annoyance in Hill's response. "We've done this kind of thing before, Mike. I have a dozen agents surrounding the hotel and we've already put a wire tap into both the main switchboard and a public phone box at the end of the corridor where his room is situated. In the last hour we've been able to establish a direct line of sight from the building opposite, and a directional mic together with infra-red motion detection equipment is trained on his room. As of ten minutes ago he was still inside."

Devon reached out and patted Hill lightly on the shoulder. "I'm sorry Don. I know your people are the best. It's just that I want this bastard so badly I can almost taste it."

"No need for apologies, I know how I'd feel if it was one of my men he'd killed. I met Mason Hunter last year and I liked him a lot. I know your team will miss him."

The talk of Hunter took Devon's mind briefly back to the last time he'd seen him, sprinting in vain for his life away from the garage block. He forced the image into the background and reached for his satellite phone, as if suddenly remembering something. Allowing ten seconds for the signal to bounce up to one of the stationery satellites and a further ten seconds for redirection back to the selected earthbound co-ordinates, Devon waited patiently as it whirred and clicked along its path to London, and eventually reached its destination. Barely thirty seconds in total had elapsed before the familiar voice of Alan Doyle filled the earpiece.

Devon brought him up to speed on his arrival in Chicago and the surveillance on Changwani, finishing with a request for an update at the other end.

"First the good news," Doyle said cheerfully. "Bill Carlisle has come out of the coma and the doctors say he's going to make it. He has a lot of injuries from the bomb blast and will need three to four weeks of recovery time, but there's nothing to stop him from climbing back in the saddle."

"That *is* good news, Alan. What else you got?"

"Not much as yet. We're trying to backtrack on Changwani's movements before he surfaced at the garage block. We're running the Dublin passport picture through the images scanned at any of the London airports during arrivals from France. We've also sent the picture to Bartran's Paris office to get them to do the same at their end. So far there's nothing but we expect to get some hits within the next few hours."

Devon listened intently and then spoke. "Any news from Claude on picking up Sylvia Flynn's trail at Monaco?"

"Not yet. His deputy says he took off himself and they haven't heard back from him."

"That's not like Claude. I'll try to raise him from my end." Devon finished the conversation with the promise of keeping in touch. Next he hit a speed-dial number for Bartran and again waited patiently while the satellite sorted out his request. After the usual time lapse there was nothing but a continuous dial tone at the other end. Devon knew that could only mean the phone was switched off, something he had never known Bartran to do.

Don Hill eased the big saloon car alongside a street pavement a hundred yards away from the hotel where Changwani was holed up. Noting the frown on Devon's face he asked simply: "What's up?"

"I don't know that anything is," Devon told him, "but I've known Claude for a long time and he never stays out of contact, even when he takes a day off to go horseracing."

"What's Claude up to?"

Devon was suddenly aware he hadn't briefed Hill on the significance of Claude monitoring Sylvia Flynn's visit to Monaco. He filled in the back-story from the time he watched her enter and leave a terrorist safe house in Manchester until she was trailed to a London investment bank. "She's part of a big puzzle and could have been heading to Monaco to meet with some of her principals. What if Claude stumbled into something that is bigger than any of us thought?"

"C'mon Mike, we both know old Claude can look after himself."

"Yeah, but just to be on the safe side, I'll think we need to take a look for ourselves at what's happening in Monaco." As he spoke he was again speed-dialling Doyle's desk number at the London office.

Dispensing with any preamble he issued a number of orders as soon as Doyle came on line. "Alan, I want you and Alfie Cheadle in Monaco on the first available flight. If everything's alright with Claude he could still do with the company, but if anything's gone wrong I want us ready to pick up the pieces without having to go through official French channels. Before you leave make sure we have a full team monitoring the bank where Sylvia Flynn worked. I want a constant check kept on everyone entering and leaving, and make sure we get full transcripts of any interesting messages emanating from that building."

Doyle recognised the urgency in Devon's voice. "I'm on it. I'll let you know the minute we have anything."

Devon was about to answer when Don Hill tapped him on the knee and directed his attention to the front of the hotel. He looked up to see Asif Changwani emerge from the entrance, dressed in white trainers, faded jeans and a zip-up jacket. Devon's blood ran cold when Changwani turned to look to his left, offering the same profile Devon had last seen at a London garage block shortly before it disintegrated.

A yellow taxi pulled up to the pavement to allow Changwani to climb into the back seat, unaware that two similar cabs were waiting farther down the street to pull out ahead of him. Meanwhile, a battered Ford pick-up truck, emblazoned with a sign for gardening services, and a silver Chevrolet Impala, fell in behind Changwani's cab in a well-rehearsed manoeuvre.

Hill gently squeezed the Dodge throttle and joined the queue of traffic six cars back.

***

Shortly before he exited the hotel, Changwani had made the last of a dozen phone calls from a pay-as-you-go mobile package bought at the airport. He began with a call to a self-appointed Imam who ran a small mosque on the city's East Side, which had seen its fair share of racial tensions down through the ages. Although dominated these days by a large Mexican population, there are still pockets of Arabs, Poles, Serbs and Croats living uneasily among longer-standing Italian and Irish immigrants who had largely moved to other neighbourhoods.

The Imam was known to Changwani and his cousin Yousaf Hasni from a successful mission they had carried out a few years earlier in New York. The cleric, who at that time was little more than a lowly sleeper, a gopher whose sole function was to provide assistance to Jihadist warriors when requested, had provided shelter for the cousins and arranged delivery of Semtex explosive for use in their New York mission. He had also laid on transportation to their target and had driven them back to Chicago hours before the bomb exploded outside a US Marines recruiting office. The bomb was timed to detonate in the middle of the night and was one of a series of explosions planned against Government and Army buildings by six two-man teams similar in origin to Changwani and Hasni.

The intention was not to kill but to cause massive disruption within the security services. The man who had sent the teams out on their mission wanted to let the American people know he had not gone away after the success of his 9/11 attacks. He had wanted them to know that he could still reach out from a cave in Afghanistan and touch their lives with a continual threat of death.

As it turned out, the bomb set by Changwani and Hasni was the only one to detonate successfully. Two others only partially exploded causing minor damage, and the other three were found after failing to detonate. The news of the attacks was largely suppressed from the American people and the world, who believed they were little more than futile gestures by disgruntled militia groups.

Unlike the other suppliers, the Imam was credited with providing good quality explosives, and as result he was elevated to a new status, which brought increased funding and standing within his community. Since his dealings with the cousins, he had immersed himself fully in the life of the mosque, leading the small congregation in their daily prayers and lessons, believing that his days of participation in dangerous missions were at an end.

He had now received two separate contacts within the space of a few weeks. He was able to tell

Asif that his cousin passed through Chicago on his way to Boston, but he had no way of knowing his final destination. He had provided a car and believed that Yousaf's instructions were to hide up in a farmhouse somewhere in the New England countryside. He could not narrow it down any further than that, but supplied Asif with a list of numbers of men who were based around the Boston area and who would likely be contacted by Yousaf. Finally, he agreed to prepare a vehicle and leave it at a prearranged spot for Asif to pick up, well away from the neighbourhood of the mosque.

The remaining calls Changwani had made from the cell phone were cagey affairs. He knew the men on the other side of the line were just as anxious as he was to avoid any words or phrases being picked up by the array of satellite listening equipment that America had in place. Everything had to be said in a way that would appear merely as innocent exchanges between friends – the trick was in getting the people at the other end to understand who he was and who he was looking for.

Satisfied he had at least narrowed down his search to a particular area of Massachusetts, Changwani decided to leave the hotel and head for the address he had been given to collect the Imam's car. During the journey across the city he was satisfied he was not being tailed, believing his entry into this so-called high-security country had passed undetected. He relaxed in the back of the taxi and thought longingly of the reunion that lay ahead.

Two hours and more than a hundred miles east of Chicago, Devon and Hill were getting an uneasy feeling as the I-90 highway thinned out across the Indiana countryside. Ahead of them the old blue and white Commer campervan, that Changwani had picked up in Chicago, occasionally blew out black exhaust fumes from a forty year old-engine, which was looking increasingly past its sell-by date. What worried the two men was that Changwani could easily pick up their tail on the increasingly deserted inter-state highway.

There were three other cars in the surveillance chase, each taking turns to leapfrog the other in an effort to provide a different rearview mirror image for the driver ahead. Eventually, Hill despatched one of the cars to overtake Changwani, with the intention of staying more than ten miles ahead in case any of the trailing cars had to break surveillance. He thought of ordering up a chopper, but knew that he couldn't risk it being picked up against the clear skies above.

Other traffic occasionally overtook the convoy, making it easier to divert Changwani's attention away from Hill's Charger, which hung back at a distance of almost two miles. At every crossing and off-ramp, Hill was forced to slow down to check for any signs that Changwani had left the main highway. It was becoming clear that unless they closed the distance they risked losing contact, so Hill stepped on the accelerator, but ordered the car behind him to stay well back.

Another two hours of monotonous tracking increased the tension until ahead of them Devon spotted the large canopy of a garage forecourt. Hill maintained his speed as they flashed past the garage, his eyes staring straight ahead at the miles of blacktop racing towards him. From the passenger seat, Devon glanced briefly across and watched as Changwani stood pumping petrol into the campervan, his back to the traffic racing by.

Hill ordered the car behind to pull in and find a vantage point as a precaution against Changwani doubling back. Then he called the forward car, instructing the driver to slow down and asking for details of the topography of the road ahead.

"There's a picnic area layby about two miles from the garage. I noticed four or five vehicles already parked up so you should be able to blend in."

Hill eased down on the accelerator and scanned ahead for the turn-off which was now being signposted as five hundred yards to his right. He clutched into third gear and moved in behind a row of cars, noticing with delight that a family of five already occupied one of a number of tables cemented into a grassed leisure area. It was an innocent scene that shouldn't cause Changwani more than a casual glance.

They waited for fifteen minutes before they heard the distinctive chugging of the campervan. Within a minute it had passed the layby, Changwani's eyes firmly fixed on the road ahead as he munched on what looked like a bar of chocolate or one of those fitness protein bars.

Devon turned to Hill. "Get the men behind to check what Changwani was up to in the garage. We need to know if he used the phone or made any purchases other than petrol and food."

Hill gave him a should-have-thought-of-that-smile and relayed the message before engaging the car and driving out of the layby in pursuit of the campervan. He called to brief the forward car to resume its journey. Ten minutes later a voice broke through the static in his radio mic. "We've just been into the garage and discovered something interesting. Our friend bought a route map for Fitchburg, which is about forty miles outside Boston. He quizzed the attendant about the distance and where he could stop over for the night."

"Anything else?" Devon asked. He had been listening to the conversation from the dashboard-mounted handset which was switched to loudspeaker.

"Just that he bought a shitload of snacks and bottled water. Looks like he's in for a long run."

Chapter 22
Monaco

IN HIS YOUNGER DAYS Claude Bartran would have given the two men a run for their money. An amateur weightlifter, with a cupboard full of trophies and medals, he also studied various forms of martial arts, preferring the many defensive moves of *Jujitsu* over most of the other disciplines he experimented with. He had become adept at using the strength and momentum of his opponents to his advantage, often disarming them of guns or knives before they had realised he had moved against them. But now he found himself in a situation that would have bordered on hopeless thirty years ago, and was well-nigh impossible in his present predicament.

He had heard them coming, their footsteps heavy on the small wooden hallway outside his room. He even had time to guess at who they might be, and time too to reach across the small bedside table to retrieve the Sig SP2022, the standard issue for French national police members. What he didn't have was time to wrap the weapon in his fist and bring it to bear on his would-be intruders.

It had taken a lot of shoe leather and most of the cash in his wallet to find a suitable hotel room where he had a view of the harbour and could monitor activity on board the *Gennady1*. That was less than two hours ago and for most of that time he was seated at the first floor window watching his quarry and ordering up reinforcements from Paris. His back-up team of agents were still thirty minutes away and he cursed himself for his lone-wolf antics, believing at the time this would be little more than a babysitting exercise.

The door of his room crashed in and flew across the confined space to bounce off the outer wall. It had been torn completely off its hinges as the result of a powerful force of nature, or more accurately, the combined boots of the two men who now stood framed in the gap that was left. The door had caught Bartran a glancing blow on his left hip as it catapulted past him, causing him to stagger away from the reach of his weapon, and wondering how he could have missed the giant twins leaving the yacht.

The Borimovs moved quickly into the room and lifted Bartran like a rag doll, their giant hands clasping under each of his armpits. As he dangled helplessly above the floor Bartran stared defiantly into the smiling faces, trying hard to ignore the reek from their breaths and the murderous look in their eyes. He attempted to twist his right leg to aim a kick at one of the twins who sidestepped it with ease and held his captive farther away from his body.

The other twin drove a fist into Bartran's midriff with such force that the little agent expected to feel it come out of his back. The air rushed from his lungs and he could feel bile rising to his throat as a savage pain raced around his insides. Then he had the sensation of flying through the air as his assailants flung him casually towards the bed, where he bounced off the mattress against the wall, his head exploding in a kaleidoscope of sparks and colours.

He drifted in and out of consciousness as he felt

his trouser pockets being invaded and heard the noise of drawers opening and slamming shut. A giant hand closed around his throat and he smelled the reek of tobacco and alcohol as a face pushed against his. "So you're a filthy French security agent," the voice screamed in a shower of spittle that caused Bartran to close his eyes.

He knew they had found his ID wallet and would now try to torture information from him. He wondered how much pain he could withstand before having to tell them everything he knew. He wondered too if he could stall long enough for his other agents to arrive. His guess was that he could at least hold out for that length of time by feeding them misinformation.

He guessed wrong.

The hand around his neck slowly tightened. He could hear a mocking voice say "This is what we think of French policemen."

And then there was darkness, total and absolute darkness.

***

Sylvia Flynn sucked in three deep breaths before knocking on Anasenko's cabin door. For the past hour her mind had been filled with all kinds of apprehensions about the possible reasons for being ordered over to Monaco at such short notice. She knew how volatile her Russian boss could be and wondered if he had suspected her growing concerns about what she was mixed up in.

She had been grateful at least to see the Borimov twins leave the yacht ten minutes before she had readied herself for the meeting with Anasenko. If he had intended any harm towards her he would have used the vile twins.

"Come in, my dear."

The voice snapped her away from the dark thoughts and she stepped into the room with as much confidence as she could muster.

Anasenko held up a remote control handset and pressed a button which activated the door lock, a gesture she knew was intended to signal his most immediate intentions.

They made love frantically over a forty-minute period with Flynn playing her part fully in bringing Anasenko to a climax on at least two occasions, although her own moans and gasps were as faked as the multiple orgasms he thought he had caused. Throughout the ordeal Flynn tried to mask her growing apprehension over the real reason for Anasenko demanding her immediate presence in Monaco. She knew it wasn't for quick shag; he could have his pick of Monaco's party-goers and hangers-on, as well as satiating his appetites with his secretary, although she had to admit that Bobkov's bony body would hardly be much of a turn-on for a man who liked a bit of meat around the frame.

In a move that signalled the end of pleasure and the beginning of business, Anasenko rolled off the bed, grabbed a silk gown, and marched out to the cabin's large drawing room, signalling for Flynn to join him. She wrapped herself in a white bath robe and made her way slowly out of the room, stopping at a mirror to finger-shape her hair. As soon as she sat down on one of the leather armchairs, he spoke with his back to her while fixing them a drink at the bar.

"I need you to kill someone for me," he said in a matter-of-fact tone, watching carefully through the bar mirror for any reaction. Flynn sat immobile, seemingly accepting the comment as casually as if he had asked her to buy him a tie.

"You know I will do anything you ask Gennady, but why bring me here instead of just telling me over the secure line in London?"

Anasenko crossed over to sit opposite her on another armchair. "This is a rather special target and I need you to understand that he must be killed in a special way. There must be no suspicion about his death, no way in which it can be traced back to me."

"There are not many ways this can be done Gennady. The advances in forensic sciences provide the police with powerful investigative techniques. I'm not sure I can achieve what you want."

Anasenko smiled at her. "My friends in Russia have developed an interesting new drug which stops the heart within two seconds of being taken orally. It has the added advantage of dissolving without trace in the body's fluids."

"How do I fit in? Surely this could be done in a restaurant in much the same way as Litvinenko was killed?"

A snarl crossed Anasenko's face. "Don't be so stupid. Alexander Litvinenko was administered with Polonium-210, which was easily traceable because it was meant to be. The Russian authorities wanted to send out a public message to all dissidents that there was nowhere in the world they could consider safe. I've just told you that this is different and that the world must believe this man died from natural causes."

Flynn reddened and tried quickly to smooth over the mistake of challenging Anasenko. She knew this man could have her killed on a whim, and for a while she had feared that was why he had brought her to Monaco. Knowing she was still useful to him had been a reprieve that she would not mess up. "I'm sorry, Gennady. I will of course do what you ask. I sense you have a plan for the way in which this is to be carried out."

Anasenko seemed to relax. "The man's name is Sir Clive Oliver. He is chairman of *Paxoil*, a very powerful cartel, which controls a lot of oil supplies in France, Germany and Britain. He is a bit of a recluse and very security-conscious, but he has one weakness...."

"Can I guess, Gennady?"

"Feel free, my dear."

She sat forward on her seat. "Can it be that this Sir Clive has a fondness for the fairer sex?"

Anasenko burst out laughing. "Precisely my dear. We will arrange introductions for you on the pretence of representing potential investors in his company. You must forge a relationship with him as soon as possible, but I will tell you when and where to strike."

"What about the drug?

"I will have it delivered to you in London. We must not risk you carrying it through customs. You will leave at first light in the morning."

GIGN Captain Georges Laurent drove with three agents from the Monaco train station to the small hostel where Claude Bartran was staying. Outside the main entrance they were greeted by two uniformed members of the principality's Urban Police Division, standing legs astride on a step above their striped police vehicle, parked up against the pavement with its lights still flashing.

Laurent felt an immediate unease, knowing that whatever had happened here must have involved Bartran, who had not responded to his radio for the past hour. The French authorities shared excellent relations with their neighbours and Laurent had no hesitation in showing his ID card to the two officers and explaining that they were due to meet their boss at this location. The officer waved him into the foyer where a third policeman was talking to a receptionist and scribbling on a small flipover notebook. Laurent told him who he was and asked what had happened.

The policeman explained that there had been some sort of a fight, but no one had seen anything. The occupant of the room, in which the disturbance had taken place, was missing. He told Laurent that normally he would have assumed it was little more than a drunken brawl, but he had found a Sig SP2022 on the bedroom floor. He held the weapon up for inspection.

Even wrapped in a polythene bag and partly covered by an evidence sticker Laurent immediately recognised the black polymer pistol as Bartran's. The policeman confirmed that it hadn't been fired.

An hour later, Laurent extricated himself from the small police station, having signed a full statement outlining that Bartran was holidaying in Monaco and had asked his friends to join him for a few days. He could not mention Bartran's reported surveillance of the yacht, or his suspicions about the large twins who had accompanied the mysterious blonde to Monaco. He knew that to do so would leave the local police with no option but to blunder in on a situation that needed to be controlled.

He emerged from the station to rejoin his colleagues, sipping coffee in a nearby restaurant, all the while cursing the time wasted searching for Bartran. When he stepped into the small dining room he was surprised to find two strangers seated at a table with his men.

One of the men stood up and greeted him as he crossed to the table. "Captain, my name is Alan Doyle. I work for British Intelligence and I'm here to help find out what happened to Claude Bartran."

Chapter 23
Fitchburg, Massachusetts

DARKNESS OVERTOOK THE small convoy six hours into their journey. They had skirted Lake Erie, passed through Cleveland, and were now back on the I-90 heading in the general direction of Buffalo. Devon took a spell behind the wheel as Don Hill fiddled with the car's satellite navigation set before announcing they were more than five hundred miles from Fitchburg, assuming that was Changwani's final destination.

"He can't keep going at this rate," Hill announced through a yawn. "We have to be prepared for him to pull in somewhere to rest up for the night."

Devon kept his eyes fixed firmly on the gloomy stretch ahead, aware that the monotony of trying to anticipate contours beyond the scope of the car's headlights was beginning to take its toll. "I agree. Unless the bastard isn't human, he has to stop sometime soon. I'm beginning to think we should just pull him over and get this done with."

Hill shared his travel companion's irritation, but couldn't shake the notion that Changwani was leading them towards other terrorists who needed to be rounded up. "There's a lot at stake here, Mike. Let's give it another hour and then make a decision. I've already called in some reinforcements to meet us in Fitchburg, but if we feel this is getting away from us then we'll settle for what we have."

Both men knew that night-time surveillance can work both ways. For the pursuers, it's easier to keep track of the subject vehicle lights ahead, provided you close the gap to a manageable distance. But there's also a distinct advantage for the hunted, who can pick up on trailing car lights, particularly when they maintain the same speed. All you've got to do is slow down and see if the other guy does the same.

The pursuers were helped by the appearance of a fourteen-wheeler which flashed past them on an open stretch and kept at an even sixty, not enough to chase down Changwani. Devon eased in behind the large truck, hauling what appeared to be loose sand, judging by the small shower of grains which escaped continuously from below a billowing tarpaulin. Devon was able to switch to dipped lights and ease off the accelerator to stay a quarter mile behind.

Ten miles down the road, the truck's indicators blinked for a left turn. The men in the car noticed for the first time a large service area, already populated by more than twenty freight trucks and an assortment of saloon cars parked up in a circle surrounding an all-night transport café. This time Devon slowed, ostensibly to allow the truck to complete its manoeuvre, but in reality to give himself and Hill the chance to spot whether Changwani had pulled in. Although they both frantically scanned the area there was too much activity to be able to pick up Changwani's Commer.

Hill radioed to the forward car to stop and instructed the driver to find a vantage point from where he could see if the Commer passed by. The occupants of the trailing car were also told to stop and await further instruction. Ten minutes crept by before Hill punched the radio and asked for an update.

"Nothing. He should have reached our position by now."

Hill acknowledged the message and turned towards Devon who had already pulled the car over to the side of the highway. "What do we do now?"

"It's quite simple," Devon told him. "You need to give me your automatic and step out of the car."

"What the fuck are you taking about?"

Devon smiled, reached around to the back seat for a windcheater jacket, and held out his hand for Hill to pass over his automatic pistol. "Look it's obvious our friend has stopped at the service station, but we need to find out for sure. If two of us drive in it will look suspicious, particularly since you're wearing a suit that might as well have law enforcement written all over it. On the other hand, I dressed down for the flight over and have a better chance of blending in if I'm alone."

Hill studied him for a few moments before snapping open the glove compartment and extracting a Glock 17. "This is a spare I'd brought along for you. Do I need to tell you to be careful?"

"Careful is my middle name."

Hill pushed open the passenger door and climbed out, narrowly avoiding the car's tail-end as Devon threw it into a three-point turn, gunned the engine and set off under a shower of roadside debris back towards the service area. Hill kicked out at a loose pebble, partly to show his annoyance, but much more to do with his frustration at being left twiddling his thumbs in the middle of nowhere. He knew Devon's assessment was right, but it didn't help him to swallow it any better.

***

Asif Changwani had no intention of breaking his journey. The thousand-mile trip from Chicago to Fitchburg was merely an operational hurdle to overcome, a means to an end which, although it would prove tiring and sore on the limbs, was nothing compared to the many privations he had suffered during his time as a soldier in Afghanistan. He had considered journeying by train, but was wary of potential security checkpoints that might be in place at various Amtrak stations. Going alone cross-country would eliminate risks and provide better options if he needed to change his planned search for his cousin Yousaf.

What he hadn't counted on was the sheer boredom of endless highway driving. On at least two occasions he found himself dozing off behind the wheel and having to fight to keep the campervan from careering into a ditch. The lights of an approaching service station helped change his mind.

He swung into large parking area filled with a variety of vehicles, many of which he guessed would stay in the compound for the night. He knew enough about the habits of Western truckers to know they slept in their rigs, preferring daytime travel which enforced their union rights for a properly-structured working day.

He parked up well away from the entrance, his eyes busily taking in all the details of his surroundings. The campervan had curtained windows and a good-sized bench which folded down into a bed. He hesitated for a moment, wondering whether to retire for the night or enter the café for a much-needed coffee. He decided on the latter, but before climbing out he rummaged in a box left by the Imam and pulled out a short-barrelled revolver which he stuffed into his trouser waistband underneath his jacket.

The café was alive with the noise of men talking, though Changwani wondered how they could hear themselves above the racket caused by music screeching from a jukebox in one corner. No eyes turned towards him, no-one seemed to take any notice as he strode to the counter and ordered a coffee in the best American accent he could muster. The girl behind the counter banged a mug in front of him and started filling it from a percolator before he had time to tell her he wanted it in a carry container to take outside. Deciding it was best not to make a fuss, he thanked her and drew up a stool, propping an elbow on the counter in as casual a manner as his nerves allowed him.

He used the time to search the faces of the people around him, all the while alert to any shifting of glances or changes in body language that would ring alarm bells. What he saw was the usual collection of brash Westerners wrapped up in their own little worlds and ignorant of any threats to their safety. He downed the last dregs of coffee, left a five-dollar bill on the counter, and headed slowly for the door. Just as he was about to step outside, a tall man mounted the step and brushed past him, forcing him to step aside. For a moment he thought about teaching the dog a lesson in manners, but merely smiled and allowed the stranger to barge his way inside.

Back in the campervan he locked all doors, and settled down to a well-earned sleep. Tomorrow he would meet Yousaf, and together they would wreak havoc in this land of the Godless.

Devon had noticed the campervan as soon as he entered the parking area. It was sat well back from the road, but had a clear run to the entrance if the driver wanted a fast getaway. His initial glance told him there was no-one behind the wheel, but that didn't mean Changwani wasn't in the rear compartment which was screened from view. After waiting a few minutes he decided to check the interior of the café.

He was just two paces short of the front door when Changwani filled the windowed partition from the other side. There was no time to turn, no time to avoid contact. Devon's hand started to reach for the Glock in his waistband, his conscience refusing to fight against the thought of putting several rounds into a face that caused the death of Mason Hunter. He suppressed the urge, dipped his shoulders, and decided to bluster his way through.

He hauled open the door and forced his way past the figure who had already started to cross the threshold. He kept his eyes down, knowing he couldn't mask the hatred he felt for this man. Then he pushed his shoulder hard against Changwani's torso before continuing into the café as if nothing had happened. Behind him he could hear the door slap against its hinges. He waited for a moment before turning to see Changwani cross the car park and climb into the campervan.

Devon knew Changwani had a perfect vantage point to watch the café from the darkness outside, so he moved into a corner hidden from view. There was a small hallway leading to toilets at the rear of the building and from there Devon hoped he could gain access to the outside.

He breathed a sigh of relief when he saw a large window in the toilet block. He quickly lifted a swing-latch and eased himself to the ground outside, careful to leave a small opening as he swung the window back on its latch. He sprinted to the side of the building and made his way towards the car park, all the time listening for any sounds coming from the direction where he judged the campervan van to be located.

He spotted the front end of the vehicle as he crept beyond a Peterbilt 387 rig that looked as if it had just come out of a showroom. Kneeling behind its large rear wheel set, Devon was less than twenty yards from the Commer and could see it rocking on its axles as someone moved about inside. He remained crouched for five minutes, satisfied the man inside had settled for the night.

Deciding to take no chances that he was being watched Devon retraced his steps, climbed back through the toilet window and emerged into the café. He ordered a coffee to go, walked back to his car without looking in the direction of the Commer, and drove to meet up with Don Hill.

The Commer passed their position at first light, both

men grateful for a return to action after almost eight hours of trying to get comfortable in the cramped car interior. Hill had received a call from his Washington office during the night, informing him the man they were tailing had now been identified as Asif Changwani, an Afghani national who had popped up on various security radars over the past few years. Hill flicked the radio to loudspeaker so Devon could hear the conversation.

"How come our so-called infallible facial recognition software didn't pick him up going through the airport? If we hadn't been tipped off about his bogus Dr Adam Seaton persona, he would have waltzed unchallenged into the country. How the fuck do things like this happen?"

Ignoring Hill's rant, the agent on the other end of the line continued his report. "Changwani is suspected of involvement in a number of incidents, both here and in Europe. Our sources tell us he was usually in the company of his cousin, one Yousaf Hasni, by all accounts a nasty piece of work who is credited with masterminding a series of suicide-bomb attacks in Israel last year."

Devon interrupted. "Do we know where this Hasni is now?"

The answer was unequivocal. "No sir, just like Changwani he dropped out of sight a few months ago. I've contacted a number of agencies to see if we can get a lead on him."

Hill banged his fist on the dashboard. "For all we know he could be here in America. Do you have men checking through airport registers and passport scans?"

"We're already on it, but there's too much of a

time period to cover. I'll keep you posted."

Before ending the conversation, Hill ordered replacement vehicles to be prepared at a rendezvous point just outside Albany. He knew the longer the trip continued, the more likely Changwani was to pick up the tail. He was also beginning to get a bad feeling about a new development that had entered the equation. He turned towards Devon. "What if Changwani is driving to meet up with his cousin in Fitchburg?"

At that moment Yousaf Hasni was pacing across a small living room in a farmhouse tucked into the countryside five miles east of Fitchburg. The previous evening he had taken various calls from men within his group telling him about odd messages they had received from a man purportedly looking for his cousin. The contacts were verified through the Imam in Chicago, but Hasni couldn't understand how Changwani could be in America when he was supposed to be in London.

A suspicious man by nature, Hasni ordered his group to join him at the farmhouse. There were now six men cramped into the small house, which had been rented by a local Fitchburg resident, an elderly second-generation citizen whose family fled Pakistan in 1931, and whose allegiance was still pledged to the cause of Islam.

Hasni had been holed up at the farmhouse for more than two weeks without any contact from the men who had sent him here. Weapons and explosives were stored in a little outhouse, but so far there was no green light to point him to his targets.

As the days passed, Hasni became more and more agitated, believing he had been forgotten and that his mission to America had been aborted. He had resolved to wait only a few more days before embarking on his own mission, anything that would provide him with action to quench a growing thirst for killing the enemies of his people.

Now he had to deal with the sudden appearance of his cousin Asif. Perhaps this was planned all along? Perhaps Asif had been sent to help him with his mission? But why should Asif know so much while he was being kept in the dark? His mood continued to darken as he ordered two men to drive to the outskirts of Fitchburg to meet Asif at the appointed place. It would be good to see his cousin again, but there would be strong words between them before he would agree to anything.

Chapter 24
Monaco

ALAN DOYLE SAT alongside Captain Georges Laurent in the prow of a motor launch cutting through the waters on course for *Gennady1*. Beside them were two more GIGN agents, busily checking their standard-issue Sig SP2022s and staring nervously across the harbour to check on the progress of the second launch, which was making a northerly approach under the control of Alfie Cheadle, accompanied by the other two French agents. Daylight was beginning to crack the Mediterranean sky, and the noise of the small Honda 4-stroke outboard engines was amplified by the stillness of the morning.

Doyle and Laurent had argued most of the night, the Frenchman finally conceding they had little option but to board the *Gennady1* to learn what they could about Claude Bartran's fate. The little chief's earlier garbled messages confirmed he was keeping the yacht under surveillance and that he suspected two of its passengers, whom he described as giant twins, of being involved in the murder of the GIGN agents in Paris. Despite their assurances to Monaco's Urban Police Division commander that they would not interfere in the investigation of Bartran's disappearance, they knew only fast and decisive action would provide the answers they needed.

Laurent recognised from their first meeting that Doyle was a highly experienced covert operative, a fact confirmed by the Englishman's calm assessment of the situation which faced them. Doyle had spent more than an hour studying the harbour scene through binoculars, provided by one of the French agents, before outlining a plan to board the yacht and interrogate everyone who was there. By the time he had finished, it was accepted that Doyle was now the de facto leader of the group.

Doyle's motorboat had meanwhile coasted to a stop alongside a silver ladder at the stern of the yacht. As they prepared to step across the gap between the two craft, a large bearded figure appeared at the top of the ladder. "What's going on here? Get away from this vessel or I shall call the police."

Doyle aimed his suppressed Glock directly into Benny Christensen's face, causing the old Captain to take an involuntary step backwards. In a whispered voice, dripping with menace, Doyle told him: "Stay exactly as you are and keep your hands where I can see them."

Christensen watched as four men, wearing head-to-toe black outfits and all heavily armed, ascended the ladder and stepped onto the deck beside him. Two of the group knelt with their gun arms extended in a sweeping motion that took in the doorway to the main lounge and a stairwell leading belowdecks. Christensen knew his boss was wrapped up in a lot of heavy-duty affairs, but this was his first real glimpse at just how dangerous the world of Anasenko had become. These men weren't party-crashers, or some kind of modern day pirates; they had the look of professional killers who would just as soon squeeze triggers as bid the time of day.

The group's leader pushed Christensen to one

side and began to question him on all the passengers, in particular whether he had any knowledge of an elderly man who might have been taken aboard the previous evening.

Before Christiansen could answer, the sound of gunfire erupted from the front of the yacht.

Igor Borimov heard the engine sounds through an alcohol-induced fog which refused to let any alarm bells ring in his normally alert brain. The Monaco port was the busiest of its size in the world and there were always idiots thrashing about and ignoring the strict no-engine rules that were imposed after midnight. He was about to turn over to continue what had been a restless sleep when he heard a distinctive thud against the side of the yacht. Moments later there was another thud, this one more metallic, and coming definitely from somewhere above and to the right of where his cabin was located.

The fog lifted quickly and Borimov sprang from the bed, noticing for the first time he was still fully clothed. He grabbed the T-33 Tokarev and made his way into the corridor, stopping outside Yevgeni's cabin just as another thud assailed the yacht. The cabin door burst open and Yevgeni emerged, tucking his shirt into his trousers and waving his pistol in the air. "What's going on?"

Igor motioned him to silence before whispering: "We appear to have company. You take aft and I'll go forward. Let's see if we can't create a little surprise for our visitors."

The two men moved away from each other,

their guns trained on the doors opening onto the corridor from both ends. Igor nudged open the door and walked silently to a stairwell leading to the top deck. Dropping onto his stomach, he inched upwards until he could see beyond the last stair towards the brightening sky above the ship's stern. As his eyes slowly fell towards the horizontal, he could make out the black-clad figure of a man climbing over the ornate railing.

Igor waited until he saw the flash of gunmetal in the man's right hand. That was all the confirmation he needed to know that this was a situation requiring the most extreme response possible. He levelled the Tokarev and squeezed off a three-round burst that tore open the intruder's head and sent his body catapulting over the rail and into the waters below.

Alfie Cheadle's launch had been first to approach the yacht. The bow stretching above him now looked a lot higher than it had from the shoreline, and as he craned his neck upwards, he began to wonder if he had fashioned enough rope to reach the ornate silver railing that ran all the way around the front of the vessel. He also began to doubt whether he could successfully throw the makeshift grappling hook that far upwards.

He cursed as the hook thumped against the bulkhead and dropped back into the motor launch. He gathered up the rope, grabbed the hook and prepared for a second throw, knowing that his first attempt had fallen at least eight feet short. He swung the hook several times in a circular motion before releasing it with all the power he could summon. This time it reached the railing, but clanged harmlessly against the top tier before again falling back to his feet.

Steadying himself against the constant bobbing of the deck below his feet, he went through the same pre-throw routine and launched the hook with a determination that almost caused him to bite off his lower lip. He watched as the hook sailed through the air, as if in slow motion, and reached out to wrap itself around the top rail. He pulled on the rope to ensure it was secured and immediately began an arm-over-arm ascent that was helped by knots tied into the rope at two-foot intervals.

At the top he bellied his way over the rail, pausing to look down as the first of the GIGN agents began his climb. Leaving the man to fend for himself, Cheadle unholstered his Glock and moved to the right to watch for any activity coming from the deck above. He didn't notice the small opening that led to the lower deck where at that precise moment Igor Borimov was beginning his careful climb up the stairs.

Cheadle sensed movement a fraction of a second before he looked down and to his left to see a hand with a gun appear from what seemed like a hole in the deck. He spun round to bring his Glock towards the target, just as the GIGN agent rolled over the railing and removed his pistol from a shoulder belt.

There was no time for Cheadle to shout, no time to discharge his weapon before the gun in the gap spewed a murderous burst towards the unfortunate agent. His peripheral vision detected the agent falling backwards and disappearing from sight, but all the while Cheadle held his focus firmly on the gun hand. He fired a burst towards it and was rewarded by seeing the gun jump from a bloodied hand and clatter across the deck.

Thump-thump noises on the stairwell told Cheadle the gunman had fallen, but he wasn't about to rush the gap in case the man might have another weapon or, worse still, have a few of his mates as back-ups. Inching his way carefully along the bulkhead, Cheadle paused at the entrance to the hatch before stepping into the doorway, his gun raised in a two fisted stance, the knuckle on his right index finger showing white in readiness for the last hairline squeeze of the trigger.

Below him, the stairwell was empty, but a trail of glistening blood was visible on the beige carpeting which covered a hallway leading to the left. Cheadle descended, one careful step after the other, until he reached the bottom. Stopping for only a moment, his back pressed against the stair wall, he pushed his head out to stare up an empty corridor, tracking a line of blood to a door that was still swinging on its hinges.

Doyle wasted no time when the first sounds of gunshots reached his ears. He bundled Benny Christensen to the deck and motioned for one of the GIGN agents to stand guard over the captain's trembling body. Without waiting to explain his intentions, he took off down a flight of stairs that led to the level where the noises had come from.

It was a mad headlong rush that probably saved his life.

As he reached the second step from the bottom,

he lost his footing and careered into a dropping roll that propelled him forcefully against a corridor wall. Above him the stairwell entrance was peppered by a sustained burst of automatic fire that tore chunks from mahogany panelling about the height where Doyle would have emerged had he not tripped.

Lying on the floor, Doyle rolled quickly onto his side to stare up a narrow hallway, his blood almost frozen by the sight that greeted him. The entire passageway seemed to be filled by a monster, the biggest sonofabitch Doyle had ever seen, and one who was redirecting his weapon from the stairwell towards where Doyle lay. There was no doubt that this was one of the giant twins reported by Bartran. There was also no doubting the murderous intentions etched across his face.

Doyle didn't give him a chance, no chance at all. With his Sig on full auto he held down the trigger and watched the giant convulse as the hammer blows raked his body. Incredibly, despite taking at least eight rounds in the stomach and chest, the giant continued to lumber onwards, although his gun hand had dropped harmlessly to his side, and he had to use the wall to keep himself upright.

Doyle jumped to his feet, the Sig trained steadily in the middle of the face that bore down on him. He watched as a steady trickle of blood escaped from the giant's mouth; watched as he staggered forward, the face contorted in his final attempts to suck air into punctured lungs. Two feet away from him, the face twisted into a contemptuous grin as he tried to spit blood at his assailant. There was just enough energy left to bubble the blood at the corner of his mouth before he sagged to his knees, the eyes searching upwards for a last sight of the man he knew had killed him.

Doyle thumbed the Sig to single-shot, squeezed the trigger, and watched the giant's right eye disappear in a fine spray of red and white.

Yevgeni Borimov's head whiplashed before his body crashed forward onto the blood-soaked carpet.

With the passageway now clear, Doyle could see a white-haired man clutching a briefcase as he stepped through a door thirty yards away. The man paused only to look menacingly at Doyle, as if trying to remember everything about him for future reference. Then he slammed the door behind him.

Gennady Anasenko had been awakened by the sounds of gunfire. Despite a deep-rooted belief in the ability of the Borimovs to protect him, an overwhelming instinct for self-preservation immediately kicked in. He leapt from the bed with the agility of a man thirty years younger, dressed quickly and attacked the dial on his wall-mounted safe. From this, he extracted a sheaf of papers and turned to exit the cabin through a door leading into his private hallway.

He heard a burst of automatic fire coming from his left. Using the retinal scan, he gingerly opened the door in time to see Yevgeni, at the far end of the corridor, stagger back from a volley of shots. Knowing there was nothing he could do, he watched as his giant protégé stumbled forward before sinking to his knees and providing Anasenko with a view of the man who had fired the shots. He was a tall well-muscled man, who carried himself with the ease of a professional. He watched almost in disbelief as the man stood over Yevgeni and calmly fired a shot at point-blank range into his face.

The stranger looked up and locked eyes with Anasenko. There was no emotion, or regret at the execution that had been carried out. It was the face of a dangerous man, a face Anasenko burned into his brain, one he hoped to see again, but with the tables turned. It would be a pleasure to look into that face to find out if the smugness would still be there if someone else was pulling the trigger.

He forced himself away from the image and bolted through the door, his thoughts now only on escaping from this madman and regrouping at his chalet in Switzerland. As he entered a second corridor leading to the helicopter deck, a door burst open and Igor Borimov staggered through, clutching a bloody rag to his right hand. Anasenko had to restrain him from running towards the rear of the yacht.

"Let me go. I must help Yevgeni," he pleaded.

Anasenko knew the next part wouldn't be easy. "I'm afraid my son, that Yevgeni is beyond help."

Igor searched his master's face looking for a sign he hadn't heard him right, but all he saw was sadness. The thought of his brother lying dead was like no pain he had ever experienced. The torment and rage slowly built up and his large frame bulged before he threw back his head and roared - a raw animal roar that seemed to echo throughout the yacht.

Anasenko knew he couldn't prevent Igor pushing past him, so instead he began to talk urgently into his face. "You will have your vengeance and much more. I have seen the man who did this vile act and we both will not rest until we corner him like the rat he is. But now is not the time, we must make a tactical withdrawal and plan how we can trap this monster."

For a moment it seemed the words fell on deaf ears, but slowly Igor's frame relaxed and he buried his head in Anasenko's shoulder, tears dripping onto the white silk shirt. Anasenko waited a few seconds before pushing the giant gently away. "Come. We must go. I have ordered the chopper to be ready, but if we don't leave now we might not get the chance to escape."

The two men turned and made their way down another stairwell into the large room where the Sikorsky's engines filled the space with a thunderous noise. The sky hatch was already open as Anasenko and Borimov climbed onto the platform and scrambled quickly through the side door of the lumbering craft.

Doyle heard the whine of hydraulics before feeling the vibration running through the entire vessel. He had reached the door through which the white-haired man had fled, but it refused to yield, despite Doyle emptying a full clip into the locking mechanism. He turned at the sound of footsteps behind him, but relaxed when Georges Laurent burst into view, closely followed by one of his agents. He directed the two men to aim their weapons at the door lock, pulled a radio from his breast pocket and began talking urgently into the small black handset.

"Alpha two, are you there? Come in."

After listening to static for a few seconds he

thumbed the send button again. "Cheadle, where the fuck are you?"

This time he was rewarded with a voice. "Sorry boss, we're stuck in a corridor. We can't get a door open."

"Make your way back onto the upper deck. Some of our targets are trying to escape."

"What's that noise?" Cheadle asked.

"If I'm not mistaken that's a chopper. If we don't get topside we'll lose the bastards."

Doyle nodded to Laurent to keep trying the door and then took off at a sprint back down the corridor. Leaping over the body of Yevgeni Borimov, he reached the stairwell, stopping only to insert a fresh magazine into the Glock before continuing upwards.

Back on deck, he was assailed by the powerful downdraft of the Sikorsky's rotors sitting atop a platform twenty feet into the air, and less than thirty yards from where Doyle had crouched to avoid being swept overboard. He looked upwards to see the large helicopter free itself from the platform and rise slowly skywards.

Doyle wedged his back against the bulkhead and tried to steady the Glock on the engine casing just below the rotor housing. He emptied the magazine, knowing the force of the wind had pushed his arms off course, making it almost impossible to direct the 9mm Parabellums towards their target.

The chopper continued to rise, swung through a one-eighty, and accelerated away from the yacht. Doyle watched it all the way, hoping a plume of smoke would materialise and the chopper would ditch into the radiant blue waters. Instead it continued to shrink against the skyline and was eventually lost to view.

Doyle scrambled over the yacht towards the opening where the platform had sprung from. Looking below, he could make out a large garage-like room strewn with all manner of tools and equipment, including two brightly-painted JetSkis. Two figures emerged from the left side of the room, Doyle recognising instantly the outline of Laurent and his fellow agent. He shouted down to them. "It's too late, the birds have well and truly flown."

Laurent kicked out at an oil drum positioned slightly apart from a cluster of similar drums, each painted black and standing about three feet tall. The drum shifted off its spot and toppled over with a hollow clang that confirmed it was empty. Behind where the drum had sat, Doyle could see two legs jutting out from the other drums. "There's someone lying there."

Georges Laurent aimed his Sig at the body and then bent down to examine a face swollen with bruises and covered in blood. "Mon Dieu, it's Claude," he shouted.

Doyle hunkered down on the deck and watched as Laurent carefully cradled Bartran's head in his lap. What Doyle couldn't see were the tears flowing down Laurent's face as he pushed strands of matted hair away from Bartran's eyes. Suddenly the GIGN agent seemed to stiffen.

"What is it?" Doyle shouted.

There was a brief pause before Laurent answered. "He's alive, he's alive!"

Chapter 25
Fitchburg

CHANGWANI'S SENSES WENT into high alert when he noticed a thick pall of black smoke rising in a straight column, about a quarter mile distant from where he crested a ridge on the two-lane highway running towards Albany. He could make out a number of vehicles, including a sheriff's car with its roof lights flashing, and a large truck which appeared to be jack-knifed, the cab bent at angle which allowed it to look back along its trailer.

His first thought was to U-turn out of there, even though it might draw undue attention from the policeman who was now looking towards his approaching van. He was driving in strange countryside with no way of knowing how to find his way to his destination from a detour, and no way of knowing whether other police vehicles might be rushing to the scene from the road behind him. It took only a few seconds for him to decide to brazen it out.

He coasted to a stop behind a small queue of cars, noticing for the first time a station wagon lying ablaze in a ditch in front of the twisted truck. He tensed as the policeman walked towards him holding out his left hand in a needless stop gesture, while his right hand rested lazily on a hip holster. When he spoke the voice was gruff. "We've had an accident here, and it will be some time before we can get traffic moving again. Please stay in your vehicle until we sort things out."

Without waiting for a response, the Highway Patrol man turned on his heels and walked back behind the truck. The sound of an ambulance siren could be heard in the distance and a number of people had left their vehicles to investigate what was going on, despite the patrol officer's instructions to remain inside.

A large tractor emerged from a field behind Changwani's Commer and pulled up to the queue with its engine on high revs and diesel fumes escaping from a funnel mounted behind the driver's cab. Leaving the engine running, a heavy-set man in filthy dungarees jumped down to the tarmac and made his way forward, stopping briefly at Changwani's open window.

"What's going on here?" he shouted, more for the benefit of the people ahead than for Changwani.

The Highway Patrol officer appeared around the truck, his face a mask of annoyance. "Who's making all the racket?"

"I am," the man responded defiantly. "I've a lot of work to be doing without wasting my time while you people close the roads to poor farmers trying to make a living."

The policeman looked shaken by the outburst. "There's been a bad accident and one person is dead. Show some respect."

"That's as may be, but I can't be standing about here. I'll be driving my tractor on the left verge where there's enough room to pass, and don't you think you can stop me."

The farmer turned to head back to the tractor,

but the patrolman grabbed at his shoulder, twisted his arm into a lock, and threw him heavily against Changwani's van. The two men grappled for a moment before falling to the ground, the larger man ending up on his belly with the patrolman's knee wedged firmly into his back. A pair of handcuffs was produced and snapped around the farmer's wrists.

Hauling his prisoner to his feet, the patrolman shoved him forward and put him in the back of his car before returning to mount the cab of the tractor and switch off the engine. As he alighted, he noted a battered Taurus pull up behind the tractor.

Holding the tractor keys in his hand the patrolman stopped at Changwani's window. "Sorry about the disturbance. You wanna make a complaint about the dent in your van?"

Changwani was startled by the question. "No officer. This old thing has so many dents that one more will not make a difference. You have enough to worry about without thinking about this. I can't understand why that man was so rude to you."

"Aye. It takes all sorts and that's a fact."

Ten minutes later the patrolman started to wave the queue of vehicles onto the verge and past the blockage. Changwani could see the burnt-out shell of a vehicle lying in the ditch and a body being stretchered into a waiting ambulance. A man, who looked like he might be the truck driver, was leaning against the patrol car, ignoring the rants of the farmer hidden partly behind the grilled-off back seat.

Changwani glanced at his watch, aware he had lost valuable time, but knowing that Yousaf's people would wait for him at the rendezvous.

The two men in the battered Taurus smiled as the Commer stretched away in the distance. They watched it disappear from view before turning to the patrolman who approached carrying a suitcase. Behind him the back door of the patrol car opened and the farmer climbed out, holding his handcuffs triumphantly in the air with one hand as he strode towards the Taurus.

The suitcase was pushed through the opened window into the passenger's lap. Don Hill lifted the lid to look at what appeared to be the screen of a laptop, and began twisting small dials running along the bottom of a built-in console. The screen came to life, showing the image of a map with a small flashing dot almost dead centre.

He turned to the patrolman and the farmer. "Good job, gentlemen. This will help us relax for a while. I must congratulate you on your accident scene; it was well staged and very realistic."

The "farmer" spoke first. "You did tell us it had to look good, although you didn't give us much time. The thanks should go to Sheriff Palmer who pulled out all the stops when I put our unusual request to him." As he spoke, he clasped a friendly arm around the Sheriff's shoulder. "I must say though Sheriff, you were a bit rough in the arrest scene. I almost didn't get the magnetic homing device attached under the Commer while you were pummelling my back."

Palmer smiled. "It's not every day you get to put the cuffs on an FBI agent."

Hill held his hand out the window. "I want to thank you Sheriff, and I promise your department will get an honourable mention when we write up our report. You've done more than you know to help safeguard our country."

"Just as long as you catch the bastards." The Sheriff shook Hill's hand and walked back to his car.

Hill watched him with a look of admiration before turning his head to John Winstanley aka the farmer. "Have you got your team in place?"

Winstanley nodded through the window. "I have a full tactical unit holding back for your instructions. Don't forget our deal – nobody moves in until we get there."

Hill had no option but to call in the Feds. Several hours ago he had put in a call to the FBI Field Office in Albany, requesting a staged diversion to allow a tracker to be placed on Changwani's van. The long trek across country was beginning to jeopardise the integrity of the pursuit; there were just too many variables to be able to follow the Commer at a safe distance, without risking the likelihood of it turning off at the many crossings they flashed past.

He had worked other cases with Winstanley and trusted him, even allowing for the fact that part of the bargain meant surrendering a piece of the action. The important thing was to make sure Changwani led them to other terrorists, and the chance to shut down another major threat to America's security.

Mike Devon had not been happy with the decision. Although he had accepted the need for a tracking device, he was not prepared to surrender first crack at Changwani.

As Devon eased the borrowed Taurus around the roadblock he glanced briefly across to Hill. "Remember, we too have a bargain."

Hill was staring intently at the flashing screen dot, but lifted his head in acknowledgement. "Don't worry Mike, Changwani is all yours."

***

Ten miles outside Fitchburg, Changwani turned the Commer off the main highway and drove north towards Worchester to intercept the John Fitch Highway before it climbed into a wooded hilly area shrouded by gathering storm clouds. It was a bleak landscape, offering little in the way of a break, except maybe the odd grazing herd of Dexter cattle or a few derelict ranch houses sitting forlornly in weed-strewn fields, long abandoned as a means of farming income.

Changwani drove slowly, keeping his eyes fixed ahead for a crossroads where he hoped to find a garage and a contact to take him to his cousin Yousaf.

He smiled at the contradiction between the bleak scenery and the so-called riches of this great land. Substitute the grass and the trees for sand and rocks, and he might as well have been in some of the darkest parts of Afghanistan, where poverty was rife, but where people were true to themselves and their God. The difference was that the Afghan people wanted to get on with their own lives, wanted to preserve their rich culture and heritage, and wanted to be free from the meddling of foreigners.

His thoughts were interrupted by the sight of a number of road signs visible about three hundred yards ahead. He shifted noisily down the gears and came to a stop at the crossroads, his eyes turning to the right to pick up the pumps and forecourt of a garage, exactly where he was told it would be. He drove slowly alongside a pump, all the while scanning the area for any hint of the men he was to meet there. The place seemed deserted.

He alighted from the van and walked in the direction of a ramshackle wooden hut, which was the only building on the lot. The door of the hut opened and an old man stepped out pushing a stout cane into the ground in front of him in an effort to maintain his balance. He looked up at Changwani. "Would yer mind serving yerself young fella? Me old bones are full of arthritis and I can't operate the pumps the way I used to."

Changwani nodded and walked back to the pumps. As he fiddled with the petrol cap he asked the old man: "Are you on your own? Have you had many other customers today?"

The old man squawked in laughter. "Customers! You're the first today. Come to think of it young fella, you're the first this week." He squawked again.

Changwani didn't seem to think the remark was as funny as the old man did. "Has no one been around?" The question underlined a growing apprehension that he had missed the rendezvous or, worse still, had he come to the wrong place?

"Nah, no-one bothers now. Used to be different back in the fifties when this was a main route through to the larger towns, but since they got those new-fangled highways everybody's always in a hurry to get where they're going. I remember I used to serve five hundred cars a day, but nowadays I wouldn't get five hundred in a year."

Changwani tuned out from the old man's reminiscences. He would have to call the number he had stored in his mobile and hope he hadn't strayed too far from the pick-up point. Just then a car roared past the garage, decelerating hard as it approached the crossroads before coming to a stop in a squeal of tyres. He could make out the figures of two men sitting in front as the car idled for more than a minute.

The seconds ticked by. Changwani withdrew the petrol gun and slammed it into the rack on the pump. He handed the old man a bunch of crumpled notes and climbed back into the driver's seat, his hand shooting out towards the cardboard box where he had stowed the revolver. He reached up to twist the rearview mirror for a view on the stationery car, and watched as it moved off in a circle around the crossroads, heading back in the direction of the garage.

The car moved slowly, giving Changwani a clear view of the occupants as it drew level with his position. He held their gaze and watched the car continue down the road before stopping about two hundred yards from the garage. Convinced these were the men he was supposed to meet, Changwani pulled out of the garage and drove slowly up to the parked car.

Holding the revolver down by his side, Changwani climbed out of the van and walked up to the driver's window of the car. He said simply: "Do you know Yousaf?"

The driver twisted to look up into Changwani's face. "Where have you been? We have travelled this road many times over the past two hours."

Changwani ignored the absence of a traditional greeting, though he pledged to wipe the smirk off the man's face in the not-to-distant future. He controlled his emotion and said simply: "Take me to Yousaf, now."

Devon was tired, a down-to-the-bones tiredness brought on by a combination of jet-lag, too little sleep, and the constant stresses of the past few weeks. As he stretched out on the tilted-back passenger seat, his mind was three thousand miles away, tuned into the smiling face of Emma, wondering what she was doing. Probably for the first time, certainly for as far back as he could remember, he wished he was back in London, watching as she hunched over her laptop, churning out some legal document. He missed her, and was silently cursing the imperative that took him halfway across the world just when their relationship had reached a new and interesting level. Things would have to change.

"You awake?"

He was instantly alert. "I am now. What's a fella got to do to get a bit of sleep around here?"

Don Hill smiled across from the driver's seat. "Listen Snow White, there'll be plenty of time for sleep later. Just thought you'd want to know something's stirring."

Devon and Hill had led the small convoy of cars in pursuit of Changwani for more than eighty miles after the tracking device was planted on the Commer. They estimated their hang-back distance was about five miles – enough to avoid suspicion or detection, but also enough to be able to respond quickly to any dramatic changes ahead. Their only anxiety was Changwani's ten-minute stop at the garage, but they pulled over and waited patiently for the screen flasher to start moving again.

Twenty minutes later the Commer stopped again. Devon studied the screen map where the flashing dot was now static - at a point a few hundred yards off the main road in what appeared to be little more than a narrow lane leading towards hilly, wooded terrain. After pulling over and waiting fifteen minutes the two men agreed to investigate what lay ahead.

They passed the entrance to the lane, noting as much detail as they could of the fields on both sides and the woods beyond. The lane dipped about a hundred yards in, preventing a view of how far it stretched or whether there were any buildings in the area. A mile down the road, Hill pulled the Dodge into a muddy verge and retrieved a pair of binoculars from the glove compartment. "Looks like we've got a bit of a walk in front of us," he said matter-of-factly to a resigned Devon.

The first field was covered in tall grass, which made it easy to move quickly to the crest of a hill. Once in position, Hill swept the binoculars over the ground leading to the road where the Commer had turned off. He was rewarded with a direct line of sight to a ranch house surrounded by four vehicles. He continued panning the area, working out possible approaches to the house, and trying to guess the distance between it and the treeline running behind to the west.

Devon grabbed the binoculars and focussed in until the image of the Commer enlarged in his eyepiece. It was parked up beside a broken down fence on one side of an overgrown square which was probably once a corral. Devon could easily imagine it filled with horses, the only practical transport to service a large working ranch back in the days when cowboys were commonplace in this remote landscape. He pushed the images from his mind and turned to face Hill with a look of determination. "This is as far it goes. No more running around, no more softly-softly; we take them here."

"I agree," Hill told him. "Let's get back to the car and rustle up the troops."

An hour later, Devon was again stretched out in the car, listening intently as Hill outlined their plan to the rest of the team, and to the incoming FBI unit, which was directed to take up position in the woods east of the ranch house. Two of Hill's team had been ordered to keep the house under surveillance from a vantage point west of the approach track. There was nothing to do but wait until everyone was in position. It was agreed they would move in under the cover of darkness, less than three hours away.

The sound of automatic gunfire blew their plan to hell in a hand-basket.

The four al-Qaeda men had watched silently as the conversation between their leader and the stranger from the garage became increasingly animated. The initial greeting between the two men had been genuinely warm, each clenching the other in an embrace which lasted more than a minute and had the onlookers squirming in embarrassment at the unusual sight of Yousaf stepping outside his normally abrupt and morose façade.

The mood had changed when the two retired alone to the kitchen area, leaving the door open as they stood against a sink unit, staring off into the woods beyond. The pitch of their voices gradually rose, and at one point Changwani could be seen placing his hands on his Hasni's shoulders.

"Yousaf, you must believe me when I tell you I knew nothing about why you were sent to America."

Hasni brushed the hands away. "I have sat here for two weeks kicking my heels while you have been operating in Europe. Why has that been so, and why have you suddenly turned up here?"

Changwani could understand his cousin's frustration, but knew he would be able to change his mood. He explained quickly what had happened in Paris and London and about his growing suspicions of the men who hid in the background and pulled his strings. He spoke of his growing realisation that these men were also Hasni's backers and were using both of them to further their own cause at the expense of the Jihadist warriors whose lives were wasted by the missions chosen for them.

Hasni was dumbstruck by the news. So much of what Changwani told him made sense; at the very least it explained many things which had tormented him for the past few weeks, although he would not have been able to guess the reasons as clearly as were now laid out for him.

The two began to exchange stories about how contact was first made with them, how they were sworn to conceal the offered support from each other, and how the logistics of their movements were dealt with. Everything they spoke about seemed to be in duplicate – the same arrangements for travel, the same methods of delivery of cash and arms, and the same kinds of targets they were ordered to attack. By the time they finished ticking all the boxes, there was no longer any doubt they had been duped by the same people.

"What we must do now," Changwani concluded, "is to join together as we once did in the mountains and plains of our homeland. We must find these people and destroy them in the name of the martyrs whose deaths have been sullied by their interference."

Hasni nodded agreement, but before he could respond one of his men burst into the room. "Yousaf, you must come. There is someone moving about outside."

They rushed into the front room towards a window where one of the other men was pointing out to the fields beyond the parked vehicles. "I have seen at least two men. They are crawling towards the house from that field," he said, pointing to an area covered in gorse bushes less than a hundred yards away.

"You must have been followed," Hasni challenged Changwani.

"It's not possible. Perhaps you have been under surveillance?" Changwani countered.

The two stared menacingly into each other's eyes before Hasni's face broke into a grin. "I think you may be right cousin. We have been holed up here for too long, certainly enough to draw attention to ourselves. At least one good thing will come of this."

"What's that?"

Hasni withdrew an automatic pistol from his waistband. "You and I will get the chance to fight again side by side. We will kill these enemies of our people and then we will unleash our might against the Great Satan."

He walked away from the window and motioned the others to join him in the centre of the room, where he began outlining a plan to deal with the intruders.

***

Carl Foreman and Todd Slater had joined *LonWash Securities* barely three months ago, following successful ten-year careers in the CIA. The prospects of doubling their salaries and getting out from under Langley's administrative shackles were too much of a lure when they were approached initially by Don Hill. The two first met in college days at UCLA and became firm friends, a relationship cemented by Foreman marrying Slater's younger sister. They enrolled together, coaxed and cajoled each other through the tough training regime at Maryland, and were assigned together to the Washington office, where they made their names as resourceful agents.

They had been keeping a watch on the farmhouse for more than two hours when Foreman suggested they should move closer. Hidden in a field of old corn stalks and weeds, they could see stands of gorse bushes offering ideal vantage points in an adjoining field. They moved stealthily across the space in a classic you-go-I-go leapfrog routine, certain they were screened from the view of anyone in the house.

Crouched behind a large gorse bush, they scanned ahead, noting with satisfaction they now had a clear view of the front and back of the house. They settled in to wait for nightfall.

Their attention was suddenly drawn to a commotion at the front of the house where a number of men were opening and closing car doors, as if retrieving items. They resisted the temptation to break radio silence, knowing that Don Hill and the Englishman would be watching the same thing from their vantage point to the west of the hill. They continued to watch as another man emerged from a lean-to shed carrying a large box towards the house.

The activity continued for several minutes, with most of the agents' attention drawn to the man who constantly moved in and out of the lean-to. There was something about the boxes he was ferrying to the house; something that reminded them of wooden ordnance cases similar to those stored in Army arsenals. They watched the activity for another five minutes before agreeing to radio Hill for confirmation that he had eyes on what was happening.

They never got the chance.

Behind them, a slight rustle of grass was followed by the unmistakeable sound of a metal slider. They spun round in tandem to stare into the brown faces of two men pointing Uzi sub-machine pistols at them from less than twenty feet away. There was no time to react, no time to dive away from the murderous bursts which erupted from both barrels.

The brothers-in-law, who had spent so much time in each other's company, who had dreamed the same dreams, and had planned the same plans, died together in a fusillade that echoed noisily across the semi-enclosed prairie.

Chapter 26
Switzerland

THE GULFSTREAM TOUCHED down in Geneva at the end of a thirty-minute hop from Monaco. Gennady Anasenko had radioed ahead for the pilots to file a flight plan and be ready for wheels-up as soon as his party transferred from the helicopter, which had extricated him from the gun battle aboard the yacht. His mood was foul. He spent the time locked in his cabin trying to make sense of the turn of events which had exposed him to a French security operation, and brought the head of GIGN to snoop around Monaco.

He cursed Yevgeni for the decision to bring the policeman aboard the yacht instead of allowing Igor to finish throttling the life out of the interfering busybody. Yevgeni had argued that the discovery of the man's identity made it imperative to torture him for information about the details of the operation he was engaged in. Anasenko agreed they needed to know the extent of their exposure, but he hadn't reckoned on the agent having back-up, certainly not the kind willing to mount an all-out assault on his yacht.

In a way, Anasenko admired the French policeman's resilience. He had been mercilessly beaten over a three-hour period, but refused to give up more than the usual name-rank-serial number response to every question. In the end they left him for dead in the chopper cargo area, intending to dispose of the body far out to sea the next morning.

As he paced the Gulfstream's private drawing room, he couldn't figure out what had alerted GIGN to his involvement in whatever they were investigating. The only thing that made sense was that suspicion had somehow fallen on the Borimov twins during their trip to Paris, and they had been followed to London and on to Monaco. There could have been any number of reasons for suspecting the twins, not least that their mere physical presence usually caused second glances. It could be as simple as that, if not for the knowledge that the man who followed them was no less than the head of France's top counter-terrorism agency. Surely a routine assignment such as this would have been delegated to an underling?

He pushed the questions from his mind and decided to look at the positives. There was no way he could be implicated in anything, certainly nothing to do with his operations against major oil companies or his involvement in the terror plots in London and Paris. He would deny being on board the yacht at the time of the shooting, and disavow all knowledge of the movements of the twins. He would pass them off as little more than bodyguards whom he employed from time to time. In any case, he would use his contacts to ensure that any French investigation into his business would be shut down.

Satisfied all angles were covered, he opened the cabin door and walked out to the main passenger area where Igor was lying asleep, no doubt from the effects of the morphine injections administered shortly after they boarded. His hand was wrapped in a fresh bandage and his arm placed in a sling as a precaution against his flailing about in a semi-comatose state.

Across the aisle, Sylvia Flynn sat staring through the window at the Swiss terrain stretching below. He had to admire the acute sense of self-preservation which had taken her aboard the helicopter, even before Anasenko reached the platform. At the first sounds of gunfire, she had rushed from her cabin into the chopper pilot, pausing only to grab her suitcase, already packed for an early-morning departure, and followed him to the cargo area.

She turned at the sound of Anasenko's approach, noticing his earlier fury had been replaced by his usual blank-faced calmness. "Is everything alright, Gennady?" she asked with a hint of trepidation.

"Yes my dear. There's nothing to worry about. When we get to Geneva you will remain at the airport and return to London on the first available flight. Your mission must be fulfilled at all costs, and you must begin to sow the seeds the minute you get there. Do you understand the importance of what you have to do?"

She knew better than to question him about the events in Monaco. Her reply was one she judged he would want to hear. "Of course, Gennady. You can trust me."

Geneva airport was busy for the start of the winter skiing season. Anasenko ignored the groups of holidayers and made his way to the lower-level train station, stopping only briefly to kiss Flynn lightly on the cheek and watch her stride towards the bookings area. Ahead of him stretched a three-hour journey to Gstaad, with stopovers to change trains at Montreux and Zweisimmen. His chalet was situated in one of the many hillside vantage points overlooking the busy little village of Gstaad – and it was from there he would implement the final stages of his plan.

***

By the time Anasenko settled into his train compartment, Alan Doyle and Alfie Cheadle were airborne, on their way back to London. Georges Laurent had convinced them to leave Monaco immediately by reasoning their presence would only further complicate an already complicated situation. The discovery of Claude Bartran on board the *Gennady1* would provide the GIGN agents with sufficient reason for investigating the yacht – or, as Laurent put it, – for making "a social call" in the search for their boss. They would tell Monaco's Police Division of their surprise at being fired upon and their understandable need to defend themselves.

After receiving an assurance that Laurent would keep them posted about Bartran's condition and any follow-up investigation, the two men climbed into a motor launch and snaked across the harbour away from two police dinghies approaching from the opposite direction. The gunfire had cut through the early morning stillness of the harbour, and everywhere people were grouped on their yachts and along the harbour walkway, craning to see what the commotion was about.

Doyle knew there was no reason for staying in Monaco. The men who had fled the yacht in the chopper had to be traced, although at this point he had no way of knowing their whereabouts. After taking the train back to Monaco airport they began questioning staff about recent flights, but were met with either stony silences or excuses about confidentiality. Since they were in a country which didn't recognise their jurisdiction - and mainly because they wanted to keep their interest low key - they were forced to accept the situation.

Once back in London, Doyle was convinced his tech boffins could hack into the relevant flight databases. Failing that, they would have to go official and demand the answers through Interpol or other inter-agency channels. He cursed the loss of valuable time, but knew he had no alternative. He would also have to wait until he got back to London to brief Mike Devon on what he knew his boss would describe "as an interesting turn of events."

Chapter 27
Fitchburg

IT WAS PROBABLY JUST as well Doyle didn't try to make contact with Mike Devon. At that moment he was busy scrambling through tall grass and weeds, attempting to get closer to the ranch house, and trying to figure out what had caused the burst of automatic gunfire east of his location. Lying alongside him, Don Hill broke radio silence by calling in a sit-rep from all agents, fearful of what he was about to find out.

One by one the calls came in, but there was nothing from the two agents sent to watch the approach lane.

Foreman, Slater, come in. Nothing.

Foreman, what's happening? Nothing

Has anyone got eyes on the east? Can anyone see Foreman and Slater?

An FBI sniper, lying on ground overlooking the scene from the treeline northwest of the property, traversed his rifle sight to the fields opposite his location. He moved slowly across a hundred yards of ground before concentrating on a cluster of gorse bushes. The Leupold 3.5 variable-power scope brought the yellow-tipped bushes into absolute clarity, allowing the sniper to see the bodies of two men half-hidden by overhanging twigs and tall grass.

I have a visual. Two men down, I say again, two men down.

It was not what Hill wanted to hear. The thought of two of his men lying injured or dead made him want to rush to their aid without caring about taking fire from the house. Instead, he fought his emotions, and tried to figure a way of storming the house and killing every fucker he found inside. His thoughts were broken by a voice on his comms.

I see at least one bandit near where the bodies are lying.

Hill recognised it as the same voice which reported the original sighting. *Are you sure it's not one of our men?*

Negative. The bandit is carrying an automatic machine pistol. Do you want me to take a shot?

For Chrissakes, make sure it's not one of our men. If you have a shot, take it.

The sniper held his aim on a gorse bush where his target had run when he first spotted him. If the man intended making his way back to the ranch house, he would likely emerge from the left, trying to find cover behind the next bush. The sniper moved his aim towards the second bush and waited.

Barely a few seconds elapsed before a man broke cover towards the bush where the marksmen had his weapon trained. The sniper watched as the texture of the bush took on a new shadow caused by the figure crouching behind it. Centering his aim on the mass of the shadow, he squeezed the trigger, fought the recoil, and watched a small cloud puncture its way through the bush. The shadow disappeared.

As an afterthought, the sniper began firing into other bushes in the area. Four times he slid the bolt to eject a spent cartridge and ram a fresh 7.62 mm shell into the breach, before another figure leapt from cover and started running towards the house, with no thought of looking for cover. The sniper sighted just ahead of his runner, judging the allowance needed to ensure the target would run slap bang into the bullet that would take his life. Just as he was about to pull the trigger the ground around him erupted as a spray of automatic fire poured from the house.

He dove for cover, released his finger from the trigger, and cursed his luck at letting the target escape.

Hasni had talked quickly to the assembled group. They had to retrieve the weapons and explosives stored in the lean-to shed, using the activity as a cover for two of the group to slip out through a concealed tunnel and deal with the two men seen close to the house. He knew there would be others, but he wanted to control the situation rather than remain like sitting ducks inside the house. His instructions to the two operatives before they climbed into the tunnel was to make things as noisy as they could in the hope of drawing attention away from his other planned moves.

Changwani listened intently, impressed by the boldness and cleverness of the scheme. The four remaining men made their way out to the front of the house, three of them making a show of searching the cars, while the fourth entered the lean-to. Using the constant movement in and out of the house as a cover, Changwani dropped on his stomach, crawled below the car he had followed from the garage, and waited for an agreed signal. The others retreated into the house. Once inside, Hasni moved to the rear and climbed into the tunnel, waiting for the same signal.

The staccato sound of the Uzis dealing death to the two *LonWash* agents acted like a starting pistol.

Changwani sprang from below the car and disappeared into the tall grass of a field stretching north of the house towards the main road. Hasni emerged from the tunnel at the rear of the house, turned right, and climbed into a field heading towards the wooded area to the west. The two men sent to deal with the intruders were ordered to circle back towards the house and search the fields to the south. The remaining two al-Qaeda men were delegated to stay behind to deal with any attempted assault on their position.

Hasni heard the sound of a large calibre rifle from somewhere ahead of him in the woods. He knew enough about the distinctive boom to recognise the trademark of a sniper, something he hadn't factored into the equation. He was heartened by the return fire of his men, and used their withering barrage to muscle his way through the tough grass at a crouching run, which took him within twenty yards of the treeline.

John Winstanley held binoculars to his eyes and smiled as he watched the grasses shake in a zigzag path towards his position. Including the sniper, sheltering behind a tree fifty yards to his right, there were five other agents strung out along the treeline. He had enough firepower to deal with a platoon assault, never mind what appeared to be just one man, but Winstanley was not one to take chances.

The assailant rushing towards them could have all manner of high explosives capable of blasting a wide swathe of destruction across their position.

He hand-signalled the men on either side of him and pointed his Ingram M6 in the direction of the area where the grass was last disturbed. Six machine pistols opened up almost simultaneously, the tall stalks of grass disintegrating under the 600 rounds-per-minute onslaught.

***

Devon and Hill had crawled to within fifty yards of the old corral fence when they heard the thundering roar of the Ingrams. They dropped on their bellies and exchanged "what-the-fuck?" glances, knowing the FBI team had somehow engaged a target from the treeline southwest of their position. Their comms units provided an answer: *Be advised we have bandits roaming the exterior.*

Hill whispered to Devon: "How did they get out of the house?"

"Doesn't much matter. We can deal with the whys and wherefores later, but right now we need to split up." Devon signalled Hill to go right before crawling towards the left side of the corral, close to the parked cars. He had gone barely ten yards when he heard a rustle just ahead – something was disturbing the grass, and he was betting the farm it wasn't a field mouse.

He lay rigid, his right hand outstretched with his index finger lightly caressing the trigger on the Glock supplied by Hill. The pistol was already chambered and cocked, unlike the movies where the bad guys always give themselves away by waiting until the last second before deciding to prepare their weapon with enough noise to alert the good guy.

Devon maintained utter stillness for more than two minutes, his senses on high alert for any movement or noise that didn't square with the normal effects of a light breeze on the tall spindly stalks around him. After a further minute he was beginning to believe the original noise had been nothing more than imagination, or maybe there *was* a snake of the more common variety slithering around the undergrowth? But Mike Devon had learned a long time ago to trust his instincts, to understand that impatience got you dead.

And so he held his position.

In the end it was not the noise of the grass, or the blurry outline of a shape hurtling towards him that caused him to roll quickly to his left. It was an inbuilt antenna for trouble and danger which propelled him instinctively away from the path of the incoming five-inch blade.

Although, in reality, he didn't make it all the way clear.

Changwani had no intention of dying today, certainly not in a dungheap of a farm where his corpse would have little more than rotting grass and weeds for eternal company. His mission for Allah would end in one of this country's great cities, somewhere his last actions would be carved forever into the memories of his enemies. He had liked Yousaf's plan, if only because it afforded him the chance to slip through the net, to live and fight another day - and at a place of *his* choosing.

He regretted that having found Yousaf he would lose him so quickly, but it was his own fault he had drawn attention to himself. His cousin must have been careless with his security, and for that he would have to pay with his life. He cared not about Yousaf's followers, particularly the one who had shown disrespect to him at the garage. He smiled at the thought of the dog dying so that he might live.

The gunfire from near the trees told him Yousaf had engaged the enemy. Judging by the intensity of the salvo, and the absence of return fire, it was clear Yousaf stood no chance. A noise in the grass ahead snapped his attention back to his own predicament.

As he expected, there were men in the undergrowth, but he credited himself with having a distinct advantage. The years of guerrilla fighting in the mountains and plains of Afghanistan and Pakistan had honed his predatory skills to a level beyond the capabilities of the men he now faced. From an inside pocket he withdrew a Colt 45 Bowie knife, a wicked-looking weapon which featured a stainless-steel Damascus blade, upswept to a curved point. He had snatched it from where it was left carelessly on a table in the kitchen.

He knew that by using a gun he would draw attention to his position. Much better to kill silently, engage any further targets he came across, and get beyond the cordon of men he was sure was closing in on the ranch house from all sides. Once free of the area he would find a way of securing transport, perhaps back to Chicago.

It was relatively easy to judge the position of the man in front of him. The noise had stopped which could only mean he had also heard something and was waiting for Changwani to approach. Instead of moving forward, Changwani crawled back along the already trampled grass before deviating to his right and inching his way towards the man's position.

He judged the moment almost perfectly. Coming from the side of the man's position, he hunkered with the weight on the balls of his feet, and sprang through the air like a tiger pouncing on his prey. Holding the knife in a downwards stabbing motion he thrust for a point at the base of the man's neck. Inches from his target, the man rolled, and the blade missed its mark. However, Changwani was rewarded by a deep guttural scream as the blade sliced across the man's shoulder.

It was the kind of pain Devon knew could only come from a bad wound. He continued rolling away from his assailant into the tall grass, feeling the hot flow of blood running down his back and chest, and aware of the nausea which was sweeping over him. The fear of passing out created a new panic, brought on by the certainty that this man would kill him if he couldn't defend himself.

He lost the Glock somewhere along the path of his roll-overs, but there was no time to search for it. The attacker had regained his balance and was on top of him, pushing the curved blade towards his right eye as Devon fought to hold his wrist with an arm weakened by the wound and loss of blood.

Devon stared into the smiling face of his assassin, recognising, for the first time, the familiar features of the man he had chased halfway around the world. The realisation gave him a fresh surge of adrenalin and renewed determination. He locked his second arm onto the man's wrist and pushed upwards with all his might. At first he thought he was succeeding in moving the blade away, but the man was just too powerful, and Devon was weakening from the injury to his shoulder.

He had to turn the tables, and there was only one way he could think of. Staring into the other man's eyes Devon spoke in a voice of utter calmness. "It's finally nice to meet you Dr Adam Seaton, or should I say Asif Changwani, murderer of innocents, and failed Jihadist warrior, who had to slink out of London with his tail between his legs."

The impact of the words was better than Devon could have hoped for. Changwani's thrust on the knife slackened as he stared in disbelief at the man beneath him. "How do you know my name? How do you know I was in London?" Even as the words left his lips Changwani realised it was not Yousaf who had been slack with his security; it was he who had brought these men to the ranch house.

Devon used the brief respite to spring into action. Releasing his right hand from the grip on Changwani's wrist, he pushed upwards and drove it open-palm into Changwani's nose. The crunch of bone and sinew was followed by a feral scream as Changwani's head rolled back, taking his knife arm with it.

It was the opening Devon needed. He torqued forcefully against Changwani, twisting him first to the right and then all the way to the left. The two bodies rolled and thrashed in the weeds before coming to rest, this time with Devon on top.

Changwani still held the knife with Devon's left hand locked around the wrist. Instead of trying to push down as Changwani had done. Devon suddenly freed his arm and leapt to his feet.

He stomped his boot mercilessly into Changwani's face, and followed this with a well-aimed kick that tore the knife free and sent it hurtling into the grass. Devon dived for the knife, expecting to be able to regain his stance over his stricken victim. But he hadn't reckoned on Changwani's amazing strength and resolve. Before he could turn back to face his opponent, Changwani was on his feet and clenching his arm around Devon's throat.

Devon dropped into a tuck-roll, taking Changwani with him. The big Afghan held his vice-like grip as the two struggled back and forth before ending on their knees, Changwani behind and pulling with all his power against Devon's throat. The strength started to ebb from Devon's body, and he began wishing Hill would suddenly appear to the rescue.

He had one last roll of the dice to play. Letting his body go slack against Changwani's, he turned the knife in his hand and stabbed backwards into Changwani's side. He heard the man groan, but his grip remained tight. Devon stabbed again and then again. On the third time attempt he kept the knife in place, twisting it as best he could in the cramped space with which he had to work. He could almost feel the gristle against the blade, and was rewarded when the arm on his neck fell away.

Devon turned to face his opponent, noting that Changwani's chin was lolled forward onto his chest.

Devon stood up, grabbed Changwani's hair, and yanked his head upwards so that he could look into his eyes.

There were a lot of things he wanted to say, but only one seemed appropriate. "This is for Mason Hunter," he uttered solemnly as he thrust the knife into Changwani's exposed throat.

***

There wasn't much left of Yousaf Hasni when John Winstanley and his FBI team closed in slowly on the spot where they had directed their fire. The body, lying grotesquely among the mown-down grass, was literally shredded by the hail of 7.62mm bullets which had almost torn it in half. There was no need to check for any signs of life.

Winstanley motioned the sniper to remain in place and provide covering power as he urged his team down towards the farmhouse. Sporadic gunfire was coming from the west-facing windows, but the precision of the sniper's actions allowed his colleagues to make good progress towards the side of the building.

Don Hill radioed to alert Winstanley to his position, the two joining up beside the broken down fence of the corral less than thirty yards from the house. "How do you want to play this?" Winstanley asked.

Hill removed two grenades from his belt. "Let's do it the easy way."

Winstanley smiled, pulled a grenade from his flak jacket, and nodded at his men to follow suit. Then he turned back to Hill. "Mind if I do the honours for the record?"

"Be my guest."

Winstanley cleared his throat and yelled: "This is the FBI, throw down your weapons and come out with your hands in the air."

A quick burst of automatic gunfire provided the response they expected. Hill nodded at Winstanley and both men pulled the pins on their M67 fragmentation grenades before lobbing them towards the side of the house, where they rolled against the wooden structure beneath the windows. The explosions had barely died down before three of Winstanley's men flung more grenades through the windows under covering fire from the other two members of the team.

***

There was no need for a follow-up operation. When the FBI team kicked open the house doors they found two badly cut-up bodies among the wreckage. Nonetheless, they went through the motions, pointing their weapons ahead and clearing each room as they searched the building for survivors.

Through the front window, Hill could see Mike Devon approach the house in obvious discomfort. He was crouched over, his arm clasping a bloody shoulder, and his stride zigzagging erratically across the parking area. Hill watched as Devon fell against one of the cars and slid to the ground.

Just as Hill reached the halfway point between the house and Devon, the last surviving member of the al-Qaeda cell burst out of the field to his right. The terrorist held an Uzi two-handed at waist level and could be heard shouting the praises of Allah as he brought the weapon to bear on the stranded Hill.

Devon caught sight of the man at the last moment, but there was nothing he could do. Even if he had been able to retrieve his Glock he doubted he would have the strength to raise it. The moment seemed to slow down into one of those freeze-frame action re-runs much beloved by television producers, as Devon waited for the Uzi to spit its death-load at Hill.

Suddenly, the top of the terrorist's head seemed to disappear and his feet left the ground. He crashed heavily onto the gravel yard, his right leg twitching for a moment before he went still.

I hope that's the last of the bastards, the voice of the FBI sniper sang in Devon's earpiece.

Chapter 28
London

ALAN DOYLE HAD GRABBED less than six hours sleep since his return to London forty-eight hours ago. The name of Gennady Anasenko was now plastered across his wipeboard, with blue-inked arrows linking numerous boxes filled with scrawled notes that seemed to be updating on an hourly basis. Streaks of sunlight penetrated the office blinds and marched across the board to signal the end of another all-nighter – but Doyle hardly noticed as he stood back for the umpteenth time, hoping that distance would rearrange the scribbles into a sensible sequence.

Tying Anasenko to ownership of the yacht in Monaco needed little more than a check on the Lloyd's Register. From this information he was able to track back to its construction in Germany, and to the payment details, which were logged against a Russian oil company address in Dzerzhinsky. Further checks into the company's activities began to create links to other companies – five in America, three in England, two in Germany, two in France. The list seemed endless, and Doyle began to run out of space on his wipeboard.

It had also been easy to track the flights out of Monaco within the thirty-minute window after the gunfight aboard *Gennady1*. A private jet, carrying Russian diplomatic papers, had taken off for Geneva shortly before Doyle and Cheadle arrived at the airport. The aircraft's registration was traced back to one of the myriad companies linked by Doyle to Anasenko. That was the easy part, thought Doyle. The real trick would be in finding where the jet passengers disappeared to once they had landed in Geneva.

A late-night telephone call to Georges Laurent at GIGN headquarters elicited two pieces of good news. The first was that his boss, Claude Bartran, was out of immediate danger and should make a full, albeit very slow, recovery. The second update was that Laurent had already traced the jet's flight to Geneva and had dispatched a team there to try to pick up the trail of the occupants. He was also liaising with the Swiss Federal Office of Police to determine whether Anasenko owned any property in the area or had booked in at any hotels or ski lodges. He promised to feed the information back as soon as he had it.

Doyle thanked him and returned to his wipeboard. He had put a small team of agents on to the task of delving into the personal life of Anasenko, but so far they had drawn a blank. All they had been able to report was a list of business interests and some sort of tenuous role as a roving ambassador for the Russian Federation. Doyle knew there had to be more to the man than that – you don't get mixed up with two oversized killers, involve yourself in the kidnap of a senior counterterrorist commander, and take off for Geneva unless your hand is firmly in some dodgy till or other.

He glanced at his watch, realising with impatience that he still had a few hours to wait before placing a call to an old KGB agent he had crossed swords with on a few occasions back in the day. Sergei Kablukov was an old-school spy, who would have shot you without remorse, but who lived by an honour code, which recognised torture and death only as a last resort in a profession where mutual respect was a far more precious commodity. Sergei had been put out to grass by the new FSB, Russia's Federal Security Bureau, but if anyone still had a finger on the pulse it was he.

Respectful of the time-zone differences, and Sergei's need for rest, Doyle resisted the temptation to contact the seventy year-old before mid-morning.

The office door opened, allowing the smell of coffee and hot croissants to precede the arrival of Cheadle and two other agents.

"Thought you could do with this boss." Cheadle smiled as he placed an oversize Starbucks container and brown plastic bag on the desk in front of Doyle. The men knew their senior operative had stayed behind when he chased them home shortly after midnight.

"You're a lifesaver, Cheadle," Doyle responded, his hand already clawing the lid from the coffee cup. He swallowed a few healthy gulps of the hot liquid before ramming a croissant into his mouth. He cleared the first mouthful, took another swig of coffee, and turned again towards Cheadle. "Where are we on the surveillance of Sylvia Flynn?"

Cheadle provided a well-rehearsed summary. "As you know we picked up her presence back in London yesterday morning. She turned up at her office as if nothing had happened, remained there for most of the day, and went back to her apartment last night. She stopped for a carry-out and hasn't left since. Through the bugs and camera in her apartment, we watched her get ready for work an hour ago, but I left to come here."

"Your team know they must not lose her?"

"They know you'll have their guts for garters if they can't account for her whereabouts every minute."

Doyle smiled. "Just checking. It's been a long night."

***

Devon was lying atop a hotel bed bemoaning the shoulder injury inflicted by the late unlamented Asif Changwani. He had discharged himself from hospital the previous day, having undergone a blood transfusion and the insertion of thirty stitches to close a gap that opened all the way to his collar bone. He had slept for the better part of thirty hours and awoke to find his arm in a sling, before remonstrating with hospital staff and discharging himself to the fussy attentions of Don Hill.

"Look. I'm perfectly alright," he told Hill before cadging a ride to the nearest decent hotel *LonWash's* money could buy.

"That arm needs to stay in the sling for at least a week," Hill barked in a commanding voice. "You heard the doctor; any undue movement will split those stitches wide open. You've still got an infection from crawling through the fields around the ranch house, and any more infections will knock you on your butt for six weeks."

"Don't worry, I'll take it easy. I need to make a few phone calls and then I'll rest up for another day.

One way or another, though, I'm on the first plane to London the day after tomorrow."

Hill headed for the hotel room door. "Just see that you keep that sling in position." As he passed through the door, he turned back as an afterthought seemed to strike him. "Thought you should know, our boss got a call from the President to thank us for the operation in Fitzburg."

"Nice to know we're appreciated."

Shortly after Hill's departure he used his sat-phone to call London, speaking first with General Sandford who wanted brought up to speed on everything. The old man was obviously delighted by the presidential citation and waxed lyrical about the great job done by Devon and the American agents. He bemoaned the loss of life sustained by the Americans and voiced genuine concern at Devon's injury.

After assuring the General of his wellbeing, Devon asked to be patched through to Doyle who, he was told, had returned from Monaco. The two men spent more than thirty minutes running through their respective operations, but only after Devon could hear a lot of whooping and hollering when Doyle conveyed the news of Changwani's demise to whoever was in his general vicinity.

"Score one for Mason Hunter," Devon could hear above the racket.

When the noise abated, Doyle completed his report. They exchanged a range of ideas and agreed on follow-up actions, the most important being the need to find Gennady Anasenko and his cronies. Devon told Doyle he would not return for two days, but wanted constant updates.

Devon purposely delayed making his next call until the following morning when he judged he would be in better shape to explain his lengthy silence to Emma. Now here he was staring at the handset and rehearsing his speech. She answered on the first ring.

"Mike, is that you? Are you alright?"

"I'm fine, darling. We got our man, but I picked up a slight injury and the hospital knocked me out for longer than was necessary."

"Omygod," she screamed. "You've been shot!"

"No Em, I wasn't shot. It was nothing more than a small knife wound."

"Where?"

"It happened near a small town outside Chicago."

"Mike Devon, you know precisely what I meant. Where are you injured?"

"Oh, sorry," he feigned innocence. "It's a shoulder wound. I've had a few stitches, an anti-tetanus jab, or suchlike, and I'm up and about trying to do a bit or work."

Her voice softened. "Are you sure you're okay? When are you coming home?"

"I've a bit of paperwork to tie up here," he lied, "but I'll be home no later than tomorrow evening."

"Tell me what flight you're on and I'll come meet you."

"There's no need for that Em. The agency is laying on a chauffeur."

"Then promise you'll come see me first."

"I promise."

There was the slightest of pauses before she spoke again. "One more thing Mike..." The voice tailed off and Devon suddenly became anxious.

"What is it Em?"

He could hear her stifle a sob. "It's just...it's nothing. I miss you and I love you."

"I love you too, Em."

As he replaced the hotel telephone receiver, the thought kept nagging at the back of his mind that Emma had wanted to say something more. Maybe the dangers of his job and the long-distance nature of their relationship were getting to her. God, he hoped not! He was still running through the options when the sat-phone chirped on the bed beside him. It was Doyle.

"Breaking news, boss. We've tracked Anasenko to Geneva and GIGN has put a couple of agents on his tail. The Swiss authorities are being very cooperative and we should know his location sometime later today."

Devon snapped out of the melancholy state brought on by his conversation with Emma. "That's great news indeed, Alan. When we find the bastard we need to sit on him. Have you been running a full background on him?"

"Even as we speak. I'm just waiting for our former Russian friend from KGB days to help fill in a few blanks."

Devon didn't need prompting. "You're not talking about Major-General Sergei Kablukov by any chance? Is that old bastard still living?"

"Alive and well, and dossing down in some rented apartment in Moscow. I've tracked down his phone number and am waiting to talk to him later this morning."

"Should be an interesting conversation. Send

him my best regards."

"There's one more thing, Mike. Sylvia Flynn has resurfaced in London. We have her under a 24/7, but wanted to check with you what we should do."

Devon didn't need to think twice. "You already know the answer to that Alan. Bring the bitch in and put the squeeze on."

***

Sylvia Flynn couldn't be described as a happy bunny. Since her escape from the gunfight on the yacht and her return to London, she had been constantly looking over her shoulder, expecting at any moment to have her collar felt by some flatfoot copper. Despite Anasenko's assurances that everything was under control she felt a sense of unease, the kind she used to experience in her days as an IRA volunteer.

She had been around too many dodgy operations in her time not to recognise that what happened aboard the yacht was not the result of some innocent meddling by a nosy French agent, who just happened to be holidaying in Monaco and decided to take a special interest in the *Gennady1*. If that was the case why did Anasenko's two goons overreact by kidnapping and torturing him? Why did a group of armed agents storm on board with all guns blazing?

The more she thought about it, the more her disquiet grew. She had listened to the news reports of the terror attacks in Paris while the Borimov twins were there, supposedly on a business trip. She didn't believe in coincidences.

What caused her most worry was the sudden

order to drop everything in London, and travel to Monaco to be given details of what appeared to be a straightforward assignment. She wasn't fooled by the notion that Anasenko missed her company or craved sex in a resort where it was virtually on tap for him. Try as she might, she couldn't shake the notion that, for some reason, she had become expendable and that her next assignment in London would be her last.

After spending an uneasy day at work, she returned to her apartment to make plans. There was only one place she could run to, one place where even Anasenko couldn't reach out for her. She would head back to Ireland, south of the border, and rebuild a new life in Dublin.

She tossed and turned throughout a sleepless night, before rising at dawn to make a number of phone calls. She secured a booking on a flight from Heathrow at midday and then rang a taxi firm to arrange a fare to the airport. She would leave her car at the apartment's underground car park and travel with only a small suitcase. For all intents and purposes it would look like she had never left.

Next she booted up her Samsung laptop and waited impatiently for Windows 7 to run through its start-up routines. As soon as the wireless icon signalled its connection, she logged onto several online bank accounts embedded in her favourites list. One by one she punched keyboard instructions to transfer funds which would bounce around countless European banks before nestling in an account she had secretly created as a slush fund in Dublin five years ago. By the time she reached the Republic of Ireland capital at around one o'clock, the

£5million syphoned off from various Anasenko holdings would be waiting for her. She had not wasted her time while working for his stupid bank all these years.

She felt a weight drop from her shoulders and hurried to complete her packing. Her hardest decisions were to choose which items of the huge designer wardrobe to leave behind. She consoled herself with the prospect of building a new collection during a visit to the noted Brown Thomas store in Dublin's Grafton Street.

Right on cue at ten o'clock the doorman buzzed her intercom to inform her of the arrival of her taxi.

"Have the man come up to collect my suitcase." There was no "please" or "thank you" just a quick return of the handset before gathering up her smaller items to place into a handbag. The apartment doorbell chimed.

She crossed the room and opened the door to an elderly man.

"Good morning, Miss."

"Yes, I believe it is," she replied with unusual airiness. She waited for the man to lift the small suitcase, waved him through the door, and slammed it behind her without glancing backwards.

She settled into the back seat and said silent goodbyes as the taxi flashed past a number of familiar buildings. The route from her apartment should have taken them through Ealing, but the driver explained about road building work which was causing thirty minute delays.

"I absolutely can't miss my flight check-in time," she told him sternly.

"Not to worry miss. I'll go by the Holborn Viaduct and through South Kensington. Shouldn't cost us more than a few minutes."

Satisfied the man knew what he was doing, she settled back into her seat and watched as the Viaduct road and bridge came into view. She was puzzled when the taxi turned left into Charterhouse Street, and even more puzzled when it banked sharply into an underground car park.

She leaned forward to remonstrate with the driver and found herself staring into the barrel of a Glock 19.

"Welcome to the *LonWash* clearing house for terrorists and malcontents," he told her with a toothy grin.

Chapter 29
Gstaad, Switzerland

THE FRENCH STOCK MARKET, *Companies des Agents de Change*, or the CAC as it's better known, almost went into freefall in the aftermath of the Paris terror attacks. Already fragile from the effects of the world banking fiasco and Eurozone bail-outs, the last thing investors needed was a further assault on the country's economy. This could only lead to dramatically higher national security costs, meaning funds would have to be diverted from other budgets and would raise the prospect of increased national debt at a time when France was only just staying one step ahead of Greece, Portugal, and Italy in the queue for hand-outs.

At one stage, the performance of the market's A-list companies plummeted almost eight per cent, wiping an estimated 26 billion euros off the share value of the top forty. The ripples from Paris rolled across the English Channel to London, where the FTSE-100 dropped four percentage points over a two-day period, before rallying at just below two per cent.

Kalnay Petro should have been more vulnerable than most to the whirlwind stripping away of the delicate and fickle outer layers of market confidence. Not only did it have to deal with the same problems faced by those around it, but there was also the tragic death of its chief operating officer, Sheik Kalid

Abu-Nayyan, to consider. Even in normal times an event of this magnitude would have caused a mild panic, leading to the dumping of shares for the safer ground of a handful of other blue-chip companies.

But an expected double whammy implosion in value never materialised. Before the Paris attacks and the death of Abu-Nayyan, the company's shares were quoted at just over 20 euros apiece. One week later, they still held remarkably steady at almost 19 euros per share. With twenty-two individual brokerages at his disposal, Gennady Anasenko saw to that.

Anasenko's plan was not to pick up cheap shares. As soon as the first signs of a selling frenzy hit the markets, his brokers stood ready to pick up every single unit of *Kalnay Petro* stock entering the market. They cleared transactions at a lightning speed, mindful of the need to keep price levels at or near their peak. The idea was to stay on top of the flow of purchases, rather than have to cope with an avalanche if investors started dumping simultaneously because of an alarming drop in value.

Sometimes the Anasenko brokers had to be more proactive, often contacting the brokerage houses of clients listed as *Kalnay* shareholders. They resorted to various scare tactics, including false rumours that Sheik Abu-Nayyan had been murdered as part of a new global Jihad against the company.

Anasenko paid top dollar for each of his newly-acquired shares. By the end of an eventful first week after the terror attacks, he had bought up 28 per cent of *Kalnay Petro*. Added to his existing stock of 10 per cent he had edged closer to being the sole shareholder outside the 60 per cent stock held by the late Sheik.

It wasn't clear what inheritance or release arrangements were in place in the event of the Sheik's death, but it didn't matter to Anasenko. He was aware of a deal between the Sheik and the London chairman of another oil company, whereby 15 per cent of the Sheik's holdings in *Kalnay* were wrapped up in a new joint oil exploration company currently operating off the South American coast. Anasenko knew that by acquiring the London company's assets he would stretch his *Kalnay* holdings to 53 per cent. Overnight he would control the world's largest oil company – and, with that in his pocket, he would also have control over entire national economies.

But for the failed attacks in London, the prize would already be in his pocket. Asif Changwani's treachery had caused him to lose valuable ground, and forced him to switch to other means to eliminate the oil chairman who now stood in his way. He was confident, however, in Sylvia Flynn's ability to get the job done.

***

Had Gennady Anasenko been able to see inside the basement cells of *LonWash Securities* he might have had a different view of Sylvia Flynn's abilities. Her arms and legs were duct-taped to a chair in the centre of a large concrete chamber which smelled of old mustiness mingled with fresh sweat and urine. The room's previous occupants – the three surviving members of the al-Qaeda cell arrested in Manchester – had been delivered to the tender mercies of Israeli

Mossad agents in a rendition transfer somewhere in the Mediterranean Sea.

Flynn had seen no one since her capture more than four hours before. She had been frogmarched to the basement's makeshift cell area by two men who appeared from behind concrete pillars as soon as the bogus taxi came to rest. They roughly tore the clothes from her body, leaving only her bra and panties to cover her modesty – but not before they searched them for any hidden items.

"What, you think I've got a Walther PPK stitched into the lining of my D cup?" she yelled at a searcher who was taking a lot longer than necessary groping around her breasts.

Since then, the cold and damp had seeped into her bones and chased away the bravado. Suddenly, she felt more vulnerable than she had for many years. She knew the chances of a new life in Dublin had gone up in smoke the minute she was grabbed by these men and, even more worrying, was the realisation that if she somehow extricated herself from this situation, her options were limited.

The room door opened and a tall man stepped through, carrying a file awkwardly across the crook of his right elbow. He walked behind a single wooden desk, pulled up a seat to stare directly at Flynn, and slammed the buff-coloured file onto the desktop. He made a show of slowly flicking through the pages.

"My, my, you have been a busy little girl these past few lifetimes." He smiled in her direction.

"Where am I?" Flynn yelled into his face. "You've no right to keep me here. I know my rights."

The big man merely smiled some more. "Let's see now," he said glancing down at the file. "Sylvia

Flynn, erstwhile IRA volunteer, murdering bitch gunrunner, mistress to the great and good in America, and lately shacked up with one Anasenko Gennady on board his yacht in Monaco."

She was gobsmacked by the breadth of the man's knowledge. The Monaco connection could only mean she had been under surveillance for some time, but this could be nothing more than a fishing expedition, despite her IRA past. She decided to bluff it out.

"I was in Monaco on business. Mr Anasenko is a very important client of the bank I work for........"

"Oh, you mean the bank Mr Anasenko owns and from which he diverts funds to a whole raft of good causes, including the new scumbags on the block, al-Qaeda?"

Things were getting out of control for her. "I'm just a humble bank teller. I know nothing of these things."

The man stood up from behind the desk and paced across the room. "It's hardly the job of a bank teller to pick up cash and weapons from railway stations and deliver them to known terrorists in Manchester."

He might as well have slapped her across the face. This was worse, much worse, than she thought. "I want a lawyer. I refuse to say anything without a lawyer present."

Doyle threw his head back and roared with laughter at the ceiling. "Lawyer? Just where do you think you are young lady? We don't play by any rules here. Even if we were so inclined, we could hand you over to the authorities on a string of murder and conspiracy charges that even the best lawyer couldn't argue his way out of."

He again returned to the table and sat down facing her. "Oh, and by the way you can't even afford a lawyer."

She smiled back at him. "I have more than enough money to make sure I get the best defence possible against these outrageous allegations."

Doyle was enjoying this. "By money I hope you don't mean the five point three million pounds you had salted away in a Dublin bank?"

Doyle watched as the woman's eyes glazed over. "What do you mean I *had* salted away?"

Doyle fished a piece of paper from the file and handed it over to her. "This is a copy of the transfer of all your holdings in Dublin to our account here in England. I want to thank you for your contribution to the fight against terrorism – I promise we'll put it to good use."

She wriggled against her bonds to get a closer look at the paper. "How did you get hold of this? How did you track it down?"

Doyle smiled. "You really should have disposed of your laptop. We placed a rather neat little attachment to it a few days ago, and it's been monitoring all your keystrokes ever since. When we retrieved it an hour ago during a search of your apartment, it was simple to follow what you had done with the wire transfers. I have to hand it to you; we would never have been able to track your tangled web without the benefit of the source of the original input."

""Fuck you," Flynn snarled.

"Not on your best day love," Doyle retorted.

"Does Gennady know you stole from him? I have to give you credit for the way you bounced it around half the world to hide your tracks. You'll be glad to know we bounced it some more so that no one knows where to come looking for it."

"Who, who are you?" There was a new tremor to her voice.

"We're the only chance you have of staying alive. Tell us what we want and we'll look at making an arrangement with you. Tell us not," he paused to look around the room," and I promise you will die here sometime in the next twenty-four hours. I'll give you an hour to decide."

***

Igor Borimov had spent a less than fruitful day trying to track down Flynn's whereabouts. He had made a routine early-morning call to her office for an update on her contact with Sir Clive Oliver, chairman of *Paxoil*. He was told she hadn't yet clocked in, probably taking a rest after her recent trip. He called her apartment without success, and then decided to leave it for a few hours, reasoning that perhaps she was already cultivating Sir Clive over a business breakfast.

He busied himself with checking the security of the grounds around the Gstaad property. Six of Anasenko's personal squad of ex-Spetsnaz soldiers had arrived from Russia during the night and were deployed around the two-acre estate. His first call was to a special surveillance room, where one man was seated in front of a bank of television monitors recording live feeds from cameras mounted at various vantage points. Three areas, selected by Borimov as vulnerable access points, were also fitted with motion detection trip wires and under-soil pressure plates.

Of the remaining five soldiers, four were deployed in two-man shift teams patrolling the grounds with suppressed MP5-Ns, part of the consignment used by the terrorists in the attack on the Eiffel Tower. The remaining soldier was tasked with staying indoors to provide ground-floor protection in the unlikely event that any intruders made it as far as the chalet.

By mid-afternoon Borimov was becoming agitated by the lack of contact from Flynn. He spent another hour on the phone, calling all the numbers where she might be, before finally issuing instructions to the manager of Anasenko's bank to go to her apartment. The man had a key and was told to let himself in to check for any signs that she had absconded.

Just before five o'clock London time the manager rang back. "She left her apartment early this morning and, according to the caretaker, she took a taxi to Heathrow."

Borimov slammed the handset against the arm of his seat. "Fucking bitch," he screamed at the room. He returned the handset to his mouth. "Do we know where she was headed?"

"It took some time but we traced her to a flight that left for Dublin at midday."

"Dublin? What the fuck could have taken her to Dublin?"

The man at the other end coughed nervously. "That's just it. She wasn't on the flight. No-one seems to know where she is."

Borimov was about to cut the connection when the man spoke again. "There's something else you should know. Her apartment was trashed. Someone gave it a right going over."

"This is grave news indeed, Igor." Anasenko fought to control his rage as he listened to the report of Flynn's disappearance. There was no doubt in his mind that she had intended to take flight; the fact she ordered a taxi was confirmation enough that she had arranged to leave the country under her own steam. But what had spooked her? Who had searched her apartment? Was it possible she arrived home to find the apartment in a mess and decided to cut and run? No, she wouldn't have waited until the next day before leaving!

Borimov watched the wheels turn as his boss stared into the roaring log fire. He decided to offer his own thoughts. "We have to face the possibility that she has been arrested. Our operation may be compromised more than we imagined after the turn of events at Monaco."

"Why then, Igor, didn't she contact us if she believed there was a threat?"

Before he could respond, a telephone rang harshly on a table at Borimov's elbow. He grabbed it and listened intently before cutting the connection. He turned solemnly to Anasenko. "That was the bank manager again. They've just discovered Flynn moved five million out of various accounts and they can't trace its whereabouts."

"What?" Anasenko exploded off his chair and

hurled a brandy glass into the fire. A whoosh of flame made him jump back, and he slumped into a chair alongside Borimov. "Now we *know* the fucking whore jumped ship!"

"It still doesn't explain the state of her apartment."

"My guess," Anasenko responded, "is that she was picked up at the airport, after which her apartment was searched. Whoever has her is welcome to her. We have other things to consider."

For the next hour Anasenko outlined his thoughts. Top of his to-do list was the assassination of Sir Clive Oliver. And right now he didn't care how messy or publicly the *Paxoil* chairman was dealt with.

Chapter 30
London

THE FIRST RECOGNISABLE face Mike Devon saw as he emerged from baggage reclaim at Heathrow's Terminal 4 was that of Alan Doyle, grinning like a Cheshire cat as he leaned against the bonnet of a Range Rover Sport SE. The sight of Devon's sling caused the briefest of frowns, but Doyle chased it away and walked forward to grab the suitcase. "Nice to have you back boss. See you've brought a little souvenir with you," he said, nodding at the grey plastic covering encasing Devon from wrist to elbow.

"Yeah, couldn't have you being the only one to boast about an arm injury," Devon countered, knowing Doyle would take no offence at the reference to the loss of his limb courtesy of an IRA shoot-out years before.

As soon as Devon climbed into the passenger seat, he started removing the ties holding the sling at the back of his neck. Doyle shot him a look. "Aren't you supposed to keep that thing on for a while?"

"Stop cackling like a mother hen. It's been on long enough and I need to get some proper circulation going. Besides it was a bit of overkill if you ask me."

As Doyle drove away from the concourse and headed towards central London, the two men settled into a lively exchange of information. Devon wanted to know how the interrogation of Sylvia Flynn was going, and was buoyed by Doyle's assessment that "she's like putty in our hands."

The early evening traffic was heavy and Devon was anxious to get back to the office. Before that he had a call to make, one which surprisingly conflicted him. On the one hand he was looking forward to seeing Emma, but there was a dark side wondering what it was that appeared to trouble her during his phone conversation from Chicago.

Doyle broke into his thoughts. "Listen up boss, I've something to say and I won't take no for an answer."

"Fire away."

"I'm taking you home. Emma's there and you need to spend the night together. You've a bit of catching up to do."

Devon was about to argue about the workload waiting at the office when a thought struck him. "Hold the fort a minute. How do you know Emma's there?"

Doyle pretended to concentrate on the traffic ahead as he signalled a left turn out of a roundabout. Finally he spoke. "She rang me this afternoon to check your flight time and I sort of got the impression you two have things to talk about."

Devon was flabbergasted. "What things? What gave you that impression?"

Doyle shifted uneasily. "Stop giving me a hard time, Mike. We've been friends too long for me not to tell you to wise up. You've got a smashing girl there and the way I see it, you need to give her a bit more care and attention."

The words hit home. Devon's unease continued to grow over his meeting with Emma, but Doyle was right. Whatever her problems were he would fix them and find a way for the two of them to move forward.

She met him at the door, careful to avoid his injured shoulder as she leaned forward and kissed him heavily on the lips. She raised a thumb to Doyle as he pulled away from the kerb, and then turned to link her arm into Devon's. She had yearned for this moment, yet felt a knot of dread in the pit of her stomach.

She had a meal already prepared and ushered him quickly to the table, avoiding his attempts at quizzing her about their telephone conversation the previous evening.

"What's wrong, Emma?"

She stood at the kitchen sink with her back to him and fought to bring her breathing under control. "Wrong? There's nothing wrong. It's just your imagination."

"I don't think so. You were definitely trying to say something to me when I was in America. Let's get it out in the open."

She paused for a moment to control the tension in her voice. "I *had* something to tell you, but it can keep. It's not important."

The anger in his reply shocked her. "For Chrissakes Emma, whatever it is you need to tell me now."

She turned slowly to face him, unable to control a tear that escaped to run down the side of her nose before she wiped it away. The carefully rehearsed words were forgotten. Instead she blurted out "I'm ...I'm pregnant, Mike."

She looked deep into his eyes. Whatever reaction she imagined her news would create, she was not ready for the one she got. She watched as Devon pushed back his chair, jumped into the air with his good hand punching towards the ceiling, and let out a yell that was probably heard all the way down the block. "Yes, yes!" he repeated through the silliest grin she had ever seen.

Her tears started to flow freely and she rushed to him. "I thought you would be mad. I thought this was the last thing you wanted to hear."

He held her away from him, stared into her face, and told her, "Don't be silly. This is the best thing that's ever happened to me. I couldn't be more pleased. This is brilliant."

Then his mood changed. "Wait a minute, are you angry? Do you not want a baby?"

She punched his chest. "Now who's being silly? Of course I want a baby, but I thought it might come between us."

He hugged her close again and then suddenly pushed her back. He dropped to his knee, looked up into her face, and switched on his serious tone. "Emma, will you marry me?"

She fell beside him. "Of course I'll marry you. I think I've always wanted to marry you."

***

Sir Clive Oliver never tired of the early morning view from the deluxe fifth-storey apartment he called home during weekdays in London. Looking out over Kensington Gardens and the snaking River Serpentine at Bayswater, he liked to be reminded of his country estate in Surrey, and the weekend escape it provided from the madness of the ever-demanding world of commerce.

It was 6.45am and, as usual, Sir Clive was dressed and ready for a chauffeur-driven ride to his offices at Gracechurch Street, close to the imposing Bank of England headquarters in the curiously-named Threadneedle Street. Trade reporting at the London Stock Exchange opened at 7.15am, and Sir Clive liked to hear the latest official bulletins before trading started at 8.00am. The markets had cooled after a tortuous week, and he was heartened by the resolve of *Paxoil* investors to hold on to their stock. Nonetheless these were jittery times.

The biggest cloud on the horizon had been caused by the death of Sheik Kalid Abu-Nayyan. Although the Sheik's main *Kalnay Oil* investments remained relatively unscathed, the joint-venture exploration company, in which they held a combined thirty per cent stake, was beginning to dip in value. If the trend continued, he would have to shore up the company's value by further "confidence" investments.

He had also received worrying news of heavy "transfer" trading in *Kalnay* stock. Although he had no direct interest in the company, it was a major competitor and, as such, he liked to know what he was dealing with. The last thing he needed were major policy shifts which might have consequences for his own company.

Turning away from the window, he was so absorbed in his thoughts that he failed to notice a car idling on double-yellow lines on the opposite side of the street. It was out of place this early in the morning – but Sir Clive was not a man trained to be aware of such nuances.

***

Sylvia Flynn was at the lowest point she could remember for a long while. Sometime the previous evening she had been moved to an army-type cot, furnished with a few hessian blankets, and had her left wrist chained to the iron bedpost. A Styrofoam cup of coffee and a bland, vacuum-packed cheese sandwich were placed on the ground within her reach, before the door slammed and the flickering, overhead florescent tube was switched off.

Eight hours of cold and darkness did little to encourage positive thoughts. She accepted the reality of her predicament – aware that even with her considerable gifts for negotiation and survival, there didn't seem a way out from under the dangers facing her. She was in a deep, dark place, in more ways than one.

The light in the room clicked on and a noisy bolt slid open on the door. She twisted in the cot to see the one-arm man enter, carrying that damned dossier again! Another figure emerged behind, this one slightly taller, and showing more menace than the first guy, if that was possible.

One-arm unchained her wrist, dragged her from the bed, and hauled her over to the desk and chairs. She noticed the new man took the only remaining seat.

When he spoke, she recognised the confidence and authority of someone used to getting their own way. "I'll not fuck around with you, Ms Flynn. You're

306

too smart not to have realised by now that we're an off-the-books operation with no time for the niceties in life. Your career history as an enemy of this country has already bought you a bullet to the brain and a nice little unmarked plot in the countryside. The only way to avoid this happening is if you tell me everything I want to know. Are we clear?"

His words sent a further chill down her spine. She didn't doubt for one moment that this bastard would do as he said – and probably get a perverse kick out of it. She tried to keep the fear from her voice. "What is it you want to know?"

"Tell me about Gennady Anasenko."

She didn't hesitate. "I met him in America a number of years ago. He was a major investor in the IRA and helped us supply arms for the struggle." She noticed his eyes narrow into a frown, but kept going. "After the conflict ceased in the north of Ireland, he approached me with a job offer in one of his banks in London. I've been working there ever since."

"What was your job in the bank?"

"I handled international investments, mostly routine stuff...."

The man slammed his palm on the table. "Stop dicking around, what was your real job?"

"I helped to set up a number of sting operations on major clients. Gennady always had competitors who had to be..." she searched for the right word..."who had to be brought on board."

"You mean blackmailed?"

"Yes, it usually always involved blackmail."

"Let me guess, you were the perfect honey trap?"

She flickered her eyelashes as if acknowledging

a compliment. "I guess so."

"Did you ever kill anyone for Anasenko?"

"No, never. It didn't work like that. These were powerful men who could prove useful to Gennady."

"Tell me about them."

"They were just the usual mix of bankers, businessmen and politicians..."

Mike Devon held up a hand to signal her to stop. "When we finish here, I want you to make out a complete list of these men. Don't leave out anyone, is that clear?"

She nodded resignedly before raising herself up in the chair and looking directly into her interrogator's eyes. "I'm cold and I'm hungry. Do you suppose I could get a blanket and something to eat?"

Devon's response surprised her. He smiled and nodded imperceptibly towards Alan Doyle, who left the room. Then he rose from his chair, crossed to the bed, and returned with a blanket, which he draped around her shoulders. After retaking his seat, the smile evaporated.

"Tell me about your relationship with al-Qaeda?"

"I don't have a relationship. I know nothing about them." She waited for him to assault the table again, but it didn't materialise.

When he spoke, the tone was exactly the same. "You know we clocked you delivering to the bedsit in Manchester. Who did you think those people were? Members of the local Temperance Society?"

"I swear, I didn't know anything about them until I got there. It was the first time Gennady asked me to do something like that. He said it was urgent and there was no one else available."

"You expect me to believe you?"

"It's the truth. When I saw who they were, I was frightened. I don't want to be mixed up in that kind of thing again. It's the reason I was leaving the country when your men picked me up."

Devon knew it didn't ring true, but decided to drop it. "Let's turn to a more pressing matter. What were you doing on Anasenko's yacht in Monaco?"

"Gennady invited me there to discuss some business."

"What kind of business?"

"Just usual financial stuff...."

The crack on the table took her by surprise. She leapt up as the sound of the slap reverberated around the room. When she fell back into her seat, she noticed the raw anger in the face of the man opposite.

"Last chance, Ms Flynn. What did Anasenko want to discuss with you?"

Instead of answering, she held his gaze. When she finally spoke, there was a renewed confidence in her voice. "What I have to tell you is big. It's something you'll want to hear, but I want something for it."

The smile returned to Devon's face. "There's no shit-creek paddle for you here, Ms Flynn. Your only options are a bullet or a long prison stretch."

"Those aren't options, you bastard. You get nothing more unless I see a way out. If you don't like it, then go fuck yourself."

Devon wasn't surprised by the venomous change in her mood. This was the old Sylvia Flynn, the former IRA killer, emerging into the true light.

But she was right about one thing – unless he offered some carrot, he could waste a lot of time forcing the information from her.

"You get a one-time deal-breaker. Tell me everything and I'll ship you back to Ireland. You can stay there and rot for all I care."

"I want my money."

"No chance in hell."

The response was too unequivocal for her to argue. At least this way she could escape with her life, knowing she was resourceful enough to make a decent living in Dublin. "Okay, here it is, warts and all."

***

Terence Hannigan watched the limousine pull up outside the apartment block in Kensington. It was right on cue at 6.50am, the same time every morning, Monday through to Friday. This was a rush job, not the kind he usually accepted, but with a quarter of a million already sitting in his bank account, and another quarter of a mill to come at the end of the mission, he wasn't about to argue.

The assignment came through his usual handler, a man who sourced the top jobs for top dollar. He was probably getting the same payment for setting up the hit, but Hannigan was happy with his cut. Two or three of these kinds of jobs per year had set him up nicely, thank you very much.

Hannigan had been fed details of the target's routines, but he liked to see things for himself. This was the second morning of his stake-out, and he had seen enough to know there were no surprises waiting around the corner, so to speak. The man had no bodyguards, no following escort; nothing but a low-paid, disinterested chauffeur who sat reading a newspaper while waiting for his employer.

It was decided. He would take the shot today.

He lifted the 357 Magnum from the glove compartment and balanced it in his latex-covered hand. He liked the raw stopping power and kill success of the heavy-duty revolver, even if the noise levels would send any nearby citizens running for cover. After all, that was the general idea!

He opened the car door gently and stepped out onto the pavement. There was no traffic to worry about as he crossed the street, holding the weapon down by his side, and timing his walk to the apartment entrance. Sure enough, right on cue, Sir Clive Oliver pushed through the revolving door of the complex and walked towards the limousine.

Just as Hannigan was raising his gun arm, the driver's door opened and the chauffeur alighted. Strange, he didn't do that yesterday morning! Hannigan tore his eyes back to his target, surprised to find that Sir Clive was now curiously on one knee and pointing, what looked to Hannigan's trained eye, as a Sig P226.

"What the fuck?" he murmured.

"Drop your gun and raise your arms!" The voice came from the chauffeur, now draped across the roof of the limousine with his left arm extended by the appendage of a Glock 17.

Before Hannigan had a chance to react, both guns fired. He died instantly from taking two rounds in his throat and two in his heart.

High above the scene, curtains on a fifth-floor

window parted, and Sir Clive Oliver looked down at what was happening, He watched as Alan Doyle removed a chauffeur's hat and walked towards the blood-covered body splayed on the pavement.

Mike Devon, wearing Sir Clive's brown panama and long tweed overcoat, looked upwards and smiled.

Chapter 31
Gstaad

THE TWO FRENCH AGENTS stepped onto the platform at Gstaad Railway Station and began rubbing circulation back into tired limbs. They had spent a long day trying to track the movements of the Anasenko party from Geneva airport, and wanted nothing more than a bed to crash out on. First, they had to confirm their quarry was where they were told he would be.

The chase involved good old-fashioned police legwork, the kind that kept them tramping up and down the airport and railway station, flashing photographs at every porter, rent-a-car receptionist, and taxi driver they could find. No one recognised the images of Anasenko. It was only while talking to a ticket-clerk that mention of the giant Borimov twin came up in conversation. They could have kicked themselves; who wouldn't remember a near-seven-foot mountain, particularly with a makeshift sling tied around his grotesque shoulders?

True to form, they found their efforts wasted when they boarded the Montreux train. A call came through from GIGN headquarters to tell them the Swiss police confirmed Anasenko's ownership of a chalet in Gstaad. At least they knew where to change trains when they reached Montreux!

Their orders were explicit; confirm sighting, but under no circumstances do anything to alert

Anasenko to their presence.

It was after nine o'clock in the evening and darkness hung over Gstaad's streets and buildings, brightly illuminated by heavy snow and the twinkling of what appeared to be a million lights flooding out from bars and restaurants, and strung on streamers floating between every available electricity pylon. The place was awash with the hustle and bustle of party-goers enjoying the crisp alpine air.

The little village had a strict no-cars rule, relying instead on the more magical alternative of horse-drawn carriages for those living beyond its boundaries. Wheeled carriages were used in summer and changed by necessity to ski-slide passenger vehicles in winter.

Located in the Canton of Berne, Gstaad had an indigenous German-speaking population – and that suited the two agents as they went in search of information about the location of Anasenko's chalet.

They hit paydirt in the first hotel. A flaxen-haired receptionist was able to provide precise directions, but also mentioned that Anasenko had called in to purchase several boxes of their finest cigars. She knew him well, she said. He was a nice man and a big tipper. Alas, his visits were all too infrequent, she lamented with a shrug.

The agents spun a story about being friends who would surprise Anasenko with a visit in the morning. The news seemed to help in finding "the last available room" and they retired after thanking her for her kindness.

Thirty minutes later they were out in the street again, looking for a ride to the Anasenko chalet.

According to the receptionist, it was less than a mile east, and would take fifteen minutes by carriage. The first driver they found said his horse was tired after a busy day, and he could be persuaded to make the journey only by the offer of a sizeable bonus.

Leaving the lights of the village behind, the open-top cab climbed slowly up a steep track running between hedges smothered in white. The heavy fall of snow in recent days helped to deaden the noise of the hooves.

Despite what must have been an exhausting pull, the big stallion maintained a steady trot. Fifteen minutes later they arrived at a small turning to their left, and could see the outline of a cabin cut into the mountain a few hundred yards along what was little more than a narrow laneway.

The agents ordered the driver to stop, telling him they would proceed on foot. They crammed another roll of Swiss francs into his hand and asked him to wait twenty minutes for their return. He simply shrugged and stuffed the banknotes into his pocket.

They made their way along the side of the lane, careful not to leave tell-tale footprints that could be easily detected in the morning. Close to the chalet, they clambered into a field and edged towards a block wall that seemed to run around the entire boundary. It was ten feet high and could be scaled only if one agent stood on the other's shoulders.

They attempted the manoeuvre several times before one agent grabbed the top of the wall and peered over a white lawn stretching all the way to the chalet. He was taking in the detail of a wooden-deck platform running around the exterior, when he saw two figures emerge from the side of the chalet. The agent crouched down to watch the men stroll across the deck. It looked innocent enough, until he glimpsed the heavy-duty automatic weapons cradled in the men's arms.

The agent dropped to the ground. "Let's go, I've seen enough."

***

The ex-Spetsnaz sergeant lolled on a swivel chair, his feet planted on a bench running below a bank of wall-mounted monitors. He continually had to swivel his head in a semi-circular arc across eight, foot-square television screens, and his eyes were burning from squinting at the grainy images. After more than two hours, he knew he couldn't maintain the concentration needed to ensure nothing escaped his notice. He would have to ask Borimov to consider two-man shifts.

Despite the difficulties, he stuck manfully to the task, although there was more than a modicum of luck about the way he picked up movement on the west wall of the front garden. He was scanning the monitors to his right when his mobile phone pulsed and danced daintily across the bench beside his left hand. As he turned, he spotted a blurring image on the end monitor, and watched as a hood-covered head dipped below the wall.

***

Captain Georges Laurent was stretched out on a tattered chaise lounge, grateful for a rest after an exhausting few days. Grab it while you can, he told himself, just as the midnight silence of his office was pierced by Scott Joplin's *Entertainer* ringtone on his BlackBerry. He glanced at the screen displaying the name of one of the agents sent to Switzerland. "Tell me some good news," he said after hitting the little green "accept" button.

"The Anasenko party is confirmed in residence in Gstaad. Our first impressions are that they have been joined by some heavyweight support. We spotted two well-armed sentries, but will need to do a further recce in the morning." It was a clipped, concise report, the kind drilled into GIGN agents by the enigmatic Claude Bartran.

"Negative," Laurent replied. "Do not risk exposure. Your job is to sit tight and make sure our friends don't move out of the area without your knowledge. Narrow down surveillance to the train station; it's their only way back out of there."

"Shouldn't we at least see how big the party has grown?"

"Negative. They must not know of your presence in the area. We need time to get back-up to your location and then we need to figure out how we're going to neutralise these bastards. You have to sit tight."

Laurent rang off and began considering his next moves. If Bartran had been around, he would know what to do, but in his absence it was up to Laurent to put together a workable plan. His biggest concern was the Swiss authorities. There were a lot of potential repercussions to operating on foreign soil, not least having to deal with the fall-out if things got messy. And, at this moment, Laurent couldn't see how they wouldn't get messy.

Finally, he decided there was one special card he could play. What was it they said about a problem shared? He thumbed his way through the office contact list looking for the number of *LonWash Securities*.

***

Sir Clive Oliver cut an imposing figure at the head of the room. The breadth of the man's knowledge of all things business and financial struck a chord with his audience, no one more so than Mike Devon. After hearing of the involvement of Gennady Anasenko in recent events, Sir Clive had spent four hours poring over the names and information gathered by Devon during his visit the previous month to the Manhattan offices of Montgomery Holdings. Finally, he broke off from his review in a side-office of the main *LonWash* executive area and insisted on addressing the waiting group of agents.

"Gentlemen, let me begin with a rather startling piece of news for you. Until this morning I believed, just like the rest of the world, that the late Sheik Kalid Abu-Nayyan was simply unfortunate to be caught up in last week's terror attacks in Paris. I now know for certain the Sheik was singled out for assassination."

He waited for the hum of conversation to die down and held up a hand as a signal to let him continue before the questions began. "The attempt on my life merely confirms a pattern and highlights a much more frightening scenario, which I've spent the morning trying to unscramble."

Sir Clive paused to sip from a glass of water before continuing. "The list of financial transactions obtained in Manhattan includes the names of a number of investors and brokers connected with *Kalnay Oil.* There's no doubt Anasenko was trying to move large sums around the world with the express intent of buying up *Kalnay* shares, should they become available. The only way he could guarantee this was by making the markets squeamish – and what better platform than terrorist attacks? The death of the Sheik was the extra push needed, but one that had to be timed precisely."

This time Devon cut in. "You're not seriously suggesting that more than twenty people had to be killed at the Eiffel Tower just to screen the assassination of an oil magnate?"

Sir Clive smiled in his direction. "The Sheik was rather more than just an oil magnate. Anyone who controls *Kalnay,* controls supply and sets the prices for crude oil. In effect, they could hold most of the world to ransom."

"Apart from obviously making a lot of money, what other motive could there be?" Devon asked tentatively.

Sir Clive rummaged through a number of note-filled pages on the desk in front of him. "Ah, here we are," he said, holding up a single sheet. "I rather think other possible motives are up your street, not mine. However, given Anasenko's political links to Moscow, you might want to start there."

The summary hit Devon like a hammer in the chest. He'd been too busy chasing down terrorists to see the wider picture. Had Sylvia Flynn not traded the news of the attempt on Sir Clive's life, they would never have known about this murky underbelly of financial double-dealing. Even then, they had been lucky to intercept Sir Clive's would-be assassin. If the hitman had acted a day earlier, Sir Clive's revelations would have remained hidden from them.

Not quite sure how to continue, Devon turned to Sir Clive. "Can anything be done about Anasenko's financial dealings? Is there any way to stop him taking control of *Kalnay*?"

Sir Clive beamed. "I've already put the wheels in motion. From what I've been able to learn, there has been considerable activity on the French CAC; less so on the FTSE. However, I've alerted stock exchange investigators in both countries about the potential fraud, and I'm hoping we can secure a suspension of trading until we get to the bottom of this."

"How does that work?" Devon asked.

"If the exchanges believe there is malfeasance in share-dealing, they have the power to de-list companies until things are sorted out. In cases where they have proof of shares being obtained illegally, they can seize the assets of the owners and conduct a regulated fire-sale. At the very least we can tie-up Anasenko in the courts for many months, even years."

Devon shot Sir Clive a puzzled look. "Don't worry about the courts. Something tells me that legal actions will be the least of Gennady Anasenko's troubles."

***

The sun glistened off the snow as the two French agents made their way out of the hotel and across the street towards the glass-encased railway station. Groups of skiers were hurrying excitedly towards the non-stop cable-car ferry to the Schonreid, the largest and most popular of Gstaad's pistes. The agents watched the passengers clamber aboard cars, envious of the day they would spend traversing the Simmental and Saanenland ranges, and calling in at the various ski bars which dotted the slopes.

The idea of sitting in a railway station watching the world go by was not one the pair relished. It was highly unlikely any of the Anasenko party would be leaving the resort so soon after arrival, but orders were orders, and they had to admit to the logic of keeping their heads down while waiting for reinforcements.

Despite the trails of steam formed by their hot breaths against the cold air, it was a pleasant, cloudless morning. A blue canopy hung over the mountains to provide a clear backdrop between the peaks where small, racing figures carved perfect lines in the hitherto undisturbed snow. From their vantage point inside the station's small café, it was hard for the agents not to be transfixed by the scene above them - so much so, that when the shadows fell across their table it took them a moment to register the presence of two men.

When the agents looked up they instantly recognised the figure of Igor Borimov towering over them, in a feet-wide-apart stance that signalled he was ready to deal with any kind of sudden movement on their part. Beside him stood another man, almost as tall, his right hand hidden under an unzipped ski jacket. A third figure was positioned menacingly at the doorway.

"I think we have something to talk about," Borimov whispered.

The agents looked around the room. An elderly couple sipped from small coffee cups at a nearby table as a waitress busied herself with wiping the tops of the remaining empty tables. The rest of Gstaad's tourist population were either in their hostels or enjoying the delights of the ski runs.

"There is no need to make a big scene," Borimov told them in a neutral voice. "If we wanted to kill you, then you would already be dead. You will come with us to meet our boss who is anxious to know why you snoop around our chalet last night."

***

General Sir John Sandford arrived at the *LonWash* offices shortly after Sir Clive Oliver finished his briefing. The two men adjourned to a small office where they engaged in conversation for more than an hour before the door opened and the General signalled Devon to join them.

"I'll get straight to the point, Mike. Sir Clive has an appointment at the Stock Exchange in an hour's time and then he's heading to Paris. I've agreed to release all our papers to him for use in any investigations into Anasenko's dodgy dealings. I want 24/7 protection for him until this thing is resolved."

It was what Devon expected to hear. "I already have two agents standing by. They're top men, but I must insist Sir Clive does everything they tell him to do. For all we know there could be another contract out on him"

Sir Clive leapt from the seat and grabbed Devon's hand in what for him was a rare show of emotion. He began to shake it vigorously, but stopped when he noticed Devon wincing. "Do forgive me, I forgot about your shoulder injury. As I've already told you, Mr Devon, you have my eternal gratitude for saving my life this morning. I saw what these people are capable of and, believe me, I will do whatever is asked of me."

An awkward moment passed between the two men before the General intervened. "There's one more thing. Sir Clive will be joining us on a permanent basis, so to speak."

Devon's jaw dropped. "Excuse me sir, did I hear you right?"

Sandford smiled and waved Devon to a chair. "Sir Clive has been filling me in on what we'll describe as financial terrorism. As you already know from his earlier briefing, there are things happening around us which are beyond our pay scale. Sir Clive's business expertise will help to alert us more quickly to the sort of things Anasenko has been up to over the past few months."

"I still don't understand."

"Sir Clive has agreed to put together a specialist unit, which will be attached to *LonWash* with the specific remit of watching the world's stock markets for any hint of activity that could be considered worthy of further examination."

Devon looked slightly bemused. "Surely that kind of thing is already happening?"

This time Sir Clive answered. "It is true that all the major Stock Exchanges have their own oversight and investigative arms, but they are limited in what they can achieve. Like everybody else, they have to follow rules, and those rules are often used against them, either to slow down investigations or to make them go away completely."

Devon was beginning to see where this was going. "I take it you mean these investigators need to stick to purely legal methods of obtaining information?"

Sir Clive smiled. "The General has assured me of his ability to use more covert means of monitoring certain individuals or companies which fall under our purview. With this kind of support, I believe I can put together a team capable of thwarting the Anasenkos of this world."

The conversation was cut short by Alan Doyle's appearance at the glass-panelled door. Devon broke away, crossed the room and pulled the handle. "What is it, Alan?" he asked, sensing the urgency in the other's face.

"I've just taken a call from our French friends. Anasenko has been tracked to Gstaad in Switzerland."

"What are they intending to do about it?"

Doyle grinned. "Whatever it is, we've just been invited to the party."

Chapter 32
Moscow

SERGEI KABLUKOV LAY under a pile of blankets, staring at the ceiling and waiting for the first rays of dawn to raise the outside temperature above the minus ten of a typical winter in suburban Moscow. It had been a long night. The ex-KGB Major General was unable to sleep after responding to calls the previous day from former contacts within Britain's MI6 security agency, a world he thought he left behind a lifetime ago.

As sunlight broke through the gloom he glanced around the sparse two-room box apartment provided as "reward" for his long service on behalf of the state. That, and a meagre monthly pension, had consigned Kablukov to near poverty, unable to afford switching on the gas heating for more than a few hours a day.

A month away from his seventieth birthday, he had little to look forward to. His once strong body had wasted away, ravaged by smoking too many cheap cigarettes, and sustained by cheap vodka which, more often than not, took the place of a decent meal.

Things had been so different back in the days when he headed an internal security department which earned a fearsome reputation among Russia's many enemies, both home and abroad. In those days, he had a decent salary and enjoyed the perks of free food and clothing supplies from businessmen anxious to keep on the right side of "the little enforcer," as he had come to be known.

Kablukov accepted the extra rations as a part of the job, but he drew the line at taking bribes or turning a blind eye for the packets of roubles he knew some officers of his rank received as a matter of routine. When they weren't being handed kickbacks from the *Mafiya* gangs, they helped themselves to the vast riches of cash and drugs in the city's evidence lockers, often recycling drugs back to the men from whom they were seized.

These former colleagues could now be seen driving around in their petrol-guzzling Gaz M23s and living out retirement in luxurious dachas. They passed him often in the streets, but never once did Kablukov regret the choices he had made.

Memories of his former life had come flooding back the previous day when Alan Doyle called from London. He had been introduced to Doyle many years ago by Mike Devon, a young MI6 operative he met in East Berlin. It was a meeting which Kablukov recalled with affection.

Devon was part of a successful ongoing British operation responsible for helping a number of prominent scientists to escape to the West. Kablukov was sent from Russia to track down the operation and kill every agent he could find. As it turned out, it was Devon who had turned the tables on him.

Kablukov recalled receiving a tip-off about a meeting in a farmhouse twenty miles from the border. Accompanied by three other agents they moved in on the location, but were spotted. In the ensuing firefight Kablukov's men were killed, and he found himself staring down the barrel of a gun held against his face by Devon.

What happened next surprised the hardbitten KGB man. Instead of squeezing the trigger, as Kablukov would have done, the young Britisher frogmarched him to a shed and bound him, careful not to tie the knots too tight for fear of stopping circulation. He then brought an oil heater which he lit to keep the harsh cold from killing his captive. Before he left, he knelt beside Kablukov and whispered. "We spies should not be killing each other because of a damn wall. Someday it will disappear and then we will live together as friends, not enemies."

When he had heard the sounds of engines disappear into the night, Kablukov used the flame from the oil heater to painfully sever the rope binding his wrists. He had rushed across the fields to where he had left his car, and had made a mad dash for the border.

Kablukov could still see the look of shock on Devon's face when he had pulled up at the Russian sector barricade two hundred yards from Checkpoint Charlie. The young agent must have had to detour to pick up passengers, and that allowed Kablukov to reach the checkpoint ahead of him.

Kablukov had stepped out of a sentry hut and marched up to the driver's window. He calmly asked Devon for his papers while scanning the interior of the car. A young man sat stiffly in the passenger seat, while his wife and three year-old daughter fidgeted nervously in the back.

After making a show of examining the papers – which Kablukov had to admit were excellent forgeries – he handed them back to Devon. Leaning through the window he whispered: "From one spy to another, make sure you stay on the other side of that damned wall, at least until such times as it disappears and we can live together."

The KGB man had stepped back, waved for the barrier to be lifted, and watched as Devon drove into the American sector.

Their paths were to cross many times over the years, and there was always a healthy respect and admiration between them, forged by the events of that night in East Berlin.

And now, after all these years, Devon was reaching out to him again. The request for information on Gennady Anasenko opened up old wounds that Kablukov thought were buried.

He had had many dealings with Anasenko in those early years fighting the Moscow gangs. On several occasions he had come close to tying Anasenko to numerous murders and extortions, but vital evidence always seemed to go missing. It was around that time his beloved wife Anna was knocked down and killed while walking home with groceries from the small store in the next street. The local police dismissed it as a drunken hit-and-run, but Kablukov saw Anasenko's hand in it.

He couldn't prove it, of course, and after months of trying to find evidence, he had to admit defeat. By then Anasenko had grown out of the underworld to become an oil magnate and international jetsetter, his presence in Moscow curtailed to only a handful of high-level meetings each year. Until yesterday, it had been more than ten years since Kablukov last thought of his nemesis.

After filling Doyle in with as much background as he could, Kablukov had paced his small kitchen and spent the night wondering what had caused Anasenko to resurface in his life.

During that long night he resolved to contact Mike Devon. After dispensing with the pleasantries Kablukov came straight to the point. "I must know of your interest in Gennady Anasenko. This is very important to me and I ask as an old friend that you be honest with me."

The solemn words took Devon by surprise. He was in the middle of planning a trip to Gstaad when the call came through. "Sergei, you seem agitated. Tell me first what has put you in this state."

Kablukov recounted his history with Anasenko and finished by telling Devon of his belief that he was responsible for the death of his wife. "You see, my friend, why I would want to know what dealings you have with this animal."

The revelation shocked Devon, and he knew he needed to be honest. "We're convinced he's been sponsoring international terrorism. He has to answer for certain atrocities carried out in recent weeks and I intend to see he pays for those crimes."

"Do you mean to arrest him?"

"No, Sergei, it will serve no useful purpose to parade this man in front of the world. From what I gather he has a lot of political clout and I'm damned if I'll run the risk of some deal being struck on his behalf."

There was silence for a moment before Kablukov responded. "Can you tell me where he is at present?"

"I'm sorry Sergei, but I'll have to pass on that

one. I *can* tell you I'll be on my way to meet with him shortly."

Silence again. When the voice came back on line, Devon detected what he thought were sobs. "Will you do me a favour?"

"Go ahead and name it, Sergei."

"Will you put a bullet in his brain and tell him it's from Anna Kablukov?"

***

Four miles from Kablukov's location the Director of FSB, Russia's Federal Security Service, felt like he'd just been torn a new one as he emerged from a meeting with Premier Vladimir Putin in his palatial office overlooking Lubyanka Square. The subject of the conversation had been one Gennady Anasenko.

"How could you not know what's going on?" Putin demanded. "I have to read a bulletin from our Paris office to learn that Anasenko is being accused of dodgy dealings and that shares in his company have been suspended pending investigations. Do I have to remind you that we have a lot of capital tied up in these enterprises? Do you realise that billions are at stake, not to mention the damage which will be caused to our international reputation if we are linked to this in any way?"

He pushed a single sheet of paper across the large mahogany-inlaid desk. The Director fumbled nervously for it and read the short statement, which had been translated into Russian:

JOINT STATEMENT
With effect from 9am today, trading in Kalnay Oil, and

various other companies in which Gennady Anasenko has share-interest, has been suspended pending investigation of possible irregular transactions. The London Stock Exchange, in partnership with Companies des Agents de Change in Paris, have removed these companies from their lists and advised other exchanges to examine their books. This action will remain in force for a minimum period of 21 days after which a further bulletin will be issued.

"What...what does it mean?" The FSB Director stumbled over the words.

"What do you think it means, you imbecile? Our friend appears to have bitten off more than he can chew, but all of us will suffer from the fall-out. We have to minimise the damage as quickly as possible."

The FSB man wasn't sure how to respond. Finally, he asked, "What do you want me to do?"

Putin slammed his fist on the desk. "Do your bloody job! Find Gennady Anasenko and bring him here immediately."

Back in his office, the Director made a number of calls listed against Anasenko's name in a rolodex which was constantly updated for him by his private secretary. The third call elicited a response. Anasenko's voice filled the earpiece. "Who is this?"

The response was unequivocal. "Gennady, you must listen carefully to what I have to say."

The Ilyushin IL-96 rolled out of a military hangar at Sheremetyevo Airport, and taxied to a runway set apart from the commercial lanes used by the national Aeroflot fleet. Its four Aviadvigatel PS-90 engines continued to purr for twenty minutes while the captain and two copilots waited for further instructions.

Looking out through the cockpit windows, the crew picked up the lights of a vehicle emerging from a light snowfall. It was a high-sided lorry, unmistakeably one used by the GRU, the country's foreign military intelligence service. It raced to the port side of the large jet and braked alongside the opened staircase.

The captain rose from his seat and walked out to greet his mysterious passengers. Six men entered the cabin, each carrying a large rucksack with an automatic rifle tied across the top. One of the men freed himself from the group and walked towards the captain, holding out a piece of paper.

"These are your orders. You are to take us to Geneva and wait until we have finished out business. We could be there only a matter of hours or we could be there for up to two days."

While the man spoke, the captain studied the official FSB orders which confirmed that the bearer of the note, Lieutenant Arkady Antipov, was in complete charge of a mission of the highest importance to state security and must be obeyed at all times.

The captain was not one to question official orders. He smiled at the lieutenant and told him to get his men to buckle in. Then he turned on his heels and strode back to the cockpit.

Ten minutes later the Ilyushin banked over Sheremetyevo and disappeared into the skies.

Chapter 33
Paris

MIKE DEVON, Alan Doyle and Alfie Cheadle strode into the GIGN offices and were greeted with warm handshakes by Captain Georges Laurent. They were ushered to a large conference table covered in an array of maps, with a coffee pot and cups in the centre.

"Before we start," Laurent said earnestly, "we have lost contact with our two agents in Gstaad. I'm beginning to fear the worst."

Devon looked nonplussed. "Don't take this the wrong way, Captain, but even if your agents have fallen into Anasenko's hands, it changes nothing."

"But if they are persuaded to talk, they will know we are coming." There was anxiety in the Captain's words, his thoughts more focussed on his men than on anything Anasenko might learn from them.

"After what happened on the yacht in Monaco, Anasenko will know we're onto him and will be ready for anything we throw at him."

While the two men talked, Doyle helped himself to the coffee pot and poured cups for everyone. Laurent ignored the cup raised in his direction. He paced across the room several times before taking a seat beside the British agents. When he spoke it appeared he had made a decision. "I have to tell you honestly that I don't know how to proceed. I'm prepared to hand command of this operation over to you, Mr Devon."

Devon hadn't figured it any other way. "Call me Mike, for goodness sake. Are you ready to listen to a plan that will involve a high degree of risk for all concerned?"

When Laurent nodded his agreement Devon continued. "Do you have any men with experience of HALO parachuting?"

Laurent smiled. "You will forgive my boastfulness, but GIGN has the best equipped special agents in Europe. As far as High Altitude Low Opening jumps are concerned we insist they can do them before they have their first shave."

It was Devon's turn to smile. "Okay, the way I see it we have only two choices. We either go in full throttle or we attempt a stealth approach. I say we hit them hard from the get-go and to hell with prancing around in the snow looking for an opening. One thing will be important, however. We will not use explosives and all our weapons will be silenced."

Doyle shot him a glance. "If we're going into a well-protected position, a few flash-bangs would come in handy."

"Negative," Devon responded. "I don't want to raise any activity from the nearby village, and we have also to consider the possibility of triggering avalanches."

"Gotcha," Doyle answered before returning to his coffee cup.

Devon stood to sort through the maps of the Gstaad area. "I've already had a look at the general area through Google Earth, but these will help pinpoint precise distances and the layout of the

Anasenko chalet and grounds. There are two obvious points of entry – we go straight through the front gate after creating a diversion at the rear."

"Sounds simple," Laurent mocked. "Perhaps you should tell me your entire plan."

Devon remained on his feet and spoke for almost twenty minutes. When he finished he scanned the faces at the table and told them: "To recap, four GIGN agents will carry out a HALO jump onto the mountains two miles from the property. They will bring all our weapons and equipment and rendezvous with us at this point east of the property." He pointed to a position on one of the maps before continuing.

"We four will travel to Gstaad by train. We can't risk bringing anything with us and will travel in separate two-man groups to avoid suspicion. When the mission has been completed we will bury our equipment and the entire group will leave by train. Extra tickets will be bought in advance for the other GIGN agents. Any questions?"

The others at the table shrugged in acknowledgement.

"Good," said Devon. "It's now time to meet with our parachutists."

***

The four men had spent most of the flight hooked into a single 100% oxygen tank designed to flush nitrogen from their bloodstreams. Without the exercise they would suffer the equivalent of "diver's bends" and most likely pass out before they had time to deploy their chutes. Beneath their heavy-duty flight suits they wore layers of polypropylene undergarments to fight the minus-fifty temperatures experienced at 30,000 feet.

They checked each other's equipment, including MBU-12 oxygen masks, Airox VIII o2 regulators, and the MC-5 Halo parachutes and reserve parachutes. Shortly before they reached the drop zone they removed their oxygen masks, strapped on MGU-55 ballistic helmets, and continued breathing through their bottled oxygen supply.

Three red lights flashed at the rear of the cargo plane as the tail opened downward. The men shuffled to the platform and watched the lights turn from red to green. On the third green, they dropped off into space, meeting up in a team formation less than a minute into their jump. They held that position for a continuous four-minute freefall, clutching between them a special cargo parachute containing the equipment needed on the ground. Speed was maintained at 115mph before they deployed their chutes at 2,000 feet.

From that point it was textbook stuff, all chutes guided to within twenty yards of each other on a snow-capped ridge midway down the Simmental range. The agents worked fast to unpack skis and attach a sled to the underside of the cargo crate. One of the men held up a compass, fixed the bearing, and nodded for the others to follow as he glided down the darkened slope. Their helmets were fitted with pull-down, night-vision shades.

Two hours later, they swooped to a stop beside a stand of trees a hundred yards from a wall-enclosed chalet. They had just removed their helmets when a low voice echoed from behind them.

"Over here."

They turned to watch Georges Laurent, Mike Devon, Alan Doyle and Alfie Cheadle emerge from the gloom.

***

Igor Borimov glanced at the large clock hanging above the mantelpiece. It was about to strike five in the morning. He reached for the Motorola walkie-talkie and thumbed the transmit button, just as he'd done every hour on the hour since midnight. One by one his men signed in with "nothing-to-report" messages that were beginning to irritate Borimov's urge for action.

He'd reasoned an assault would take place over one of these next two nights. Since he knew from the captured GIGN agents that reinforcements were on the way, he calculated they would not hang about after arriving in Gstaad. A daytime assault was out of the question, so that left either tonight or tomorrow night for any action.

He brought his men in from perimeter duty and deployed them around the house, leaving two to constantly monitor the CCTV feeds. He would draw his opponents into the place he could best defend, and he would take great delight in watching them die.

The walkie-talkie pulsed in his hand and an urgent voice broke the eerie silence of the large drawing room. "We have intruders. Two, three, no four men have scaled the west wall."

As Borimov rushed to the communications room, the glass in the windows to the rear of the house shattered, sending ornaments crashing to the floor. It was a sustained burst, obviously from silenced weapons, and as yet there was no return fire from his men positioned at that part of the building.

He ran past the communications room and slid into the rear kitchen area where one of his men knelt below a sink unit. Bullets continued to rip into cupboards and plasterwork above his head. "Return fire, return fire you yellow bastard!" Borimov yelled as he stood above the units and aimed a burst from his MP5N into the garden. The other gunman immediately joined in.

When his gun jammed on empty Borimov dipped below the window and fumbled for a fresh magazine. He lifted the radio to his mouth and screamed orders to no one in particular. "Get to the first floor rear windows. Stop those bastards from getting any closer."

He was about to rejoin the firefight when the radio cut in again. "Intruders to the front, intruders to the front!"

***

Devon counted down from sixty when the action started at the rear of the building. The idea was to make the enemy believe the assault was one-dimensional; pull them one way before forcing them to go back another way. Timing and confusion were the bywords.

He knelt with Doyle beside a column holding a sturdy wooden gate in place at the main entrance to the chalet grounds. Opposite them, Laurent and Cheadle rested behind the other pillar. When the countdown reached zero, all four men stood and aimed steady bursts of fire at the four separate gate hinges. One powerful kick by Doyle and it collapsed inwards.

They broke into a run up the sloping driveway; Devon and Laurent moving right to fire at the downstairs windows; Doyle and Cheadle running left to engage the upstairs windows. There was no return fire.

Devon reached the decking area first and pressed his body against the timberclad wall. He waited while the others moved into position around him before removing a black box from his jacket pocket. It was a small image intensifier with a four-inch screen designed to highlight body heat inside a building. Nothing registered from the room to the right of the door. Across the way Doyle held a similar box towards the room on the left, and signalled the all-clear.

Devon held up three fingers and began a silent countdown. When the third finger folded, he dived through the broken window and rolled across a carpeted floor, quickly followed by Laurent. He pointed the box at the next wall and was rewarded with a red blur moving towards their location. They remained perfectly still as the outline closed in on the room door.

As the knob handle made a slow turn, both men in the room open-fired on continuous auto. The door panelling virtually disintegrated, to reveal a gunman flying across a hall with most of the middle part of his body missing.

Doyle ducked behind a settee just as a volley of fire

raked the room from a service hatch, built into a partition wall between the room and the kitchen area beyond. Whoever was firing had not registered on the intensifier and must have reached the location after Doyle and Cheadle hurtled through the window.

He glanced across the room to see Cheadle wedged against an ornate bookcase, barely able to protect himself from flying splinters being gouged out of the wood by a hail of 9mm bullets. Unless Doyle acted quickly, the bullets would chew their way through to where Cheadle was trapped.

It was at that point he wished he had a few grenades; the very sight of one flying towards the serving hatch would have sent the gunman diving for cover. That was it, he thought! He put down his weapon, pulled the intensifier from his pocket and hurled it over the top of the settee. As it flew through the air he shouted "Grenade" as a warning to Cheadle, before rising to his feet to fire a steady burst in the direction of the hatch.

He didn't expect to hit anything other than the wall. The intention was to drive the gunman away from the opening long enough to allow Cheadle to scramble for better cover. The ploy worked perfectly; Doyle could see the top of the gunman's head disappear below the gap.

Doyle vaulted the settee and sprinted towards the hatch, with Cheadle in hot pursuit. They kept their fingers tight on the triggers, peppering the hatch and surrounding wall with a murderous spray.

At the far end of the adjoining room, one of the ex-Spetsnaz troopers hunched below a sink unit to avoid incoming fire from the GIGN agents in the garden. He was exposed to the salvo coming from the opposite direction, through the serving hatch. His back was shredded by a stream of bullets which pitched him heavily against the sink, where he hung in a weird suspended animation, before sliding lifeless to the floor.

Doyle knew the gunman who had fired at them was crouched somewhere below the hatch level, possibly even crawling for safety to the side of the kitchen. He quickly ejected the Uzi magazine, rammed in a fresh one, and pushed the weapon one-handed through the gap. Pointing downwards, he sprayed the room from side to side and was rewarded with the sounds of a man in his death throes.

Just as Doyle was about to pull the pistol back through the gap, it was wrenched from his grasp by a three-round burst that tore through his hand.

Igor Borimov had just crawled away from below the rear kitchen window to help the shooter at the service hatch, when a shower of bullets streamed through the gap. He saw his man drop to the ground and roll away from the opening as a hand reached in to unleash a spray of death across the kitchen floor.

Borimov slithered to the corner of the room, narrowly avoiding a tracer which tore over the marble tiles close to where he crouched. He could do nothing but watch as his hired hand crawled into the line of fire and died instantly from two rounds that ploughed into the back of his head.

He knew his plans for the defence of the house had been shattered by the swiftness and boldness of the two-prong attack launched against them. He could only guess at the number of assailants and cursed himself for underestimating their ability to assemble such a determined force. At best, he believed no more than four or five French agents would be sent to Gstaad, instead of a group that must be twice that number, judging by the barrage coming from both sides of the house.

He steadied his aim on the arm extended though the hatch, and smiled as all three-rounds found their mark. *At least that's one of the bastards out of commission.*

Devon found himself at the bottom of a stairwell when he pushed through the shattered door. He signed for Laurent to lie flat on the left side and train his automatic on the landing above. Careful not to block Laurent's line-of-sight, Devon hugged the right hand wall as he inched his way upwards.

When he reached halfway, a figure loomed into view at the top of the stairs and began firing. He managed only two rounds before a burst from Laurent cut him down; his body thrown backwards to crash against a wall.

The blur of movement made Devon drop to the stairs, trusting Laurent would do his job and remove the danger. The gunman's bullets flew inches over Devon's head and he remained crouched until Laurent shouted the all-clear.

He continued his climb to the top and, after a moment, risked a glance round the corner. Ahead lay a corridor running thirty yards towards a large window overlooking the east side of the chalet grounds. He waved Laurent to join him.

They had no way of knowing how many gunmen, if any, remained on this floor. Three doors opened into the corridor and they would have to assume a threat lay behind each one. They would have to clear them one at a time.

***

"Fuck that," Doyle howled as he surveyed the shattered prosthetic. "The clinic will be tired of replacing this, and God knows what the old man will say about the bill."

Cheadle knelt beside him, realising for the first time that it was Doyle's false limb which had taken the hits. "Thank God you didn't stick your good arm through the gap."

"Are you kidding?" Doyle responded. "One of the perks of having this is that I can replace it whenever I like. A regular Bionic Man, that's what I am."

The pair had crawled to the side of the room to inspect the damage. They didn't expect any further fire through the hatch, but there was no point in taking unnecessary chances of being caught underneath it. Doyle motioned Cheadle to help him remove his jacket so he could get at the strapping holding the arm in place. The wiring mechanism was shattered and the limb flopped uselessly at his side.

Cheadle unhooked the straps and followed Doyle's direction to pull wires from a small unit fixed inside the prosthetic. This completed, Doyle used his left hand to wriggle the limb free from the stump. He glanced at Cheadle to watch the young man's reaction, but there was no flicker of emotion. Good

343

guy to have in your corner, Doyle reflected.

He flung the limb across the room, nodded at Cheadle to help him back into his jacket. He withdrew his favourite Glock 17 from his waistband. "That's more like it," he said as he cradled the weapon. "I feel whole again."

The words had barely been uttered when the door to the room crashed open to reveal Igor Borimov standing in the gap. He clutched an MP5N two-handed, the business end pointed directly at Cheadle standing with his back to the door. Veins bulged in Borimov's neck and head, and he screamed a maniacal roar as he squeezed the trigger.

The four French agents at rear of the building continued to lay down a steady barrage as they advanced on the building. The only return fire had come from a downstairs room, which had gone strangely quiet in the past few minutes. The leader of the group decided to break radio silence. "Snow Leopard One, the rear downstairs is secured. Advise."

Devon's voice responded. "Break formation and surround the building. Concentrate fire on the upstairs windows. We are moving to the upper floor. Do not let any tangos escape the building. Copy?"

"Roger. Cover fire in sixty."

The GIGN agent motioned to his men who crawled off through the snow to take up their new positions. A minute later he began raking the first floor window. He could see flashes to both sides of his location, and heard the tinkling of glass and cracking of wood as his team joined in."

Borimov's MP5N was still on its three-round setting when he fired into the middle of Alfie Cheadle's back. Doyle saw shock and pain register on the young agent's face as he flew past to crash against a wall.

Doyle sidestepped Cheadle's flailing body and raised his Glock towards the menacing figure advancing into the room. Borimov's finger contracted on the trigger a fraction ahead of Doyle, but the big man didn't flinch. *Make it count, you bastard*, he mumbled as he waited for the destructive force of the 9mms to assail his body.

The slide on the MP5N clicked against an empty magazine. The noise reverberated around the room as Borimov frantically thumbed the eject lever. He lifted his eyes to glance at Doyle. The smirk on the one-armed man's face was the last thing he saw. Doyle fired and watched his round enter Borimov's left eye.

Without waiting for the giant to thunder to the floor, Doyle turned and ran to Cheadle. The body was twisted in a heap, the head resting peacefully in the crook of an outstretched arm. Doyle sat down and began rubbing his hand through the shock of blonde hair, caressing the locks and ignoring the tears streaming down his cheeks. It had been a long time since Alan Doyle cried.

He stayed like that for several minutes, acutely aware how much the young agent had come to mean to him. If only he had acted sooner? If only he had secured the area before asking Cheadle to help him out of that damned prosthetic?

At first the soft murmuring voice didn't register with Doyle, but gradually he realised the body beside him was moving! He leaned over to look into

Cheadle's face and saw the eyelids flicker. Then the lips moved: "Jeez, Alan, it's sore. Get it off me, I can't breathe."

It took several seconds for Doyle to register what was being said. Suddenly he remembered the bullet-proof vest, and began tearing at Cheadle's jacket. He uncovered a Kevlar wraparound waistcoat with ceramic plates sewn into its padded layers. The layers were chewed by Borimov's bullets, but an inspection confirmed none had penetrated through to the skin.

***

Pavel Jakov was no coward, but neither was he a fool. The silence of the guns around the house told him all he needed to know – either the rest of the team were dead or captured, leaving him to confront a substantial force with just three men still standing. To make matters worse, they were trapped in two upstairs rooms with no hope of escape. He made a decision.

"Soldiers! You people in the corridor, we wish to surrender." He looked at the face of the man sharing the room with him, and registered the nod of agreement. Across the corridor he knew his cousin Nikita would follow his lead.

After a moment he heard a voice from the corridor. "Open the door slowly and throw your weapons into the hall. Come out one at a time, with your hands clasped behind your heads. If any of you make one wrong move we will kill you all."

The offer of surrender surprised Devon, but he was happy not to have to go through with a series of "clear room" manoeuvres, particularly without the use of flash-bangs. He watched as two doors opened on either side of the corridor and three men emerged after tossing their weapons ahead of them. Without being ordered, they knelt on the floor and eased facedown into the carpet.

"Are there any more men on this floor?"

"No," Pavel assured him.

Devon nodded to Laurent to keep his gun levelled on the prostrate group. He stepped over the men and examined the rooms they had exited, before making his way to the third room, and kicked open the door. Again there was nothing.

He returned to the group and began tying each man at the wrists and ankles with plasticuffs. As he knelt over Jakov he spoke into the man's ear. "Where is Gennady Anasenko?"

The man twisted his head to look at Devon. "He's gone."

"What do you mean he's gone?"

"He receive phone call last night and leave on first train this morning. I think he was ordered back to Moscow."

Chapter 34
Geneva

THE ILYUSHIN WAS PARKED among a sea of private jets in a remote corner of Geneva airport. The passengers had stowed their equipment in a false locker and changed into business suits, to await the arrival of an officer from the Swiss Federation Customs Administration. Lieutenant Arkady Antipov glanced at his watch, calculating how long he would stay in Geneva before striking out for Gstaad. He gave himself an additional 30-minute window.

The customs officer was a stern-faced woman in her forties, although the greying hair tied back in a severe bun added at least another ten years. There were no smiles and no greetings as she entered the main cabin; everything was sharp and businesslike. She examined the papers and surveyed the faces of the men seated in the generously-sized leather armchairs. None returned her stare.

Antipov was in no mood to attempt to soften this annoying jobsworth. "As I've already explained, we are an official trade delegation acting on behalf of the Russian Federation, and as such, I expect to be shown the proper courtesies and support from your government."

She answered without looking up from the paperwork. "You cannot remain indefinitely aboard this plane. You must explain why you would wish to do so, when Geneva has some of the finest hotels in the world. Surely, you do not expect to receive trade orders if you do not go out and meet some potential customers."

Antipov tried not to let his exasperation show. "I think I've already told you that we are awaiting a visit from the head of commerce at our Embassy in Bern. He was due to be here ten minutes ago."

"And if he does not arrive?"

"Then we are to go to the Grand Hotel Kempinski and wait for further instructions. At this point, we do not know what itinerary is laid on for us. If no potential sales leads are available in Geneva, then we will fly to Germany without troubling your sweet little country."

She ignored the obvious sarcasm in Antipov's voice and handed over the passports. After taking a further glance around the cabin, she turned and marched back down the stairs onto the tarmac.

Antipov glanced at his watch again. Gennady Anasenko was now forty minutes overdue, despite explicit warnings about what would happen if he failed to show up at the appointed time. If "his guest" didn't arrive in the next ten minutes, Antipov's team would travel to Gstaad and forcibly remove him from his chalet, eliminating any resistance they might encounter.

He walked to the rear of the jet and knelt below an empty seat. He traced his fingers around the deep-pile carpet until he found a small bump, which he depressed to release a built-in compartment. He withdrew a large canvas diplomatic pouch containing their equipment, which had been transferred there during the flight from Russia.

As he walked forward to the cockpit, past the open passenger door, he could hear the sounds of footsteps approaching the plane. He moved to the top of the stairs and looked down on a solitary figure walking hunched over to ward off a biting wind sweeping across the service area beside the private hangars.

He watched as the figure slowly ascended the steps, moving aside only at the last second to allow him to enter the cabin. "You're late," Antipov said brusquely.

Gennady Anasenko looked up from under his Fedora to study the young man standing insolently in front of him. "I am a senior official of the Russian Federation and I demand to be treated accordingly," he shouted. "Wipe that smirk off your face or I'll see to it that your next posting is somewhere north of Siberia."

Antipov held the angry gaze. "If you had been ten minutes later I would have come looking for you. I would have smashed my pistol across your smug face, trussed you up in a diplomatic bag, and dumped you in the cargo hold for your trip home. I may yet feel inclined to do it, so if I were you I would shut up and do exactly as you are told."

"This is preposterous!" Anasenko's face contorted into a red mask of fury. "Forget another posting; I will have you shot for your insubordination."

Antipov's men stirred in their seats, but he waved at them to remain silent. "It's funny you should mention executions, because my orders were somewhat similar."

"What, what do you mean?" Anasenko's voice dropped to a whisper.

"Just that I was told if you didn't come willingly I was to shoot you and leave you in this country where you have made a second home."

The words drove all fight from Anasenko. He knew the message he received in Gstaad from the FSB Director couldn't have been more explicit, and that he would be in a world of trouble if he did not return to Moscow. But, he had reasoned, it was nothing he couldn't handle, nothing he couldn't put right. He would meet with the Premier and restore his considerable influence. There was still time to save the *Kalnay Oil* deal, despite the interference of the stock exchanges. But why these drastic orders? Why was a special operations team sent to "escort" him home?"

He flopped into the nearest empty seat and watched the young lieutenant close the outer doors. It would be a long ride home and he would need to spend the time figuring a way out from under the mess he had created.

***

Devon spent most of the day supervising a clean-up of the Gstaad chalet. He put Borimov's surviving henchmen to work on digging a large grave at the rear of the building where the ground was still surprisingly soft, despite the winter onset. The remoteness of the property and the screen of the high walls kept the work hidden from view, even in the unlikely event of any tourists passing by.

The debris inside the house was gathered into large plastic bags and deposited in a cellar. Throughout the house, exterior wooden shutters were closed over to hide the shattered windows. With the residence barely used for more than a few weeks a year, it was unlikely anyone would investigate the lack of activity in the coming months.

Devon's next job was to sit down with the Russian survivors and spell out a few home truths. "We have spared your lives, but do not underestimate our ability to reach out and find you whenever we want. When we leave here, you will stay behind for at least six hours, after which time you are free to go on your way. You will be locked in the cellar and should have little trouble breaking down the door. Beware, however, that we will booby-trap the door, making it foolhardy to attempt opening it before the stipulated time. When the six hours have passed, the firing mechanism will be deactivated. If you don't believe me, feel free to try escaping before the deadline; your deaths will make things a lot easier."

Pavel Jakov looked resignedly into Devon's eyes. "What are we supposed to do after we escape the cellar?"

Devon nodded at a desk in the drawing room while his team kept their weapons trained on the Russians. "I am leaving your passports and some money, enough for you to buy train tickets to Geneva. After that you are on your own, but I would advise you do nothing to raise suspicions. The Swiss authorities are not known for going easy on people who shoot up their country, and would almost certainly leave you to rot in the Strafanstalt Prison at Regensdorf – I'm afraid it would put your Lubyanka to shame."

As the men turned to leave the room under the direction of the GIGN agents, Devon shouted after them. "One more thing. I would suggest you make no attempt to contact Anasenko. Quite apart from not caring what happens to you, Anasenko will have his own hands full."

As the group departed, Devon turned towards the pale figure of Alfie Cheadle, who was huddled in a chair close to the roaring fire, his arms wrapped around his body. Although none of the bullets had penetrated his armour, the young agent's back was covered in ugly black and yellow bruises, and he was having difficulty breathing. At the very least, Devon guessed, he had a few busted ribs and would need a complete physical examination. For now, he was swathed in bandages and protected from the worst of the pain by a morphine injection from the medikit supplies brought in by Laurent's agents.

Overall, they had been lucky, Devon conceded. He had expected the opposition to be better organised, and it had surprised him that the perimeter patrols had been withdrawn. They had allowed themselves to be boxed in, something even the most basic defensive strategies preached against.

Yes, things couldn't have been better, except that Anasenko had escaped the net. Devon wondered whether he would get another chance at the mass murderer.

***

A lot of water had passed, literally and figuratively, under the O'Connell Bridge since Sylvia Flynn last crossed into Dublin's Southside district. She had a mile to go before reaching Donnybrook, a mainly residential suburb nestled against the Grand Canal, and home to the Aviva Stadium, the revamped national centre for rugby and soccer.

It was an area with an eclectic mix of old Dublin aristocracy and welfare-state residents, trying to hold their ground against the Johnny-come-latelies of the Celtic Tiger boom years. Men and women, who had made fortunes in property speculation, had ploughed their new-found wealth into high-rise condominiums and private compounds, which cocked a snoop at the traditions of a neighbourhood once populated by families stretching back six generations.

Rented estates owned by Dublin City Council were immune from the privateers. As the "for sale" signs and window boards went up in the wake of the global financial crisis, the Donnybrook "locals" smiled at the disappearing SUVs, and turned back to the affairs of their own world.

These thoughts now occupied Paddy Flynn, as he stared out through a large bay window, idly trying to recall the names of the original tenants of Hope Street where he had lived for all of his sixty-two years. His gaze fell on a woman who turned the corner beside the Centra supermarket, crossed the narrow roadway, and walked up to the front gate of his small terraced house.

There was something vaguely familiar about the way she carried herself, the blonde hair flowing behind a head-held-high arrogance that reminded him so much of his long-lost younger sister. He pushed aside a lace curtain and stared at the stranger as she strode up the short path, hesitated for a moment, and pushed the dimly-lit button of the doorbell.

"Sweet Jesus," he moaned, as the face took shape

on the other side of the window.

He rushed from the room into a small hallway and fumbled at the door handle. His hands were shaking and it took several attempts to twist the knob all the way clear of its locked position. Finally it gave way, and he stood with tear-filled eyes, willing the vision in front of him to be real.

Sylvia Flynn looked up at her older brother and said simply: "It's me Paddy, I've come home."

The two fell into an embrace, his arms locked in a bear-hug which swept her off her feet. He held her in a tight squeeze for thirty seconds before releasing her and wiping a grizzled hand across his eyes. Then he pulled her into the hallway and slammed the door firmly shut.

It took the better part of an hour for her to fill in the twenty-five years since they had last seen each other. At intervals, she dabbed the corner of her eyes with one of his patterned linen handkerchiefs, but she was determined to tell him everything, warts and all. When she came to the events of recent weeks, her face assumed a bewildered expression.

"I still can't believe they let me go. The leader was a tough bastard, but a man of his word. What I told them about Anasenko seemed to help, because when they came back on the third day they handed me my suitcase and told me they were shipping me back to Ireland. They took all my money and personal belongings but returned my passport and drove me to Heathrow."

She paused to sip from a mug of tea prepared by her brother. "They issued dire warnings about not setting foot in England again, but they needn't have any worries on that score. I'm finished with that life for good. I've been given a chance and I intend to make use of it."

"What about the Gardai?" her brother asked tentatively.

"That's another thing I don't understand," she told him. "When I arrived in Dublin airport, I expected the Guards to be waiting to arrest me on some charge or other dating back to my days in the IRA, but no one bothered me. It looks like I really am free of everything."

Paddy Flynn rose from his seat and sat on the arm of his sister's chair. "This is your home now. It's still jointly in your name and you can stay here as long as you like."

She reached up and kissed him on the cheek. "Thank you Paddy, but I might have enemies in the IRA after the way I walked out on them in America all those years ago. I could be putting you in danger."

He rubbed his hand through her hair and smiled benevolently. "You're forgetting I'm still a big cheese around here. You done your part and nobody'll be bothering you. And anyway, don't you know there's a glorious peace on the island these days? You get yourself settled in and we'll see about getting your life back together."

***

Gennady Anasenko was kept waiting in the outer office for forty-five minutes while the Director of FSB attended to "some pressing business." It was a classic let-'em-stew ploy that he himself had used many times, but at least the delay gave him the opportunity to sort through his options.

The news of the actions taken by the stock exchanges had floored him; he couldn't work out how the *Kalnay Oil* transactions could have raised any flags. He had used scores of different brokerages to pick up small share portfolios, mostly under the names of shell corporations, so how had they traced his involvement? He had timed things to perfection with markets awash in dealings as investors constantly shifted their assets in search of safer ground, so why the focus on him? He just couldn't figure out why he should have been placed under the spotlight.

His thoughts were interrupted by the opening of the office door to his left. Director Yuri Basilevski hooked a finger in Anasenko's direction and beckoned him like a truant pupil to a headmaster's office. By the time Anasenko walked into the room and closed the door behind him, the Director was already perched on a high-backed chair behind a desk cluttered with files and notepads.

Basilevski was a small, wizened-featured man whose eyes bulged in magnification behind plain, wire-framed spectacles. He was completely bald, his head mottled by freckles and splotches of unsightly red circles caused by the bursting of tiny blood vessels. To many people, the sixty-five year looked more like a bingo-caller in an old people's home than the head of one of the world's most feared state security departments.

He motioned Anasenko to a chair in the centre of the room and returned his gaze to an open file on his desk. There was no welcome, no hint of warmth behind the bland façade. Without lifting his eyes, he spoke in a low monotone voice. "You have caused quite a stir by your antics of recent weeks and have placed a great many people in an extremely awkward position. The time has come to put an end to your lawlessness."

"What!" Anasenko roared. "Who in the hell do you think you're talking to? I believed I was meeting with the Premier and I demand you make an appointment immediately. I'm not sitting here to be insulted by some pipsqueak who has to be told how to dress properly in the mornings."

Basilevski lifted his eyes to stare at Anasenko. "A meeting with the Premier is out of the question. Count yourself lucky you are not already facing a firing squad. You have dragged Mother Russia's name into the gutter, cost us untold billions, and undermined our fragile dealings with the rest of the world."

"This is nonsense. The issue of the stock exchange embargoes is a minor irritation that can be overcome. When the dust settles, all my investments will be safeguarded and I will have control of the world's oil supplies. All this I have done on behalf of Russia. You are out of your depth Yuri, and I suggest you allow me to discuss these matters with the Premier."

Basilevski slowly turned the pages of the file. "We know it all, Gennady," he said simply.

"Know all what?"

"We know of your involvement in the recruitment of al-Qaeda to mount attacks in Paris and London. We know of your assassination of Sheik Kalid Abu-Nayyan and your rather crude attempt to kill Sir Clive Oliver. We know you murdered two French agents and kidnapped and tortured their boss in Monaco. We know the names of every politician and financier with whom you've had dealings while you prostituted the name of Russia around Europe these many months. Do I need to go on?"

Anasenko was flabbergasted. He couldn't bring himself to believe that all his actions had somehow been monitored, and that his situation had now become extremely dangerous. When he spoke, it was in a more conciliatory tone than before. "Yuri, you know me. Whatever I did was for the good of the Russian Federation."

"What you did was for your own benefit, and now you must face the consequences."

Anasenko tried to ignore the menace in the other man's words. "Yuri, you need me. I can help figure a way out of this...."

"We don't need your help, Gennady. We have your secretary, Anna Bobkov, going through all the transactions and we are working out our own solutions to these problems."

"Traitorous bitch," Anasenko mouthed, recalling the mistress he left behind when he fled the yacht in Monaco. "She knows nothing. You need me to protect the deals I have already secured. I know of ways to move these transactions around the world and keeping them protected."

Basilevski ignored the pleas. "You delude yourself, Gennady. Do you not think the British and French authorities know as much as we do about your actions? Do you not understand the pressures we will come under to hand you over to face trial for the atrocities carried out in your name?"

Anasenko jumped from his seat. "What are you

saying? The Premier would not allow such a thing."

"Sit down, Gennady, and I will tell you what has to be done."

When the crestfallen billionaire resumed his seat, Basilevski sifted through a pile of papers. "You will be placed under immediate arrest and an announcement made to the effect that you are an enemy of the state."

"You can't do that!"

"Shut up you fool," Basilevski retorted in a rare show of anger. "Arresting you under federal charges is the only way of keeping you from the clutches of the west. It also allows us to make a rather generous offer to the stock exchanges which have frozen your accounts."

"What kind of offer?"

"We will announce that you pilfered your original holdings from the Russian Federation and that these have now been returned to us. We will hand over all additional stock bought by you as a gesture of good faith to allow trading to reopen and to smooth the way to a return to the status quo."

"But you're talking about giving away millions, not to mention control of one of the world's biggest oil companies."

Basilevski consulted his notes. "The actual figure transacted in recent months is almost two billion American dollars. By writing this off, we will at least protect more than ten billion tied up in original stock. There are no other choices."

Anasenko looked a beaten man. Slouched in his seat he whispered: "What is it you want me to do?

"You will sign over to the Federation all shares, company ownerships, and all other assets held by you. This is effective immediately." As he spoke he pushed papers across his desk and made a show of holding up a pen.

As Anasenko signed the sheets, there was a nervous stammer to his voice. "What is to become of me?"

"I'm afraid, Gennady, you must disappear permanently."

Chapter 34
London – three months later

"DO YOU WANT TO know what it is?"

"Maybe if you told me what you're talking about I would be able to tell you whether I wanted to know."

Emma thumped Devon playfully on his shoulder. "Don't be so obtuse. You know perfectly well I was at the doctor's for a scan this morning. They've confirmed I'm 26 weeks pregnant and they took a photograph of our son kicking in the womb."

Devon threw down his newspaper and leapt from the seat. "We're having a son!" He hugged her and whispered in her ear. "Thought you asked me whether I wanted to know?"

She pushed away and laughed in his face. "Silly, how do you think I could have kept this to myself? When the doctor asked if I wanted to know, I didn't stop to think, I just heard myself shouting yes. Oh, Mike, you are happy aren't you?"

He took her by the hand and led her to a chair. The swell of her belly suited her and the radiance in her face was infectious. "Looks like we should now finalise some plans," he told her earnestly.

"Yes," she said excitedly, "we can prepare the nursery now that we know it's blue for a boy. I would like to get started right away; it will keep me occupied during the day when you're not here."

Shortly after Devon's return from Gstaad he had asked Emma to move in permanently. He took a week away from the job and they spent their time rearranging the house the way she wanted. He liked what she had done to the place, particularly the decluttering of old furniture and ornaments. Many had belonged to his parents, but it was time to move on.

Emma had sensitively bubble-wrapped a lot of items and packed them in large crates for storage in the basement. Six or seven trips to charity shops removed the best of the furnishings, with the rest going into a large builder's skip which had to be replaced twice. In the final few days they temporarily moved back to Emma's apartment to allow a team of decorators carte blanche to repaint the entire house.

The only room to remain unscathed was Devon's private gym on the top floor. Lately Emma had taken to joining him there, working her way slowly through a routine of power-walking as she brushed aside Devon's constant warnings to take things easy.

"I have my eye on the loveliest cot in the John Lewis store on Oxford Street. Why don't you come with me on Saturday?"

Devon smiled down at her. "When I said it was time to make plans I wasn't talking about the nursery."

She looked at him quizzically. "What *are* you talking about?"

"Now who's being obtuse? I'm taking about getting married. I've already proposed and you've accepted, but we didn't decide on a date."

She held her hands to the sides of her face. "What are you suggesting?"

"I'm suggesting, my darling, that we do it as soon as possible. How does next month grab you?"

She erupted from the seat and threw her arms around his neck. "I would say that grabs me just fine."

"Good," he said. "We can't have Michael Junior being brought into this world knowing that his parents aren't married."

***

Doyle could usually interpret all Mike Devon's moods. It was a discordant whistling sound that drew his attention to the lift as Devon stepped out saying "Good morning" to everyone as he strode smiling across the room.

"And what has put our fearless leader in just good form this gloomy December day?" he asked, as Devon sat at the edge of the desk.

"I have a favour to ask," Devon responded.

"Shoot."

"How do you fancy getting out of those rags for a day and standing beside me while I marry the woman I love?"

Doyle, for once, was lost for words. "Does this....does this mean what I think it means?"

"Yes, you chump; I'm asking you to be my best man."

Doyle came out of his seat like an athlete from a starting block. He grabbed Devon's hand and began pumping it furiously. "This is great.....when, when is the big day?"

"We're still trying to work out whether to have it before Christmas or afterwards. Em likes to spend the festive season with her folks so we'll probably go for early January and honeymoon in the Seychelles while you lot are suffering heavy snowfalls."

Doyle let go of Devon's hand and returned to his seat. "I couldn't be happier, Mike. You make a great couple..."

"Hold the fort a moment," Devon cut in. "You haven't answered me yet. Are you going to agree to be my best man?"

"You just try getting someone else in my place!" The smile faded from Doyle's face as he looked up into Devon's eyes. "It's an honour and privilege, Mike. I owe you so much and I can't think of a prouder moment than to be watching you get married to a great girl."

Devon was thrown momentarily by the seriousness in Doyle's voice, but he recovered quickly. "That's just the big softie in you. Just make sure you bring a flask of the best brandy with you on the day. Your job is to keep the nerves from eating away at me."

They were so engrossed in their conversation that they failed to notice an excited Alfie Cheadle rush from a side room waving a piece of paper. He spotted Devon and made straight for his desk. "Boss, this has just come in. According to reports in Moscow, Gennady Anasenko has committed suicide in a cell at Lubyanka prison."

Devon snatched the paper from Cheadle's hand and began reading aloud a print-out from the English edition of Pravda's online newspaper:

Security services in Moscow have confirmed that disgraced oil billionaire, Gennady Anasenko, has been found hanged in his cell in Lubyanka Prison. Anasenko, who was facing multiple charges of treason, murder and federal fraud, was due to stand trial next month for his part in a conspiracy to destabilise world stock markets. A spokesman for the Ministry of Justice of the Russian Federation said the former tycoon's suicide has robbed the people of Russia of the opportunity for a public trial which could have uncovered the part played by co-conspirators in other countries. Sources close to Pravda have revealed that Anasenko is to be buried later today in a pauper's grave.

Doyle let out a whistle. "That's the best news we've had for some time. Looks like we can close the book on the whole, sorry Anasenko affair."

"Yeah," said Devon, "if nothing else it lets Moscow off the hook. I'm betting someone put the rope around Anasenko's neck and persuaded him to take the drop. Can't say I'm bothered either way."

Doyle rose from his seat and began cleaning the large wipeboard. "Look on the bright side, boss. That's another successful mission accomplished."

Devon was still staring at the Pravda announcement, his mind running back through events of recent weeks. He had to hand it to the Russians for the way they tackled the share-trading scandal, handing back millions of shares while retaining major investments in some of the world's top companies. The intervention of the Russian Federation and the prospects of Britain and France being tied up for years in a messy diplomatic furore, meant the offer of returned shares could not be refused. It was a masterstroke which allowed a potential scandal to disappear while Russia claimed the moral high ground.

Until now Devon hadn't believed Anasenko was in any danger from his countrymen. He thought the arrest was little more than a publicity stunt designed to underline Russia's determination to make things right. He half expected to hear of Anasenko resurfacing after the spotlight dimmed in a year or two. Just goes to show, he thought.

"You still with us, boss?"

Devon glanced across at Doyle. "Sorry, Alan. Did you say something?"

"Just asking if there's anything else you want us to do before we look at some other assignments waiting in the queue?"

"There are still some loose ends to be tied up on this one," Devon told him. "We need to process all the blackmail names supplied by Sylvia Flynn before handing the dossier over to the Metropolitan Police. I've a feeling some of the gentlemen on that list have been guilty of fraud on a massive scale, but it's not our concern any more. Let the Met get a bit of the limelight for a change."

***

Claude Bartran was reading the Pravda report at about the same time as Mike Devon. He was less than a week back at work, his frail body wedged into a wheelchair parked against a low desk cluttered with paperwork. He had reluctantly accepted early retirement on health grounds and was trying to tie up a few loose ends before finally leaving at the end of the month.

He suffered semi-paralysis down his left side; a condition which doctors assured him might improve with rest and rehabilitation over the next year. His spleen, ruptured by the pounding inflicted by the Borimovs, was removed in a ten-hour operation, which was more concerned about relieving the pressure of blot clots on his brain. Twice the surgeon thought he had lost him on the operating table, but somehow the old man's will to survive pulled him through.

During his lengthy hospital stay, he was heartened by the news of the deaths of the Borimovs and the subsequent unmasking of their boss. The news of Anasenko's fate was the icing on the cake, but something kept nagging at the back of Bartran's mind. The idea that someone had provided the Russian with Intel, which led to the deaths of his two agents in the bookstore stakeout, was something Bartran could not leave unresolved.

His intelligence team had worked for weeks trying to trace the mysterious Francois Balliol, the name supplied by Mike Devon from the list of financial transactions he unearthed at the Manhattan brokerage firm of Montgomery Holdings. There was little doubt the name was an alias, and that somewhere a bank account was sitting stuffed with cash, waiting for the owner to pick up his blood money.

Bartran's team had sifted through every database they could find for any trace of the alias, in the hope it was used to rent a post office convenience address or the purchase of homes or cars, anything that might have been needed in the construction of a double identity. They checked credit card companies, phone records and utility services. Everywhere they turned, they drew a blank.

Finally, Bartran decided to approach the banks. Armed with anti-terrorism warrants they ploughed through mountains of paperwork on account holders and safety-deposit box renters, an amorphous underbelly of confidentiality and false paper trails. It was a tedious bank-by-bank slog that yielded nothing until the second week when an agent checked the records of a small, independent bank in Vierzon, a mainly rural town in the country's centre region.

The name of Francois Balliol jumped out from a list of twenty renters. According to the scant details held by the bank, Balliol was listed as a Belgian national who opened the account a year previously. The account identity papers included copies of a Belgian passport with an address in Bruges. What intrigued the agent most was the grainy copy of the passport photo, showing a dark-haired, serious looking individual with thick, horn-rimmed glasses which did little to disguise the well-known face hidden behind.

Bartran insisted on interviewing the man at his place of work. He was driven there by Captain Georges Laurent, already tipped to take over the elite squad when Bartran retired the following week. There was little chat between the two men as Laurent drove the wheelchair-adapted Renault people carrier past the Eiffel Tower and across the Pont d'Iena towards the Palais de Chaillot. They completed a ninety degree turn around the famous maritime museum and pulled into the forecourt of a large administrative complex.

Laurent wheeled Bartran down the metal ramp at the side of the vehicle and both men showed their badges as they entered the lobby area. Bartran waved aside the protestations of a receptionist, who insisted on checking the appointments book, and ordered to be directed immediately to the offices of the man he had come to visit. On the tenth floor they exited onto a lobby area, and were informed their subject was in a private meeting and could not be disturbed.

Bartran nodded at Laurent, who pushed the wheelchair towards a boardroom doorway. He stopped to allow his boss to turn the handle, and smiled as Bartran kicked open the door which slammed against an inner wall. All heads around a large table turned to look at the source of the interruption.

At the top of the table Andre Fabron blanched.

"Everybody out," Bartran shouted. "I have urgent business to discuss with the Minister of the Interior."

Heads swivelled to where Fabron was slumped in a high-backed chair. He waved a hand dismissively and kept his head bowed as the men and women in the room filed bemusedly past the little man in the wheelchair. When the last of them had gone, Laurent closed the door and pushed the wheelchair across to the end of the empty table.

"I think you know why I'm here, Minister."

"I...I have no idea. This is inexcusable."

Bartran ignored the attempt at bluster. "You are a traitor to France. I have evidence linking you to Gennady Anasenko and to the recent terror attacks in Paris. Not only were you directly responsible for the deaths of those poor people at the Eiffel Tower, but you also sold out two of my agents."

Fabron stared in horror at the GIGN chief. "My only dealings with Anasenko were of a financial nature. I have no idea what you're talking about."

"Then let me explain," Bartran told him in a calm voice. "You betrayed our surveillance operation on a terrorist cell. This led to the deaths of my agents and allowed an al-Qaeda cell to escape from our clutches. That same cell took up station at the Eiffel Tower and mowed down defenceless citizens. They were able to do so because you made a phone call for no reason other than to line your greedy pockets..."

"Please, I'll tell you whatever you want to know. I had no idea what was going on."

The colour of Bartran's face slowly changed to red. "You have nothing to bargain with. We know it all, and I'll see to it that you face a firing squad for what you have done."

Fabron buried his face in his hands and began weeping. When he looked up again it was the face of resignation. "Will you permit me to collect a few personal possessions from my office?" He nodded at a door behind him.

"By all means, but we need to hurry."

Fabron slowly rose and pushed his seat away. As he walked to the door, Laurent moved to follow, but was stopped by a firm hand from Bartran. The little chief looked into his deputy's eyes and shook his head.

Fabron closed the door behind him and strode, trance-like to the windows. He pushed open the largest of the swivel windows, climbed up on a metal radiator, and looked down ten storeys to a cobbled courtyard. Behind the courtyard, the Seine weaved its way through a number of the familiar landmarks of Paris, the most prominent of which was the nearby Eiffel Tower, now reopened for business.

With barely a pause, Fabron stepped through the opening, momentarily balanced on a narrow window ledge, and launched himself into space.

The sounds of screams from far below the boardroom, galvanised Laurent into action. He rushed into the adjoining office and over to the opened window. The scene below was not a pretty one.

When he returned to the boardroom Bartran was smiling. "A dishonourable end for a dishonourable man."

Laurent looked quizzically. "You knew there was a chance of him doing that. Why did you not let me stop him?"

"I think, Georges," Bartran replied, "that France has suffered enough these past few weeks without setting the weight of a traitorous minister on Her shoulders."

Chapter 35
Moscow – the following year

HUNCHED OVER, HIS breathing coming in short, rapid gasps, Sergei Kablukov placed his faltering steps carefully into the tracks of other walkers as he negotiated the icy, snow-covered pavement. He should not have ventured out in the sub-zero temperatures, but he needed to stock up the bare cupboards in the one-bench area of his apartment that was laughingly called a kitchen. The last of his stale bread and supplies of tinned soup had been used up the day before yesterday, leaving him to exist on biscuits and coffee. Now they too were gone.

A bitter Siberian wind had created daytime chill factors ranging from minus ten to minus fifteen over the past week, forcing Kablukov to stay indoors and turn the gas heating up to its maximum setting. The combination of dry heat and layers of woollen clothing constricted his airways, and sapped energy from his frail body. This, he told himself resignedly, would be his last winter.

It had taken almost an hour to reach the main thoroughfare at Kutuzovsky Prospekt, less than a mile from his home. The thick diesel fumes from the traffic clogging the five-lane highway, added to the smog which seeped through the woollen scarf and burrowed deep into his ravaged lungs.

As he turned a corner to make his way towards a small supermarket, he glanced across at the grandeur of the Radisson Royal Hotel. International flags fluttered above the white-marble building, surrounded by generous, well-kept gardens and rectangles of parking areas, bordered by snow-capped hedges. It was another world to Kablukov. He stood for a moment watching fur-clad figures enter and leave the building, and wondered what might have been if only he had pocketed the bribe envelopes when he held sway over the city's gangsters.

He shook off the thought and watched as a gleaming, powder-blue Mercedes pulled up to the kerb near the entrance. A tall figure emerged from the driver's door and walked to the rear of the car where he retrieved a briefcase from the boot. There was something oddly familiar about the shoulders-back erect stride, though from what little Kablukov could see of the man's face, it was not someone he recognised.

His head was covered in a brown astrakhan hat and most of his face was hidden by large black-rimmed glasses perched on a bulbous nose. There was an air of authority about the way he walked up the steps towards the hotel entrance and handed his car keys to a uniformed valet. The walk, the shape, the mannerisms – they were hidden in the recesses of Kablukov's mind, but he just couldn't bring anything to the surface.

Two hours later, hunched over a steaming cup of vegetable soup, Kablukov continued to run the image of the man through a lifetime of memories. He blotted out the distraction of the gas boiler's tinny throbbing on the outer wall of his apartment and tried to put a name to the mysterious figure.

It was probably just one of the many politicos or military bosses he had come across during his service. Maybe it was one of more than a hundred criminals he put behind bars, some of whom were the leading lights of Moscow's underground at the time?

It was late in the evening, with Kablukov settled in bed under a mound of blankets, when an image jumped to the forefront of his mind. He spasmed upright, as if hit with an electrical charge, and wiped drops of perspiration from his forehead.

"My God, it can't be....it can't be!" He rocked back and forward on the bed, intoning the thought over and over again, wishing it away. But the more he re-ran the encounter at the hotel the more convinced he became that he was right. There was no other possibility.

The man he had seen that afternoon was Gennady Anasenko.

***

The suite was one of three which took up the hotel's entire fifth floor. A large reception room equipped like a modern office was dominated by a rectangular desk turned at an angle to maximise the window view of the Moskva River. Ornately carved wooden doors built into the leftside wall led to a master bedroom, a guest bedroom and a toilet/shower room. It all came with a monthly price tag that put it beyond the reach of all but the fabulously rich.

The man lying on the bed had little care about money. In truth he could have rented the entire hotel without a second thought about depleting his bank balances. True, they were a lot less than he was once used to, but when measured in the billions, what was a few million here or there?

Life had changed dramatically for Gennady Anasenko during the past year. Certain that he was facing death after his meeting with the FSB Director he had gladly accepted the options placed before him. All his assets were "transferred" to the state and he had to undergo plastic surgery as part of the construction of a new identity. He cared little that some unknown miscreant was strung up in the Lubyanka as part of the cover story surrounding his suicide.

He bemoaned the loss of his estates at Dzerzhinsky and Gstaad, accepted the impounding of his yacht, and had gotten used to living without the foreign travel, which had once been the main part of his activities. What he couldn't come to terms with was the new face created for him under the strictest security at a private Moscow clinic.

Small silicone implants were used under his eyes and on his nose and lips to dramatically alter the facial structure. Where once he was gaunt he was now puffed out in a way he found grotesque. His hair was coloured and reshaped after being allowed to grow out to a new length which covered his ears and caused him to continually brush it aside. Coloured lens were fitted over his eyes and he was ordered to wear unflatteringly large black-rimmed glasses to complete the transformation.

A new name and false papers were provided, together with bank accounts totalling more than three billion dollars, a fraction of what he was once worth. He was permitted to trade in financial markets and to continue to provide investment advice to the Treasury. Unlike before, however, all transactions had to be approved in advance and he received only fifteen per cent of any profits.

He glanced at a calendar on a noticeboard above his desk and noted with satisfaction that he would be free to leave the hotel in two weeks' time. Under his deal with the government he would be allowed to purchase a new mansion on the expiry of a one-year probation. He had already agreed on a price for a property outside the city limits and was looking forward to enjoying the lord-of-the-manor lifestyle of his previous existence. He would be allowed new cleaning and security staff, though he still missed the company and companionship of the Borimov twins.

Above all else he looked forward to planning the destruction of the men who had brought down his empire.

***

The baby's cry woke him from a deep sleep. Six am, right on cue. "Your son is demanding attention," the voice whispered from under the sheets to his right.

Mike Devon smiled, threw back the covers, and headed for the kitchen where a prepared bottle was standing sentry-like in the first rack of the fridge door. Well used to early rising, he had volunteered for the first feed of the day, knowing there would be many occasions when his job kept him away from his new family. In any case he welcomed every opportunity to spend time with Michael Jnr, now fast approaching his first birthday.

He filled a kettle and poured the hot water into a

saucepan. He immersed the bottle and checked continuously on the rising temperature of its contents. Satisfied it was at the right level he carried it through to the nursery and watched with pride as his son's face lit up at his approach to the cot. He sat the bottle on a dresser and hoisted the boy into the air, swinging him around several times and relishing the giggles of delight that filled the room.

He laid Michael Jnr on a changing platform and unhooked his clothing. After fitting a fresh diaper he sat the boy on his knee, and held the bottle to anxious lips. Ten minutes later the two of them were in the home gymnasium, the youngster tossing toys around a playpen as Devon pummelled the treadmill. It was the same routine every morning.

By the time Devon carried his son through to the bedroom Emma was already up and dressed. She grabbed the child, smothered him in kisses, and headed to make breakfast while Devon showered and changed. He had barely finished when the BlackBerry on the bedside cabinet lit up and sang out his Scott Joplin ringtone. He glanced at his watch, knowing that an early morning call was never good news. The caller's name in the window of the handset made him frown even more.

He sat on the edge of the bed and hit the answer button. "Sergei, this is an unexpected surprise."

The phlegmy Russian accent filled the earpiece. "Mike, I'm glad to speak with you, but I have grave news. Gennady Anasenko is alive."

At first Devon thought he had misunderstood. "Sergei, what are you talking about? Anasenko has been dead for almost a year."

"No, no. I have seen him. His face is different, but

I know it was him."

"Are you sure?" Even as he asked the question, he knew the old spymaster was not likely to make such a mistake.

"It was him. I have no doubt. He has tried to alter his look, but you can't hide certain things about a man. Do you think I would mistake the animal that killed my wife?"

Devon was gobsmacked. He'd had his suspicions about Anasenko's so-called suicide at the time, but had no way of verifying it. His agent in Moscow had confirmed the death of a man in Lubyanka and bribed a night cleaner into divulging that he had seen a body taken from the cell area, placed in a coffin, and buried in the grounds of the complex. Although this could have been stage-managed, Devon was forced to accept the official announcements, and had closed the Anasenko file.

"Sergei, where did you see him?"

Kablukov recounted his sighting at the Radisson Royal Hotel and how the man's mannerisms had alerted his attention. When he finished, Devon told him: "I will get our agent to follow this up and confirm if Anasenko is staying at the hotel. We will have him followed and see what he's up to these days."

"There's no need for you to put your people in danger. I only called you as a courtesy. I will handle this myself."

Devon exploded. "That's out of the question. With the greatest respect, my old friend, you are in no state physically to be running around. We will conduct the surveillance."

There was a momentary silence before

Kablukov spoke. "You must understand that I do not need to go into surveillance. I know what must be done."

"What are you talking about, Sergei?"

"I intend to kill him."

Devon jumped off the bed. "Don't Sergei. It's too dangerous for you. There's no way you can pull this off on your own."

"Look my friend, my life is nearing an end. What better way for me to go than to know I have avenged my Anna?"

Devon was about to launch into a tirade against the old man when he realised the connection was cut.

***

Alan Doyle was in the gun range booth when Devon stormed through the door. "I need you upstairs now," he yelled just as Doyle removed the earmuffs.

"Somebody got out of the wrong side of the bed."

Devon smiled as Doyle pretended to repair the damage to his auditory senses. He waited until the Glock 19 was re-magged and shoved into the shoulder holster before telling Doyle about his conversation with Sergei Kablukov.

"You're fuckin' joking! There's no way we can let that bastard run around free, not after what he did. Just say the word, Mike, and I'll gladly hop over to Moscow and finish him once and for all."

"In good time," Devon told him. "Let's figure out what's been happening and what Anasenko's been up to this past year. Who've we got in the Moscow area?"

Doyle followed Devon towards the lift. "Pete Tolliver's on station. He's a good man. Still does a bit of work for the CIA, but he's as loyal as hell to *LonWash Securities*. If we get him to mount surveillance on Anasenko, we can rest assured the job will be done professionally. He's a tough bastard, knows how to take care of himself."

They emerged from the lift and headed for Devon's office. As soon as the door was closed, Devon laid out his plans. "I need Tolliver to intercept Sergei. The old fool is hell bent on trying to assassinate Anasenko."

"Maybe we should just let him get on with it."

"Come off it, Alan. Thirty years ago he would have been able to do it with his eyes closed, but now he'd be lucky to lift a weapon, even assuming he could lay his hands on one. If he goes after Anasenko he's likely to get himself killed and blow any chances we have of mounting an operation quietly under the radar."

Doyle nodded agreement. "It'll be hard to keep the old bastard out of it."

"I don't intend to keep him out of it. For a start we need him to point out the man he saw. Apparently Anasenko got a face job and only Sergei will be able to identify him. Once we have the target in our sights, we can figure out the best way of eliminating him."

Doyle smiled. "I still don't see how Sergei will step aside and let you get on with it."

Devon reached for the phone to make contact with a small publishing business which acted as a front for *LonWash* in Moscow. "That's just it, Alan. I don't intend keeping Sergei on the outside. I owe it to him to be there when I pull the trigger."

Doyle jumped out of his seat. "Hold the fort! What do you mean when *you* pull the trigger?"

Devon cupped his hand over the phone. "I'm heading for Moscow."

Chapter 36
London

EMMA DEVON HOISTED young Michael in her arms, and pushed the supermarket trolley through the sliding doors leading to the rear car park. She was able to get a handy parking spot in the bays reserved for mothers and toddlers and had less than fifty yards to walk through a light early evening drizzle. She left the trolley at the rear of the car, pinged the unlock button with the remote control key, and began strapping Michael into his special seat.

From a vantage point in an adjoining bay, her every movement was watched from inside a black Range Rover Discovery 4, its tinted windows shielding the occupant from outside scrutiny. Behind the wheel was a dapper little man, barely five-five in height, and sporting a full head of wavy sandy hair despite his sixty-two years. He wore a tan corduroy sports jacket over a pink floral shirt, opened at the top to reveal a braided gold necklace. It was rare to find him on surveillance work, but Trevor Aspinall wasn't about to risk a potential payday of four million pounds on some minion making an elementary mistake.

Aspinall watched as the woman deposited her shopping bags into the car boot, pushed her trolley against a walkway ramp, and climbed into the driver's seat. He smiled as the little Renault Clio drove across the front of his car and headed towards the exit. This would be easier than shelling peas, he told himself.

What a pity, he thought, that the husband was not with her. He had followed Mike Devon that morning, assuming he was heading to his office, as he had done for each of the previous five days he had tailed him. This time, however, his target had gone straight to the long-stay car park at Heathrow. Aspinall was forced to hurriedly ditch his car and follow Devon into Terminal 1, watching closely as he booked in and made his way to the departure gate for flights to Moscow.

His latest assignment had come out of the blue just over a week ago. His specially-encrypted email service received a familiar message from a source he believed was dead. There was, however, no mistaking the agreed lengthy password or the pre-set coding which instructed him to retrieve an envelope from one of his well-used post-box mailing addresses. Inside the envelope he found a new contact number to be dialled at precisely midnight London time. He knew the number would engage a secure satellite link to his lucrative Russian client.

Aspinall began to sweat profusely as he watched the clock on his mantelpiece tick towards the appointed hour. The failure of his agent to eliminate Sir Clive Oliver on the instructions of the Russian had severely dented Aspinall's reputation. There was also the little matter of a pre-payment of half a million pounds for a hit that hadn't taken place. Maybe the Russian wanted his money back? Or maybe he was after more than money as retribution for failure?

At the time of the attempted assassination,

Aspinall couldn't believe his eyes as he watched the events unfolding on the road outside Sir Clive's Kensington apartment block. Watching from his Range Rover parked across the river, Aspinall could see his hitman, Terence Hannigan, approach Sir Clive as he exited the building. After that everything happened in a blur, as first the chauffeur and then "Sir Clive" drew concealed weapons and cut Hannigan down before he had the chance to bring his weapon to bear.

Aspinall studied the two gunmen as they dispassionately checked the dead assassin and then whisked the real Sir Clive away from the scene before the police arrived. To this day he still couldn't figure out how the security of his operation had been breached.

The chimes of the clock brought him back to the present. He lifted the satellite phone and began to punch in numbers that were typed across the single sheet of paper retrieved from his mailbox. When the connection was made he read off a coded set of letters which informed the listener he was alone.

A familiar voice cut through the static. There was no preamble. "Your failure to carry out your last mission has cost me dearly. You are extremely fortunate to be still living, but I may yet decide that is a situation which needs to be changed."

Aspinall blanched. "I'm, I'm sorry about what happened. They were waiting for my man. Someone at your end must have tipped them off or made a mistake." Aspinall found himself blurting out the full story of what had happened.

"Enough! I am not here to listen to excuses. You were paid handsomely to guarantee a simple job."

Even as he spoke, Gennady Anasenko knew the man at the other end of the line was right. The only way in which the authorities could have been alerted to the attempt on Sir Clive's life was through that bitch Sylvia Flynn. She had spilled her guts to protect her own ass.

"If it's a question of money, I can arrange to refund...."

Anasenko exploded. "Money! You think this is about money? Your failure exposed me to my enemies and I've had to live like a recluse for the past year. My businesses have been closed down. I've been shunned by political allies, and I've lost a number of people who were very dear to me. All this I've suffered because you failed to honour your commitments. And you talk to me about money!"

Aspinall tried, without success, to guess where this outburst was leading. He had little doubt this man could arrange for some unsavoury things to happen to him and he couldn't imagine spending the rest of his life looking over his shoulder. When he settled his nerves to speak again there was pleading in his voice. "What can I do to make it up to you?"

"I would have thought that was obvious," Anasenko told him in a calm voice. "I want the men responsible. I want you to find them and I want them erased. In particular I want you to trace a one-armed man who was part of the team sent against me and who killed a very good friend right in front of my eyes."

"What you ask will not be easy," Aspinall smiled to himself. He omitted to tell his client that he had watched the one-armed man in action outside Sir Clive Oliver's apartment block and had followed him and his partner to an office complex on Charterhouse Street.

"If you are not up to the job, then we have no further business. I suggest you start looking for a hole to crawl into."

"No, no," Aspinall replied too quickly. "I will start on this immediately. I have a lot of contacts, people who can be bought...."

"Good answer. Ring me at the same time two nights from now and let me know what you have." The line went dead.

Forty-eight hours later the two men had engaged in a similarly curt conversation.

"I've found the one-armed man and his accomplice," Aspinall said excitedly. "I know where they work and where they live. I have spent over one million pounds paying off a number of high-ranking people who......"

"Tell me about the targets."

Aspinall referred to notes he had hastily scribbled on a jotter before making the call. "They seem to work for some anti-terrorist organisation, but I have not been able to find out which one. Everything is very hush-hush but they seem to have a lot of resources and manpower."

"Forget who they work for. Tell me about these two men."

"The one-armed man lives alone, but the other, who I think is the boss, is married and has a young baby."

There was silence for more than thirty seconds before Anasenko spoke. "I want you to take them all out."

"Both of them?"

"I said all of them. I want you to eliminate the family as well."

Aspinall was dumbstruck. After several seconds he regained his composure. "We have not talked about payment," he said anxiously.

"Four million pounds. One million for each of your targets, but this time you will be paid only when all four are eliminated. If you fail on any one of your targets you will receive nothing."

"I understand," Aspinall replied.

There was laughter at the other end. "No, my friend you do not fully understand. Should you fail me this, you will pay a forfeit. And I promise your death will not be a pretty one."

***

Devon carried his bag through to the Federal Customs Service desk at Sheremetyevo and planked it down in front of a bored looking official who had already started thumbing through Devon's fake passport. "What is purpose of your visit?" he said without looking up.

"I'm here on business. We have an office in Moscow, but we supply printing services in many of your fair cities," Devon replied in a well-rehearsed speech. To confirm the legend, his bag was crammed with brochures on new printing presses and the latest price lists of paper products from many of Europe's leading suppliers.

The information was ignored by the official who stamped the passport, handed it back to Devon, and turned his attention to the next person in the queue.

Devon walked through to the main concourse

and instantly spotted his contact, Pete Tolliver, standing in a thin line of people scanning the faces of the passengers emerging from the arrivals corridor.

"Good to see you again, Mike. I have your friend with me," he said, nodding towards the outside parking area where Sergei Kablukov was sitting in the passenger seat of a grey Volkswagen Golf Estate. As they walked towards the car, the door opened and Kablukov rushed to meet them, his hands wrapping tightly around Devon's chest in a bear hug.

After exchanging genuinely warm greetings, the men climbed into the car and settled down for a thirty-minute drive through Moscow's notorious afternoon traffic. Tolliver drew up alongside a print-shop building in a side street and ushered his guests through a rear door that led directly to a spacious upstairs apartment.

Kablukov whistled as he took in the plush surroundings of an open-plan reception room with window views across the city. He removed his large overcoat and sank into a leather armchair, looking appreciatively at the rest of the furniture and wall coverings. "I'm not used to so much heat and comfort," he said by way of explanation as the other two men stared at him.

"Well, you'd better get used to it," Devon told him nonchalantly as he settled into a seat beside him.

"I don't understand." Kablukov looked flustered.

Devon ignored him and turned to Tolliver. "Did you manage to get all the things I asked for?"

Tolliver picked up a folder and passed it to Devon. "It's all here. It just needs a few signatures."

"Will somebody please tell me what's going on?" Kablukov pleaded.

Devon smiled at the old warrior. "I bring great tidings from a firm of solicitors in London who are dealing with the estate of your uncle's grandson, who sadly passed away a few months ago. Apparently he left you everything, and with your new windfall, you have bought these premises, including the print shop. There's enough left to keep you in luxury and you'll have a steady income from the printing business, which turns a nice annual profit."

Kablukov looked puzzled. "But I don't have any relations living in London, or anywhere for that matter."

"Of course you don't! We've created them for you. I can assure you the paperwork is exceptionally tight and will hold up to any scrutiny. You'll be glad to know that the money comes from funds we liberated from our friend Gennady Anasenko. I think it's only right that he should repay you for the miseries he's caused."

Kablukov jumped from his seat. "I don't want that bastard's blood money. I know you mean well, but I just couldn't accept it."

Devon expected as much from the proud Russian. "Sit down, Sergei and listen. These funds come from my company, which exists by taking it from those who shouldn't have it. If you want a clear conscience, then be assured that what we took from Anasenko is a drop in the pond compared to the vast sums we extract from other sources around the world. My people sanctioned this transfer in recognition of your work for us over many years. It is money you've earned and it's still only a fraction of what you deserve".

"I still don't understand why you do this."

Devon put a hand on Kablukov's shoulder. "Partly because of what I've already said but mostly because it will be a convenient way to tie up a lot of loose ends in Moscow. When this is over, Pete here will be accompanying me back to London for other assignments, but that leaves us needing someone here to keep an eye on things for us. Who better than you?"

Kablukov looked directly into Devon's eyes. "I will help all I can, but I will never betray my country."

Devon burst out laughing. "You silly old fool, this is not about espionage. Our mission against Anasenko is the only type of work we get up to. You have my word that your honour will never be compromised. Now, do we have a deal?"

Kablukov looked around the apartment, taking his time to drink in as much detail as he could. "When do I move in?"

***

Anasenko didn't know what to make of the touching reunion he witnessed in the car park of the Sheremetyevo. He had received a call from Aspinall alerting him to Devon's flight to Moscow, and could only wonder what business would bring his enemy to his doorstop. Aspinall had supplied a detailed description of Devon and he had no difficulty in picking him out as he emerged through the airport's sliding door exit. But who were the other two men?

Propped on the backseat of a taxi directly facing the doors, Anasenko watched as the trio piled into a Volkswagen and set off for the city centre. He had the driver follow at a discreet distance and park at the end of the side street as the occupants made their way into a building fronted by a print shop.

He waited for a half hour before ordering the driver to take him to a well-known nightclub in one of Moscow's seedier suburbs. The driver raised an eyebrow but knew better than to question his menacing passenger.

Anasenko was returning to his roots in gangland Moscow. He knew that here he would find the men willing to carry out any job for a price. He smiled as he remembered that the sleazy London broker, Aspinall, would be down a million pounds, and that it would cost a lot less to have this part of the job carried out in Moscow.

Back in his hotel room he telephoned Aspinall and ordered the other three hits to be carried out immediately.

Chapter 37
London

ALAN DOYLE JOGGED through Hyde Park on his fourth and last lap of a mile-long circuit. It was rare for him to leave the office during the afternoon, but the frustrations were building and he needed to clear his head. He had pleaded with Devon to accompany him to Moscow, but knew his boss was right about two men drawing extra attention. Besides, Doyle was needed to keep an eye on things back at the office. He could see Devon's point, but it didn't make his mood any better.

Things were relatively calm, though he had a number of agents tracking what was supposed to be a shipment of musical instruments to Germany. The office suspected the shipment was a front for the transport of automatic pistols to a group with links to the Hungarian Mafia. It was known that Hungary was a fertile ground for al-Qaeda cells and, if this shipment could be traced to them, a full-scale *LonWash* operation would be mounted. If it was nothing more than an underground smuggling operation, then the details would be passed on to the German and Hungarian authorities.

It would be days before Doyle heard anything concrete from his agents. In the meantime he was left twiddling his thumbs, and waiting for news from Moscow.

He exited the park at the Bayswater Road, in

time to notice a black Range Rover pull rather too quickly away from the kerbside. He hated cars with tinted windows, and cursed the police for not enforcing the ban on their use. He thought he had seen the vehicle earlier when he had entered the park, but dismissed it as a coincidence. There must be a hundred similar vehicles running around London.

Despite his reasoning, Doyle decided to go with his instincts. He sprinted up the pavement towards traffic lights at an intersection, praying they would turn red to hold back the Range Rover. They stayed green.

Doyle dashed out into the stream of traffic, hurtled over a Ford Fiesta by sliding his backside across the bonnet, and ignored the cacophony of horns as he forced other drivers to swerve away from him. He watched as the big 4 x 4 disappeared over a hump in the road, but not before he read off the details on the number plate.

***

"It's registered to a Trevor Aspinall at Wood Green Road," Alfie Cheadle shouted over the top of the screen. He was logged onto the police ANPR database, and was reading the standard six-line entry of every vehicle registered in Great Britain.

"What can we find out about him?" Alan Doyle shouted from across the room.

Cheadle cleared the Automatic Number Plate Registration programme before switching to the log-in for the National Crime Database. He entered Aspinall's name, and waited while the search engine roamed around more than ten million entries. Two seconds later the screen announced five entries matching the name. In the search sub-section Cheadle typed in the address from the ANPR, and the screen changed to a single sheet, dominated by a head and shoulders photograph in the top right corner.

"Looks like you're on to something here, Alan."

Doyle sprinted across the room and stood behind Cheadle's desk as they both scanned the screen details. "Read it out," Doyle said as he walked to sit in the chair opposite.

Cheadle hovered the mouse over a menu offering page enlargement. As the type expanded, he began reading.

Trevor James Aspinall, aka Tom Bradbury, aka James Burdette, is suspected of involvement in a number of murders and conspiracy-to-commit-murder cases in London and the Midlands. Arrested in 2004 and 2008 in connection with apparent gangland wars in South East London, he was released without charge because of lack of evidence. He leads a lavish lifestyle despite no apparent means of support and has been investigated on a number of occasions for potential unpaid income tax. Purports to own an image consultancy agency, but records filed with Revenue and Customs show this has recorded substantial losses for each of the last three years. Previous associates include John Carlisle (deceased), Patrick Turner (deceased), and Felix Moriarty (deceased). File last updated February 2012.

"Holy fuck!" Doyle banged his fist on the table. "What's a bastard like that doing following me?"

Cheadle was about to ask Doyle if he was sure

he was being followed, but thought better of it. Instead he offered: "What do you want us to do about it? Should we mount surveillance on him?"

Doyle was out of his chair and pacing the room muttering. Cheadle could only snatch fragments as his boss began talking out loud. "How have our paths crossed? How does this fucker know me? No it couldn't be that......the answer must lie in some of our recent cases....We need to find out what this fucker's game is."

Cheadle stared expectantly, waiting for a direct comment. Doyle rushed towards the elevator and turned back to look in the young man's direction. "What are you sitting there for? Grab your coat and let's see what Mr Aspinall has to say for himself."

***

At that moment, Trevor Aspinall was chucking clothes into a large suitcase, and cursing himself for the stupidity of being spotted by the one-armed man as he came out of the Hyde Park entrance. He had seen the look of curiosity on the man's face as he pulled away from the pavement and knew, for some reason, he was giving undue attention to Aspinall's vehicle.

The tinted windows precluded any chance of being recognised, but he worried that the man had gotten his car registration number. Through his rear view mirror he could see the man sprint up the street after him, and he was sure he went through the intersection before his pursuer could read the plates.

But Aspinall knew what the man was capable of.

He wasn't about to hang around to find out if he was right about the registration number. He would do the woman and child, ditch the car, and lie low for a while until he found a way of killing one-arm. He still had three million coming to him, and he wasn't about to walk away from that.

He emptied cash and passports from his wall safe, filled a holdall with his laptop, satellite phone and weapons, and ran out through the front door, not caring that it failed to close behind him. He threw his cases into the back of the Range Rover, jumped into the driver's seat and turned the ignition. When the big 4-litre engine roared into life, he pushed hard on the accelerator and tore away from the pavement in a screech of burning tyres.

At the corner of the street he turned left into a busy arterial route, heading for the anonymity of the central London.

Less than a minute later Alfie Cheadle eased the *LonWash* Mercedes into the opposite end of Wood Green Road, and pulled into the kerbside spot recently vacated by the Range Rover.

Doyle spotted the inswinging door immediately. He nodded at Cheadle and withdrew the Glock from his holster. Both men climbed out of the car, carefully making their way up the short path leading to the front door. Doyle silently signalled Cheadle and smashed his foot hard against the door. The young operative tuck-rolled into the hallway and brought his gun to bear, as Doyle aimed towards a stairwell to his left.

Silence closed around them and Doyle knew the bird had flown. Despite this, they went through the motions of checking every room before meeting up again in the front hallway five minutes later. "Let's go, "Doyle said. "I'm beginning to get a bad feeling about that bastard running around loose. Get an APB out and tell all agencies to approach with caution."

***

Aspinall edged the Range Rover into metered parking spots on the Bayswater Road, mindful to stay away from the glare of street lights which illuminated the dark London evening. It was seven o'clock and the area was still busy with pedestrians returning from work, or others taking the opportunity for a stroll in the unusually balmy March temperature.

As he screwed a suppressor into a Taurus M19 automatic, he glanced across the street to the steps leading to Mike Devon's house. He had decided to get this over with quickly. He would simply cross the street, ring the doorbell, and shoot the bitch when she answered. He would then drag the body into the hallway and go looking for the baby. He knew no one else lived there and he would have time to do what he had to do. The thought of firing point-blank into the baby's face repulsed him. No, he would cover the face with a pillow and suffocate the child. That way he wouldn't have to look at him and it would be over relatively quickly.

Just then the door to Devon's house opened to spill light onto the steps. The woman emerged carrying two suitcases, which she deposited onto the pavement while she fumbled in a jacket pocket for the car keys. She hefted the cases into the boot and returned to the house. A minute later she came back out cradling the boy in her arms.

"Where the fuck's she going?" Aspinall muttered to himself. He thought about jumping out and shooting her on the doorstep, but just then an elderly couple stopped to talk to her. He watched as the couple walked with the woman to the car and continued to chat as she strapped her son into the back seat.

Aspinall was forced to hang back as the woman climbed into the driver's seat, waved goodbye to her neighbours, and pulled the car out into the road. He waited until she had travelled about two hundred yards before starting his engine and following. He would get his chance somewhere, he told himself.

***

"It's been nearly a fucking hour. Is there nothing back from the APB?" Doyle realised he was shouting at Cheadle, who had spent most of the time on the phone since they had returned to the office.

"Nothing yet, Alan. There were a couple of false alarms, but the registrations didn't fit when the uniformed boys pulled over a few Range Rovers."

Doyle banged his fist on the table for the umpteenth time. "Registrations can be changed. Are they checking all occupants?"

"Yes," Cheadle replied evenly. "We issued a full description from the database record, but nothing remotely matching our quarry has been reported."

"The bastard can't have disappeared."

"Don't worry, if he's out there they'll find him. We have people monitoring all street cameras, as well as extra mobile patrols on all roads leading out of the capitol."

Doyle stared at a hard copy print-out of the database record. He looked into Trevor Aspinall's photographed eyes and muttered to himself. "Why did you run? What are you up to?"

Emma Devon eased the Renault through the Hyde Park Corner junction and headed towards Charing Cross. As expected, the evening traffic had thinned, and she hoped to complete the journey to her parents' house outside Basildon in little more than two hours. She knew they would be delighted to see their grandson, more so when they heard she would stay for a few days.

The visit was a spur-of-a-moment decision after talking to Mike when he had landed in Moscow the day before. He told her about meeting up with his old friend and of his intention to try to complete his business within forty-eight hours. As usual, she hadn't pushed him about the reason for his sudden departure, but knew it was something that would once again put him in danger. Since the birth of their son her anxieties over his absences had spiralled almost out of control. A few days with her parents would help focus her mind on other things.

Michael was fast asleep in his chair and she reached across the seat to hit the mute button on her mobile. She kept her speed to a steady thirty miles per hour and was careful to avoid sudden stops for fear of waking the boy.

"We've got a confirmed sighting."

Doyle glanced across the room at Cheadle. "Is it a secret or are you going to tell me?"

Cheadle looked suitably admonished. "Sorry, boss. The Range Rover has just been clocked at a camera on the Victoria Embankment. The registration was confirmed."

Doyle leapt from his seat and crossed to a large map pinned to a noticeboard. He began tracing his finger across the surface. "Do we know which direction he's heading?"

"I'm just waiting for confirmation. There seems to be...." Cheadle stopped in mid-sentence as his desk radio console lit up. He snatched up a set of earphones and listened intently before turning to face Doyle. "The Range Rover has just gone through Tower Hill. It appears to be heading for the A1203 out of town."

Doyle continued to study the map, and after a few seconds shouted over his left shoulder. "I want the entire area north and west of Tower Hill covered by mobile patrols. Get everyone out there to report at one-minute intervals, even if they don't see anything. I want this fucker caught."

As Cheadle issued instructions into the radio mic, Doyle beckoned to two agents at the other side of the room. When they arrived at the desk he instructed them to take over the radio monitoring and patch everything through to him on his mobile. Then he nodded at Cheadle to follow him to the lift.

"Are we joining the chase?" Cheadle asked excitedly.

"Damned straight we are. I've a feeling we'll do a lot better out there in the streets than sitting here on our asses."

Chapter 38
Moscow

"THERE HE IS, there's the bastard who........"

Devon winced as Kablukov thumped him in the thigh, and pointed across the car park towards a man climbing the steps of the Radisson Royal Hotel.

It took barely a second for Devon to shrug off the effects of a jet-lagged induced sleep, but he was already out of the car and hurrying across the park before Kablukov could finish the sentence.

As his quarry disappeared into a lift opposite the concierge's desk, Devon entered the foyer as the doors ping closed on a man he had travelled across Europe to kill. Using all his trade craft, he rushed towards the lift, and then turned dejectedly to the concierge. "Damn it, I think I've just missed an old friend. Did you see him go past you?"

The concierge, an eager young man in his late twenties, lifted his head and smiled. "Do you mean Mr Potenko?"

"No, I thought that was someone else. Are you sure it was Mr Potenko?"

"Quite sure," the concierge replied with a trace of smugness. "Mr Ivan Potenko is one of our most valued guests. I would not mistake him for anyone else."

Devon made a show of looking bewildered. He had gone through the charade as a means of learning Gennady Anasenko's new name, and now he had it. He thanked the concierge, and crossed the foyer to a large marble-topped receptionist counter, where he booked in for two nights. While the receptionist completed the registration, Devon removed a plain white envelope from his pocket, scribbled across the front of it, and handed it over the counter.

"Would you be good enough to leave this for Mr Ivan Potenko?" he asked in a businesslike tone, watching as the receptionist inserted the envelope into a small compartment marked Room 402. Devon grinned at the thought of Anasenko opening the envelope to discover a colourful business card for one of Moscow's leading call-girl agencies.

Devon was escorted to his room by a bellhop, who left beaming after receiving a generous tip. For the next two hours Devon wandered the hotel, checking stairwells and fire escapes before heading to the fourth floor. He noticed the corridor layout was different from other floors, and it took him a while to figure out there were only two guest rooms, numbered 401 and 402. A single security camera was mounted on the corridor wall at the farthest point from room 402. The distinct lack of a security presence was something Anasenko would not have countenanced a year ago.

The next few hours were spent back at Tolliver's apartment, running through a plan for the evening ahead. It was now just a matter of waiting.

Devon glanced at his wristwatch and then at Tolliver and Kablukov. "Time to go, gentlemen. We have dinner booked for nine o'clock at the Royal Radisson and we don't want to be late."

He knew that London was three hours behind and that Emma would soon be starting out to visit her parents. He was glad she'd decided to go; glad she would have something to occupy her while he tied up the loose ends of the Anasenko case. Probably for the first time in his life, he desperately missed being away from home, knowing that the arrival of a son brought new responsibilities for him. Perhaps it really was time to look for a new career.

Kablukov looked relieved when Devon rose, put on his coat, and led the trio down the narrow back stairs.

Devon stepped out of the building's rear door ahead of Tolliver and Kablukov. A single overhead light provided poor illumination across a yard cluttered with waste bins and skips, and bathed in eerie shadows. It was the slightest of changes to one of the shadows that put his senses on high alert.

A volley of muted automatic fire raked the doorway a fraction of a second after Devon pushed his colleagues roughly to the ground. All three scrambled behind the cover of a double-width commercial waste trolley, as a second fusillade of bullets pinged off their aluminium shelter.

"That makes at least two them," Tolliver said matter-of-factly, and withdrew a Glock 19 from his shoulder holster.

"They appear to be behind the skips in the right corner of the yard," Devon responded, grateful to note that his two colleagues seemed to be still in one piece.

"If we stay here they'll shred this cover to mincemeat," Tolliver whispered conversationally.

Devon tried to weigh up the options. "Give me a hand to manoeuvre this trolley back against the door. I have an idea."

The trolley was inched sideways as bursts of fire

continued to rake their position. When they were directly in line with the doorway, Kablukov crawled through the space and lay flat in the hallway, careful not to disturb the still-open door and betray his position. Devon was gambling on their assailants being unaware of what had just happened. If things went according to plan, they were in for a fatal shock to the system.

Devon and Tolliver each grabbed a handle of the trolley and used it for cover as they broke into a squat-run away from the door towards the apparent safety of the access road entrance. The gunmen had no option but to break cover and give chase.

Two large men, cradling silenced Uzi's against their hips, emerged from the shadows and peppered the trolley as they rushed forward. The waste receptacle was taking a terrible pounding, causing chips of aluminium to fly in all directions. The lid sprang open and the contents began to dance in the air.

As the dark-clothed figures passed thirty yards from the apartment door, Kablukov aimed his Makarov from the shadows and let loose two bursts. It was the signal for Devon and Tolliver to spring from their cover and bring their weapons to bear. It was all over in a few seconds.

The assailants had just turned to face the threat from Kablukov, when they were cut down by the combined fire from behind the wheelie bin. Both were dead before their bodies slammed against the hard concrete.

"I recognise the tattoos on their forearms," Kablukov announced as he rose from inspecting the bodies. "They're from a Mafiya group on the east side of the city."

Devon made a quick decision. "Let's bundle them in the boot and get them as far away from here as possible before the police show up. We don't want your new home associated with gangland murders."

Driving away from the scene two minutes later, Kablukov leaned across from the back seat and spoke into Devon's ear. "I can't understand why this group would attack us."

"Could it be a throwback to your days of hunting the gangs? Maybe someone's son is trying to get even for you putting his old man behind bars?"

"No," Kablukov said emphatically. "There's something else. That particular gang used to be in the pocket of Gennady Anasenko."

***

Rimsky-Korsakov's *The Flight of the Bumblebee* filled the apartment as Anasenko sank into an armchair and waved his right arm as if conducting the frantic piano interlude. He sipped from a glass of brandy, closed his eyes in appreciation of his favourite composer, and allowed a feel-good warmth to pervade his mood. By now his Mafiya cronies would have disposed of the Englishman who had caused him so much anguish and disruption. *Rot in hell you bastard*, he whispered as his arm movements synchronised perfectly with the tempo erupting from the expensive surround-sound system.

The volume of the music, and the fact that Anasenko was lost in another world, meant he had no chance of hearing the low-tone ping of the doorlock, or the sounds of two pairs of feet crossing the lush carpet. His eyes were still closed when Mike Devon kicked him in the leg and snapped him out of his reverie.

The brandy glass fell onto the carpet as Anasenko attempted to spring to his feet. The menace of a silenced Sig P226 motioning him to remain in his seat caused him to think again, and he slumped against the leather backing. He looked beyond the silver-plated pistol into the eyes of the holder, and immediately stiffened.

"Surprised to see me Mr Potenko, or should I say Mr Anasenko?"

The words were like a dagger to the heart. "How do you know…how did you get in here…what do you want?" The words tumbled out in a torrent of confusion and fright.

Two hours had elapsed since Tolliver had driven to a secluded wooded area and disposed of the bodies of the gunmen. Then the trio had made their way to the hotel and joined a throng of diners for the late-evening supper menu. At the end of the meal they retired to a lounge where Tolliver grabbed a corner booth while Devon and Kablukov had headed for the east wing.

When they had exited the lift, Devon used an aerosol paint spray to disable the security camera, knowing that the chances of it being constantly monitored were negligible. Tolliver had supplied a universal hotel key card, meaning that getting into Anasenko's room would be a doddle.

Devon remained standing, the Sig aimed directly at a point between Anasenko's eyes. "We know all about you, Gennady. You almost had us fooled for a while, but thanks to my good friend here, we've been able to catch up with you again."

For the first time Anasenko's gaze moved from Devon to the man standing slightly behind and to the right. Watching the change of direction, Devon spoke softly. "Where are my manners? I haven't yet introduced you to Sergei Kablukov."

Devon saw recognition slowly spread across Anasenko's features. "You, I thought you were dead."

"Not hardly," Kablukov spoke for the first time. "You did manage to kill my wife and I have willed myself to keep living for this moment. I've come for my revenge."

"Your wife! What has that got to do with me?"

"I can understand why you wouldn't remember," Kablukov replied without a trace of bitterness. "She was just another pawn in your grand scheme. You probably don't remember why you ordered her death, why you felt it would serve as a warning to me and others. You probably don't even remember the manner of her death, but you were responsible, just as if you were behind the wheel on the night she was mowed down."

The memories came flooding back to Anasenko. Now he remembered wanting to teach the irritating policeman a lesson by setting up his wife's death to look like an accident. How could this be coming back to haunt him after all these years?

Instead of cowering at the news, Anasenko sneered back at Kablukov. "So now you betray your countrymen to foreign agents. You think this man cares about your wife? No. But he does care about his own wife, and if he wants to see her alive again he would be advised to get out of here as soon as possible."

The movement of the Sig was a blur. The arc swept across Anasenko's temple, opening a three-inch wound that spurted blood over the front of his silk dressing gown. Devon pressed a knee against the slumped figure. "What the fuck are you talking about? Talk fast you bastard or I'll finish you here and now."

Anasenko held a hand to his head to stem the flow of blood. His face was contorted with pain and he had to fight against a wave of nausea to stay conscious. "If you kill me, you'll never see your wife and son again."

Devon was completely thrown at the mention of Emma and Michael. For a moment he thought the man was bluffing, but how could he know about his family? He lifted his arm as if about to swing the Sig into Anasenko's head again. "You've got about five seconds to talk."

Anasenko held up his hand to ward off a possible strike. "I put out a contract on you, your family, and your one-arm friend. The man who has agreed to fulfil this contract will already be on his way. The only chance you have of saving them is to let me make a phone call. But first you must agree not to inflict any further harm on me, and then you must kill this Russian traitor." He nodded towards Kablukov.

"You're fucking insane!" Devon yelled. "How do I know you're speaking the truth and not just trying to save your own miserable skin?"

A smile flicked across Anasenko's face. "You must ask yourself how I know about your wife and son, and about the one-arm man who attacked my boat in Monaco. How would I know about your organisation and your base of operation in Charterhouse Street in London?"

Devon stared blankly into Anasenko's face, trying to come to terms with what he had just heard. His mind drifted off to thoughts of Emma and Michael, trying to measure how real was the threat to their lives. He tried to rationalise the information and was lost in a tangle of emotions when he became aware that Anasenko was speaking again.

"The man who is to carry out the contract is the same man who followed you to the airport and warned me you were coming to Moscow. How else would I have been able to lay on a little reception for you this evening? Judging by your presence here, I take it those idiots I sent to the printing shop premises have been dealt with?"

"So it was you who arranged tonight's fireworks?" Devon asked sombrely, knowing the answer was also confirmation that there was indeed a contract in force back in London. His heart sank.

He cracked the Sig off the side of Anasenko's head, leapt from the chair, and grabbed for his satellite phone.

Chapter 39
London

EMMA DEVON JOINED the A127 dual carriageway that would carry her past Basildon to her parents' countryside manse four miles outside the town centre. She had less than forty minutes journeying time still to go, and was wrapped up in Radio 2's evening folk music show hosted by Mike Harding. She was oblivious to the gentle throbbing and flashing lights of her mobile, tucked under the flap of her handbag discarded on the passenger seat.

She was also oblivious to the light traffic, and failed to notice a black Range Rover manoeuvre menacingly a hundred yards behind. Whenever she did glance in the rear view mirror, it was to check that Michael was still fast asleep, his pacifier wedged determinedly between his lips.

She maintained a modest forty miles-an-hour pace, allowing traffic to overtake. She was in no hurry.

Nor, it seemed, was the black Range Rover travelling in her wake.

Five miles behind the two-car convoy, Cheadle looked quizzically at Doyle as they approached a large roundabout with five possible exits. Which way?"

Doyle knew the area vaguely from previous

journeys and pointed his finger straight ahead. "Let's take the obvious main road towards Basildon. I'll radio in for other units to cover the other routes. Keep the pedal to the metal."

The *LonWash* Toyota Land Cruiser blasted through the junction, staying in the outside lane as it hurtled past other startled drivers. Doyle was busy shouting orders into the car's RT set, when he became aware of the buzzing of the satellite phone in the inside pocket of his coat jacket. He grabbed for it immediately, knowing the call could be coming from only one source.

Before he had a chance to speak, he heard Devon's familiar voice. Only it wasn't so familiar, it was more a scream, the words stretched tortuously across the miles that divided them. "Alan, Alan, you've got to help me. It's Emma; someone's trying to kill her. You've got to find her...she's in danger...he's sent a hit man after her..." The words kept tumbling out.

Doyle came bolt upright on the seat. "Mike, what the fuck's going on? You need to calm down and tell me everything."

The voice that came back was wracked with pain. "There's no time to explain. Emma's in danger and you have to find her. She's not answering her phone, something's not right."

"Mike we're miles away from your house. We'll break off and head there now..."

"Wait, no. She's not at home. She'll be on her way to her parents. You have to go there."

Doyle was about to signal Cheadle to stop the car. Instead he asked: "Where do her parents live?"

"They're in Basildon."

"Holy fuck!"

There was a fraction of a second of silence before Devon's voice cut through again. "What do you mean? What's going on?"

Doyle tried to gather his thoughts. "Mike, we're on the road to Basildon now, and I think I know who's after Emma."

Trevor Aspinall kept a patient distance behind the Clio. Four miles ahead he knew the carriageway opened into a wooded hilly area, with large drop-offs to low-lying farmland. One good shunt would send the Clio hurtling over the edge.

He glanced at his watch for the umpteenth time in the last twenty minutes. He was getting edgy, impatient to finish this, ditch the Range Rover, and go into hiding. He was certain the one-armed man would be looking for him, and the bastard would have plenty of resources at his disposal. All he had to do was lie low for a few days and then resurface to complete his assignment.

He recognised the change to the terrain on both sides of the carriageway. The flat grazing fields were giving way to rocky terrain sweeping down into hollows and rising towards a forest about a mile ahead. This was what he'd been waiting for.

He checked the rear view mirror and eased down on the throttle as he moved into the outside lane. He drew alongside the Clio and noticed the woman staring intently ahead, oblivious to the danger.

He turned the steering wheel and nudged the big 4 x 4 into a spot just beyond the Clio's driver door. He smiled at the tortured screech made by the two cars slamming together.

"More, more, give her more!"

"For Chrissakes, I'm at the maximum, Alan," a nervous Alfie Cheadle shouted as the needle shook on the one hundred and fifty mark on the speedometer.

Doyle was bent forward on the passenger seat, rocking to and fro as if trying to coax every last ounce out of the powerful 3-litre engine. Everything seemed to rush past them in a blur, Doyle staring intently ahead, and willing the black Range Rover to come into view. The screaming siren and flashing lights helped clear the outer lane, but still there was no sign of their quarry.

Doyle kept shouting into the RT, demanding updates from patrols on the other roads that led away from London. Nothing. The fucker had vanished!

If Emma Devon was Aspinall's target, then Doyle was certain they were on the right road. He ordered a roadblock to be set up at the end of the carriageway on the outskirts of Basildon, and screamed at a hapless motorway traffic constable to take off from Basildon in the hope of spotting the Range Rover from that direction.

There was still two miles to go before the road block when Doyle noticed car lights ahead. The gap narrowed surprisingly quickly and Doyle could make out the shape of a Range Rover in the outside lane. He quickly killed the flashing lights and siren as they closed in.

Doyle's heart leapt when he saw the little Clio sandwiched in the left lane between the roadside kerb and the Range Rover. It was Emma's car!

He watched in horror as the Range Rover cut across the Clio and forced it against the kerb. "Do something!" he screamed at Cheadle.

Cheadle jammed hard on the throttle and crashed the Toyota into the tail of the Range Rover. The combination of speed and impact shot the Range Rover forward, away from the Clio. Doyle looked out the window as they passed the Clio, and could see Emma's mouth contorted in a silent scream as she fought to control the steering wheel.

The two larger vehicles quickly opened a gap on the Clio. It was obvious Aspinall had gunned his engine and was intent on evading his pursuers. Doyle twisted in his seat in time to see the Clio mount the kerb, twist in the air, and disappear over the edge of an embankment.

"Stop, stop!" Doyle roared, even as Cheadle stood on the brakes. They skidded to a halt almost two hundred yards away from where the Clio left the road. Cheadle threw the vehicle into reverse and zigzagged wildly back to the scene.

Before the car had fully stopped, Doyle was out of the passenger seat and racing to the top of the embankment. Through a haze of steam and exhaust fumes, he could see the little Clio flipped on its side and wedged into a tangle of wires and bushes fifty feet below.

The single strands of wire were straining to prevent the car from sliding into an abyss beyond. Even as Doyle vaulted over the edge of the embankment he could see the car moving forward, tearing itself free from the safety of the wires.

He set off on a headlong run, unaware of the tears streaming down his cheeks as he hurtled towards the wreckage.

***

The past forty minutes had been the worst of Mike Devon's life. He kept staring at the sat-phone, willing it to ring, knowing that his world depended on the next news he heard.

Anasenko had regained consciousness and was lying moaning in the chair, clutching a blood-soaked towel to his head. He spoke plaintively to Devon. "Let me make a call. I can stop this if you agree to my terms."

Devon ignored the words, his mind far away on a stretch of road leading to Basildon. He knew he couldn't accept Anasenko's offer, knew there was no way he could satisfy the man about his safety in time for him to call off the assassin. He had to put his faith in Alan Doyle, had to believe that somehow Doyle could make things right."

Anasenko was still talking. "I have more than one million in American dollars locked in my safe. Take it and go. I'll make the call." Desperation grew with every syllable. Anasenko knew that whatever way the events in London panned out, he was a dead man.

Devon stormed across the room, intent on administering another pistol-whipping, only to be stopped in his tracks by the urgent tone of his sat-phone. He sucked in a deep breath and hit the answer button.

Devon rose from his seat, checked and chambered the Sig, and crossed to Anasenko. He looked down at the pathetic figure and said simply: "It ends now."

Anasenko cowered into the back of the seat. "You can't kill me, please don't do this."

Devon smiled. "You're right I can't. The honour should go to one more deserving than me." With that he motioned to Kablukov, and handed him the suppressed weapon.

Kablukov fired one round clinically into the pit of Anasenko's stomach. "That's so you know you are dying," he spoke without emotion.

As Anasenko slid off the seat and lay writhing on the floor, Kablukov stood over him and brought the weapon close to the terrified Russian's face. "And this is from my dear wife, Anna."

"Mike, Mike they're okay! Emma's in hospital with cuts and bruises but little Michael slept through everything without a scratch...."

Devon couldn't contain himself. He threw the phone in the air, fist-pumped several times, and slumped into the nearest chair. He retrieved the phone from the carpet at his feet, and felt himself choking with emotion as he spoke. "I can't thank you enough, Alan. I don't know what to say. Tell me everything that happened."

Doyle launched into a detailed account of events from the moment he spotted Aspinall while out for his afternoon jog, and ending by describing how Emma was saved from serious injury by the deployment of the Clio's airbags. The secure strapping on Michael's seat held him firmly in place when the car overturned on the embankment.

"Where are you now?" Devon urged.

"I'm at the hospital. They've given Emma a few stitches, but she'll be discharged shortly. One of the nurses is feeding your son, and he loves the female attention. Just like his father, I'd say."

Devon smiled. "What about Aspinall?"

"We've got him. He ran straight into the road block and is currently kicking his heels in the local nick. I'll head over there after we've finished here."

Devon ended the call with a series of thanks and glanced murderously across the room at Anasenko. The Russian oligarch was curled foetal-like in his seat, his eyes a mask of terror. He made a last attempt to save his life. "Take the money, I can get you more. I have twenty million in a safety deposit box. I can take you to the bank in the morning."